BLOOD BINDS

DENISA MIH

Contents

Author's Note

Dear reader,

Before you step into the world of *Blood Binds*, know what you're walking into. This story doesn't pull its punches. It contains graphic violence, gore, blood magic, and battle scenes. There are depictions of death, loss, grief, and parental death. Sexual content is explicit and includes blood play. Emotional manipulation, trauma, and PTSD are woven throughout. Mind control and loss of bodily autonomy occur. Alcohol use is present.

If you've faced trauma, proceed with care. While every effort has been made to handle sensitive topics with respect, each person's experience is unique. The narrative explores anxiety, depression, survival, and the weight of impossible choices.

Your mental well-being matters more than any book. If something hits too hard, step away. Take breaks. Protect yourself first.

This story is built from research, conversations with those who've lived through darkness, and an understanding that sometimes the monsters we face aren't the ones with fangs. It's for readers who want their fiction raw and real, who understand that love doesn't fix everything, and that sometimes choosing to keep fighting is the bravest thing you can do.

If you're not okay right now—if you're struggling, grieving, or wondering if it gets better—this book won't have all the answers, but it might remind you that survival looks different for everyone, and there's no shame in how you get through.

You're not alone in the dark.

With love,
Denisa

Dedication

For the ones who refuse to go quietly.
For everyone who's ever wanted to burn the world down and start over.
For the monsters who choose love over vengeance—
and the lovers who choose vengeance anyway.

Glossary

GODS

***Bendis** (BEN-DEES)* - The Mother Goddess. Ruler of the earth and magic.

***Zalmoxis** (ZAL-MOX-IS)* - Firstborn. Demi-god.

***Sabazios** (SAH-BAH-ZEE-OS)* - Secondborn. A thunderbird. God of the Sky.

***Kotys** (KO-TIS)* - Secondborn. A hydra. Goddess of the Sea.

***Gebeleizis** (GEH-BEL-AY-ZIS)* - Secondborn. A dragon. God of Fire.

***Derzelas** (DER-ZEL-AS)* - Secondborn. A demon. God of the Underworld.

The Great White - A wolf. Zalmoxis becomes a god.

CREATORS

Derzelas' Enforcers on earth. Vampires.

***Dracula** (DRA-KU-LAH)* - Creator of the Tepes Coven.

***Lucian** (LOO-CHEE-AHN)* - Creator of the Wurdulak Coven.

***Marcus** (MAR-CUS)* - Creator of the Hansen Coven.

NATIONS

Crowned Republic of Transylvania - Founded by the three Creators.

***Tsardom of Russkaya** (ROOS-KA-YA)* - Founded by the Great White. Rival nation to the Republic.

***Aerothria** (A-EH-RO-THRI-A)* - Iele Kingdom. Founded by Sabazios.

***Solanthia** (SO-LAN-THI-A)* - Human Kingdom. Founded by Bendis. Zalmoxis/Great White as Protector.

RACES

Pureblood - Plural is purebloods. Immortals. Citizens of the Republic. Blood Magic.

Original - Plural is originals. Immortals. Purebloods. Citizens of the Republic. Wield the Darklings. Blood Magic.

Halfblood - Plural is halfbloods. Mortals. Former citizens of the Republic. Ieles, varvas, balaurs, or humans. Magic specific to their races.

***Varcolac** (VUR-CO-LAK)* - Plural is varcolacs. Mortals. Citizens of Russkaya. Great White's children. Werewolves. Magic unknown.

***Iele** (YEH-LEH)* - Plural is iele. Mortals. Citizens of Aerothria. Sabazios' children. Air Nymphs. Air Magic.

***Varva** (VUR-VAH)* - Plural is varvas. Mortals. Unknown location. Kotys' children. Water Nymphs. Water Magic.

***Balaur** (BAH-LAU-R)* - Plural is balaurs. Mortals. Unknown location. Gebeleizis' children. Half-dragons. Fire Magic.

Humans - Mortals. Solanthia. Bendis' children. Thirdborns. Earth Magic.

STALKERS

Russkaya's creations to defeat the Republic.

***Limus** (LEE-MUS)* - Plural is Limuses. Sand Manipulation.

***Glacie** (GLAY-CHEE)* - Plural is Glacies. Ice Manipulation.

***Nebula** (NEB-YU-LA)* - Plural is Nebulas. Pressure Manipulation.

***Ignis** (IG-NIS)* - Plural is Ignises. Magma Manipulation.

OTHER

Zmeu *(Z-MEH-OO) -* Plural is Zmei (z-may). Dragons dwelling high up in the Carpathian Mountains.

Kafea *(KAH-FAY-AH) -* Homemade blend of roasted dandelion root and ground chickpeas.

Plosca *(PLOSH-KAH) -* Flask or flat bottle used for carrying liquids.

Pronunciation Guide

LOCATIONS
Sibiu - SEE-BYOO
Sighisoara - SEE-GYSH-OH-AH-RAH
Brasov - BRAH-SHOV
Medias - MEH-DEE-ASH
Dumbrava - DOOM-BRAH-VAH
Postavarul Massif - POH-STAH-VAH-ROOL Massif
Targoviste - TAR-GOH-VEESH-TEH

MAIN CHARACTERS
Aurora Rada Tepes AW-ROH-RAH RAH-DAH TSEH-PESH
Radolf (Radu) Lowe RAH-DOHLF / RAH-DOO LOH-VEH
Selena Popescu SEH-LEH-NAH POH-PES-KOO

BLACK GUILD MEMBERS
Sabin Cantemir (SAH-BEEN KAHN-TEH-MEER) - *Terraknight*
Tudor Steros (TOO-DOR STEH-ROS) - *Hummingbird*
Horia Bratu (HOR-YAH BRAH-TOO) - *Quakelord*
Karina Bulwark (KAH-REE-NAH BUL-WAHRK) - *Pearl*
Alina Wyrm (AH-LEE-NAH WERM) - *Gale*
Lena Longtail (LEH-NAH LONGTAIL) - *Ember*
Ditoa Firestarter (DEE-TOH-AH FIRESTARTER) - *Phoenix*

TEPES FAMILY
Vlad Tepes (VLAHD TSEH-PESH) - Aurora's father
Elena Tepes (EH-LEH-NAH TSEH-PESH) - Aurora's mother
Victoria (VEEK-TOH-REE-AH) - Aurora's cousin, Marcel's betrothed
Traian (TRAH-HYAHN) - Aurora's great-grandfather

HANSEN FAMILY
Marcel Hansen (MAHR-CHEL HAHN-SEN) - Master of Keys, the Obayifo
Anastasia Hansen (AH-NAH-STAH-SEE-AH HAHN-SEN) - heir
Octavian Hansen - sculptor

LOWE FAMILY
Conin (KOH-NEEN) - Radu's younger brother

WURDULAK COVEN
Lev Wurdulak (LEHV WUR-DOO-LAHK) - antagonist

COUNCIL MEMBERS/ELDERS
Elder Armand
Elder Viktor
Elder Nicolae

OTHER CHARACTERS
The Shepherd - main antagonist
Olaru (OH-LAH-ROO) - Projector
Bodgan Enescu (BOHG-DAHN EH-NES-KOO) – Commander
Stefan Luchian (SHTEH-FAHN LOO-KEE-AHN) – artist
Katerina (KAH-TEH-REE-NAH) – Lev's sister

Sevastyan (SEH-VAHST-YAHN) – Wurdulak loyalist

Alexandru (AH-LEK-SAHN-DROO) – Wurdulak loyalist

Tristan (TREES-TAHN) – Wurdulak loyalist

Joseph – Outlier

Rosebud – Outlier

Mandrake – Outlier

Shadow (Boy/Sugar) - the zmeu (baby dragon) that lives with the Black
Guild

Summary

I'm Aurora Tepes, heir to Dracula's throne and next in line to inherit his powers. I'm also Projector of the Sparrows—a guild of mixed-breed outliers fighting monsters beyond our borders.

For almost a century, the Crowned Republic of Transylvania has been at war with the Stalkers—Russkaya's abominations fused with elemental magic. Limuses manipulate sand, Glacies wield ice, Nebulas crush with pressure, and Ignises throw bulwarks of lava.

While immortals remain secure, mixed-breeds are sent to die on the battlefield. Under the *Total Rendition* Act, they were stripped of their civil rights and branded "Russkaya's supporters." The government seized upon the initial Stalker attack as justification to reinstate mandatory conscription and intern mixed-breeds in detention camps.

My coven fell into ruin after Father's death. The Wurdulaks orchestrated our downfall, turned our allies against us, and stole my crown. Mother's solution? Marry me to Lev Wurdulak, their heir, to secure an alliance. For my hundredth birthday celebration, that bastard gifted me five mortals to drain at dinner—a power play designed to break me into compliance.

I refused. Told him I'd never accept his hand, sent him where the sun doesn't shine. Things went downhill fast.

Rather than submit to a forced Blood Pact under the Red Moon, which would bind us for eternity, I fled with Selena Popescu, my best friend and medical lieutenant, to the front lines. Commander Enescu helped us fake our deaths and assigned us to investigate the Black Guild, specifically their captain, Harbinger, who'd been harming his projectors.

The Black Guild operates from an abandoned mansion in the Tenth Ward—the first Republic territory to fall and now our warfront against the Stalkers. Harbinger commands seven outliers: Terraknight and Quakelord (earth magic), Hummingbird and Gale (air manipulation), Pearl (water control), and Ember and Phoenix (fire magic).

They despised us on sight. Can't say I blamed them. Immortals had treated them like disposable weapons for generations. I made it my mission to prove that not all of us shared those bigoted views.

Before our first mission, Harbinger revealed what he was—half-varcolac, something that should be impossible. His varcolac father and pureblood mother had both died in the war's early years.

I discovered he predicts Stalker movements with disturbing accuracy and speaks their language—Russkayan. Selena suspected treachery, but I defended him. What spy would slaughter hundreds of his own?

During a brutal battle, I tried to save Phoenix from two Ignises while weakened from our dwindling blood supply. A Nebula captured me, crushing my bones to splinters. Phoenix died anyway—magma ball to the chest—and Harbinger saved my life by cutting the creature in half.

I woke disoriented and starving, attacked him, thinking he was Lev come to finish me. When I recognized those amber eyes in the candlelight, everything changed. I fed from him. His blood—rich with both immortal and varcolac heritage—satisfied me in ways I'd never experienced. The feeding turned intimate, ignoring every line I'd sworn not to cross with someone I was investigating.

He told me about his younger brother, Conin, who died thirty-five years ago on the Eastern Front. Harbinger's been searching for him ever since. His brother had been the outlier who saved my life so many decades ago.

I also learned their real names—Phoenix was Ditoa Firestarter, Harbinger is Radolf Lowe (Radu for short), Terraknight is Sabin Cantemir, Hummingbird is Tudor Steros, Pearl is Karina Bulwark, Gale is Alina Wyrm, Ember is Lena Longtail, and Quakelord is Horia Bratu. Using call signs instead of names was just another way the Republic stripped away their humanity.

During our final battle, while connected through the Harmonization link, mysterious voices invaded my mind, agonized screams I couldn't understand. The pain tore through my consciousness until I thought I'd shatter.

Then a Nebula approached Radu and spoke one word: "Brother." Over and over, calling to him while those tortured voices grew louder in my head. The agony fractured my awareness completely.

My story ended with me drowning in those screams, Radu shouting at me to cut the mental link, and darkness swallowing everything whole.

THE GLOOM
DRACULA
THE CARPATHIANS
BRASOV
SIGHISOARA
BLACK GUILD
SIBIU
10TH WARD
9TH WARD
8TH WARD
N
W
E
S
CROWNED
REPUBLIC OF
TRANSYLVANIA

Harbinger

Thirty-five years ago.

Blood paved my passage through Medias like a curse upon the snow. Each step bled a darker shade into the white, a stain that the monsters would track come dawn.

The gash across my chest had soaked my shirt rust-red, and my right shoulder burned where the Glacie's ice shard had punched through muscle and scraped bone. Ma's immortal blood, strong and defiant, fought to knit flesh back together with reluctant threads, but even that ancient power faltered, as if the night conspired to end me right there in the ice.

The Chronoportal had drained my magic reserves to nothing. I'd managed thirty miles from the slaughter near Sibiu before my legs gave out and I lost control of the portal.

Half of my guild lay dead in Dumbrava forest. Good people. Experienced fighters who'd survived a decade of this war.

The Stalkers had known exactly where to strike. Where we'd be vulnerable. Like they'd studied our formation, understood our tactics. If I didn't know better, I'd think someone had sold us out, or given them a goddamn map.

I shook my head and passed through the massive stone gates of the 8th Ward, where Republic words sculpted in relief gathered dust and bird shit. 'Scientia potentia est'—Knowledge is power. Rich coming from the leeches who excelled at ignoring the truth. What good was knowledge when you systematically buried your head in the ground and refused to act?

Bunch of stupid zealots.

I stumbled into the city, boots slipping on ice-slicked stone, and coughing more blood. At this rate, I'd leave a trail a child could follow. Fucking brilliant.

Medias after dark belonged to scavengers, but the library offered shelter. Granite walls that were three feet thick. Heavy oak doors with iron reinforcement. A defensible position if I could make it that far without bleeding out.

My boots slid in the thin sheen of my own blood and icy cobblestones. The shadow of Medias Library rose ahead. The outer iron gates gave little resistance, which I was grateful for. Then I hefted the main doors open with my shoulder, panting, allowing the weighty fuckers to amble shut behind me as I entered.

The main library chamber stretched into shadow, thick beams arching overhead. Shelves loomed, towering as if acting as my very own gallows. I raked in a stuttering breath, glancing around.

Dozens of brass lanterns hung from chains, their glass covers clouded by grime. Dust motes danced through moonlight from broken windows, and the air reeked of parchment and decay—or perhaps the decay was just me, my wound open and festering.

Dad used to drag Conin and me here when we were young. Before the Total Rendition, when halfbloods could travel between wards without papers and interrogations. Before everything went to shit.

I collapsed between the stacks, back against cracked spines and moldering pages. The musty books reminded me of better times. When the worst threat was some prissy librarian lecturing us about proper text handling.

Pretentious bastards.

The night's chill cut through my clothes. Winter in this part of the continent meant killing temperatures, especially after losing too much blood. My teeth chattered. I clenched my jaw and leaned my head against the shelf, focusing on the sharp pain instead of the cold seeping into my bones.

At least the walls would hold against whatever prowled outside. For now.

Howls drifted through the ruins. Distant, but closing in. My blood trail would draw them into the city like a dinner bell. Either they'd find me here, or dawn would force them back to their holes.

Fifty-fifty odds. Maybe worse.

Then I heard it.

A voice needled my head. Not my guild's usual chatter through the Harmonization. Something else. Someone calling to me. Familiar.

Static hissed through the mental link, like two radio frequencies overlapping. I dragged a bloodied hand over my face. Fresh blood welled from reopened cuts.

"Harbinger?" Gale's voice cut sharp and clear. *"Are you alright?"* Wind whipped past her—she was airborne. Still alive.

My chest tightened. The Chronoportal had worked. Got them out before the massacre.

Worth burning through my reserves if it kept them breathing.

"I'm fine," I said, teeth gritted.

"*You don't sound fine.*" Pearl's voice was steady as always. "*Where are you?*"

"8th Ward library."

"*Stay put until we reach you.*"

Static filled the link. Then the other voice took over, pulled deeper. Multilayered echoes that bypassed my ears and went straight to the bone. Recognition hit like a sledgehammer to the gut.

I knew that voice. Would know it anywhere.

"He's calling me." I pushed against the shelf, forcing myself upright. Torn muscles screamed. Vision blurred. My knees buckled, and I braced against the frame as a book thudded to the floor. "I need to check—"

"*Don't you dare leave that building,*" Terraknight growled. "*You're half-dead, and those bastards are circling the city.*"

But I couldn't ignore *him*. My brother's voice carried childhood words he'd used when storms made him afraid.

"*Radu? Radu, where are you? I can't find you in the dark.*"

I'm coming.

Wind struck my face as I rushed through the library's doors. Medias had been transformed into a white grave. Ice cracked overhead, and I jumped back as a massive icicle shattered to the floor where I'd been standing.

Close. Too fucking close.

I stepped over it and pressed forward, Conin's voice buzzing in my head, drowning out my guild's protests to stay inside. Stay inside. Stay inside.

The storm had passed, leaving killing cold and silence thick as death.

I passed the ward's Postal Office, squatting on the corner, its red brick facade split down the middle. Across from it, the Tax Registry's timber-framed walls leaned inward, the upper floors jutting over the street.

Wrought-iron lanterns stood dark on every corner. The electrical grid had failed decades ago when the power station in the 9th Ward fell to a Nebula pack.

"Cap, we're tracking your position," Hummingbird said during a break in Conin's summons. *"Just wait—"*

But the voice called again. Stronger now. Desperate. The same tone my little brother used when fever dreams made him cry for me to find him in whatever nightmare had claimed his sleep.

"I'm scared, brother. It's so cold here. Why won't you answer me?"

My boots crunched across powdered ground toward the central plaza. Each step sent electric jolts into my shoulder. Didn't matter. Couldn't stop. Not when my brother needed me.

Hendrik's Bakery sign—*Fresh Bread Daily Since 1847*—creaked on rusty hinges as I followed the voice to the Founders' Memorial Fountain. The three-tiered marble structure had once sprayed water from the mouths of three carved dragons. Now the top tier was blown to smithereens and the northernmost dragon's head lay in pieces in the basin.

"I'm here, brother," he said.

I looked past the broken fountain. Through the curtains of white, a dark shape slumped against the memorial wall.

My heart stopped.

No. Please, no.

I lurched forward, white drifts swallowing my legs to the knee. The figure sat motionless, winter settling on familiar shoulders. That tilt of his head. Platinum-blond hair almost lost in white.

My throat closed. I couldn't breathe.

I rushed to him. Waded across sleet. The wind bit my face, but I felt as if I were moving in quicksand.

"Conin." His name came out cracked. Broken.

He lay against frozen stone, the snow rising over him like it meant to bury the last warmth he'd ever given the world or given me. Like a shroud. It clung to his dark-blond lashes, his face, his chest, his still hand—that same hand I had once steadied when it was too small to lift a weapon. It now, in a frozen fist, clutched Dad's sunsteel blade.

Moonlight glinted and bled over the frostbitten steel, appearing pale as death itself.

My body failed me.

Knees hit the cobbles hard enough to send a crack into the silence. Then there was nothing. No wind. No breath. Just the quiet ache.

And beneath the snow, older layers were soaked with *his* blood, dark and frozen. It seeped up through the newer frost as if it needed me to witness it.

With trembling hands, I brushed powder from his face. Couldn't look at his eyes. Not yet. The cold had preserved him. He looked as if he were sleeping. Like any moment he'd complain about me waking him too early for training.

Please wake up. I'm here now. I found you.

His skin held the blue-white of marble statuary. The birthmark on his right temple—the stupid thing I'd always poked fun at—stood stark against bloodless skin. His lips curved in a ghost of a smile, as if he'd found peace before the cold took him.

Silver shone at his throat. The black opal necklace Ma had given him on his twentieth birthday. Twin of the one I'd lost in a camp fight.

My fingers closed around the gemstone. Biting cold. Like the rest of him.

The chain snapped with a brittle ping.

Something cracked in my chest.

I pressed the pendant against my ribs and doubled over. No sound came out. Grief had stolen my voice, left me hollow and shaking beside my little brother's body. It built and built like the downpour of snow until it was crushing, suffocating me under its weight.

He'd fought until the end. Died with Dad's blade in his hand, defending himself against the monsters.

And I hadn't been there.

I took the Sunsteel too, prying his frozen fingers from the pommel. My throat burned, but nothing came.

A thunderous crack split the air.

The distinctive hiss of Hummingbird's air wave sliced the snow. Terraknight's roar shook the ground, and for a split second, silence reigned over the plaza before agonized howls echoed into the night.

The bastards had sniffed my blood and made it into the city.

Pearl reached me first. Her breath caught when she saw what lay in front of me. The others gathered close.

"Radu…" Pearl's voice quavered.

"He's gone," I whispered, and my stomach churned. "Conin's gone."

"He shouldn't have died alone," Hummingbird hissed. "Not like this."

"Captain." Gale squeezed my shoulder. "Look."

A few feet behind the monument, a barren tree rose from the ground. I tilted my head, and my breath caught at the sweep of branches reaching skyward.

"Cherry blossom," she whispered. "You always said they reminded you of home."

"The tree where you and Conin sparred as boys," Hummingbird added, his voice soft. "You told us about the petals falling around you."

I could only nod as the world blurred. All I wanted was to gather my little brother and carry him home. But the Gloom lay too thick between here and there. We'd never make it together.

Terraknight kneeled beside me, gripping my other shoulder. "It's fitting. A guardian from your childhood to watch over him."

The branches reached over the monument. For a heartbeat, I saw them heavy with pink flowers. Heard Conin's laughter as we sparred together.

The frozen earth would deny him burial now. But here, under these familiar branches...

I looked to the east. The sky was already lightening.

Dawn would take him away, leave nothing but dust beneath this tree. But in spring, I'd return for whatever remained.

"I'll come back when the blossoms wake. You'll rest beneath home, brother." I cupped his frozen cheek one last time. "Wait for me here. Just until spring."

I love you, little brother.

Aurora

I'D ALWAYS WONDERED WHAT dying would feel like. Turns out, it's loud as hell.

Death had finally caught up with me, and this time Pearl wasn't here to intervene.

The Voices were building a fortress of madness in my skull, each cry laying another brick in the wall of my closing tomb. The pressure mounted behind my eyes, a gnawing heat that ate away at the edges of reason until even my own thoughts began to scream.

My body betrayed me. Blood gushed from every pore, turning my skin into a canvas of crimson rivers. The metallic tang filled my nose and drowned out the acrid smoke that clung to Brasov's ruins. It sought to suffocate me, perhaps bury me.

Through the haze of agony, I clung to the glimpse of moonlight filtering through the skeletal remains of the clock tower. The structure that had dominated the square since fourteen-twenty now lay twisted across the ground, its clock face shattered. Fire magic had melted the stone spires of Lucian's Temple. Down the alley, a shop sign creaked on rusted hinges from what had been Petrov's Blood Works.

The Council Square reduced to nothing.

Just like I'd become another pile of ashes scattered across these war-torn cobblestones by dawn.

My intestines twisted into knots, my body trying to squeeze itself into a fist, desperately preserving what little life remained. The Deep Sleep kicked in—a pureblood's last defense against complete exsanguination.

Or the 'death box.'

All because I'd trusted him.

The Voices infiltrated my mind deeper—Harbinger's precious secret—tearing through my mental barriers like acid through paper. High-pitched wails stripped away layers of my sanity. My identity dissolved. Blood bubbled past my lips, the last cavity it hadn't been pouring from, and the wet heat felt final.

Then—

CRACK!

Something shattered inside my skull. The monster chorus died, but the damage was done. My soul ripped free as my spine arched off the stone. This wasn't agony anymore; this was existence becoming undone. I reached for something—anything. A memory. Meaning. Mercy. And found only the echo of my unraveling clawing its way out of me.

In the void that followed, my screams were captured in infinite loops until understanding dawned.

Harbinger had saved me. He had severed the harmonization, knowing it would hurt like hell. Why would a traitor show mercy? Was this how Projector Olaru had met his end, driven mad by these Voices?

He should have let me die.

The thought jump-started my failing heart. Because the alternative meant a reckoning. I'd extract every truth from his lying throat, even if it killed us both.

I was done with his games. Done letting him call the shots while people died for his secrets.

Fire erupted from my nape and threaded through my spine. Each breath felt like inhaling broken glass. The hunger wrung my insides, turned my veins to liquid lead.

My fingers slipped against the blood-slicked metal at the back of my neck. The Bloodthorn Nexus burned my skin, but the pain dimmed beside my flaring rage. I twisted onto my knees, clawing at the device. Then my head knocked against the wall as I tried to scrape the Nexus off against the rough stone.

A scream ripped from my raw throat, carrying all my fury at Harbinger, at the Republic, at my own stupid trust.

"Aurora, stop!" Selena's shadow fell over me, her obsidian hair catching starlight, sharp cheekbones set in determination. The fear twisting her elegant features reminded me of Sibiu—of finding out Harbinger was one of them. A varcolac. "You'll hurt yourself!"

"Get it out!" I slammed my fists against my temples. "Get this fucking thing out before it fries my brain!"

"Hold still." She locked my shoulders between her thighs, tangled her fingers in my hair, and yanked my head forward. Her other hand clutched the Nexus. With a soft click, my harmonization link to the Black Guild died. "This is going to hurt."

I lurched forward onto my hands. "Just rip it—"

My words dissolved into blackness as she pulled, vision failing. The Nexus clung like a parasite. With each tendril that disconnected, white-hot bolts shot through my brain.

Then, something snapped, and the burning vanished.

Without Selena's support, I crumpled forward, blood dripping onto stone.

"Easy." She braced me as I pushed up on shaking legs. "Did that bastard do this to you?"

My mind was already putting pieces together. "Sel, Harbinger can communicate with them. The Stalkers. I heard them—hundreds of Voices screaming through our mental link." My voice cracked. "I heard Phoenix."

'I don't want to die...'

Her eyes narrowed to slits. "Phoenix is dead, Aurora. Everyone saw—"

"I know what they saw!" I snapped. "I watched her die. I heard her heart stop. But that was her voice. The same desperate plea from that night, before the Ignises got to her."

Selena's grip tightened on the Nexus until her knuckles went white and my blood pooled between her tight fingers. Panic flickered in her eyes. She thought I was losing my mind.

An explosion rocked the ground. Battle sounds crashed in as if someone had uncorked my ears—screams, blasts, bodies hitting stone. Through the gaps between buildings, I caught flashes of combat: Ember's flames painting the night orange, earth magic reshaping the landscape.

The outliers were still fighting.

It wasn't over. I almost doubted it ever would be.

Selena's ice-cold hands gripped my face. "Aurora?" Her pulse spiked, and the sound made my mouth water. "Are you alright?"

"I'm fine," I lied.

The emptiness in my gut was getting harder to ignore. Every cell screamed for blood, and Selena's proximity wasn't helping.

Her lips thinned into a grim reprimand. "That's bullshit!" she snarled. "The Nexus stays with me."

"On that, we can agree. Give me your Transmitter."

"Are you out of your fucking mind?" she said, her voice suddenly honed to a razor's edge as she yanked away. "You almost died again. And by the way, your veins are showing, so stop lying to me. You really want to keep fighting like this?"

I raked bloody fingers through my hair, feeling the raised black lines snaking from my hairline. A searing cramp almost doubled me over.

"I need to do this. Yes, I need to sate myself. Yes, my head feels like it's going to explode." I met her eyes. "But we have minutes, an hour at most. If we don't act, we're both dead. Either the Stalkers will kill the Black Guild and come for us, or I'll lose control and you'll have to deal with both me and them. Your choice."

Her jaw hardened as she slapped the Transmitter into my palm. "Fine. But take my blood first."

My insides twisted. I couldn't refuse.

"Just a little," I warned, grasping her arm. The pulse beneath my fingers jumped like a trapped bird. "If I take too much—"

"—It'll be me who slips into bloodlust. I know. It won't get to that. Now, feed!" She thrust her wrist at my mouth, the scent of jasmine and vetiver filling my nostrils.

I pierced her skin with measured care, but nothing could have prepared me for the rush. Her blood hit my tongue, ancient and powerful, and I hummed in pleasure. My knees almost buckled as the first swallow blazed down my throat, igniting every depleted cell in my body. The world transformed. Darkness gained texture, colors bled into impossible new shades, and even the stone walls seemed to pulse with life.

Five swallows. That was my limit. Any more and I'd risk pushing her over the edge. I forced myself back, licking the wounds closed with trembling lips. Her blood crackled through my veins, but it was barely a drop in an endless void.

We couldn't risk two purebloods in bloodlust. Not with the growing Stalker numbers I sensed gathering in the square.

"Better?" Selena asked.

I wiped my mouth, tasting the last copper traces of her blood. "It'll do. Let's go finish this so we can call it a night. I know I need it over yesterday."

My fingers shook as I positioned the Transmitter beneath my ear. The device latched onto bone with a sharp bite. "Black Guild," I commanded.

The device hummed to life, connecting me to the outliers fighting in the square.

Another cramp twisted my gut, hot as a knife and sharp enough to blur my vision. On a scale of one to for-the-love-of-god-this-hurts, I would've given this a twelve. I was running on borrowed time.

But the others needed us. Even Harbinger, the lying bastard.

"Ready?"

She fixed me with a flat stare. "No."

Despite the pain, I snorted. Neither was I.

"Love the spirit. Let's go kill some Stalkers. Then we'll deal with me."

The alley squeezed us between crumbling buildings, barely five feet wide. I stumbled over debris, my elbow cracking against stone. The little blood in my system might as well have been water for all the good it did.

The alley mouth opened to chaos.

Three fireballs—Ember's handiwork—streaked across the sky. My Blood Manipulation reached out, categorizing the seven essences around us: clear blue auras of outliers against the dark presence of Stalkers. Everyone was unharmed. But that knowledge came at a price.

Their scents slammed into me, and my gums split open. My fangs descended without permission, so I clenched my jaw to stop myself from giving in. A gust of wind carried the reek of decay and ashfall, temporarily clearing the red haze creeping at the edges of my vision. But the smell of spilled mortal blood was hard to ignore.

Selena halted in front of me and shot me a knowing look. "You okay, partner?"

"Never better," I muttered through tight lips.

In the square, agonized wails splintered the night. Through the gap between the ruins, I glimpsed dozens of Stalkers swarming Harbinger, his silver hair flashing as he moved between their ranks. He'd sheathed his mysterious sword in favor of a more effective weapon.

Where his portal-born blade slashed, Stalker parts disappeared.

Somewhere in another realm, it was raining severed monster limbs and heads. The surrounding air rippled with temporal distortion as his strikes tore holes between worlds, feeding Stalkers piecemeal into the void. His Chronoportal was as terrifying as it was majestic.

He took a sharp turn, slid beneath a Nebula, and hamstrung the four-armed beast with a quick movement of his hand. Gore sprayed the cobblestones from the stumps he'd left of its legs.

My breath caught, and bile rose to my throat. *Why fight them if they're his allies?*

On the other side of the square, thirty feet from where Harbinger danced with death, four Limuses crouched on their forelegs. Twice as wide in the shoulders as an average pureblood, the hellhounds almost matched my height. Some very old ones even did. Their maws gaped to reveal endless rows of yellowed fangs, sharp as sickles and strong as steel. The barrier of sand writhing from their ridged spines wavered like heat mirages, thick enough to blind.

They were preparing to attack.

My body moved before conscious thought could intervene.

I launched myself into the fray, hunger forgotten. Harbinger's eyes locked with mine, ice-cold and furious. How dare he? The bastard had lied, manipulated, nearly killed me, yet *he* was upset?

My fangs dropped fully. This time I welcomed them.

Then he vanished, leaving empty air where the Stalkers' jaws snapped shut. Black ichor sprayed as the Limuses collided, their own momentum turning them against each other in a tangle of claws and fangs.

"Goddamn, he's quick," Selena breathed behind me.

The Transmitter buzzed with a chorus of shrieks, whimpers, and groans, not as overwhelming as before but enough to splinter my focus. I tried to adjust the device, but the Voices only grew clearer. Each cry distinct and urgent. Though only an echo of the torrent Harbinger had channeled through our link.

And where I'd collapsed in agony, spewing blood and sanity, he moved without the slightest sign the Voices affected him. No nosebleeds. No screaming. Just another normal day in his rampage.

My fingers curled into fists, nails cutting crescents into my palms. I would immobilize him, send him to his knees again, and—

"I don't want to die! I don't want to die! I don't want to die!" Phoenix's voice rose above the noise, clear as the night she died.

A whisper of fear fluttered in my belly, my knees buckling.

"Holy shit," Hummingbird's voice echoed through the Transmitter. "That—that was Phoenix!"

My head snapped up. They heard her too.

"Aurora?" Selena gripped my elbow. Her keen eyes scanned for wounds she wouldn't find. "What's happening? Are you hurt?"

I shook my head. "Phoenix is out there somewhere." I forced myself to voice the horrifying thought. "And if she is... what about the others? All our dead—where are these Voices coming from?"

AURORA

SELENA'S FINGERS TREMBLED AROUND the needles she'd let slide from her coat sleeve, knuckles bleached white. "A... I-I think I heard her too... before. And the others." Her voice dropped to a whisper. "But it can't be Phoenix. She's gone. Even if she somehow survived those Ignises, she wouldn't have made it past sunrise."

The rogue fires painted stark shadows across her face, and her eyes blazed with an intensity I'd only seen once before—when she discovered her parents had arranged her marriage to a noble pureblood more than ten times her age.

She swallowed hard, her jaw stiff. "I don't know what's happening, but those aren't our dead speaking, they can't be."

The line connecting me to the Black Guild exploded in an uproar.

"Phoenix...?" Terraknight's familiar rumble filled the Transmitter. *"Those bastards took her?"*

Dove-white wings beat furiously above as Hummingbird circled over the square. *"Didn't Cap handle this already?"*

"There was no time, you idiot!" Gale snapped, her airstrike scattering a pack of approaching Stalkers. *"It was an ambush! And the projector was critical."*

A lone Glacie broke through the iele's assault, its massive black wings carrying it straight for Harbinger. The creature passed right over Terraknight and Pearl as if they were invisible, its nightmarish face—a grotesque fusion of human skull and satyr—fixed solely on its target.

My pulse spiked.

Ice crystallized along the Glacie's arms as it readied its strike. I reached out with my blood magic, but Terraknight's vines erupted first, ensnaring the beast mid-dive. The ground shuddered. Pearl stepped forward, eyes blazing azure, raised her scaled arms, and drove an ice spear through its core. They returned to their positions without a backward glance, protecting their captain with the seamless efficiency that came from years of fighting at his side.

I tracked Harbinger's movements through the square, his form blurring between portals as he carved through the horde. His lips moved in a pattern I recognized—counting, just like in Sibiu. But this time he circled the same cluster of Stalkers once, twice, searching.

"Ember. North-east, five-hundred yards," his voice came loud and clear through the din. *"Front row, second Nebula from the right. Group of ninety-five."*

"Got it."

The crack of Ember's shot split the night. The Nebula's leprous head snapped back, dark blood spraying from the hole between its beady eyes.

My fingers dug into Selena's arm. "The Voices... they're coming from the Stalkers."

Then realization hit.

Harbinger had tracked that single voice through the chaos, hunting the creature that dared steal Phoenix's final words, all while fighting to avoid getting killed.

He stood in the center of the square, monsters closing in, shoulders pulled back and muscular arms relaxed at his sides. A muscle twitched on his forehead as he tilted his head skyward. His battle-rage had morphed into ice-cold calculation.

"So now you're after my friends?" The words carried the glint of a double-edged sword.

Phoenix's mimicry still echoed its desperate plea, but fainter now, nearly lost among the other tortured souls. More shots rang out as Ember methodically eliminated each Stalker that carried sounds of the dead.

Harbinger vanished in a glitch and materialized thirty feet from the Nebula still speaking in Phoenix's voice. The creature struggled to its feet, riddled with bullet holes. From her perch on the roof, Ember continued firing. The fury in her rapid shots betrayed how desperately she wanted to silence the monster wearing her friend's voice.

Metal clicked empty, but Ember kept pulling the trigger until Harbinger stepped into her line of sight. He waited, watched the Nebula struggle upright, then raised his arm in a wide arc. The halfmoon portal that shot from his hand cleaved the creature's hairless head clean from its shoulders.

"I don't want to—" Phoenix's voice died mid-scream.

Time stopped. No one moved. No one breathed. The change in atmosphere was palpable, like the calm before a devastating storm.

Then it hit.

An invisible wave that made every muscle in my body tense. Hundreds of glowing eyes turned as one and fixed on a single target: Harbinger. The ground trembled as Stalkers converged on him from all directions.

Limuses howled, releasing the Gloom.

Glacies took to the skies by the dozens, dark leathery wings blotting out the moon. Gale and Hummingbird landed, flapping copper and silver wings to disperse the thickening sand rising around them.

Fear struck deep in my gut as I grabbed Selena's arm and charged toward them. Instead of trampling us, the Stalkers split like a massive river, gray, rotten bodies writhing past.

My magic responded, rising to the surface with surprising ease despite the throbbing in my head. Pain seemed to fuel it rather than hinder it.

"Holy shit," Hummingbird gasped as we reached them. His wings stuttered, nearly dropping him on his ass. "Projector—your face!"

Gale folded her crimson wings tight behind her back and pressed her palms together. Magic sparked under her hands as a shimmering barrier expanded from the contact, creating a Stalker-free air bubble.

Her gaze landed on me and traced what I supposed were the black veins spreading across my skin. "Those markings... they're like Cap's when he needs to—"

"Move!" Terraknight burst through the barrier, dripping dark blood everywhere. He skidded to a stop when he saw me, muscles tensed. "Fucking hell, you look like death warmed over. What happened to you?"

Your lying captain happened, I almost yelled at him, but the hunger twisted deeper, and their racing pulses made my fangs ache. "Focus on the Stalkers," I managed through clenched teeth. "Just don't let me die."

"She's in bloodlust," Selena snapped, positioning herself between me and the others. "And we're wasting time."

An Ignis smashed against the wall, and a wave of static pulsed through the shield. The fine hair at my nape stood up. The clock was ticking, and we needed a blunt approach to lower the Stalker numbers, or none of us would go home tonight.

I'd lost my harmonization with the guild, but nothing stopped me from trying to establish a one-way connection with these hollow-brained monsters. Without the Nexus, I'd have to rely purely on Blood Manipulation.

"Sel, I need you to hold as many as you can," I said, squaring my shoulders. "If I slip, you know what to do. At my command."

Her grunt held a universe of disapproval, but I trusted her to snap my neck if I became a threat to the Black Guild.

Terraknight shifted closer. "Projector, what's your plan?"

I didn't respond.

Jasmine and cuscus grass—Selena's magical signature—swirled around us as she summoned her power. My own magic rose to meet it.

What little blood remained in my body surged through my veins, awakening tired muscles. My heart raced, but the spike in adrenaline made the hunger cramps hit harder. I gritted my teeth, using the next wave of pain to push my control outward, searching through the sea of Stalkers. Red crept into my vision. My fangs pierced my bottom lip as I held back a scream.

The world slowed to a crawl.

I pressed a hand against the air shield and squeezed my eyes shut. "Now, Sel!"

Selena's magic took hold. Three-quarters of the Stalkers in my radius froze, their viscous blood slowing, heartbeats stuttering to a halt.

"A," Selena's voice strained, "I-I can't... hold them for long."

She didn't need to.

Their mental barriers were paper thin, some nonexistent. Slipping into their empty minds was easy. It was their sheer numbers that stretched my blood magic to the breaking point.

I couldn't stand the dried blood cracking across my cheeks. The itch was unbearable.

I felt Selena's control slipping, her magical threads snapping one by one. She might have called another warning, but it was lost under my heart slamming in my ears and barbed wire tightening around my stomach.

Taking a ragged breath, I focused. *Just take over, kill them all, then feed.* Warm, metallic liquid trickled down my upper lip. More blood I couldn't afford to lose, but I licked it anyway, desperate for every drop.

I zigzagged my magic between the Stalkers, snagged their black, gelatinous auras with a ruthless fist. My Blood Manipulation moved with the speed of lightning, bright red and branching in hundreds of different paths. It acted like a magnet as, one by one, it claimed their minds.

Six hundred and fifty-five Stalkers swarmed the battlefield. Far more than Harbinger had predicted. And every single one was now under my command.

Acid squirted up my throat. Burned my tongue.

"Holy shit, is that Projector's doing?" Hummingbird's voice threatened to break my concentration.

My legs trembled under me. The hunger wrangled my insides, and my head weighed so heavy it felt like I carried each Stalker's weight.

The Transmitter buzzed again.

"She's separating them by type. What the fuck?" Terraknight's shout pierced my skull.

I forced my eyes open. Through the red haze clouding my vision, I saw dozens of Stalkers laid impaled on his earth creations, ichor mixed with ice shards melting in puddles.

Good Derzelas! Had the Stalkers retaliated before I took control?

My first priority: stop breathing. The outliers' proximity pushed me over the limits of starvation. I needed to resist the temptation before I lost focus.

I commanded the Nebulas toward the idle Limuses. Some Stalkers still fought back, a spark of intelligence trying to expel me, but I pushed harder, crushing their defiance. Fresh blood gushed from my nose. My focus narrowed to a pinpoint; the world beyond fading to shadow.

Someone shouted, "Kill at will," and the night lit up.

Another of my commands forced the Nebulas to wrap their powerful arms around the stocky necks of the hellhounds. They squeezed. The Limuses' black claws sparked against stone as they thrashed, their agonized wails rising above the chaos as bone shards erupted through flesh.

Something snapped inside me. I crashed to my knees.

Voices shouted, but my sluggish heartbeat drowned them out. My awareness slipped. Then numbness spread throughout my body. No more pain. Only unfeeling bliss. But I couldn't stop now.

Just hold the magic. Save everyone.

Focus.

I redirected the Ignises' power toward the remaining Stalkers. Fissures split the ground, belching smoke. Their screams reached me through the haze, but none were familiar.

Red dripped from the corners of my eyes, and the last thing I saw before squeezing them closed again were geysers of lava devouring the monsters.

Voices argued behind me.

Selena's angry pitch raised above all. "Let her finish! No, don't touch her. She needs to feed—move away." Footsteps withdrew. "I swear to Derzelas, Sabin, if you don't let me down, I'm going to kill you!"

A laugh caught in my throat and emerged as a bloody cough. I found myself on my hands and knees, heaving. The bloodlust cleaved at my sanity. My mind frayed like old rope.

Fire erupted in my veins as another drop of blood fell from my nose. Claws ripped through me. My insides contracted, withering, rearranging beneath my ribs. My spine snapped and cracked as my body folded inward. The scream that tore from my throat sounded wrong, incomplete, unnatural.

Darkness called to me once more.

When awareness returned, a pair of dark boots filled my vision. I tried to blink away the red haze, but my eyes were too dry to close.

I tried to speak, to warn him, but my throat was scorched sand. My trembling hand waved weakly. *Run, save yourself.*

He remained still.

With my last coherent thought, I sent one final command to the Ignises in my grasp.

Just like the monster who killed my father, I willed them to lengthen their fingers into razor claws and tear their own throats. Quick. Clean.

The ground shook with their falling bodies, and the pressure in my head lifted. I heaved a euphoric sigh, forgetting that empty lungs would draw in the scent of fresh blood.

Decay and humidity hit first. Someone grabbed my elbow, hauling me up. Ozone and rain wafting from him hit next. My mouth watered.

"Remind me to never piss you off again, Projector. Captain, did you see this?"

Something screamed danger in my fogged brain, but his thundering pulse drowned all reason. I turned, drinking in the bleeding gashes across his lean body with my gaze. Most had healed, but deep cuts still soaked his shirt. Blood dripped over dense lashes and high cheekbones, drawing my attention to his generous smile—white teeth, sharp fangs.

Hunger exploded through me, rattling my bones.

"Fuck, your eyes," he backed away, hands raised.

Too late.

The hunter awakened. My head fell back as I took a long breath. Scents intensified. Reds shifted, glowing vividly against living flesh. One mortal perched on a rooftop a hundred yards away, another flying from the opposite direction—both honey-sweet.

Rocks crunched nearby. I snapped toward the sound, filtering through rot for prey. Two mortals within reach. Others lingered but too far to be worth it.

I seized the first one's mind. He tried to flee, light-colored wings flapping, but my magic held him in a vice. He crashed to one knee, veins bulging as he fought my invisible leash. Something in my chest purred at his fear. It poured out of him in sharp waves and licked at my skin, calling to me.

I commanded his essence forward. Step by step, his heart raced like a wild horse. He shook his head, causing his curls to bounce against his cheeks.

"Guys, something's wrong with the projector!"

I crushed his airway. I didn't need him talking.

"Aurora, stop!" Someone—another predator—launched at me. I twisted away, her sharp nails grazing my neck as I ducked.

Unyielding bands wrapped around my chest from behind, lifting me. I snarled at the interruption. No one stood between me and food.

"Let Hummingbird go. You don't want to hurt him." The voice was barrel-deep and raspy.

I gripped the strong arm curled around my throat, threw my weight forward, and hurled him over my shoulder. He crashed somewhere with a loud crunch, but my winged prey drew all focus.

I stalked toward him. My gums ached as his scent filled my lungs. Just a few steps remained.

A dark, smoking knot materialized between us, writhing and growing. Shadows arched and smoked until they formed an impenetrable wall. Lightning bolts zigzagged within, converging at a distant point and carving out a tunnel that stretched endlessly.

Cold air rushed past me, carrying whispers from nowhere and everywhere at once.

A tantalizing scent rose above all else: coffee and roses. I forgot all about my trapped prey and loosened my bonds.

From the darkness, a figure emerged, and my blood magic slammed against steel barriers a foot thick.

He stepped through easily, tearing away his blood-soaked shirt to reveal golden skin marred by fresh battle wounds. Fury sizzled around him. The scowl twisting his features promised violence.

The predator in me purred.

I craned my neck to meet eyes that blazed like twin suns. Fangs flashed behind his snarl. This was the prey my monster craved. My stomach knotted into a spiked ball, thrashing against my ribs in desperation for the ultimate hunt.

"Take flight, Hummingbird," he commanded, voice like thunder. Platinum hair fell across his forehead, shadowing eyes that burned into mine with lethal focus.

It would bring untold satisfaction to take down such a strong specimen. My muscles tensed as I rose onto the balls of my feet. Everything faded except the steady drum of his pulse. Mine to claim. To draw life from.

The mortal's hesitant voice barely registered. "But—Will you be alright?"

The dangerous creature drew his blade, inch by inch, the metal singing against its sheath. Without breaking our stare, he pressed the tip to his chest. My nostrils flared at the promise of blood.

"NOW!" His roar echoed as he carved a deep line into solid muscle.

HARBINGER

BLACK MIST EXPLODED FROM the last Ignis as Aurora's Blood Manipulation tore through its throat. My jaw clenched, watching her rip them apart with a savagery that made my blood freeze and burn at the same time.

She was the end of the world in leather.

That damn suit was drenched. Ichor spread across the material like oil on water. Slithering up her neck and across her face was a network of black veins that melded with raven hair.

Raw fury coursed through me. I'd warned her to cut the link, to turn off the Nexus. But no, the princess always had to prove something. Had to throw herself into danger. Like I hadn't spent decades hearing projectors scream their hearts out.

The ground beneath us moaned, soaked and still trembling from the slaughter she'd orchestrated. Limuses, Glacies, Nebulas, Ignises. She'd gone through them like wooden puppets. Five, maybe six hundred of the fuckers, all reduced to mist and gore.

And she'd had the nerve to yell at me in Sibiu for losing control. The hypocrisy was staggering.

Hummingbird gathered his wings, gave an upward push, and was airborne. His massive wings beat like thunderclaps in the silence.

Aurora whirled toward me, chest heaving, fangs bared. A sea of red had crawled across her eyes, conquering the whites and almost successfully shocking me out of my fury. It was like watching the wings of the night close out the sun. Feral. Untamed. For a split second, I saw what the rest of the continent feared—an original pureblood in her true form, stripped of sanity. The starved animal beneath the marble skin and noble breeding.

My body tensed. Ready to move. Ready to fight. Part of me wanted to shake her until her teeth rattled, make her understand she couldn't keep doing this. Couldn't put herself and my guildmates in danger with her reckless stunts.

The other part wanted to gather her close, to erase that wild look from her eyes, to shield her from the pain the Voices had brought.

When the fuck did I get so soft?

She wasn't some damsel in distress. She was a goddamn Tepes; the most dangerous bloodline in the Republic. She'd just annihilated Stalkers with nothing but her mind. And yet here I was, wanting to protect her when she was knee-deep in their remains.

The cold air carried the stench of death and Gloom, thick and cloying like a coating of fur on my tongue. Moonlight filtered through the clouds, casting dark shadows across her blood-spattered face. Beautiful, in the way a wildfire consuming a forest was beautiful. Terrifying. Mesmerizing.

Glass and stone crunched beneath our feet as we moved closer. Her scent was an ache in my throat—spilled blood mixed with vanilla and peaches. My wolf paced behind my ribs, wanting out. Wanting her. The beast didn't give a damn about timing or consequences.

"You will feed, princess," I snarled, hoping she was still in there enough to hear me. "And then we'll talk."

Aurora let out a low growl that sounded like it should've come from a much bigger creature. The sound sent shivers down my spine. Zalmoxis, help me, but even drunk on bloodlust, she was magnificent.

She launched at me like a panther, all teeth and claws. I staggered back, breath rushing out as her weight slammed into me. Pure instinct had my hands flying to her thighs, ready to throw her off, and my blade clattered to the ground, forgotten.

Her fangs sank into my neck. I couldn't bite back the groan. Sharp pain bloomed, then melted into heat coursing through my veins. My grip on her tightened, fingers digging into softness that yielded just enough to drive me crazy.

"Fuck," I hissed as she pressed closer, her body molding against mine like she was made to fit there. Like all the jagged pieces of me had finally found their match.

Every pull of her mouth sent ecstasy racing through me. My blood burned. Those feral snarls turned to soft, desperate moans, and I almost lost my head. My hands slid up her thighs, to the curve of her hips, and squeezed, needing her closer.

Rain started falling. Cold water trickled down my chest, but I barely felt it. All that existed was her—the way she moved against me, the heat of her mouth on my neck, her body grinding against mine.

Between the hunger and the downpour, a connection blazed between us. I could feel her, not just physically, but in my head. Her thirst. Her need. Her pleasure as she drank. It was invasive as hell, but I couldn't deny it felt good. My cock strained against my leather pants, and she felt it. She started moving with purpose, rolling her hips in a way that would make even a monk lose control.

"It's enough, Aurora," I rasped.

The wild hunger in her dimmed. I could sense her awareness seeping back in. She pulled back from my neck, tongue darting out to catch the last drops of blood from her lips. The sight sent another searing jolt through me, but that smug satisfaction in her eyes killed it fast.

Her smile, lazy and pleased, reminded me of what she'd done. Disobeyed orders. Nearly died. And she didn't seem to give a damn.

"Are you well?" I asked, swallowing my anger.

I set her on her feet, trying like hell to ignore how her body slid against mine. How her breasts pressed against my chest through the wet leather.

She leaned forward, that pink tongue flicking out to taste the blood on my skin. My muscles locked up, teeth clenching so hard it hurt.

"I am now—" The words died in her throat.

I watched the change sweep over her as memory hit. It was like watching storm clouds roll in. Fear replaced the post-feed bliss. Her eyes went wide, pupils dilating, pulse jumping as she stared at her blood-caked hands.

The reality of what she'd done crashed into her.

My hands tightened on her hips, pulling her close until our breaths mingled. "Good. You're starting to remember," I seethed.

She tried to pull away.

I allowed it and released her, watching her retreat.

Her eyes met mine, wary now. Smart girl—she should be afraid.

"You know what? I'm glad you fed," I spat, picking up the blade and sheathing it as I stalked toward her, "because I'm so fucking pissed at you right now, you'll need all your strength."

My fangs pressed against my lip as I bared them, copper flooding my mouth. The urge to grab her was almost overwhelming, but then I felt a push on my mind. My mouth dried; my heart closed into a tight shell. Her magic brushed against my consciousness, ice-cold fingers probing at a locked door.

The fucking audacity.

"I won't fall for that shit again, princess," I hissed.

Ma had taught me to strengthen my mental shields when I was a boy, before the conflicts, before everything went to hell. I didn't inherit her blood magic, but I could defend myself against it. I'd be damned if I let the projector trap my mind again.

Her eyes blazed when she realized her efforts were futile as she launched herself at me.

I stepped aside, feeling air displace as she flew past. "Aurora," I warned, my voice dropping an octave.

"You can communicate with them!" She spun, leading with a kick aimed at my head. Her movements were fluid despite what she'd been through, so I ducked. "All this time." Her voice broke as she feinted left, then slammed her palm toward my sternum.

I jumped back, barely avoiding her strike.

She continued, "You knew what would happen with the Nexus."

Something gleamed in her other hand, silver catching firelight from a nearby blazing pile of dead limbs. I caught her wrist and made her drop the needle with a pained gasp, but she twisted free like a cat, dancing back out of reach. The last time she'd pulled that thing out, she'd driven it into my hand.

"Those Voices were tearing me apart from the inside," she snarled. Diving low, she swept at my legs. "And you knew!"

I jumped over her leg, but she anticipated it, rolling to her feet behind me. Rage bubbled up in my chest. "I told you to cut the fucking link!" I roared, whirling to face her. "I warned you! But you just had to prove something, didn't you? Had to show how fucking brave you are!"

Her chest heaved, water streaming down her face. Or were those tears? I couldn't tell anymore. All I knew was that the fear that had gripped me when I saw her collapse from that roof, when I heard her screaming in my head, had paralyzed every nerve in my body. I'd felt her pain echoing through the Harmonization, sharp and jagged, and for one terrifying moment, I thought I'd lost her.

That fear—cold, absolute—had gutted me more effectively than any Stalker ever could. I'd stood there, useless, helpless, hearing her suffer. Just like I'd watched Ma die. Just like I'd failed Conin.

I couldn't feel that again. Couldn't bear another loss. Another failure.

I couldn't afford the distraction. Not her scarlet eyes, not her stubborn pride, not the way my body responded to her. Because if I did, none of us would survive this war.

She threw a punch.

I grabbed her arm and used her momentum to spin her against my chest. Her back slammed into me, soaked leather squeaking against bare skin. "But no, the mighty Princess Aurora knows better than everyone else, doesn't she?" I said into her ear, lips brushing wet hair. "Do you get off on going against my orders?"

She drove her elbow back into my ribs with enough force to crack bone.

My hold broke. I grunted, pain lancing through my side.

"That's rich, coming from you." Her bitter laugh echoed across the ruins. "Master of secrets and lies."

I pursued her. When she leaped at me again, I caught her in the air, pinning her arms to her sides.

"Tell me," she hissed, struggling against my grip. "Is that why you disappeared after that night? Why you bottled your blood instead of letting me feed from you? Because you knew I'd eventually catch up with your lies?"

The memory of our night together tore through my defenses. She used my distraction and hooked her ankle behind my knee. We both went down hard. The impact knocked the breath from my lungs as we rolled across uneven stones.

"What a great laugh you must have had!" she spat.

That sobered me worse than a punch to the gut.

"You want to talk about that night?" I growled, rolled on top, and trapped her wrists above her head. Mud, blood, and water soaked through our clothes, but the heat between us could have dried an ocean. "Fine. Let's talk about how you used me to satisfy your curiosity. I make a good 'blood source' as long as I don't jeopardize your royal status, right?" I scoffed. "Don't be a hypocrite."

Her eyes went feral. I could feel the anger rise inside her, simmer and bubble just beneath her perfect surface. "Look who's talking." She bucked her hips, nearly throwing me off. "Used YOU?!" Her knee shot up toward my groin, but I blocked it with my thigh. "I trusted you, you bastard!"

She twisted, slipping from my grasp. We jumped to our feet and circled each other, both breathing hard. Predator versus predator.

"And I tried to protect you!" I roared.

"Protect me?" She charged again, but I deflected, catching her arm and spinning her away. Her hair whipped across my face, carrying that maddening scent of peaches even through the rain and gore. "By lying? I defended you! You're a varcolac, and I was on your side. And all this time—" Her voice caught, hurt bleeding through the fury. "It doesn't matter. You made me want things I didn't think I'd ever get. But it's over now." Her tone turned bitter. "Thank you, Captain, for opening my eyes and showing me how misguided I was."

I stared at her, words choking my throat. The quiet hitch in her breath told me some of the droplets on her cheeks were tears. I had no idea my absence would upset her so much. She tried to hide it, but her scrunched nose and flattened lips gave her away.

The way she avoided my gaze.

My chest tightened like someone had wrapped steel around it and was slowly constricting. I hated that I was the reason for her pain. That I'd put that wounded look in her eyes.

How the hell had we ended up here? We were supposed to barely stand each other.

I dragged a hand over my face, stubble scraping my fingers. "Let me explain, there are things you don't understand."

"I'm tired of your lies." Her voice dropped, harsh and cold. "Nothing you can say will make me trust you again."

"So now I'm the bad guy? Ironic, considering you ended us before we even had a chance to start." The words burst out before I could stop them. "I didn't lie. I omitted things, yes, but I was only trying to protect—"

"And there it is." She sneered, throwing her arms wide. Her eyes zeroed in on me, ice-sharp. "He admits it. Let me spell it out for you: omitting things is the same as lying, especially if you've been plotting with the enemy all this time!"

"I'm not plotting!" I took a step forward, frustration raising my pulse. "Will you let me fucking explain? I deserve a chance, don't you think?"

"You deserve nothing, traitor."

The accusation hurt more than I cared to admit. After everything: all the blood spilled, the battles fought, the friends buried. After a century spent keeping these lands safe while the purebloods cowered behind their walls.

Traitor. As if I hadn't sacrificed everything for this fucking war.

And hearing it from her—from Aurora of all people—twisted the knife. She'd been there with me when I carved Phoenix's name on the pendant. She'd tasted my blood, been inside my head. She'd seen what drove me. She, more than anyone, should have known better.

"You want me to grovel? Is that it?" I rasped. "I hurt you, and you're letting it cloud your judgment. But throw that word at me again, princess, and we're done. For good."

She lunged and kicked. This time, I made no move to avoid it. "I put my life in danger to keep your identity secret," she hissed. "Selena's, too. Do you know what the Republic will do to us for not reporting you?"

I was pretty fucking aware of how those damn leeches treated their citizens.

Her boot connected with my chest, but I didn't budge. Just stood there, absorbing the impact.

Her foot smashed into my stomach next. Like being kicked with a crowbar, the force rippled through muscle and bone. I backed up a couple of steps. The wolf inside me grew impatient, scratching at my ribs from within.

"Is that supposed to hurt?" I grunted. Blood trickled from the corner of my mouth, and I spat it at her feet like she had spat her accusations.

She pivoted on her heel, gathering force, and launched a roundhouse kick that caught me square in the temple. The world tilted; colors bled into one another. Buildings swayed like trees in a gale. Sound faded to a distant hum before roaring back with painful clarity.

She stood there, chest heaving. "Did that get your attention, Captain?" That smirk made me suddenly crave her blood. Made me want to sink my teeth into that smooth column of her throat until she gasped my name.

How long had it been since I'd fed? Six months? A year?

I shook my head and spat more blood onto the ground. The wolf prowled to the surface, rejoicing in the challenge, begging for more. I started toward her, jaw set.

She'd had her chance.

It was my turn now.

Aurora launched a vicious jab to my ribs.

I sidestepped and reached for her wrist. She spun away and slammed her elbow into my kidney. I pivoted and took the blow on my lower back instead. She drove her boot heel down toward my ankle, putting her full weight behind it. I shifted, absorbing the impact, refusing to show pain.

With nowhere left to retreat—the old storage house of Brasov's market square loomed behind her—she feinted right, then struck with lightning speed. Her knuckles connected with my diaphragm.

Not cool.

Air rushed from my lungs in a pained hiss, but I surged forward, driving her into the wall. Stone crumbled beneath the impact. Then, I trapped her left arm with my elbow, pressing it against the rough surface. She punched my ear, sending shockwaves through my skull.

A guttural sound tore from my throat as I captured her flailing wrist, forcing it high above her head. She was completely immobilized, caged between my body and the ruins.

Checkmate.

She writhed beneath me, fighting my hold. Her body trembled with exertion. For all her immortal strength, she couldn't break my grip.

What I hadn't counted on was how having her at my mercy would affect me.

I was pissed, and aroused.

"You done?" I asked.

"Not even close," she hissed and snapped at my windpipe.

She didn't get far.

"Want to see if I'm lying?" I tilted my head, leaned over, and exposed my neck. "Here you go, princess. Do your worst. Sink your fangs in my throat."

I felt her breath against my skin. Warm. Soft. An electric jolt shot through me straight to my groin. I couldn't stop my cock from reacting, and her little pants against my ear weren't helping.

My voice turned into a ragged snarl. "You haunt me."

She stiffened. Her heart hammered in her chest, loud as the thunder overhead.

"I can't get you out of my head." Dipping my chin, I looked into her eyes, those bright depths that followed me into my dreams. "I lie awake thinking about all the ways you could get yourself killed, and it fucking terrifies me." My voice turned to a whisper. "Every time you charge into danger, something inside me breaks. You've burrowed beneath my defenses, princess. You're under my skin. And it's driving me out of my damn mind."

We stared at each other, neither willing to break first. The space between us felt too hot, like standing in the path of a Magma Lance. Her chest rose with each breath. My wolf howled and shoved against his restraints.

Our breaths created small clouds in the chilled air. "Do I make you miss me, Aurora?" I asked. "Do you feel this—this fucking tearing inside when we're apart?"

She took a long breath and closed her eyes. Her chest stopped moving. She was trying to shut me out.

I grabbed her shoulders and shook her once.

"Look at me, damn it!" I snarled. "Do you crave me? Think about me until you can't sleep? Until your skin feels too tight and nothing makes sense anymore?" I pressed closer, our foreheads touching. "Do you think about me until there's nothing left but to give in because if you don't, you feel like suffocating? Do I make you as fucking crazy as you make me? Answer me!"

Her long lashes lifted, exposing glittering irises that burned through the darkness. She pinched her lips—stubborn to the end—but her racing pulse and the way her thighs clamped against each other was answer enough. I could smell her arousal, even through the blood and death surrounding us.

"Good to know I'm not the only one drowning here."

I grabbed her waist and hurled her over my shoulder. Her forehead hit my ass, and satisfaction washed over me. She weighed next to nothing. All that lethal power packed into such a deceptively delicate frame.

"Put me down, you Neanderthal!" she shouted between bouts of pounding fists.

For the first time in days, I felt my lungs expand fully. A chuckle slipped past my lips as she squirmed against me, her struggles only making me hold her legs tighter.

"Not a chance. You behave like a brat, you get what you deserve."

I called on my magic. It responded with cool eagerness. Chilly winds whipped my hair as the portal started to form, and lightning zigzagged deep into its depths like veins of frost across black glass.

The disk behind my ear vibrated, sending a buzz through my skull. Terraknight's voice filled my head, clear despite the writhing portal—and projector.

"Cap, perimeter's clear. No Stalkers within a five-mile radius." His deep baritone rolled through the connection with a hint of static. *"Looks like they've pulled back to their territory. Whatever's left of them after your princess turned them into mist. We're good to head back to base."*

I paused, one foot already in the portal, and choked on empty air. My princess? She squirmed on my shoulder, oblivious to the verbal landmine Terraknight had just dropped. Was I that obvious? Had everyone seen what my wolf decided from the moment I first saw her?

"Everyone alright?" I forced out through clenched teeth, adjusting my grip on Aurora's thighs. She'd gone still, no doubt trying to listen. Fat chance without her Nexus to eavesdrop.

"All accounted for. Ember's got a nasty cut, but Pearl's already patched her up. Hummingbird's wings got singed, nothing serious." A pause, then a low chuckle. *"Need backup with the princess, or are you two finally working out all that... tension? Gotta say, Cap, never seen you this wound up over someone before. It's almost cute."*

Cute, huh?

I tried to pinpoint his location, but the bastard was hiding from me. I made a silent vow to punch those perfect teeth down his throat next time I saw him. Even through the Transmitter, I could sense that shit-eating grin spreading across his face.

"We're fine," I hissed.

"Sure you are." Terraknight's voice shook with amusement. *"I'll keep the children distracted so you two can have some* quality time *alone. Should I tell them you're conducting an interrogation? Or perhaps"*—his voice dropped to a theatrical whisper—*"a thorough physical examination? I hear that neck-biting thing you two do gets pretty intense."*

"Fuck. Off."

His laugh rumbled through the connection. *"Just don't break her, Cap. And remember—she's royalty, so maybe try using your words instead of just grunting. The ladies like that sort of thing."*

The barbarian would know. Probably learned his moves from the trashy romance novels Pearl kept hidden under her bed. The Transmitter went silent before I could craft a response that wouldn't dig my grave deeper.

Aurora remained still, but I could practically feel the fury radiating from her.

"If you're done with your little boy talk," she snarled, "I'd appreciate being put down."

"Not happening." The portal pulsed before me, a swirling vortex of ice and darkness. "Hold your breath."

She stiffened. "You impertinent ass—"

But the void was already compressing around us, cutting off her scream and claiming us both.

AURORA

THE COLD SANK ITS teeth through my suit, nipping at me like a juvenile zmeu. My breath crystallized in my lungs. I tried to scream, instinct overriding reason, but the sound twisted into an eerie whisper that echoed through the frigid emptiness.

My limbs felt heavy, movement like wading through molasses. I'd intended to pummel his backside until he put me down, but my fists barely made contact. Not that it would have mattered—the man's posterior was as thick as his head.

Survival instinct kicked in. I stopped fighting the void and surrendered to its pull, conserving what little energy I had. I'd resume defending my dignity once we emerged.

If we emerged.

The seconds stretched into an eternity of cold and pressure, the blackout seeming to seep into my very essence.

Just as panic began to claw at my throat, the real world snapped back into focus. We burst into open air. Harbinger released me, keeping one steadying hand on my shoulder as I doubled over and expelled ice crystals from my lungs.

"Derzelas' blood," I gasped, eyes watering. "You could have given me more time to prepare."

I looked around through watering eyes. He'd brought us to a secluded glade nestled deep within the forest. A light drizzle misted the atmosphere, and though the rain had let up, dense clouds hid the stars, leaving only the faint glow of moonlight filtering through the canopy. Ancient pines guarded the perimeter, their needles glistening with raindrops from the earlier downpour. In the center, a massive angel oak stretched its gnarled branches outward, as if trying to cover us in a protective embrace.

Under different circumstances, perhaps with someone who hadn't just abducted me through a dimensional rift, the setting might have been romantic. The thought only added fire to my rage.

"You had warning enough."

I glowered at him, my hand reaching for my hair, seeking needles that weren't there. Damn it. Coughing and tears ruined any attempt at intimidation, as did the curses and accusations jammed in my throat.

What emerged was a bastardized growl and a whine—a squeal that was so undignified I wished the portal would swallow me whole, again.

"What in the endless pits were you thinking?" I hissed, my voice still hoarse from the cold. "Why have you brought me here?"

"Good. You're well enough," he said and curled his warm hand around the back of my neck.

Bastard.

I twisted away, but he spun me around so fast it gave me whiplash. My boots tripped over the exposed roots before he pressed me against the massive tree trunk with enough force to steal what little breath I had managed to recover.

The sharp taste of panic bit my tongue. But overlaying that was a deep, deep anger. I slung my head back and caught him in the chin.

"I am not your plaything to manhandle," I spat.

His chest vibrated against my back. Every inch of him pressed harder against me. The rough bark dug into my cheek as his breath fanned over the shell of my ear, sending cold and hot shivers down my spine.

"If I were to slide my hand between your thighs right now, I think I'd find evidence to the contrary."

Heat flared low in my belly, but I strangled it with cold fury. His voice might be honey and gravel, but every word was a lie wrapped in velvet. Old fear spiked through me, yet even as Radu caged me, the difference blazed clear. I could break free if I wanted to. My body could want him all it liked; my mind knew better.

His hands tightened on my hips. "Do you enjoy tormenting me, Aurora?"

"I don't know what you're talking about?" I bit down on my lower lip to keep from giving him the satisfaction of a reaction. Damn him. Why did he have to smell so good?

"Your reckless decisions, the disregard for your own safety, your stubbornness." He captured my wrists and drew them above my head, higher until I had to rise onto my toes. "If I hadn't severed the harmonization, the link would have turned against you."

His breath made my skin pebble, and I arched my back, melting under the scorching heat radiating from his skin.

I might as well brand myself a fool and be done with it.

"Is this your idea of reconciliation? Asserting dominance?" I asked with a shaky breath.

"Sex and power have always gone hand in hand. But power shared differs from power taken." He transferred both my wrists to his left hand, using his right to grasp my chin and tilt my head. "Your scent betrays you. The hunger, the desire. I can smell it on you." His voice roughened. "Besides, I need to feed."

Whatever response I might have offered dissolved as he dragged his fangs along my fast-pulsing vein.

Panic melted into pure lust. I was still furious, but my body rode the adrenaline high of nearly dying. Some primal part of me wanted him to bite, to taste my blood. My vision blurred as he tormented me with gentle nips that never broke skin.

"You used your magic on me again," he whispered. "I don't know if I should punish or fuck you right here." Disapproval toyed with excitement in his tone.

My pulse stuttered.

Then his mouth claimed mine.

Strong arms crushed me against his chest, blocking out the world as I clutched the tree trunk. His scent penetrated my skin, winding through my body to pool between my thighs. My breasts ached for his touch. My lips burned for more.

Seconds stretched into minutes. When he finally allowed me air, I gasped. My head fell back as he traced kisses along my jawline and down my neck. One large hand gripped my hip, lifting me until his hard length pressed against my bottom.

He was pure masculine power. Beautiful in his strength. Making me feel feminine by contrast.

"Your kisses will get you nowhere, varcolac," I said, but I tilted my head further, inviting him to bite.

"And that sharp tongue of yours will get you into trouble." His palm moved beneath my breasts, fingers splaying across my abdomen. Sparks of pleasure ignited deep in my belly. "Still feeling dominated?"

"Completely."

Maybe this was necessary. A way to move beyond mistrust and betrayal. I needed this. If not for us, then for myself. I craved the release a Blood Pact would bring. He tasted of sex. If I denied myself tonight, I'd regret it forever. I was already damned for not reporting him to the Council. One more night wouldn't change anything.

Traitor or not.

He adjusted his hold, supporting me with one arm around my waist while his other hand cupped my breast. Lightning shot through me, and combined with the scrape of his fangs against my skin, it drew a moan from my parted lips.

"Tell me to stop," he demanded against my neck.

"No," I breathed.

He nipped harder. "Tell me to stop, Aurora."

I forgot how to speak, so I shook my head, urging him on, pressing myself against him. Desperate to eliminate any space between our bodies, I rocked against his hardness. Too many layers separated us, and a frustrated moan escaped me. If this was his punishment, it was exquisitely cruel.

"Good," Radu said before sinking his fangs into my neck. He held me as if I weighed nothing, pinned me against the tree. His strength, both protective and possessive, made my heart race. The rough bark against my palms, the cool night air, Radu's heat—all of it intensified as he fed.

Pleasure rushed through me in bursts so intense they could have lit the night. The way he called to my blood made every part of me respond. Addictive. Obsessive. Drawing out sensations I'd never felt before, making me beg for more. With each pull of his mouth, my body yielded further, surrendering to instinct.

I never wanted this to end.

Standing on tiptoes, I pressed harder against his erection. I longed to be so utterly lost in him that the boundaries between us would blur into nothing. To be consumed by him until all that remained was the steady pulse of our heartbeats—raw and inseparable and infinite.

The vibration of his growl traveled through my bones and struck directly at my core. It drove me to move with greater urgency against him. Savor the feel of him through the frustrating barrier of our clothing.

When his mouth released my neck, the sudden absence left me quivering. I realized with a start that he had bitten me on the other side of Lev's scars, and the thought sent a different kind of thrill through me.

Perhaps sensing my need, or guided by the shameless sounds I couldn't contain, he moved a hand up to the collar and pulled at the concealed zipper of my suit. He drew it downward with such deliberate slowness, I nearly sobbed my frustration.

Uncertain what to do with my free hands, I reached behind his neck and threaded my fingers through his frost-white hair. I tugged slightly, scraping my nails against his scalp.

The sound that escaped him was feral. His fingers dug bruisingly into my hip as he pulled me harder against him.

Liquid heat flooded my center as he grinded against me. My eyes fluttered closed, his dominance awakening desires no man had ever stirred in me before. Another complication to examine later, when my brain functioned again and I could properly analyze these feelings.

I moaned. "I don't want to rush you, but we are rather exposed out here."

My breasts spilled free from the confines of my suit, heavy and aching with need, and I arched like a cat to meet his eager hands.

"The Stalkers are deep in their territory," he said, thumbs circling the sensitive peaks. "Nothing will disturb us tonight."

A breathless moan escaped me when those skilled fingers pinched and twisted, finding that exquisite edge between pleasure and pain. He continued his exploration, exposing more of my skin to the night air until the zipper halted. But his hand didn't stop there. It slipped inside, glided lower, and cupped me between my legs.

"So wet." He tugged at my suit to trail fervent kisses toward where neck met collarbone. His teeth scraped my skin, marking me. "I want to bury myself inside you, Aurora."

I gasped at the shock of pleasure as his finger found my wetness. Ecstasy speared my center and boiled in my core. "You're such a romantic."

His other hand kneaded my breast. "Would you prefer poetry and courtship, Your Royal Highness?"

I laughed and pressed against his hand, inhaling the electrifying scent of him. The thought of this dangerous, powerful man composing sonnets was absurd. But his use of the formal title, even teasingly, made me realize something. He wasn't the captain anymore—Harbinger with his cold distance and barbed comebacks. This was Radu, the man who touched me like I mattered.

"No, honesty suits you better." Especially when that honesty came wrapped in raw need focused entirely on me.

"Good—because I intend to fuck you, princess, and I will fuck you hard." He thrust two fingers deep inside me just as his fangs pierced my skin again.

Oh. My. God.

A helpless whimper escaped me as I bared my throat to him, yielding completely. The sensations coursing through my body set me ablaze. I was standing at the edge of an awakening volcano. Responding to Radu's command, I was merely the vessel for his hunger.

"Let go," he commanded, brushing his lips to the sensitive cord of my neck. "Give me all of you."

Sharp, consuming pleasure made the decision for me. Radu claimed my mouth in a fierce kiss, our tongues hunting for sensation even as his fingers moved in quick, merciless thrusts.

I shattered around him, my inner muscles clenching so violently it bordered on pain.

As the waves subsided, I felt him tugging my suit down over my hips. The fabric bunched around my boots. Cold droplets peppered my bare back, but my skin burned so fiercely they might as well have landed on scorching coals.

The sound of his pants opening sent my pulse galloping. Then Radu repositioned my hands against the rough bark, spread my legs as far as the constraining fabric would allow, and aligned himself with my entrance.

"Final warning, Aurora. Tell me to stop."

A snort tickled the back of my throat at his belated attempt at restraint. Instead of answering, I pushed back against him, and took him in.

The stretch was divine, but his deep groan rumbling against my back was what sent shivers down my spine. Something fragile blossomed between us, a link that felt like finding something I hadn't known was missing. Whatever this had started as—punishment, release, desperation—we were equals now, locked in this moment together.

As his warm fingers traced along my ribs, tremors followed. Then he settled his hands on my hips and thrust into me, sheathing himself to the hilt.

I gasped his name.

Radu withdrew only to drive forward again and again. Fierce. Tireless. Possessive. He claimed me with every powerful slide, sending shockwaves of pleasure down to my curling toes.

His scent surrounded me in silky veils, tempting me with the velvety petals of a dark rose infused in sweet coffee. A desperate thirst rose within me. The need to taste him was absolute.

"Don't stop," I gasped, climbing toward magnificent heights.

A grunt vibrated in his chest as I tightened around him. The way our bodies molded together, as if Dark Father himself had designed us to fit this way, enforced this feeling of righteousness between us.

"Fuck, you'll be the death of me," he rasped as his fingers curled around my throat, pulling me flush with his body, while his other arm wound around my waist, anchoring me to him. He spread my legs wider, wider... until my suit protested and split the seams. But still, I couldn't find it in me to care. I was his and he was mine.

Then his mouth found my neck again, his fangs breaking skin once more, and the world beyond us ceased to exist. I shifted beneath him, lost in the dual sensations as he pounded and fed, overwhelming every thought except one: here, with him, I was exactly where I belonged.

Flashes of his thoughts—extreme pleasure, frustration, fear—rolled inside my head too quickly to make sense of them. He had been blocking me from entering his mind, but his pleasure weakened his grip on his defenses.

"Fuck, she feels like heaven... can't get enough... shouldn't want this... shouldn't need her..."

His powerful body covered mine, and I sensed every sinew and muscle tensing with each controlled thrust. His varcolac heat radiated through me, turning my thoughts to smoke in the wake of impending release.

I drowned in the sensation, unable to surface, unwilling to try.

"Mine," his thoughts whispered inside my head.

I arched beneath him as ecstasy ruined me, my body contracting around him, desperate to draw him deeper and never let go. The rhythmic pulses of my climax wrung a guttural sound from his throat that reverberated through his chest and into mine. Our frequencies aligned.

But as his control slipped in the wake of my release, his mental barriers wavered. The world around us blurred and shifted, replaced by images flickering through our Blood Pact connection. Not my memories, but his.

I saw through Radu's eyes. I—he—was crouched behind a column in a grand hall. The architecture appeared familiar: the distinctive stone walls, the Republic banners, the ornate marble pillars that depicted the faces of our Creators. The colossal chamber of the Tribunal looked different somehow, less worn by decades of use.

A muscled arm stretched out protectively. Radu crouched behind one marble column, his hand clasped over his younger brother's mouth. Conin, who was a couple of years younger than the last time I saw him.

The memory shifted focus to the center of the hall, where a man who looked exactly like Radu faced three imposing figures in Council robes. Same angular features, same platinum hair, same powerful build. Their father. Beside him stood a woman of breathtaking elegance, with raven-black hair cascading over her shoulders, the classic features of an original pureblood. Radu had inherited his father's face, but his unique eyes were a gift from both parents—citron rimmed with his mother's red bleeding inward in tiny flecks.

"—promised safe passage for all mixed-breeds," their father was saying in the same commanding tone I knew so well. "The detention camps were supposed to be temporary."

"It's been three years, councilors," his mother added, maintaining the perfect poise I'd been taught at court. "Our people are dying behind those fences"—she pointed viciously with her manicured hand—"while you debate politics. Children, elders—dying of disease, starvation, despair."

Elder Armand stepped forward, his silver-and-onyx hair shorter but his angular face unmistakable. "The situation is complex, Lord and Lady Lowe. These relocations take time to implement properly, it would be premature to rush the process before all facets are aligned appropriately."

"Relocations?" she asked, and I felt young Conin's terror spike through the memory as her voice rose. "You mean extermination. We know what's really happening. The mass killings, the unmarked graves—"

"You're mistaken," Elder Viktor interrupted. "Perhaps you should reconsider such inflammatory accusations. We wouldn't want matters to escalate unnecessarily."

Behind the pillar, Radu tightened his arms around his brother as the three councilors moved away from his parents. Their voices dropped to urgent whispers, but both brothers could hear every damning word.

"She knows too much," wiry Elder Nicolae hissed. "If word spreads about the real purpose of the camps, we'll have riots on our hands."

"The cleansing initiative cannot be exposed," Armand agreed quietly. "Not when we've come so far."

"Handle it," Viktor said with flat indifference. "All of them. Tonight."

Cold dread pooled in my stomach as the terrible truth sank in. Radu had told me the Republic executed his parents, but I'd assumed there had been a trial, charges, some semblance of justice. All executions were public affairs, the condemned's crimes read aloud to gathered crowds, their sins catalogued for history.

But this... this was assassination. Murder in the shadows to silence inconvenient truths.

The horrific memory warped and fractured.

Radu's physical pleasure had overwhelmed his mental defenses, but I felt his consciousness fighting to suppress the vision even as his body surrendered to climax. His ecstasy and the echo of ancient terror crashed through our connection in devastating waves. Then the vision shattered completely as Radu's release finally claimed him, his mental walls slamming back into place.

I gasped, dropping back into my own body.

The forest, the rain, his weight against me—everything rushed back, and I resurfaced.

His movements stuttered, then stopped. I felt his jaw clench, teeth still embedded in my flesh, and realized he had no idea what I'd witnessed. The secret he'd guarded so carefully had spilled through the Blood Pact without his knowledge or permission.

My limbs felt heavy, my muscles liquefied. I collapsed against him, shaking and boneless, surrendering completely as the final pulses subsided.

Sweet. Dark. Father. Almighty.

But even as pleasure ebbed, that horrible memory burned in my mind. High-ranking councilors—men who still held power in my Republic—had ordered his family's assassination for threatening to expose the truth.

The knowledge sat like acid in my stomach; it warred with the lingering euphoria of our connection. Part of me wanted to pull away, to process this earth-shattering revelation, but another part craved the escape only he could provide.

I couldn't change the past. Not his family's murder, not decades of Republic lies. But here, now, in his arms—this was real. This was mine. The rest of the world could burn; I just wanted to lose myself in him until the horror stopped clawing at my mind.

Radu's blood still rushed through my veins and mixed with my essence. I'd experienced Blood Pacts before. They were clinical, perfunctory exchanges with other purebloods. Nothing like this consuming fire. Forget the volcano. This was a supernova, catastrophic for the mind and soul.

I felt like I'd been reborn.

Radu's fangs slipped from my neck with exquisite care. His tongue traced the punctures and soothed the sting before blazing a scorching path up to that spot just below my ear.

He turned my face toward him, and what I saw in those gold-rimmed eyes nearly stopped my heart. The same eyes I'd just seen in his terrified brother as they watched his parents' be sentenced to death. He gazed at me through heavy lids, as if I were his salvation in the endless damnation. As if I were his entire universe condensed into flesh and blood.

His lips found my mouth, and I kissed him fiercely, letting our mental link carry the weight of my rage for his murdered family, my shame for my Republic, my need to give him something beautiful to replace those memories.

Before I could catch my breath, he'd shifted our positions, and I found myself astride him, my thighs—and what was left of my ruined leather suit—bracketing his narrow hips as he filled me once more. I would never have enough of him.

We moved together in perfect rhythm, our bodies and souls devouring each other, lost in a dance as old as time yet somehow entirely new between us.

I braced my hands on his large shoulders, dug my nails into the hard planes of muscle, and drew him closer. I feathered light kisses along his jaw, working my way toward that tantalizing pulse at the side of his neck. My fangs ached with need, saliva pooling in anticipation of tasting him again.

Then, I hesitated, waiting for him to deny me this pleasure, but he tilted his head, exposing the golden column of his throat. The gesture, so vulnerable, so trusting from a man who trusted no one, sent warmth spreading through my chest. I needed no further encouragement and sank my teeth into his waiting flesh.

His gruff moan vibrated against my lips as the universe contracted to a single point of sensation—his blood flooding my mouth. Blinding lights exploded behind my eyes, stealing my breath. When awareness returned, he still moved inside me, and my body trembled, caught between agony and need.

My fingers tingled where his hand hovered over mine. I couldn't resist the pull. When he finally cradled my wrist and lifted it to his mouth, the piercing of his fangs was both a claim and a caress.

We became one.

The mental barriers Radu had maintained crumbled to dust, and his thoughts crashed into my mind like a cloudburst. The desperate need for release contended with the desire to extend our pleasure. Beneath that roared his unexpected addiction to my blood, the sweetness of it overwhelming his iron self-control. But deeper than all of this lay the terror he'd felt earlier tonight—fear for his guild, fear for me.

This need to protect me stunned me. I was immortal; I didn't need protecting. Then I saw myself through his beautiful, unique eyes, and it nearly broke me.

Powerful. Fearless. Beautiful.

Not a princess, not a pureblood, just... Aurora.

Complete.

My climax broke like the earth's crust finally giving way to the magma that had been fighting its way to the surface.

I pulled back from his neck with a gasp. Lines of scarlet trickled from the corners of my mouth and down my chin and neck. Shuddering, I felt him pulse inside me, and cool air misted from my lips into the night as I moaned my satisfaction.

At the same time, a deep, masculine growl rumbled through my wrist. Radu tightened his arms around me and emptied himself, his own release as vocal as mine.

Spent and euphoric, I collapsed against his chest. Blood—his and mine—smeared between us and mingled with the scent of rain. Never in my one century of existence had such complete contentment flooded my veins. We remained like that, clinging to each other as our racing hearts slowed to a steady rhythm.

The storm had passed unnoticed, silver moonlight bathing the glade through scattering clouds. An owl called from somewhere above, announcing its presence while remaining hidden from view.

Slowly, Radu lowered me to my feet and tucked himself away before helping me remove what remained of my tattered suit. His touch was unexpectedly gentle as he tilted my chin up with a knuckle, forcing me to meet his burning gaze. The anger that had driven him earlier had vanished, replaced by an expression of such stark vulnerability it stole my breath. His eyes, normally so guarded, now revealed every emotion raging within him. Like an uncut gem, Radu was rough, natural, devastatingly beautiful.

Something clenched in my chest.

"I've never lost control like that before," he whispered, voice scraped low in his throat.

The worry threading through his voice pulled me back to reality. Was he apologizing for what we'd shared?

"I haven't either," I whispered back.

"This wasn't supposed to happen." His thumb brushed the delicate skin beneath my eye, then traced along my lower lip, collecting droplets of blood. "I shouldn't have crossed the line between us."

He slipped his finger into my mouth, and the hot-wet pulse between my thighs renewed with violent intensity.

I gently nipped the soft pad, watching mesmerized as the crimson rim of his irises flared. His varcolac emerged in the golden feathers swirling around his enlarged pupils. Those amber-flecked eyes would forever draw me in, keep me captive, hypnotize me.

A smile bloomed across my face before I could suppress it. Radu and I had bonded through our first Blood Pact, and it surpassed my wildest imagination. The world had shifted beneath my feet, and I had no desire to find solid ground again.

"Neither should I," I whispered as his fingertip followed the path of my smile.

From the swift glance of his mind, I understood why he'd lied to me—to avoid frightening me, to protect me. He wasn't a traitor, but that didn't excuse the lack of communication. So much pain could have been avoided. Perhaps thousands of deaths if he'd opened up to his previous projectors and told them about the Voices. Another failure on the Republic's part: not fostering enough trust with the very people protecting its walls from the monsters.

"Did I—" He cleared his throat, his jaw flexing as he struggled with the words. A man who butchered Stalkers and sent them into other dimensions now wrestled with a simple question. "Are you—okay?"

The uncertainty in his voice touched something deep within me, something I'd thought long dead.

After everything that had happened tonight, I was a mess. My body still hummed with pleasure; my mind reeled with revelations. I needed somewhere quiet to process the entire night, to understand this monumental shift between us.

But first, I had to erase that concern from his features.

I studied him with new clarity. Yes, he possessed a ruthless edge, a dangerous strength that had first made me wary. But now I saw beyond that. He wasn't handsome; that was too tame a word to describe him. Radu was magnificent in his rawness, in his power barely leashed. Everything about him called to the predator in me, an equal in every way that mattered.

My smile widened as I offered him honesty in return for his vulnerability. "No," I said, leaning forward to press a soft kiss against his still-flushed lips. "You've shattered me completely. I never imagined anyone could make me feel what you just did." I held his gaze, letting him see the truth in my eyes. "And I can't help wondering how soon we might do it again."

"Insatiable." The tension around his eyes melted away, replaced by a smoldering heat. His gaze dropped to my lips and lingered there. He was looking at my mouth as if he wanted it wrapped around him. "There are many things I want to do with you. But first, I owe you some answers. Come, Projector."

Shock held me in a chokehold, and I forgot how to fill my lungs with air.

Projector. Not Aurora. Not even princess.

He took my hand, weaved our fingers together, and stared at them. A muscle jumped in his brow and the beginnings of a frown formed.

Several paces away, the air rippled and tore open, not a sleek doorway, but a jagged tear in reality itself. The edges pulsed with pitch-black energy that frosted nearby leaves and grass with delicate crystals. The sound of splintering glass filled the clearing as the portal widened, releasing a rush of frigid air.

I stared at the portal, then at Radu, the joy of moments before reduced to a cold knot in my chest. Just one word—Projector—and the walls between us had risen again.

I bit my lower lip, fighting the unwelcome sting of tears.

My inexperience with matters of the heart left me unprepared for this emotional whiplash. One moment he looked at me like I was his salvation, the next he retreated behind formality and rank. His oscillation between intimacy and distance was infuriating.

I reminded myself of the truth: I was destined for a throne, and he was a varcolac, an enemy to my people. Having him as my blood source made tactical sense.

One thing became crystal clear in my mind, though. I needed to be more careful with my heart. I'd work with him, I'd defend his outliers, and I'd do everything in my power to hold the Stalkers at bay from the Republic, but I couldn't let myself get swept away again; he could push and pursue until his face turned violet, but I needed to remember who we were when the passion faded.

An unwelcome thought slithered from the depths of my consciousness before I could suppress it.

The way he kisses, what he can do with his body will certainly destroy my sanity. He is the finest blood blend, rich and decadent. Just that sample has spoiled me for any lesser experience.

Clenching my fists, I mentally stabbed those traitorous thoughts and buried them where they couldn't resurface. My pride bristled beneath the hurt. The lingering sweetness of his blood could not compensate for the confusion he stirred.

But egotistical asshole or not, I couldn't deny that Radu had granted me a second chance at life. He'd rescued me when he could have easily abandoned me to face dawn's lethal rays and disintegrate into dust. In his own frustrating way, he had shown me there was more to life than struggling under the constant threat of war.

A chilled breeze from the portal lifted strands of his silver-white hair as he stepped toward the swirling darkness. But his hand remained firmly locked with mine, his thumb caressing the back of my hand, a contradiction I couldn't reconcile.

This conversation wasn't over. Far from it. We would either set ground rules, or I might just kill him out of exasperation. Straightening my spine, I swallowed the hurt and followed him.

AURORA

I straightened, blinking frost from my eyelashes as Radu's bedroom materialized. The familiar olive walls, the cherry wood bookshelf lined with dog-eared volumes, the desk cluttered with maps and reports, all flickered in warm candlelight. My stomach lurched, still rebelling against the passage through Chronoportal.

"That was..." I swallowed, willing my insides to settle, "efficient."

The air still carried traces of our last encounter, and his scent was so thick it made my fangs ache. Somewhere in the house, muffled voices carried heated conversations—Selena yelling at Terraknight about how he'd handled me during the bloodlust.

Shame burned through me. I needed to apologize to Hummingbird. To all of them, for what I'd done.

Then, a map atop a pile of papers caught my attention, and I stepped further into the room. Tactical formations marked in Radu's elegant cursive handwriting, terrain sketches that looked like they'd been drawn from memory.

"Your portal points are too predictable," I said, studying the battle plan spread between stacks of reports. It was a standard 'hammer and anvil' approach. He as the hammer, the guild as the anvil. The outliers positioned in a defensive arc behind him.

Radu's eyebrow arched as he pulled the cover from his bed. "Excuse me?"

"Here." I traced his three X's marked on the map. "You're thinking linearly. Strike the center, push outward. But what if we used multiple insertion points?"

He handed me the thin throw from his bed to cover myself, then moved to stand beside me. His warmth felt good against my chilled skin. I sketched new positions with my finger.

"Portal here first, draw their attention. With my Blood Manipulation, we can turn their front line against their own rear guard. While they're confused, you portal to their flank. Here." I tapped the map. "Strike their command structure."

"The coordination timing would be impossible."

"Not with my magic." I traced connecting lines between positions. "I can sense every Stalker in my range. I coordinate when you portal, when the outliers advance, when enemies turn on each other. It's like conducting an orchestra instead of playing solo."

Radu studied my modifications, brow furrowed in concentration. "Multi-point strikes. Staggered timing." He paused, then nodded appreciatively. "That's actually brilliant. Where did you learn formation strategy?"

"My father. He used to quiz me on historical battles against Solanthia while the ladies at court learned embroidery. Said a future queen needed to understand war, not just politics."

"What was your favorite campaign?"

"The Night Attack at Targoviste. He faced an army fifty times his size, so he struck their camp at midnight from multiple points. Created chaos and confusion until the Ottomans didn't know who was enemy or ally." I pointed to my revised formation. "Same principle. Let them think they know where you'll strike while your real attack comes from unexpected angles. Terror and confusion can defeat superior numbers." I gave him a pointed look. "Patience being something you could work on."

"And you could work on not being such a know-it-all, princess." But he was grinning as he said it, dimples making an appearance, and when I laughed, something changed in his expression.

"What?" I asked, suddenly self-conscious.

"Nothing. Just... you should do that more often."

"What, correct your battle tactics?"

"Laugh like that. Like you're not performing for anyone."

Heat crept up my neck. Before I could respond, he marched towards the bathroom, only to come out a moment later with a wadded cloth pressed against the cut in his chest. Every muscle and sinew rippled as he dabbed at the wound.

I clenched my fists and willed myself not to breathe him in.

Silver hair tumbled over his forehead, mussed like he'd just rolled out of bed. Glorious didn't begin to cover it. Bronze skin gleamed like gold in the candlelight. My gaze followed the dark blond hair dusting his chest, trailing it down past his waistband like an arrow pointing straight to forbidden territory.

Territory I'd recently visited but hadn't fully mapped in our passionate haste.

I dragged my gaze upward and found him watching me. The amber-rimmed eyes, flecked with red, burned with barely leashed hunger.

His full lips curved in that arrogant smirk I knew too well. "See something you like?" Rough and velvet, his voice sent a shiver down my spine. I fought the reaction and focused on the angry gash across his chest.

The wound looked fresh, which made no sense. Radu was immortal, but even if he hadn't been a pureblood, albeit only half, he'd consumed my blood. It should have accelerated his healing.

Making my way to him, I raised a hand to his chest and 'accidentally' pressed too hard against the tender flesh.

A sharp hiss escaped his lips. "Careful, princess," he warned, though there was a dangerous edge to his tone that wasn't entirely pain.

"Oh, did that hurt?" *Pettiness, thy name is Aurora.*

I trailed the carved ridges of his abdomen with the sharp tip of my fingernail. Muscles jumped beneath my touch as I applied more pressure, leaving a faint pink line in my wake.

His body's response left me pleasantly surprised and more than a little excited. The quickening of his breath, the blown-out pupils, the unmistakable bulge growing beneath those leather pants.

Let him suffer a little.

Radu clamped a hand around my wrist just as my fingertip traced the sharp *V* leading down to his leather band.

"That's one thing I want to talk to you about," he growled, a salacious warning glimmering across his handsome face. "If you could stop touching me like that... we might actually get somewhere."

His other hand moved to work the buttons. My heart rate spiked.

"What are you doing?" I stammered and yanked my arm free.

Keen eyes tracked down my body and fixed on where I'd knotted the throw between my breasts. His smile was devastatingly wicked, all gleaming teeth and predatory intent. "Don't tell me you're suddenly shy."

He slipped his thumbs into the top of his pants, holding my gaze as he pulled them down. Buttons popped free, one after another, slowly, tantalizing, revealing where those fine dark-blond hairs thickened and darkened below his navel.

He wasn't wearing anything underneath.

I groaned internally. Of course he wasn't.

"Stop that." The heat in my cheeks could have set the curtains ablaze. "We're supposed to be talking."

"That's exactly what I'm doing," he drawled, somehow making the inoffensive words sound utterly indecent. "I may have been living in this shithole for decades, but I still have my manners. What we're about to discuss requires clean clothes and all this blood and gore off." He gestured broadly at the dark, crusty stains clinging to his pants and boots, including me in the sweep. "But if you want to join me... there should be enough hot water for both of us."

The rain had washed the worst of the filth, but I didn't even want to think about what might be tangled in my hair after rolling across Brasov's cobblestones.

Stalker bits. Ugh.

My mind warred between maintaining distance and giving in. But the blood and grime coating my skin made the decision easier.

"Trying to distract me?" I raised a brow. "It won't work."

"Won't it?" His eyes gleamed in challenge. "Then those hard nipples have nothing to do with it and everything to do with the temperature in the room, right?" His grin stretched wider.

The arrogant bastard.

"Is that what this is about?" I retorted, crossing my arms. "You think a Blood Pact and some flattering words are all it takes to make me forget you lied to me? That you kept secrets that nearly killed me tonight?"

Radu's smile dropped. "No. I think you deserve the truth. About the Voices. About what's happening. About me." He took a step closer, and despite everything, I didn't retreat. "But I also think you should know what you're getting into first." His jaw muscles feathered as he seemed to struggle to say the last sentence. "You deserve the chance to walk away."

I held his gaze, reading the truth there. He might be a liar, but in this instance, he meant every word.

"Fine," I said at last. "You talk. I'll listen. But I'm not joining you in that shower."

"Afraid you won't be able to resist me?"

I rolled my eyes, ignoring the fire spreading down my neck. "More like you drowning me to avoid answering my questions."

Radu laughed, and it transformed his face, making him appear younger, less burdened. "Suspicious little thing, aren't you?"

"Cautious," I corrected. "And you still haven't explained why that wound isn't healing."

His expression turned severe. "Because it's not meant to." He looked down at the cut and drew his eyebrows together.

I frowned too. "But why wouldn't it—"

"Let's get cleaned up first. Then we'll talk. You have my word."

"Your word doesn't mean much these days," I muttered.

I wanted to argue, to demand answers now, but I was filthy, sore, and mentally drained. A short delay wouldn't matter.

Before I could react, he caught my waist and hauled me against his chest. It was like falling into a furnace, his heat wrapping around me from all sides. I melted against him when I should've stepped back.

"Turn around." His voice a low command.

Against my better judgment, I obeyed. All the hurt and irritation I'd been nursing began to dissolve as he gathered my hair and swept it aside, exposing my nape.

Then his mouth was at my ear. "How does your head feel?"

Cautiously, he traced the area where the Nexus had been, and my knees almost buckled under his tender touch. Somewhere in the back of my mind, I was grateful for his concern.

"Better," I croaked and turned into him.

He ghosted his fingertips over my bottom lip, feather-light but burning, his face intense with concentration. When his finger grazed my teeth, I bit down gently and drew the tip into my mouth, tasting the salt of his skin. A sharp breath escaped his lips. He pressed his forehead to mine, eyes squeezed shut, and fought for control while I sucked his finger deeper.

He didn't quite succeed, because his arm shot out to brace against the dresser and pinning me there with a low groan, his free hand suddenly around my throat.

My body ached in a way that drowned out all other senses. An ache that only his touch could soothe.

"I'm glad," he whispered, breath labored. "Because I wouldn't have forgiven myself if I'd been the reason my projector suffered permanent damage."

"Try again." I wanted to sound dismissive, but failed miserably. "I'm not yours."

"You sure?" His hand skimmed down my arm. "You have my blood flowing in your veins, my seed trickling between your thighs."

A raging inferno blazed from the top of my head to my toes. The memory of his body moving against mine, inside mine, overtook any rational thought. I gulped and fought the urge to clench my legs, to feel that delicious friction again.

Then he slid his fingers over my scars, and my body went from molten to ice in an instant. I stiffened. The touch was gentle, questioning, but it scraped against nightmares I'd spent months trying to bury.

He noticed immediately and pulled back, taking his warmth with him. "As long as I live," he said, close enough that I could feel his breath against my cheek, "no one will ever hurt you like that again."

I squeezed my eyes shut, fighting the burning sensation behind them. "Why are you saying these things?"

"What things?"

"I don't know... sweet things." I sighed. "Like you actually care."

His chuckle held no humor. "One might argue that's how a proper blood source should behave."

"Is that all this is? A source and a receiver?"

"What do you want it to be, Aurora?"

The way he said my name, like it was something precious, something sacred, erased any trace of lingering shadows.

"I want the truth," I said. "No more games. No more evasions."

He tilted his head to the side, fixing me with his sharp gaze. "The truth isn't always a kindness."

"I didn't ask for kindness."

His hand came up to cup my cheek. "No, you wouldn't. That's what fascinates me about you. All that power, all that privilege, and still you reach for truth, no matter how ugly."

I tried to reinforce the shield around my heart. Easier said than done when he talked like that. "Then tell me. What were those Voices? Why did the Nebula know you?"

Conflict stained his features. Then his hand dropped, and he stepped back. "The water gets cold fast. Last chance to join me."

"Radu—" I wanted to say more, reject him again, but something stopped me. The night had officially caught up with me.

Who was I lying to?

The pull of him was undeniable and maddening. The train of terrible ideas was screaming down the tracks, and I didn't want to jump. I wanted to ride it all the way in.

"This doesn't mean anything," I said, even as I bent forward and made quick work of unfastening my boots.

His attempt to hide his grin was lousy at best. "Of course not."

"We're just conserving water." I took a step toward the bathroom, unfastening the throw.

He followed me. "Absolutely. Very practical."

"And I'll still expect answers."

"I gave you my word."

I stopped at the threshold. "No funny business."

Radu gave up and let his lips stretch in a thousand-watt smile. "Wouldn't dream of it, princess."

I let the cover pool at my feet and put an extra sway in my hips as I marched inside, but not before shooting a furtive glance over my shoulder. A petty victory kicked up my pulse when his heated gaze collided with mine and I caught him biting his lower lip.

Inside, the state of the bathroom matched the rundown state of Radu's bedroom. Cracked subway tiles in washed-out cream covered the walls, while the paint on the ceiling bore similar dark water stains and peeled from the corners. A shower stall with a corroded brass showerhead stood in the corner. Half-melted and smelling of lavender, Gale's candle flickered atop the marble vanity, casting just enough light to see my reflection in the spotty mirror above.

I was right.

Hair matted with Stalker blood stood in stiff clumps around my shoulders. Dirt and gore streaked my face and neck. I looked like I'd crawled out of a grave or had been digging one all night.

I didn't wait for the water to warm, knowing better than to expect any heat remained after the guild's return. Without electricity, none of the houses in the Outer Wards had proper hot water. The outliers had rigged an ingenious system of rooftop tanks heated by sunlight, but the Black Guild either hadn't bothered to expand it or simply hadn't had time.

I turned the rusty knob and stepped under the spray, bracing for the cold—only to gasp as hot water cascaded over my skin, loosening my rigid muscles.

I moaned. "Oooh." Liquid heat. Pure heaven.

The glass door squeaked open behind me, and Radu's presence filled the small space even before his chest pressed against my back. He gave me a gentle nudge further under the spray.

"I don't think I've ever seen you smile like that before," he murmured, lathering soap onto a cloth.

I hadn't realized I was doing it.

I shrugged, tilting my head back to let the water run over my face. "It's the warm water. I'll never take the simple things for granted again." I raked my fingers through the tangles in my hair, grimacing as knots caught and pulled. "But you're right. It's been so long since I felt pure joy over anything that when I do, I feel like I don't deserve it. War has a way of making us bitter, I suppose."

"Don't rob yourself of simple pleasures, Aurora." His voice was a low rasp as he drew the soapy cloth across my shoulder, down my arm, and back up again with maddening slowness. The way his slight accent rolled the r's in my name had burrowed into my memory.

"You were so brave today. Although you did fucking drive me insane." He took a deep inhale, pressing harder against my back as if shielding me from the world. "I've never seen anything like that. You were a goddess out there."

The simple praise, delivered in that husky voice, kindled something warm in my chest. Not the heated desire from earlier, but a deeper feeling, more profound. Dangerous to my wary heart.

I turned to face him. Water trickled down the hard planes of his face and spiked his blond eyelashes. A dewy sheen covered his bronze skin in the steam rising between us. He wasn't just a man, but a weapon forged from flesh and bone.

"You're doing it again," I murmured. "Saying sweet things."

"Do you want me to stop?" A challenge drenched in sin as he traced a slow circle over my chest and dipped the washcloth between my breasts. "Being sweet, I mean. Though you seemed to enjoy yourself earlier."

"Derzelas, you're such an arrogant asshole," I huffed.

He clutched at his chest in mock pain, the sharp tips of his fangs showing with his smile.

"Ouch. You've wounded me."

It was hard to stay angry with him. My own lips curved upward.

"But you're also a loyal friend," I continued in a softer tone. "A good captain. A beast on the battlefield. And a—"

"Great lover?"

I raised a hand to stop him, shaking my head. "An infatuated lover," I corrected.

"You didn't object, from what I remember," he purred, and I felt the vibrations down to my toes.

"You're impossible."

He pressed his hips against me, leaving no doubt about his current erect state... and what he thought of my opinion.

"Say what you want about me, princess, but you want me as much as I want you." His breath fanned hot against my pulse, and I had to gulp down the moan working its way up my throat. "I can smell it... feel it."

He raised his head until his lips hovered just above mine. "Deny it all you want. Your eyes can't lie."

'Fuck, your eyes.'

The memory crashed through the heat building between us, and guilt turned my limbs to lead. My bloodlust might have hazed most of the night, but Hummingbird's fear burned clear in my mind.

"Do you think Hummingbird will ever forgive me for what I did to him?"

"Don't worry about him. Despite how much I dislike the idea of sharing you, I don't think Hummingbird would have minded you feeding on him."

"How could he not? I hurt him, forced him to yield."

"Projector." He cupped the back of my head, pushing me to meet his gaze. "I think I speak for all the halfblood male population when I say that no matter how much they hate your guts, they wouldn't complain having your body squirming in their arms." As if trying to prove his point, he cinched my waist with his steel-banded arm and crushed me to him. His hard shaft pressed against my stomach. "See? It's a win-win."

I shoved against his chest, but my mind circled back to his possessive claim.

"Pretty territorial for someone who doesn't even acknowledge my rank," I said, pushing wet hair from my face.

His eyes darkened, and not in a good way. "When you've spent decades fighting in this hellhole," he said, "you learn to seize what matters. The rest is just noise."

Curiosity got the better of me. "So you don't feed from your guild-mates?"

A tendril of jealousy snaked its way up my body. Before I could process it, his hands had lifted and secured me against the cool tile. I draped my arms around his neck while my legs wrapped around his waist.

"I've shared with them in the past, but we agreed to keep our feedings separate from guild business," he admitted, adjusting me against him.

Sucking in a breath, I raised an eyebrow, feeling bold. "So you've never tasted pureblood before?" I rocked against him, relishing the friction of his hardness against my heat. 'Good' was such a pathetic word for how he felt. For how we felt together.

There went my voice of reason. To never fall for his sexy tricks again.

Instead of his usual smirk, his expression remained intense. "I've never had *you* before."

The pure honesty in his voice stripped away my defenses.

I needed to feel him again.

Radu's hands moved to support my weight, lifted me gently, and entered me in one powerful thrust. The fullness made me gasp, my head falling back against the tile.

"You're unlike any immortal I've known," he breathed into the nook of my shoulder.

Butterflies swarmed in my stomach, and my heart gave a worrying lurch. I began to move against him, finding our rhythm. "What exactly did you expect when you met me?"

His movements never hesitated as he pressed me harder against the wall. "Another useless, self-absorbed projector who'd retreat at the first sign of trouble."

"Not all projectors are cowards," I countered, though we both knew most were.

"You're nothing like them." The water had long since gone cold, but the fire between us more than compensated. His hand cradled the back of my neck—possessive, carnal—drawing me closer until our lips nearly touched. "You're fierce, compassionate, loyal to a fault, and still believe things can change. You're a dreamer."

"A dreamer?" I whispered, but he claimed my mouth, and time blurred.

The universe became meaningless until we finally parted.

"You dream of a better world," he whispered against my lips, panting. His voice, rich and velvety like aged wine, thrummed a string somewhere deep inside me. "And in this hell, that's rarer than you know."

Desire coiled tighter with each powerful stroke. Waves of pleasure radiated through my core, building toward devastating heights. My nipples hardened to painful points; my legs trembled as they clutched his waist. The pressure inside me swelled beyond bearing, a dam ready to burst.

"I want to come with you inside me," I gasped against his mouth.

"Whatever the princess commands."

His pace quickened, strong hips rocking me with every thrust.

When release finally tore through me, it shattered everything. My composure. My control. My very sense of self. I cried out, uncaring who might hear. Radu followed moments later with a guttural sound and emptied himself inside me.

Underworld's balls. Had I truly been alive before feeling Radu move inside me, before knowing what my body was capable of experiencing?

We remained locked together, my head resting above his thundering heart. I savored these quiet seconds, knowing they wouldn't last. Soon enough the spell would break, and reality would intrude. One of us would do or say something cutting, and we'd be back to circling each other like starved predators.

I felt his throat work, preparing words, and braced myself.

"We need some boundaries," he murmured against my throat.

I froze, uncertain I'd heard correctly. "Boundaries?"

"While this lasts, you don't feed from anyone else and don't take other lovers."

My inner muscles clenched at his commanding tone. He responded with a small thrust that sent aftershocks rippling through me.

"While what lasts, exactly?"

"This craving." He met my eyes.

"Only if it works both ways," I answered and, right then, I couldn't imagine that fire ever burning out.

And that terrified me.

Satisfaction flashed in his gaze. "Deal."

Too late, I realized. I'd let myself get sucked into his energy again. I needed space. Needed to breathe air that wasn't saturated with his scent.

Slipping from his grasp, I pushed the shower door open. He wrapped a large hand around my wrist just as I reached for a towel.

"You look good wet."

I fought to control my racing pulse. "And you owe me answers."

Sweet Derzelas, help me from falling head over heels for this man.

HARBINGER

I braced my palms against the cold tiles to keep from dragging her back and burying myself inside her again. Ice-cold water hammered my back, but it wasn't substantial enough to serve as a distraction.

She was becoming a weakness. Every time she fired back with that sharp tongue or fixed me with those crimson eyes, the beast inside me lost its mind.

I should've cut her out of my life the moment I realized what was happening. Before she consumed me completely.

But I needed her.

Her blood, her magic, her quick mind that caught details others missed. Even things that I missed; I felt oddly proud that she had revised my plans within moments of reviewing them. And the way she threw herself into danger for my guild, for Phoenix, without a second thought. She was nothing like I could have imagined.

I stilled under the freezing spray, letting the rush of feelings course through me. Damn it all to hell.

I'd had women before. Plenty of them. But none had ever made me question my sanity. Aurora fought like she was born for war, yet I'd seen her eyes fill with tears over Phoenix's stolen voice. She was brutality and tenderness in the same breath, and somewhere along the way, she'd become essential. Not just wanted, but needed. And that made her dangerous.

I gritted my teeth, forcing my thoughts away from her and onto the soap in my hand. The lather swirled down the drain, carrying away blood and grime but not the weight of what I'd just promised her.

Had I really vowed exclusivity? To her? It was like some stranger had inhabited my body and spoken those words. I hadn't made promises like that to anyone, not even before the war had started and tomorrow's dawn was a sure thing.

But even now, with her scent fading and clear thinking returning, I couldn't bring myself to regret it.

The warmth spreading through my chest had nothing to do with lust. Not the electric jolt when our skin touched or the sweet burn of her blood in my veins.

This went deeper. It had crept up on me between arguments and battles. While I'd been trying to figure out her angles, assess the threat of her magic, she'd been dismantling my walls piece by piece. I'd watched her fight for my guild like they were her own family. Seen her rage over injustices that had nothing to do with her. Witnessed her stubborn refusal to back down even when it meant risking her life.

Somewhere in all that chaos, I'd stopped seeing her as just a powerful ally or a dangerous enemy.

I'd started seeing *her*.

And I was fucked.

The road ahead would try to kill us both. First, I'd hunt down my brother, and with Aurora's abilities, I might actually stand a chance. Her

Blood Manipulation would call to him like a beacon. Then I'd put the Shepherd in the ground. Aurora's power could tip the scales, but I'd be the one to end that bastard.

After that? I'd walk away.

She belonged back in her Republic, wearing the crown she was born for. Making real change instead of bleeding out in the Gloom. Millions relied on her. Keeping her here would destroy everything good in her—or get her killed trying to save me.

I'd already decided. Use her power to free Conin. Kill the Shepherd. Then cut her loose before I dragged her down with me.

It was a simple plan. A clean break.

So why was I already dreading the moment I'd have to watch her leave?

I shut off the water with more force than necessary and combed my fingers through my damp hair. Time to face her questions. She'd earned her answers.

The glass door creaked as I pushed it open and reached for the towel rack. My hand hit bare wall. Right. Laundry day wasn't until the weekend, and I'd only had one towel.

Which Aurora currently had in her possession.

I turned to ask for a corner of it and stopped dead. Every muscle in my body locked up. Stark naked, she dabbed the towel across her damp skin, chasing water droplets that gleamed in the candlelight. My mouth went dry. My wolf howled, restless and wanting.

I forced my jaw shut before I made an ass of myself.

Narrow waist, elegant spine, shoulders that looked fragile enough to snap under pressure. Pure fucking lie. Beneath that flawless ivory skin lived concentrated death.

Her midnight hair clung to wet shoulders, trailing water down curves that could lure a man right into his grave. Soft in all the right places, deadly everywhere else. The gentle dip of her back led to a firm ass, but those slender legs could shatter stone. And I'd still choose them any day wrapped around my head while I feasted on her.

She bent to towel her calf, and my blood headed south once again.

Fuuuck.

She knew exactly what she was doing to me, and I was falling for every second of it.

I braced my hands against the copper bar above the glass door and stretched my torso just to have something to do with myself other than stare. My cock jutted proudly, and I couldn't do anything about it.

She straightened to her full height—still eight inches shorter than me—and tilted her head back, devouring me with her eyes.

Firebolts zinged down my spine.

"Eyes over here, Projector," I drawled, snapping my fingers to break whatever spell had her staring. The heat in her gaze satisfied my wolf, and a smug grin spread across my face.

She blinked hard, like she was snapping out of a trance, just as I reached for the towel.

She jerked it away, clutching the fabric against herself.

I raised an eyebrow and gestured around the bathroom. "My room, my bathroom, my towel. Unless you want to dry me off, hand it over."

Her pupils dilated for a split second, long enough to show me she wouldn't have exactly minded that, before her eyes narrowed to slits. "Keep it," she snarled, and whipped the towel straight at my head. She actually growled at me, a low throaty sound that seemed contradictory coming from her slender throat.

I caught it with a laugh, and oh boy, how freeing that was. The flash of annoyance on her face was worth the chill of standing there dripping wet. Aurora had a wildcat's unpredictability that kept me constantly guessing.

I liked that about her.

"Nice aim," I said, snapping the towel with a sharp crack just to rile her up. "Though your follow-through needs work."

"I wasn't aiming for your hands," she shot back.

Beaming, I dragged the towel over my hair. She was fighting so hard not to look below my neck that her jaw muscles were twitching from the strain. But when I passed the fabric over the slow-healing wound on my chest, her lust shifted to sharp curiosity. The cut burned like hell, but I kept my expression blank.

Her eyes narrowed. "Why hasn't it healed?"

I shrugged. "It will. Just needs time."

I wrapped the towel around my waist and stepped out. My body had definite ideas about what to do with Aurora naked in my bathroom, and none of them involved conversation. But with her, nothing ever went according to plan.

"It's the blade, isn't it?" she asked, cutting through my wandering thoughts. "Something to do with your varcolac blood?"

Too perceptive for her own good. But wrong this time.

I shook my head. "Opposite, actually. My varcolac blood will heal it."

"But how? We're both—"

"Immortal?" I cut her off with a bitter laugh. "Cut off our heads, we still die, princess." I leaned closer, catching the sweet scent of her hair. "Set us on fire, cut out our hearts: dead. Unless you're talking about full-blooded originals, centuries old. Then beheading's the only sure bet." I tried to keep my voice level, but talking about her people always brought out the worst in me. My wolf was even less forgiving when it came to those leeches. "Being immortal doesn't mean invincible. Ageless? Maybe. Deathless? Not even close."

A flash of outrage sparked in her eyes.

Good. I wanted her angry. Anger was safer than whatever else was building between us.

"What about keeping them connected long enough to fry their brains?" she fired back, stepping into my space. Her head tilted back to meet my eyes, face set with stubborn pride.

I scowled. Guilt punched through my gut. The memory of her convulsing on the ground, blood streaming from her nose and eyes, haunted every moment I closed my eyes.

"In Sibiu, when you broke our link," she continued, jabbing her finger in my flesh, "then again tonight."

My chest tightened, but she didn't give me a chance to speak.

"You should know... you've broken a few projectors yourself by now."

She spun away and bolted from the bathroom. I followed, catching her elbow as she grabbed a wool blanket from the chair.

"I didn't break them," I growled, desperate for her to understand. "It was the Voices they heard during connection. And I always warned them."

"Like you did with me?" she hissed, yanking her arm free to wrap the cover around herself. "Giving me that bullshit order in the middle of battle? Projectors died because of you."

"Only one, and he killed himself!" The words exploded from me before I could stop them. I shouldn't have raised my voice like that. Every muscle in my body went tight, shoulders hunching like I was bracing for a blow.

Neither of us spoke, our ragged breathing loud in the sudden quiet.

"He stepped into the sun," she whispered. "Purebloods don't just throw away their lives."

I ran a hand through my wet hair, hollow abscesses of guilt spreading through my chest. Her words hit too close to home, ripping open wounds I thought had healed. The memory rushed back. Finding Conin's body frozen under snow, alone in his final moments, bleeding out with no one to comfort him.

I went still, trying to lock it away again.

"That's unfortunate," I snarled. "Halfbloods die on the front every day." I met her eyes, knowing I was being an ass but unable to stop. Conin had deserved better than dying alone. "I don't know what you want me to say."

The tension between us made me want to punch something. Aurora stared at everything except my face, and it was eating at me.

"Tell me about the Nexus," I said, desperate to change the subject. "I need to understand what happened to you."

She sighed and sank onto the edge of my bed. "It's the frequency. Works as a conduit to expand our magic when we tap into more than one of an outlier's senses."

I nodded for her to continue.

"The Nexus has a blocker now to prevent us from taking full control over mortal consciousness, but apparently it hasn't been tested enough." A shadow crossed her face. "I just found out before coming here." Her voice turned hard, but for once the anger wasn't aimed at me. "Selena knows more. She's researched Nexuses for decades. Warned me about staying connected too long on high settings." Her lip curled. "Could cause permanent damage or death. Add that to your list."

My eyebrows shot up. Fucking brilliant. Those idiots didn't need Stalkers to kill them. They were doing fine on their own.

"How many senses do you usually use?" I asked, leaning against the desk.

"Hearing, mostly. Sometimes sight."

I remembered Sibiu. Felt her presence in Terraknight's mind. Not just the mental link, but her essence melding with his. Like a ghost slipping through walls. I hadn't said anything then because I wasn't sure what I'd sensed. But now I knew. The more she increased the frequency, the more senses she used and the easier it was to spot her in someone's mind.

Terrifying. And fascinating.

"I know this sounds like excuses," she continued, voice barely above a whisper, "but I couldn't just stand in that empty command room listening to my guild struggle. It drove me insane not being able to help beyond feeding them scanner data. I keep thinking... if I can't protect the people under my command, how can I ever hope to end this war? I had to be there, see what they saw, feel their pain. It was the least I could do."

"You don't need to explain yourself," I said, moving closer to sit beside her. "I understand wanting to protect your people."

Her shoulders relaxed slightly.

I reached out, touched her cheek. Cold under my fingers. "And the..." I tapped her temple. "What do you call it?"

She looked at me with wide, vulnerable eyes. "Transpection."

"That," I muttered. My fingers flexed against my thigh as her screams echoed in my mind. "Were you in pain while you Transpected?"

She shook her head. "Nothing worse than a headache. Today was the first time the Nexus tried to kill me, and I wasn't even using a higher frequency than normal. I wanted to preserve energy. But as soon as I heard those Voices, my blood felt like it was boiling, every nerve screaming in agony."

A shiver wracked her body.

"I imagine that's what dying feels like," she murmured.

I fell silent, remorse spreading through me. All this time I'd thought the Voices gave projectors a little zap, sharp enough to spook them about harmonizing with me.

Not for a fucking second had I imagined the pain could kill them. Could kill her.

"Do you still plan to use the Nexus?" I asked, unable to keep the edge from my voice.

Over my dead body would I let her risk her life again.

She shrugged. "I don't know." Her expression turned thoughtful, like she was weighing whether the risk was worth it.

Something dark unfurled in my chest, the beast sharpening its claws. I knew my face gave me away when her expression turned defensive.

"I'm not suicidal," she blurted. Then she shook her head and thoughtfully added, "I never want that agony again, but Blood Manipulation doesn't work as selectively as the Nexus. I can't just borrow one of your senses. Without it, I can only take full control over your minds, and trust me. It's not pleasant."

"Like you controlled the Stalkers today?"

"Yes."

Relief washed through me, clearing some of the dread anchored in my gut. At least she wasn't set on using that double-edged sword.

"Then it's settled. You don't need the Nexus anymore."

"Didn't you hear me?" She huffed, a soft flush creeping up her neck. I caught myself stroking the vein pulsing there. "Blood Manipulation is one-way, all or nothing. Only the Nexus lets the recipient project back. Through it, I choose the channel. Hearing, sight, both together or apart."

I tsked and slipped my fingers under her chin. "The Voices can hurt you regardless of what sense you choose."

The possessive beast inside me roared, demanding I lock her somewhere safe, away from the Voices, away from anything that might dim those fierce eyes. My grip tightened, but she didn't pull away.

"I know, but—"

"No buts, Projector." My voice came out harsh. I didn't care. Better she hate me than end up dead on my watch. I straightened to my full height, looming over her, letting her see I wasn't fucking around. "You want to stay here? You follow my rules. This is one of them. No more Nexus."

AURORA

A RUSH OF IRRITATION flashed through me, although deep down I agreed with him. He was right, but I'd rather let the Nexus kill me than say it to his face. Only through a miracle had I not catastrophically hurt Hummingbird in my bloodlust, or snapped Terraknight's neck when he intervened. I couldn't risk injuring innocent people if the monster inside me surfaced the next time the Voices drained me of blood.

"Enough about the Nexus," I said, my attention drawn to the weapon lying on the floor, its hilt peeking from beneath Radu's discarded leather pants.

Rising to my feet, I secured the blanket with a tight knot between my breasts and marched straight to his weapon. I could feel Radu's eyes tracking me, burning into the spot between my shoulder blades.

The knob had the unmistakable pale gleam of bone. I reached for it, drawn by an irresistible curiosity. Encased in a wooden scabbard wrapped in black leather, the weapon spanned twenty-five inches—a sleek line of danger from tip to pommel. Intricate silver threads wove through the leather and intertwined with gilded scrollwork and inlaid metal that shimmered in the candlelight. Brighter in some places where time and use had polished away the aged patina.

Tracing the bone handle with my fingers, I felt the grooves carved into its surface. Practical design, even slick with blood, it wouldn't slip from the wielder's grasp.

I tilted my head. What truly captivated me was the large ruby adorning the pommel, a perfect droplet of blood captured in stone. The gem's color shifted with the flicker of the candle flame, morphing from rich claret to vivid pink, a unique trait I'd seen only once before. Many, many decades ago.

When a mysterious silver-haired outlier jumped through fire and slashed the Ignis that had killed my father, saving my life in the process.

I wrapped my fingers around the grip and drew the blade free. It came loose with a soft whisper.

"Tell me about this," I said, keeping my eyes on the gleaming steel.

He leaped across the room and snatched it from my hands. "Careful with that," he said, his tone light but his eyes deadly serious. "This is not for your delicate fingers."

Before I could react, he leaned over my shoulder and reclaimed the scabbard as well. He moved so fast I couldn't stop him.

I wanted to throw something at him. Preferably something heavy and with sharp edges.

Twirling on the balls of my feet, I raised my index finger at him and warned with slitted eyes, "If you don't start talking, I swear to Derzelas I will find creative ways to hurt you."

His grin returned along with those sinful dimples. My stomach did a ridiculous little flip that I refused to acknowledge.

"I didn't peg you as this violent, princess," he said, tossing and catching the dagger with one hand.

The double-edged blade caught the light, revealing silvery inscriptions along the dark crimson steel. Even his weapons had to be beautiful, damn him.

"Choose one," I demanded, crossing my arms over my chest.

I could make out what looked like Russkayan words: Justice, Honor, Virtue. Possibly a family motto.

He caught the blade mid-flip. "Choose what?"

"Projector or princess. Pick one and stick with it."

"Can't do that," he said, suddenly serious.

"And why in the Underworld not?"

His exotic gaze bore into me. "Because you're both." His voice lowered to a gravelly rumble that sent inappropriate shivers through me. "You're 'Projector' when you're commanding and brave, facing down challenges without flinching. And you're 'princess' when you're curious and impulsive, touching things you probably shouldn't." A corner pulled at his mouth. "I like both. Both stay."

I opened my mouth to argue, then snapped it shut. What could I possibly say to that?

Sweet darkness, it would be so much easier if he remained the infuriating, arrogant captain I'd first met. That Harbinger I could handle. But Radu? This man, who alternated between maddening me and making my pulse race with nothing but a glance? Every glimpse he showed me made it harder to resist him.

Nothing changed that he was half-varcolac, and I had a throne to reclaim and a people to unite. But I'd been so wrong about him. Underworld's tits, I'd been so blind. All this time I'd thought he was playing some cruel game. Hot one moment, cold the next, as if testing how far he could push me before I broke. I'd convinced myself his attentions meant nothing, that I was simply another conquest, something to amuse himself with during endless nights of battle.

But the truth was staring me in the face. He'd given real thought to what he called me. Separated the different facets of who I was as both the soldier and the woman underneath. No one had ever made that distinction before.

The realization sent butterflies dive-bombing through my stomach. If he could see these things in me so clearly after such a short time, what else might he come to understand? And how could I possibly maintain my defenses against someone who looked at me like I was his lifejacket?

Crap.

I was in trouble. Deep, inescapable trouble. Because if I couldn't even win an argument about what he called me, how could I hope to stop myself from falling for him completely?

Ignoring the riot in my stomach, I crooked a brow. "And what impulsive thing did I do now?"

"You've just held the only object known to kill an immortal—a sun-steel blade." Radu's eyes darkened. "A single cut won't end you, but it will bleed you dry, and I've put in considerable effort to keep your veins filled and happy."

Though his words wore a thin cloak of humor, the gravity behind them left me cold. Dread squished the flutter of wings and knotted my insides.

"Liar," I accused.

Scarlet flared around his irises. "I'm not lying. But if you need proof, by all means, test it yourself."

He tightened his grip on the hilt and raised the blade to his forefinger. The tip punctured his skin with unassuming control. A single drop of blood welled on his fingertip. Just that one drop, and his exotic scent flooded the room as if he'd opened a vein.

My fangs dropped with a painful snap. The hunger I thought I'd sated roared back to life.

Radu lifted both the weapon and his bleeding finger between us. "What's it gonna be, Projector? 'Cause I'll be more than happy to feed and fuck you again when you're drained."

The confidence in his tone raised goosebumps on my skin. I drew in a shuddering breath, feeling a hard tug low in my belly. Warm and dangerous. The kind of pull that made my blood run hot and scattered my thoughts.

"Playing dangerous games, varcolac?" I countered, unable to take my eyes off the incision.

"Ah, but you're already caught in my web, princess." He pressed his finger to my lips, watching with rapt fascination as the crimson smeared across them.

My tongue darted out before I could stop it and captured his blood. The taste exploded across my senses.

"Your mouth... it captivates me," he murmured, his voice a rough growl.

The hunger in his eyes was purely carnal. "If it's not breasts, it's lips," I said, trying to sound unaffected. "What is it with men and their weird fixations?"

A smile that resembled the searchlights on the Republic walls flashed across his face. "If I had that clever mouth of yours wrapped around my cock," a salacious warning glimmered across his impossibly handsome face as he leaned close enough that his breath caressed my ear, "I assure you, I'd appreciate it thoroughly."

Electricity shot through my body. I forced myself to look away from his smoldering stare and ignore the temptation. We had lethal weapons to discuss, not to mention the Voices still haunting my mind.

I studied the blade again, if only to regain some control. Every instinct screamed at me to back away from those sharp edges, but I held my ground.

"And how, may I ask, did you acquire such a weapon?"

His easy smile vanished. "It's a family heirloom."

"Conin had one exactly like it," I breathed. I'd been too young, too consumed by shock and grief to question how a simple blade could be that effective on a Stalker.

He nodded. "This is the very same one. I found it on his body."

Knuckles whitened around the hilt as he tightened his grip. My chest ached for him. We both lost someone dear to us in this war, but I'd had almost a century to mourn my father. Radu's wounds still bled fresh.

Despite my growing unease, I studied him carefully. Something didn't add up. I was skeptical of what he claimed the sunsteel blade could do. A weapon that could kill purebloods? Hard to believe when any cuts closed before the blood had a chance to swell on the surface.

The blade gleamed in his hand, ominous, as if challenging me to put it to a test.

"You're telling the truth, aren't you?" I whispered.

"Yes."

Just one word, but powerful enough to shatter worlds.

My heart plummeted like a stone. "You could have used it to kill Selena and me," I said. "No one would have ever known."

His attention snapped back to me, some of the darkness retreating from his gaze. "What makes you think I need a special blade to do that?"

A weak smile pulled at his lips, but it didn't reach his eyes. There was no teasing in his tone, and I believed him. After witnessing him in battle, I had no doubt that if he had wanted us dead, we wouldn't have made it out unscathed, especially without my Darklings to match his speed.

But I'd never been one to cower, and I needed him to understand where I stood.

"Direct that blade anywhere near Selena," I retorted, "and I will destroy you." I meant every word. If it came down to it, I wouldn't hesitate. Not that he had given me any reason to believe he'd hurt us.

Radu gave a curt nod, his expression impassive. "I wouldn't expect anything less from you."

"Good. Because you really don't want to make me angry." A weak grin slid across my face, attempting to ease the tension choking the room.

The tight smile on his face softened, making his eyes crinkle at the corners.

"Now that," he drawled, "is something I'd like to see. What exactly would it take to make you see red?"

Very little, when I'm this close to you. The thought came to the forefront, but I decided not to give it voice and derail the conversation any further.

"I think it's time we address the elephant in the room," I said, gesturing toward the blade in his hand. "We clearly don't have time or willing volunteers to test your theory about sunsteel." I cleared my throat. "What I want to know about are the Voices, and why you *conveniently* failed to mention there are dead people trapped inside the Stalkers."

He strode toward the dresser and set the blade down. The pommel made a soft thud against the hardwood.

"You promised." I followed him. "I'm good at putting things together. If you had told me about them, we could have prepared differently for tonight's battle."

"And what exactly would you have done differently?" he asked, his voice calm as he rifled through the drawer. "Would you have cut the link?"

He pulled out a dark-gray tank top, muscles rippling in his back as he rolled it over his head. The armholes were so loose they reached the middle of his ribs.

"I would have taken precautions," I said. "Hummingbird and Terraknight got hurt. Because of me." A sigh escaped my lips. "I need to know what I'm working with so I can adjust my magic. I never want to become a danger to you and the others again."

Without warning, he unfastened the towel around his waist and pulled on a pair of sweatpants.

My windpipe stopped working.

"You want to know what you're dealing with?" he asked, turning around. The shadows in the valleys at his hips caught my attention. They shifted as he took a step forward, tying the drawstring at his waist. "Fine. First thing. They aren't called Stalkers."

I gave myself a mental slap to stop gawking at the way those sweats hung so deliciously low. Mending my voice, I asked, "What are they called then?"

Radu bit the inside of his cheek, trying to kill me with suspense. When he finally spoke, his voice had dropped to a barrel-deep rasp. "Souleaters. They're called Souleaters." He ran a hand through his still-damp hair, his skin pulling taut over sharp cheekbones. "The lieutenant should be present for this discussion. She needs to hear it as much as you do."

Aurora

Souleaters.

My stomach dropped. I clutched the blanket tighter around my body, as if the rough wool could shield me from whatever horror Radu would unleash.

Again.

He reached the door and shot over his shoulder, "Be in the war room in ten minutes. I'm going to gather the others." His tone went flat and distant. Nothing good ever came from his mouth when he shut down like that.

"Okay," I mumbled, catching his stare before he vanished into the hallway.

My skin prickled. Dawn approached. I could feel it in my bones, that internal warning every pureblood carried.

Did Harbinger sense it too? Another question on my never-ending list.

A yawn caught me as I dragged my exhausted body back to my bedroom. Ten minutes later, dressed in black leather pants and a white tank top, I headed for the war room. My mind wasn't ready for this conversation. I hadn't even dealt with tonight's events yet.

Their voices hit me before I reached the stairs. Sharp, impatient, everyone talking over each other. The bitter tang of kafea saturated the air. Gale had been busy pumping everyone full of that swill they called a beverage.

At the doorway, I took in the scene. The Black Guild plus Selena had gathered around the battered oak table. Maps and weapons lay pushed aside for a cluttered array of chipped mugs and Terraknight's homemade bread. Chunks were already missing.

Selena's piercing gaze zeroed in on me the instant I stepped inside. The boulder on my back rolled away at the sight of her unharmed. She lounged in her chair with deceptive casualness, but the set of her jaw and white-knuckled grip on the armrest told a different story.

She shot from her chair and crossed the room in a blur, crushing me against her. "You absolute idiot," she hissed into my shoulder, but her arms wrapped around me tight enough to crack ribs.

I slouched and returned her embrace. We'd figured out the height difference long ago.

When she pulled back, her onyx eyes glistened with unshed tears despite her scowl. "If you ever disappear on me like that again, I swear to Dracula I'll put a leash on you."

"I'm so sorry, Sel," I croaked, my posture collapsing inwardly. "On a scale of one to ten, how furious are you right now?"

She raised her head to look me in the eyes. "A, do you honestly believe I'm angry with *you*?"

I blinked, thrown off balance. "Well... yes? I broke every promise I made to you. Did everything I swore I wouldn't."

"I would've been *livid* if you hadn't made it back. But you fought through the bloodlust and saved our asses instead." She gave a sharp, humorless laugh. "I've always known how stubborn you are, your remarkable talent for finding trouble, but you're still you. Still my best friend."

Her face transformed into a map of worry lines as she continued, "I'm not mad about the Nexus or even the bloodlust. I'm terrified because you think you're invincible when you're not." Her lips flattened into a white line. "I can't—no, I *won't*—lose you, A. So, I'll do my damned best to watch your back whenever that hero complex of yours rears its suicidal head."

The naked emotion in her voice caught me off guard. A lump formed in my throat, inconvenient given the discussion awaiting us, but I needed to tell her how I felt. Before it was too late. Before Radu shared another world-shattering revelation and proved we were no more immortal than the people living beyond the Gloom.

"I love you, Sel," I murmured. "I wouldn't have made it this far without you. I can't promise something like this won't happen again, but knowing you have my back makes facing whatever comes next possible."

She tightened her hold until my lungs protested, said, "I love you, too," then returned to her seat.

I felt the weight lift from my chest. I couldn't bear another cold war like the one after Sighisoara.

Terraknight's rumbling baritone pulled my attention to him. "Good to have you back, Projector."

The vice-captain stood behind Selena, his thumbs working small circles into her back muscles. The leather cuirass he still wore from Brasov gleamed with Stalk—*Souleater* blood, the stench of rot scrunching up my nose. Standing well over six feet, he looked like a bear ready to crush your skull with a single blow. Dark circles shadowed his hazel eyes, but his lips quirked in a half-smile when our gazes met.

Shame clawed at me as I remembered how I'd nearly broken his arm when he tried to stop me from tearing out Hummingbird's throat. I stepped toward him, my throat suddenly dry.

"Sabin," I said, using his real name, "I'm so sorry for what happened. I wasn't myself, but that's no excuse—"

"Don't," he cut me off with a gentle shake of his head. "You were fighting it. I could see you struggling against the hunger. Besides," a wry grin carved lines around his mouth, "I've taken worse hits sparring with Cap."

Hummingbird peeked around Terraknight's broad back, his dusty-white wings pulled tight against his body. A vivid purple bruise bloomed across his throat where my magic had choked him earlier. My stomach twisted itself into a knot at the sight.

"Tudor, I—" my voice splintered, "I'm sorry."

"Save the waterworks, Projector," he interrupted, though his tone lacked any real bite. "That was some crazy shit you pulled on those bastards. Never seen anything like it." He rubbed the back of his head, a nervous gesture I came to recognize. "Worth a little choking to see you tear through them like that."

I frowned. Apologizing wouldn't change the fact that I had hurt him.

"If you need to hear it," he added, as if catching my thoughts, "here it is. You're forgiven. Stop beating yourself up over it. I'm fine." He extended his wings with a dramatic flourish, flashing a smile bright enough to rival the moon. "See?"

I returned his smile with a weak one and surveyed the room, checking on everyone else.

They were all here, all accounted for.

"I'm glad you're all safe," I said and sighed as the weight on my chest lifted.

"You handled yourself well." Ember's exotic lilt drifted from the other end of the table. "For a pureblood."

Coming from her, that was practically a declaration of undying friendship.

She sat ramrod straight, staring into the cup of kafea cradled between her fingers. Her golden hair was pulled back in a tight, practical braid. When she glanced up, her vivid green eyes caught me off guard. They held a hint of respect that hadn't been there before.

Across from her, Quakelord sprawled in his seat, one leg propped up on the table. He raised his mug in mock salute as I moved further into the room. "Your Bloody Highness, nice of you to join the party."

"Don't start," Pearl warned, elbowing him in the ribs and making him slosh kafea all over himself.

"What?" he protested, lowering his leg. "She decapitated half of Brasov's Stalker legion without pulling a muscle and made the rest implode. Even Cap was impressed. And he's never impressed."

A flush of pride warmed my cheeks. Now I just needed to figure out how I'd done it so I could repeat the performance again.

Gale perched on the windowsill, copper wings draped loosely around her. They looked like a metallic cloak, each feather gleaming red-gold in the candlelight. Her dark eyes tracked me as I pulled out the only empty chair besides the one at the head of the table.

"Harbinger's getting more kafea. We're going to need it," she said, then jumped from her perch to open the patio doors.

The man in question stepped inside, carrying a steaming pot as mugs hung from his fingers. Through the narrow crack between the closing doors, I glimpsed the faded gray of pre-dawn, and another yawn escaped my lips.

Harbinger's eyes fastened onto me and held until he reached the table. Hard and apologetic at the same time.

"You ready?" he asked, and I knew he wasn't talking about being late. He meant if I was ready to find out the truth.

Nothing ominous about that at all.

He propped a hip against the table, mere inches away from me, and folded his bulging arms over his chest. The worn fabric of his shirt bunched between his pectorals, and I had a first row view of his nipple.

Warmth spread low in my belly from all the inappropriate thoughts bombarding my mind.

"Ready for what?" Selena demanded, bringing me back to reality with an ice-cold fist. Her tone had a steel edge that helped her maintain the high-ranking position in a profession overrun with testosterone. "Are you finally going to explain why my best friend bled out screaming her lungs out?"

A muscle ticked in his jaw. "Lieutenant, I promised Aurora answers, and that's exactly what I'm about to deliver. You both deserve the truth."

"The truth?" Selena pressed, a mean scowl pulling at her eyebrows.

Unease skittered down my spine, light and cold as mice feet. I swallowed past the barbed wire in my throat and forced myself to speak.

"Tell us about the Souleaters." The new name tasted strange on my tongue.

Selena's head snapped toward me so fast I was surprised I didn't hear her neck crack. Her lips parted, froze, then pressed into a bloodless line as her gaze darted between Radu and me.

Radu gave a curt nod and braced his palms against the table. "I told you earlier, Projector, but for your friend's sake, I'll say it again," he started. "The Stalkers have a different name. Russkaya calls them Souleaters, because that's what they are. Stolen and trapped souls."

My heart punched against my ribs. I'd already pieced together my own theory from the Voices in Brasov and what he'd told me in his room, but hearing him say it aloud again hit me smack-dab in the face.

How had Russkaya even managed such a thing?

Nothing in our intelligence suggested they possessed that kind of magic. Then again, we hadn't known about Radu's Chronoportal ability either.

I filed that question away and forced myself to speak. "So, the Voices I heard in Brasov... They were the souls they've taken?" I couldn't keep my voice steady as I asked, "They have Phoenix trapped inside one of those... things?"

"What the actual fuck are you two talking about?" Selena snapped. When no one immediately answered, she shot me a wide, terrified look. "Tell me this is some sick joke."

I could only shake my head. None of the words would come out. Nothing made sense anymore. Had the Republic been this blind all along? Or did the Council know and choose to ignore it?

Radu's voice sliced through my spiral of questions. "You've got it right, Projector. And you heard them because of me. Because I'm connected to them."

The sting of betrayal reared its ugly head again, sinking its fangs into my heart. "How?" I demanded. "How is that even possible?"

This was the one piece that didn't fit. Through our Blood Pact, I'd sensed, as clearly as I sensed my own intentions, that he wasn't a traitor. The resentment he harbored against the Republic stemmed entirely from what happened to his family, but I hadn't tasted the foul poison of vengeance in him. He wasn't working against us, so how could he possibly be connected to our enemy?

His teeth ground together as he took a long, deliberate breath. "I'll get to that."

"Is this the reason you can always tell when the Stalkers are coming?" Selena asked, frost coating every word.

Harbinger laid golden eyes on her. "Yeah. I can sense them. Always can. Even when I sleep."

"Wait," I cried out, my voice rising to a pitch that made everyone freeze in place.

He made it sound trivial, but there was no way it was that simple. My mind worked better when every piece of new information was dissected and laid bare, so I decided to dig deeper.

It was either that, or throw a fit.

Radu could detect Souleaters long before my Blood Manipulation could sense them. I already knew this. Sibiu and Sighisoara both fell within a hundred-mile radius from here, but Brasov stretched much further, and he still heard them coming. Not even the Republic's most advanced scanners could catch them from three hundred miles away.

A terrible chill settled in the pit of my stomach, and my foot began tapping against the floor. The voices of the ghosts—that terrifying sound I'd heard when I harmonized with him... The Nexus had been set to a low sync ratio when the Voices started screaming and moaning in my head, loud enough to paralyze my body with pain. If I could hear them so clearly through a mere fraction of our connection... what did they sound like to him?

"What can you hear right now?" I asked, unable to contain my concern. "How far can you sense them, and what does it sound like?"

"Don't know the exact distance," he answered with a half-shrug. "I hear every Souleater in the Gloom and the Outer Wards. But when they're far or moving together, they blend. Can't tell one from another."

My eyes met Selena's, and what I read in them matched the turmoil in my chest. Every single inch of my body turned stiff as rock, my breathing catching on a silent gasp.

Because what he implied defied all logic, reason, and common sense.

He hadn't told me what the Voices sounded like to him, but even if they came across as mere whispers, it was every single Souleater living in and outside their territory. That was like saying he could hear the thoughts of every outlier on every front. Twice as many, since our specialists had forecasted a slight decline in their numbers, indicating that there were now at least two monsters for every mixed-breed in service.

And he felt it. Every single moment of every day. Even when he slept.

"Isn't it... difficult?" I asked, my fingers tightening around the edge of the table. "Living with that constantly?"

His eyes remained fixed on me as he shrugged again. "I'm used to it by now. It's been a long time."

"How long?" I pressed.

"Since Conin died." His voice dropped, gravel over glass. "I've always had a connection with him. Like a mental bond." He sighed as if this discussion bored him, as if the burden meant nothing. "I told you I was looking for him."

I nodded, recalling our conversation from my bedroom.

"He's one of *them* now," Harbinger said, and the words fell like stones. "That's why I hear them."

AURORA

The world tilted beneath me. My ears started ringing with a high-pitched noise, and I leaned forward slightly to stop the room from spinning.

"He's—" My voice cracked, and the words died in my throat. I swallowed, tried again. "But I thought he was dead."

Conin. The silver-haired outlier who'd pulled me from the wreckage of Father's zeppelin. The varcolac who'd spoken of duty and proving our commitment to the Republic with such fierce conviction that his words had carved themselves into my bones. Now trapped inside one of those... abominations.

Derzelas, have mercy.

I'd witnessed what Souleaters could do—their savage glee when ripping through flesh and bone. My pulse thrummed in my ears. The thought of Conin's soul imprisoned in that twisted shell made me want to retch.

"We have to do something!" I blurted. My hands trembled, blood buzzing beneath my skin like a thousand angry wasps. "We have to save them—your brother, Phoenix, everyone else."

The silence that followed crushed down like an iron weight. My thoughts raced in dizzying circles, each one coming back to the same horrifying question: Was Phoenix—Ditoa—aware when she died? Was some part of her still trapped, conscious, watching through eyes that no longer obeyed her will?

God. Every mission report, every battle strategy suddenly felt like a cruel mockery. We'd been killing our own people.

I'd been killing them.

Selena steepled her fingers together, her face turning analytical. "Is this 'mental link' you have with your brother a clan thing? Like your magic?"

Radu dragged his fingers over his eyebrow. "You could say that." He poured himself a cup of kafea, unaware—or unperturbed—he spilled the liquid on the table. The bitter scent filled the air between us. "The closer the ties, the stronger the connection."

He took a measured sip, then stared at me over the rim. That look carried volumes that words couldn't touch. "The Republic believes this war ends when the Creators awaken, correct?" he asked, too calm for someone who already knew the answer to that.

"Yes." I nodded, if only to humor him. "When the Creators are scheduled to awaken."

The tension in his shoulders, the careful neutrality of his tone—Radu was leading somewhere, and I wasn't sure I was ready to follow.

"And your Creators' blood powers will defeat these creatures?"

"Of course," I answered without hesitation. The Sons of Derzelas were the most powerful immortals to ever walk the earth. This wasn't blind faith, but cold, hard fact.

Radu's features turned hard as stone. "And what would happen if the enemy's army carried full immortal blood? Would the First Originals, powerful as they may be, stand against thousands of such creatures? Possibly even more?"

The way his chin lifted slightly in a subtle challenge sent fire through my veins. I wanted to refute his outrageous claim, to cite the countless tests conducted on Souleater blood samples. None had ever come back with full immortal blood.

Not that he gave me a chance to answer.

"But first you need to understand how these creatures harvest their victims." His penetrating gaze swept from me to Selena and back again. "How they capture what you might call the soul."

"It's not the actual soul they take, but an impression of it—a copy," Pearl interjected. She shrugged at my confused expression. "It's difficult to explain in simple terms."

Harbinger nodded. "They perform what we've named 'the kiss of death,'" he said. "But they require functioning brain tissue. They can't feed on just any corpse."

"I imagine intact brain matter is scarce on the battlefield," Selena barged in, her voice taking on that detached, clinical tone she used when discussing her work. Brain physiology always captivated her, for some peculiar reason.

"Very scarce." Gale's gentle voice broke through. "That's why we often run into multiple creatures sharing identical voices. Phoenix is likely still out there, trapped in another Souleater."

Ember's sob broke the silence.

My chest tightened for her. She and Phoenix had been inseparable since conscription—two balaurs forged in the same fires. I couldn't fully grasp her loss, not when I still had Selena, but the thought of losing my best friend was unbearable.

Pearl wrapped an arm around Ember's trembling shoulders, murmuring soft reassurances in her ear. Quakelord ducked beneath the table, emerged with an unmarked bottle of mead, and splashed a generous portion into a clean cup. He took a deep pull himself before sliding it toward Ember.

Harbinger's commanding voice snapped my attention back to him before I could see if she accepted the offering.

"Pearl's right," he said. "They don't harvest souls in the way people imagine. What they take are echoes, fragments of consciousness. Even when they carry these pieces, communicating with mimicked voices is impossible. They only replicate the final seconds before death."

"Black Sheep," Terraknight rumbled from across the table.

My head jerked toward him in perfect sync with Selena's. The vice-captain's massive frame practically vibrated with tension, his jawline set and unrelenting. And despite the reasonable air, my mouth dried.

"Explain," she demanded, narrowing her onyx eyes at him.

We'd been trying to decipher this sheep nonsense ever since I'd eavesdropped on their private conversation through the malfunctioning Transmitters.

"Black Sheep are Souleaters who feed off fallen outliers," Terraknight said. "They hide among the regular Souleaters—the White Sheep." He shot a glance at Harbinger's, then added, "They're the ones who remember fragments of who they were."

My mouth opened and then closed again. All Terraknight had managed to do was raise even more questions. Before I could voice them, Harbinger took over.

"I've been tracking their patterns for decades." Eyes the color of the deepest amber gleamed as they zeroed in on me. "The Republic has been their primary target from the beginning, and now I understand why." He drummed his fingers on the table. "When the purebloods fell in that first attack, they were left for the sun to dispose of them. Strategic choice during a crisis, but a damn costly one in the long run."

He paused and gave me a look that wasn't quite condescending, but not impudent either. It carried the bitter knowledge that came from anger and grief. He'd lost people too. Fought this war longer than anyone should have to.

I swallowed my pride and nodded for him to continue.

"When White Sheep found those purebloods before dawn," he continued, "they got themselves the only immortal brain tissue on the battlefield. And since they share a basic hive mind controlled by something higher, any Souleater that fed on purebloods gained fragments of immortal consciousness. Pieces that grow stronger with time—"

"That's impossible!" Selena's face drained of color. She shot to her feet, palms slamming flat against the table. Her eyes darted back and forth; that telltale sign her brilliant mind was already racing, piecing the theories together with terrifying speed.

The sight of her even considering Harbinger's words set a cold weight in my chest.

"Sweet Derzelas," I whispered, "it can't be true."

"—and when they finally breach those walls..." Harbinger continued, unmoved by our reactions, but I couldn't hear his voice anymore.

The image of an army of sentient monsters flooding through the Seventh Ward's gates tore through my mind. My stomach churned, though nothing came up. This was beyond a war crime. This was a defilement of the most fundamental kind. Dark Father, what had Russkaya unleashed?

"*You*'re going to lose this war, princess." The certainty in his tone broke through the fog of horror.

My nostrils flared. "The hell we are!" I joined Selena and bolted from my seat.

His choice of "you" instead of "we" wasn't lost on me, but I bit back the burning remark. He'd made his feelings about the divide between mixed-breeds and purebloods painfully clear from the beginning. His hatred of the Republic ran bone-deep.

Terraknight circled the table with slow, measured steps, his expression made graver by the shadows playing on his face. "You both need to understand what we're facing. This isn't just about winning the war. It's about stopping them from ever reaching the Republic's walls."

"He's right," Harbinger agreed. "The Souleaters grow in number every day. But what about the halfbloods? How many of us remain to fight them?"

To anyone else, he might have appeared calm, almost detached. But I'd learned to read the signs—the slight tightening around his eyes, the tension in his jaw, the way his fists clenched at his sides. His rage wasn't directed solely at the Republic, I realized. It was at the entire situation, at the senseless waste of lives on both sides.

I clenched my jaw, forcing my eyes to stay locked with his instead of dropping to the floor as shame threatened to pull them down. I didn't have an answer to his question. The Republic didn't track those statistics. I had barely kept count of my own fallen outliers.

His mouth tightened into a knowing line, a fleeting sadness crossing his face before the hardness returned. "At this rate, we'll all be gone within five years," he said. "People are dying faster than they reproduce in the detention camps. And those who don't... they fall on the battlefield." He paused, tilted his head, and stared at me, probably waiting for the information to sink in.

It did. Like a sledgehammer straight to my skull.

But even though my brain acknowledged his words, my entire being refused to believe him. Because he was talking about the end of the world. And I wasn't ready to accept that truth.

When he spoke again, his voice softened, even for just a moment. "If the Republic hadn't turned on its own people, perhaps there would still be hope. Your precious nation died years ago, princess—by its own hand. It perished the moment its citizens decided to persecute innocents who were supposed to be their equals."

For all their quietness, his words carried a weight that seemed to bend the air between us. Freedom and equality. Solidarity, justice, nobility. The five values the Republic once cherished, each represented by a color on our flag, one for every race that had made our democracy great. The values Father had instilled in me from my earliest days.

The values I vowed to return to my Republic.

A fissure split open in my chest to reveal the hollow pit I'd covered with years of duty and blind commitment. The war. The Total Rendition. The camps. How easily we'd abandoned everything we claimed to stand for.

I sank back into my chair, lungs struggling to pull in enough air. The question I'd been avoiding for so long clawed its way to the surface. Does a nation that imprisons and discriminates against its own people without cause, that's responsible for countless deaths without a shred of remorse... does it deserve to survive?

Everything I loved existed within those walls. The answer should have been simple. But as I sat there, watching the pain etched into the faces of people who'd fought and suffered for a country that had betrayed them, I wasn't so certain anymore that we deserved a second chance.

I'd been so lost in my spiral of thoughts, I hadn't noticed Quakelord moving around. Not that this would be the first time he'd crept up on me.

The black jacket he wore had a subtle oriental influence, high-collared and tailored to emphasize his narrow waist and broad shoulders. His fox-shaped eyes gleamed like fire agate as his mouth twitched in a way that meant he was either about to drop some philosophical bomb or crack a joke to break the tension.

"Damn," he muttered, wrinkling his nose. "The air in here is thick enough to choke a zmeu." His voice aimed for lightness, but the tightness around his mouth betrayed him. I supposed you never truly adjusted to the knowledge that your loved ones had been transformed into mindless killers, no matter how many years passed. "Think we could all use something stronger than kafea. What do you say, Projector?"

He moved between us, distributing drinks—Terraknight's 'new and improved batch.'

I declined politely, and he simply nodded, moving on. My stomach was upset enough without me pouring gasoline over it. Quakelord paused beside Selena, extending the tray.

To my surprise, she accepted, but fisted her hand for a second to stop the trembling in her fingers before drowning the entire thing.

He followed in her steps, cheered to everyone at the table, and emptied another cup. The hiss that followed was the perfect rendition of a cobra poised to strike.

"Lieutenant, since we're having a party," he said, shaking his pitch-black hair about his shoulders, "do you know the infant mortality rate in camps without medical facilities?"

She looked at him with a dumbstruck face. I was sure mine wasn't any different.

"When I was interned," he said. "Barely any babies survived their first winter. Pretty sure it was the same everywhere. And those who lived were often... repurposed."

Selena's jaw clenched, but for once my reaction came faster than hers.

"What do you mean 'repurposed'?" I choked out and gulped the dread pooling in my stomach.

"Guards, and sometimes halfbloods, tore those babes from the arms of their mothers and traded them for profit," he replied, passing a cup to Terraknight. "Can't say if they got coin or supplies in exchange."

Blood drained from my face. He didn't need to elaborate who they traded them with.

Citizens of the Republic—people who claimed to despise halfbloods—had used their infants as blood bags.

My stomach lurched violently. Acid shot up my throat. It burned, but numbness spread from my fingertips up my arms as the horror crashed through me. I'd found out in the worst possible way that the Wurdulaks fed on outliers who'd completed their service, but babies? What kind of sick minds did we harbor in the Republic? And why the hell had I been so blind to what was happening a stone's throw from our walls?

Radu kneeled before me, his hand a brand against my thigh. "Very soon, the halfbloods will cease to exist. And when they're gone, will the purebloods step forward? When you've never known true combat, when none of you knows what it means to survive on the battlefield, will you be able to continue the fight without them?"

His voice remained gentle, but the reproach beneath was unmistakable. Not the bitter satisfaction of someone watching deserved punishment unfold, but the frustration of a teacher watching students ignore critical lessons. We'd fixated on petty divisions while blinding ourselves to the approaching catastrophe. We'd severed our own defensive limb.

Radu shifted in his new position, the slight squeeze of his hand pulling my focus back to him. "With no volunteers to fill the ranks, compulsory service becomes inevitable," he continued. "But without our early defense, you'll rely solely on the scanners. And by the time those detect the enemy..." I could see the fires of destruction in his golden eyes. "It will already be too late."

I sat frozen, unable to even recoil. The repercussions and the chaos of forced conscription would unleash rolled before my eyes. Another fracture line through our already splintered society. The wealthy would buy exemptions, while the common purebloods faced slaughter. Civil unrest would tear us apart before the Souleaters even reached our gates.

My head shook in denial, though I had no counterargument to offer. I simply couldn't accept this apocalyptic future Radu painted. And it was a mere blink of an eye away. Nowhere near enough time to implement enough change to stand on our own.

"The numbers don't support that," I muttered, racking my brain to prove him wrong. "Our intelligence reports show repeated failures on Russkaya's side. Their attacks lack the coordination you're describing."

"Not to mention, Souleater numbers have been dropping significantly," Selena added, her voice ratcheting up. She, too, had a hard time accepting Radu's morbid forecast. "They've been reduced to half their former strength from just decades ago."

"To the extent of what you can observe," Harbinger countered, rising to his full height with that menacing ease that always made me think of wolves lurking in the woods. His fingers traced the back of his neck, squeezed his nape in frustration. "Your Republic's surveillance extends only to the edge of what your scanners reach."

He zeroed in on me, the blood-red ring pulsing in tandem with his heartbeat. Not angry, but resolute.

"You have no means of knowing what gathers in the depths of their territory, where the Gloom shrouds everything," he continued. One finger tapped his sensitive ear—a subtle reminder that he could hear them. "Yes, fewer Souleaters come to the front these days, but that's tactical, not weakness. They need only commit enough forces to exhaust us bit by bit, while their primary strength grows in the shadows, waiting."

The cold certainty in his voice left no room for argument. I felt like crying and fainting at the same time, but I couldn't shake his words. Because that pattern of behavior could only mean one thing—Russkaya wasn't losing. They were conserving strength, building numbers, preparing for the moment they'd abandon this war of attrition and launch an overwhelming offensive that would shatter our defensive lines in a single, devastating blow.

"They couldn't possibly possess the intelligence for such a sophisticated strategy," I blurted.

He held my gaze for exactly five rapid heartbeats before delivering the final blow, his voice unnervingly calm. "They've already developed strategic intelligence. And that's another reason why your Republic will lose."

"You arrogant bastard!" Selena erupted, slamming her fist against the table. Wood splintered under the impact. Mugs jumped and clattered, kafea splashing across maps as Terraknight's bread scattered to the floor.

The wild look in her eyes promised violence, and part of me—that stubborn fragment that still wanted to dismiss everything Radu said—wanted to join her fury. I wanted nothing more than to slap him into my reality, yell at him to take his words back.

But deeper instincts prevailed.

Harbinger never spoke without purpose or evidence. He'd proven his ability to hear the Souleaters was real. His long service was a testament of that.

We'd already confirmed the Republic's plans for 'welcoming' mixed-breeds home as a solution to our own stupidity. Why should we doubt the rest?

"Sel, please," I begged. "Let him finish." I didn't know if it was because I hadn't wet my throat in a while, or if adrenaline and anxiety parched my insides, but my voice felt rough like sandpaper.

Terraknight righted her chair——another victim of her out-burst——and steered Selena to sit. She glared at me, teeth savaging the inside of her cheek, but finally dropped back into her seat.

"Continue," I told Harbinger.

He acknowledged with a barely there nod. The hard angles of his face tempered as he registered the naked fear I couldn't hide. My heart galloped. Every nerve in my body screamed at me to flee, to abandon this room and its terrible truths.

But where could I possibly run?

"Even if intact corpses are rare," he stated, "this remains a bat-tlefield where the dead lie uncollected. The sun means little when millions have fallen." He made a dismissive gesture with one hand as if the mere statement amused him. He often did that, smile against a world he thought full of fools.

"Halfbloods carry immortal blood, diluted as it may be. Black Sheep who consume them develop more slowly than those who feed on purebloods, but they'll, too, peak in their evolution one day soon."

A spike in the pulses gathered around the table made my own rocket to the point of making my head spin. I barely caught Radu's question through the noise.

"What happens when they reach our level of intelligence?"

"We call them Shepherds," Terraknight took over without leaving Selena's side. He used his fingers to soothe the throbbing vein on the side of her neck. "While standard Souleaters operate on basic instinct and command, Shepherds provide direction. They coordinate the Black Sheep with real tactical awareness. We've encountered them a few times." His jaw clenched and unclenched. "The legions under a Shepherd's command fight with a strategy that makes conventional Souleaters seem like mindless beasts in comparison."

"You're telling me these monsters exist? They aren't hypothetical?" I shouted, panic clawing up my throat. *Derzelas, it was already too late to save us.* The room spun, taking me with it. "Harbinger, can you hear—?"

"Yes." He nodded. "I distinguish them by their voices. Shepherds speak with remarkable clarity, even within a horde. We've eliminated dozens across various fronts," a darkness seeped into his luminous eyes as he set his full lips in a straight line, "but there's one left, here in the Tenth Ward, and it's the most advanced of them all."

Terror slammed into me, and I felt myself slipping into a trancelike state, unwilling to face up to what I'd learned today. It had been one straw too many. My brain was in danger of overloading. I did mental calisthenics after mental calisthenics, trying to process the revelation.

Our first battle together flashed through my mind. Radu shouting in harsh Russkayan across the battlefield, challenging someone——the Shepherd, I now realized——to come and get him.

"It's your brother," I whispered. "The Shepherd took your brother's consciousness. That's why you keep fighting. You want to destroy it and free Conin yourself."

The shadows shifted across Harbinger's face as he gave a single, sharp nod. For a moment, the flickering candlelight seemed to play tricks on my eyes, his skin fading to ash-gray. Strange golden lines that might have been cracks or markings flickered along his neck and arms.

I blinked hard, and everything looked normal again. Just Radu's bronze skin, unmarked and solid. My exhausted mind was clearly playing games with me.

I dragged in a ragged breath, held it until my lungs burned, then exhaled slowly. Stress gnawed at me, but one thing was clear. Harbinger and the Black Guild represented our best chance against the Shepherd. If they succeeded, everyone won. Conin could finally rest, the Stalkers would lose their advantage, and the Republic would gain time. The Voices tormenting Harbinger would be silenced.

If I could help them, maybe...

Raising my chin, I met the center of the storm brewing in Radu's eyes. "Would having a Creator's magic fighting alongside you improve your chances against this Shepherd? Could it buy the Republic time to prepare?"

His brows arched in surprise. "It would, yes."

"What are you plotting, A?" Selena's voice was sharp with suspicion.

"If we eliminate it, we delay their advance. Black Sheep need time to evolve into new Shepherds." The more I thought about it, the more convinced I became of my plan. I held her stare, knowing she would understand what I intended to do. "I need to return. Dracula needs to know what's happening."

Fear pooled in her eyes. She knew what that would mean. Her mouth opened to argue, but Gale cut her off.

"You can't go back there!" Gale shot up from her perch by the window. "That bastard prince won't let you leave if he catches you. He'll force himself on you again, he'll—"

The unwelcome image of Lev Wurdulak backing me against a wall—fangs bared, that vile bloodlust flaring in his eyes—tore through my mind. A shiver crawled up my spine in response and raised every hair at my nape.

I crushed the thought as quickly as it came. Next time, if there was a next time, I'd be ready. I'd snap his damned neck if he tried to touch me again. And if need be, I would kill him without a moment's hesitation.

"I'll handle Lev," I retorted through clenched teeth. The memory of his fangs at my throat, of being powerless against his strength, sent rage flooding through me. "He puts his hands on me again, it will be the last thing he does, I promise you that." I let my gaze sweep the room, softening slightly at their concerned faces. "You need reinforcements. You've been operating at barely a third of your capacity for months, pushing yourselves without rest between missions. Dark Father's mercy, you haven't even had proper time to mourn Ditoa!" My voice cracked, and I paused, forcing myself to stave off the burning tears.

I was so strung up that it would take a slight breeze to make me lose control.

Raking fingers through my hair, I began pacing, quick strides to burn off the nervous energy sending both my mind and heart into overdrive. "I'll convince them to send support," I said. "I'll make them commit the moment I return. This can't continue." I gestured to their diminished numbers. "This is beyond unacceptable!"

"Projector," Radu said quietly, but his call brushed past me.

"I'll petition the Commander directly and have him back our request. And if that fails, I'll do whatever it takes to—"

"Projector Tepes." His voice hardened just enough to slice through my rambling.

I fell silent, suddenly aware of the absolute stillness that had descended over the room.

Harbinger pulled away from the table and turned to face his guildmates. "We're all in agreement?" he asked them.

They nodded with hapless expressions, but it was Terraknight who voiced their consensus. "Yeah."

A suffocating weight pressed against my shoulders at the dimming resolve in their eyes.

"What are you talking about?" I murmured.

He turned back to me, his face a work of stone. Crimson-flecked eyes studied mine for one long breath. "You can stop now, Projector. No matter what you do, it's meaningless at this point."

The defeated note in his voice weakened my knees. "What are you saying, Harbinger?" I pressed, fisting my hands.

"Reinforcements won't come," he said, matter-of-fact. "Not any-more."

My frantic heartbeat swallowed his next words, but I read them on his lips, regardless. "We'll all die here. This ward, this guild is our last stop. It's our execution ground."

Aurora

KILLED? THEIR EXECUTION GROUND?

I might be a century old, but even my mind had its breaking point. Today, it reached its quota of hard truths and hidden secrets buried under decades of willful ignorance, so when Radu's words finally pierced my denial, they detonated inside me with the force of a zeppelin crash. A stupefying kind of dread fired my synapses and flooded my nervous system. Disjointed fragments of thought ripped my mind apart, like shrapnel tearing through what remained of my faith in everything I'd been raised to believe. The air turned thick as molasses.

The outliers... they had chosen to fight to regain their families' rights. But what about veterans like Harbinger and the Black Guild members who refused to return to Republic soil?

"What happened to the outliers before you?" I asked, though a part of me already knew the answer. My voice sounded like it belonged to someone else, hollow and distant. "Where are they?"

My lungs seized. The room tilted sideways, walls pressing inward. Choking me.

Gale's hand touched my shoulder. "Breathe, Projector."

I couldn't. Each year, thousands of freshly Changed mixed-breeds marched off to the front lines. Where were their families if they hadn't returned to the Republic? Surely not all had fallen to Souleaters?

Or bloodthirsty Purebloods? the cruel inner voice tormented me.

Unless—unless the Republic had found a more efficient method of disposal.

Bile surged up my throat. I doubled over, but nothing came out.

Had they been herding outliers into the Tenth Ward—the first line of defense—only to deny them reinforcements, effectively killing them under the guise of duty?

My gaze shot to Selena. "Did the Commander know?" The words scraped out between heaves. "Did he lie to us?"

I should have checked the returning outliers myself. Should have visited the lower wards instead of trusting Brother's empty promises.

Her face went ashen, despite her head shaking in denial.

A strangled sound tore from my throat. "Impossible."

Metal clanged against the table as Quakelord slammed his cup down. His hazel eyes blazed with suppressed rage. "Damn right it's possible," he said. "Those knife-ears never planned to honor jack shit. They dangle promises like treats for dogs, work us till we're bones, then toss us into the meat grinder." He gestured broadly at the room. "Welcome to the Republic's *final solution* to eradicate the vermin, Your Bloody Highness."

But the Council... they wouldn't... they couldn't...

"We're not blaming you," Hummingbird was quick to assure me. Like I needed him to soften the blow when I had done nothing to save them all these decades. "But have you ever seen a halfblood in the Seven Wards?"

I opened my mouth to speak, then stopped.

After a century of war, there should have been thousands, if not millions of them returning home. Families reunited. Rights restored. But I'd never seen one. Not a single one.

Surely our paths would have crossed at some point, even if the guards rarely let mixed-breeds pass through the gates of the First Ward.

How could I have been so blind? I squeezed my eyes, fighting off the burn of tears. All this time I'd clung to faith in the Republic's infallibility like a desperate fool.

No more.

"Most outliers don't survive their conscription, so the Republic weasels out of the deal clean," Terraknight said, his deep voice resolute. "The problem is stubborn bastards like us who refuse to die. Our survival makes us heroes to other halfbloods—enough to spark dissent in the camps. So, they shuffled us off to the Eighth and Ninth Wards' first defensive guilds, expecting the Souleaters to finish what they started. Most of the time, even the best don't make it out." His massive shoulders rolled back, chin lifting with quiet pride. "But we did, and we'll keep doing it. This is our way of flipping them the finger. We do our fucking best to stay alive and make them regret every day we draw breath."

"This is where it ends, though. The Tenth Ward's first defensive guild." Quakelord leaned back in his chair, a contemplative look crossing his face. "Think of it as the Republic's elegant answer to an inconvenient problem. They can't openly execute us. That would look bad. But they can send us somewhere we'll die defending the kingdom." His shoulders lifted in a shrug. "Clean hands, clear conscience, and all the halfbloods conveniently buried in unmarked graves. If we're lucky."

Betrayal and anger churned inside me. Everything I'd fought for, everything I'd believed in. All of it, built on lies. A systematic slaughter disguised as patriotic duty.

Pain soaked through my middle as tears followed down my cheeks. I turned toward the patio doors so they wouldn't see.

They weren't defending anything. They were cattle being led to slaughter, fighting with the knowledge that death was their only certainty. Not conscription—extermination.

I wiped the tears with the back of my hand. Crying wouldn't help them.

"But what if you manage to survive?" I asked.

Quakelord's laugh was sharp. "Survive? Sure, some of us are too pig-headed to die easily. But it's like sitting in the executioner's waiting room. You know the axe is coming, just not when."

Sentenced to die. That's all they'd ever been.

Rage erupted in my chest, white-hot. My homeland. How deep did the rot go? Memories crashed through me. Hummingbird complaining about boredom, Radu's blank stare when I'd asked about his post-war plans. He'd never even considered surviving.

They'd never had futures. No dreams beyond the next battle because all they possessed was a death warrant with no execution date.

"You all knew?" I murmured.

Gale's voice wavered. "We're sorry. Harbinger, Terra, and I... we didn't know how to tell you." Her eyes shimmered with tears. "You looked at us like we mattered."

"Since when?"

"We've known since the beginning." Pearl, who'd been quiet until now, fixed her azure eyes on me. They reflected years of accumulated pain. "Ember's sister, Quakelord's parents, Captain's brother... They all marched to their deaths believing they could earn their families' rights. But the Republic never kept its promises." She paused, tracing the rim of her mug with her index finger. "When you see the same pattern repeat over and over, it becomes impossible to ignore."

"But if you knew…" my voice cracked, "why continue fighting? Why not run? Seek vengeance?"

Radu sighed, and a tired smile ghosted across his lips. "Run where, princess? There's a legion of Souleaters ahead of us whose numbers far outmatch all the hordes we've seen before. Led by a Shepherd smart enough to coordinate. We're trapped between the Republic's efforts to kill us off and becoming monsters." He crossed his arms over his chest. "Rebellion sounds appealing, but halfbloods are too busy dying to organize."

"Our parents' generation might have stood a chance," Quakelord said, fingers steepled in front of him. "But they chose survival over revolution. Can't blame them. They had families to protect, basic freedoms to secure. They clung to the Republic's honeyed lies because the alternative was watching their children starve." His expression grew distant. "When our parents died, our siblings fought to reclaim honor from a nation that had already written them off."

"Bigoted pigs, the lot of them!" Ember spat, her earlier sorrow replaced by raw fury. "They should all burn."

Their words carved chunks from my soul. The previous generations of outliers had bled for the Republic, sacrificed everything for a chance at a better life. They were more citizens than I'd ever be. But Radu and the others? They'd been stripped of even that bitter privilege.

They knew only wire fences and killing fields. The mixed-breeds had become natives of this wasteland; lived and died surrounded by monsters. They didn't care about the Crowned Republic of Transylvania.

And for good reason.

Something fundamental shifted in my heart, like bones settling after a break. The naïve princess, who'd believed in the Republic's righteousness, cracked apart.

A visceral craving to go back and take my crown burned through me. Not for power, but for justice. I wanted to drag every Council member from their ivory towers, force them to look at the faces of the people they'd condemned. Make them explain to Quakelord why his sacrifice meant nothing. Make them justify to Ember why her sister died for lies. Or Hummingbird and Gale, why they'd been tormented in the internment camp.

My hands clenched into fists. For almost a century I'd been an unwitting executioner, every mission, every strategic decision—I'd been complicit in their genocide.

The taste of bile coated my tongue, but underneath it, a new purpose emerged. These people deserved a reckoning, and I was the only one positioned to deliver it.

The crown wasn't just my birthright anymore. It was a weapon I could wield for them.

"I knew purebloods who sheltered halfbloods, hid them so they wouldn't be conscripted," Terraknight said. I distanced myself from the noise in my head and focused on him. "Cap's parents were murdered, his brother shipped off to die. You heard what happened to Quakelord's projector." His warm eyes held no accusation. "We've seen the worst of both sides."

"If it's revenge we're after," Hummingbird added from his spot near the mantle, "it wouldn't be difficult. Just step aside when the Souleaters come." His boyish voice hardened, thick with a cruel streak I hadn't heard from him before. The tip of his dusty-white wings brushed the floor as he turned to study the rusty weapons on the wall, speaking to the steel rather than us. "We die, sure, but so does the Republic. Might be worth it, watching those bastards finally get what's coming to them."

"It wouldn't solve anything." Quakelord slouched in his chair, tipping it back on two legs. "There're purebloods out there who don't deserve to die. Hell, some are probably just as clueless as you were, Projector." He propped a boot on the table and laced his fingers behind his head, staring at the ceiling. "If the Souleaters take over the Republic, every nation on this continent becomes their feeding ground. Revenge might taste sweet, but extinction? That's forever."

Hummingbird glanced over his shoulder. A deep scowl darkened his pretty face. "Projector, you're too innocent for this world," he said, that unfamiliar edge still coloring his tone. "Bet you've never even thought about getting someone back for hurting you. But hatred isn't as simple as killing your enemy." His shoulders shifted restlessly. "True revenge is watching them realize how wrong they were, making them crawl and plead for forgiveness that'll never come."

"After everything the Republic has done, a rebellion or massacre wouldn't make them regret anything." Selena's voice cut through the air like a blade.

"Exactly." Pearl nodded. "They'd close their eyes to their crimes, blame someone else, then play the victim even as they died." Her fingers tightened around her mug. "All it would do is feed their sense of martyrdom."

I bolted upright and started pacing the length of the room again. My hands clenched and unclenched at my sides. The thick silence that followed amplified the thundering in my ears.

"They sealed themselves behind walls and pretended the war didn't exist," I spat. "Built a fantasy where they were heroes while others bled for their comfort."

Their smug superiority, their blind faith in their own virtue, fed the inferno building in my chest. My blood felt like it was boiling beneath my skin.

Brother's voice echoed in my memory—so certain the government was doing right, protecting their people's interests. Such noble duty.

Bullshit. All of it.

I shook to my core, the anger sparking within me, catching fire and flooding the room with the energy pouring out of me. I grabbed the kafea pitcher and hurled it against the wall. The crash of shattering ceramic barely registered underneath the roar of fury. In a word, I threw a fit.

"They lied about the Nexus being safe! Betrayed their own citizens while refusing to honor their agreements!" My voice broke with the force of my anger. "And they have the audacity to claim righteousness? They're drowning in their own hypocrisy!"

"She finally gets it," Ember muttered under her breath, and I whipped around to glare at her. She met my stare without flinching, her green eyes blazing like the Northern Lights.

A firm hand clamped around my bicep and yanked me back toward my seat. I spun, ready to unleash my fury on whoever dared manhandle me, only to find Selena glowering at me. Without her usual heels, she had to crane her neck to meet my eyes, but her glare could have melted steel.

"You're supposed to be the level-headed one between us," she snarled and jabbed her sharp nail toward my face. "Stop throwing a tantrum and accept that the Republic fucked us." She planted her hands on her hips, anger sharpening her features. "What are we going to do about it? Let them all die, or do whatever we can to save those bastards?"

The rational part of my mind knew she was right, but the rage still burned too hot. "If we stoop to their level, we become just like them," I hissed, biting into my lower lip until I tasted copper.

The metallic sweetness flooded the room. Selena's pupils dilated, but she wasn't the only one whose hunger flashed across their faces.

We were all running on empty. Blood, food, sleep—everything we needed to function properly had been pushed aside for the mission in Brasov.

"Cut that out!" She swatted my shoulder just as Hummingbird spoke again. Something in his tone made us both freeze. A grim finality I'd only heard from the Elders preparing for their eternal rest.

"When your choices are to fight the Souleaters and maybe die, or to quit and definitely die, it's not really a choice at all. We keep going. Survive as long as we can."

"We'll fight until our last breath," Gale said. She drifted closer to Harbinger and Terraknight in a sign of solidarity. "And live with our pride intact."

Nods rippled around the table. My chest constricted under the weight of crippling helplessness.

"Even if death is all you have to look forward to?" I asked.

Quakelord's laugh held no humor. "What kind of fool throws in the towel just because the end's coming? Even when you're facing a firing squad, you can still decide whether to stand tall or fall to your knees." His sharp jaw clenched. "We've made our choice. All that's left is living by it."

My spine straightened, every muscle in my body tensed as if primed for battle. "I won't let any of you die. Not anymore."

Harbinger leaned against the table and crossed his powerful arms over his chest. "And how exactly do you plan on saving us, princess?" His lips moved, but I could only hear the mockery in his tone. "By crawling back to the man who forced himself on you?"

Annoyance seared through me. His underestimation of me grated against every nerve I had. He didn't understand how things worked in the Republic. Had no idea what I was truly capable of. And using that endearment was a low blow. This wasn't about naïve dreams; this was about me taking action to save his stubborn ass.

"He won't know I've returned," I said, restraining myself to mirror his pose and cross my arms in defense. "Once Dracula hears the truth about what's happening here, Lev becomes irrelevant. Our Creator is just—he'll grant me the Blood Aura." He wouldn't let the Republic fall without giving it a real chance to defend itself.

The muscle at Harbinger's temple twitched, but the man stayed silent. Terraknight glanced between him and Selena, both of whom were staring at me with hard, scrutinizing eyes.

"How certain are you about him?" Terraknight asked, hope warring with doubt in his voice.

I wasn't, but I didn't have anything else. Underworld's endless pits, I wasn't even sure I could reach Dracula's Sleeping Chamber without getting killed first. But looking around the room, at the faces that had become important to me, what choice did we have?

"He's our only hope," I said, holding his gaze. "I'd rather die trying than allow this slaughter to continue."

HARBINGER

THE VOICES WERE SCREAMING tonight.

I pressed my palms harder against my temples, as if I could crush the sound, as if pressure alone could drown out the chorus of agony that had been building since we left the war room. Phoenix's desperate plea echoed loudest. *'I don't want to die! I don't want to die!'* But hundreds of other souls wailed beneath it, an endless loop of their final moments.

Some nights were worse than others. Tonight ranked among the worst I'd endured in months. Every voice demanded justice, recognition, peace I couldn't give them.

And it was Conin's voice that cut deepest. *"Brother! Brother, where are you? I can't find you in the dark!"*

The same words he'd cried during childhood thunderstorms, when he'd crawl into my bed begging me to chase away the monsters in his dreams. The Shepherd had been peeling away at his consciousness for years, mining deeper into his memory center. Stealing him from me day by day.

Now Conin was the monster, and I was the one lost in the dark.

I'd fled to the balcony when my room's walls started closing in. The sun had dipped below the horizon, leaving shadows in every corner I looked. Woodsmoke drifted up from the fire pit Terra had lit last night to burn the trash. Just a few more minutes and full darkness would swallow what remained of the day.

"Brother, I'm scared. The darkness is so cold."

"Shut up," I muttered, digging my fingers into my hair. "Just shut the fuck up."

But the Voices never listened. They couldn't. Trapped in their death loops, they replayed the same terror, the same desperate pleas for salvation that would never come.

Phoenix's voice rose again. *"I don't want to die!"*

Then Rosebud. *"Ma, I want to go home. Please, I just want to go home."*

Mandrake. *"The fire burns. Oh gods, the fire burns so much."*

Three decades of this torment, and it never got easier. If anything, it grew worse as more souls joined the hive. I could hear every Souleater within hundreds of miles, predict their movements, warn my guild of approaching danger. But I couldn't silence the one voice that mattered most. Couldn't reach through the darkness to comfort my little brother one last time.

"Big brother, you promised you'd take me with you. You promised."

Those words shattered what was left of my composure. I knew it wasn't really Conin—just the thing wearing his conscience, using his memories as weapons. But hearing my brother's voice from when he was eight, disappointed because I'd broken another promise to take him on my expeditions, cut like a dagger between my ribs.

I ran a hand over my face and pinched the bridge of my nose. The Shepherd knew exactly which memories would hurt most, unearthed decades of childhood moments to find the perfect blade.

It wasn't him. But it sounded exactly like him.

"Radu."

The softest voice penetrated the chaos in my head. I jerked upright, shocked to find Aurora emerging from my room. Her scent—vanilla and peaches with copper underneath—wrapped around me like silk. Those crimson eyes that always undid me held depths I'd never fully plumb. Tonight she wore simple clothes. Dark pants and a long-sleeved top that hugged her curves. Nothing fancy, but on her it looked like armor.

A weapon disguised as a woman.

"You should go inside," I told her, though that was the last thing I wanted. "It's not safe yet. Still too much light."

"Neither is it for you." Those penetrating eyes studied my face so intently I felt exposed. She saw too much, understood too much.

The silence stretched between us. A nightjar called in the distance, as wind moved through the dense leaves. Aurora didn't press for explanations. Just waited with the patience of someone who'd lived long enough to know some wounds couldn't be rushed.

"The Voices are worse tonight, aren't they?" she asked, settling beside me on the cold stone.

I nodded. How could I explain that some nights the dead refused to rest? That their anguish fed on itself until it threatened to tear me apart?

Fatigue seeped into my voice. "They're restless," I said. "More desperate than usual. Phoenix keeps repeating the same words."

Pain flickered across her features. Since Phoenix's death, I'd watched guilt eat away at her. She blamed herself for not being fast enough, strong enough. It was a familiar weight—one I'd carried far longer.

"I don't want to die," Aurora murmured. "I heard her, too." She touched her nape, referring to Brasov when the harmonization linked her to the Voices. I'd been so focused on severing the connection to save her that I hadn't considered what else she might have absorbed in those terrible seconds.

"I'm sorry you went through that," I said. "Wish I could take it back."

Aurora shifted closer until our arms touched. I felt the chill of her skin through the thin fabric of her top. "You saved me. Without your quick thinking, who knows what the Nexus would have done to me."

"I love you, Brother. If there's someone I want to be when I grow up, it's you."

I flinched as Conin's words bled into our conversation. Words from our last trip to the Republic, before the Council ordered my parents' assassination. Before they sent him to the camps and I inherited Dad's Chronoportal.

Aurora noticed immediately. She was too observant not to.

"It's your brother, isn't it?" she asked. "He's the one you heard just now."

Most people looked at me and saw the Harbinger—captain of Black Guild, the outlier who survived decades against Souleaters. They saw strength, leadership, control, because that's what I let them see.

Aurora saw the man drowning beneath it all.

"Not him," I said, clearing my throat. "The thing that took him. It has his memories, uses his voice to mess with my head." I dragged my hands through my hair. "Knows exactly what to say to hurt me most."

Without warning, Aurora reached out and pressed her palm against my temple. The contact sent electricity through my veins.

"Let me help," she said.

"You can't use your Nexus."

"I won't." Her irises began to glow scarlet, the same light I'd seen in Brasov when she'd torn through the Souleater hordes. "Trust me."

The first time I met her, I wouldn't have trusted her past spitting distance. She was an original. Her people had killed my family. But after all these months together... I'd never met anyone more determined to change the world.

I gave her a nod.

Her presence slipped into my mind. Not the brutal invasion I'd expected, but careful. Gentle. Her Blood Manipulation wove around the jagged edges of my consciousness, creating a buffer between me and the worst of the screaming.

The relief hit so suddenly and completely I nearly sobbed. Finally, I could hear my own thoughts clearly. The Voices were still there, but muffled now, pushed to the background where they couldn't claw at my sanity.

"How?" I breathed.

"Think of it as insulation," she murmured, offering a soft smile. "I can't silence them completely, but I can muffle the worst of it."

The delicate pressure never wavered. Without the constant noise, I became aware of everything else. Her steady breathing, lips parted in concentration, the breeze carrying wisps of her hair across my neck. Nicotiana from the garden mixed with her natural scent.

"Tell me about before," she uttered. "When you and Conin were children. What was he like?"

For decades, I'd avoided thinking about the past, about the brother I'd lost. But with Aurora's magic wrapped around my mind, the memories didn't hurt as much. I could remember Conin without feeling like phantoms of the past were carving my chest open.

"He was fearless," I found myself saying, "absolutely fearless in the most reckless way possible. Used to climb the tallest trees in our dad's territory just to see what was on the other side of the mountains. Ma would lecture him about safety, and he'd listen with this serious expression, nodding along like he was taking it all to heart. Then the next day he'd do something even more dangerous."

Aurora's lips curved in a smile. "Sounds familiar. I knew someone like that once."

"Did you now?" I raised an eyebrow, surprised to find humor creeping into my voice. "And what happened to this reckless person?"

"She grew up. Learned that sometimes the people depending on you are more important than the thrill of taking risks." Her expression grew wistful. "Though I suspect she still has that streak buried somewhere."

Another piece of herself offered freely. Aurora didn't share personal details easily. Everything I knew about her past had been hard-won through observation and patience. The fact that she was opening up now, while shielding me from my demons, meant more than she probably realized.

"Conin had this theory," I continued, letting the memory wash over me. "Said the stars were tiny holes in the sky where the gods had poked through from the other side. If you wished hard enough, your dreams would slip through those holes and come true in other realms."

"What did he wish for?"

"Peace. To every corner of every world." My throat tightened despite the buffer Aurora had created. "Said when he inherited our clan's magic, he'd travel to each realm beyond the stars and bring back stories for children who'd never seen anything but the battlefield."

Aurora's free hand found mine, weaving our fingers together. The simple contact sent my pulse racing.

"He sounds wonderful," she whispered.

"He was. Even as a child, he had this way of making everyone around him want to be better. More hopeful." I turned my head to face her, struck by how the shadows played across her features. "The Shepherd knows this. Uses those memories to torture me with what I lost."

She moved closer, rising to her knees without breaking the connection at my temple. Her other hand braced on my thigh, and my cock stirred despite myself.

"Thank you," I said, meaning it more than any words I'd ever spoken.

Her smile was radiant, transforming her from beautiful to breathtaking. She cradled my head in both hands, circling my temples with gentle pressure.

"Close your eyes," she murmured.

I obeyed and nearly bit my tongue when I felt her moving to straddle me—not quite where I wanted her, but close enough. She traced a line with her thumb over my cheekbone, and I released a shuddering breath.

"Let me in."

I lowered my mental defenses, melted under her ministrations, gave myself over to her entirely.

Then I felt it.

Her magic changed, liquefied somehow. The buffer around the Voices remained, but now I could feel her in every part of me. Not just my mind, in every molecule in my body.

When Aurora's consciousness slipped deeper, euphoria hit me like a drug. She dismantled every wall I'd built, not forcing her way through but sliding around the labyrinthine pathways of my mind, navigating passages I'd thought were sealed. When she brushed the most intimate part of my consciousness, the core of who I was, lightning bolts sparked at the contact.

The screaming Voices dulled to whispers as her magic wove through my thoughts, down my spine, settling in my chest. Every nerve came alive under her touch.

My skin tingled, tightened. My blood boiled as her power carved new paths through my veins. The constant agony in my skull vanished, replaced by the warm weight of her mind pressed against mine.

Then her magic pooled between my legs, cupping me in a firm grasp that moved, stroked, milked me toward the edge.

My muscles locked and released in waves I couldn't control.

I needed more than this ghostly connection. Needed her beneath me, around me, her voice breaking on my name as I buried myself so deep inside her she'd never be free of me.

"Aurora," I growled and opened my eyes to find her watching with dark fascination.

Her pupils were blown wide, lips parted as she breathed hard. Whatever she was doing to my mind was affecting her too.

"I can feel what you feel," she said under her breath. "Your pain, your need." Her hand slid down to rest over my racing heart. "Everything." Hunger consumed her face. She licked her lower lip, looking at me like she wanted a taste—of my blood, of my cock. I didn't care which.

"If we do this, there's no going back," I warned, grasping her hips and pulling her down against my erection. "You'll be mine."

My wolf snarled, urging me to claim her. I wouldn't—not when I might not survive tomorrow—but her agreement would suffice.

For now.

The moan that escaped her lips should be forbidden. Aurora flashed her sharp fangs as she started grinding against me.

Fuck. It felt so good.

"Then stop talking and take me," she said and bit down hard on her lower lip.

Crimson welled. The scent of her blood nearly made me come in my pants. My fangs descended with debilitating need.

She kissed me, and her blood flowed into my mouth as our tongues met.

The moment I tasted her, the world exploded.

Her essence flooded through me like a dam bursting, torrents crashing over me until I couldn't tell where I ended and she began. If she'd felt like ecstasy before with just her Blood Manipulation, now she was pure icy fire in my veins.

The connection worked both ways. Her desire blazed through me as my touch sparked tremors down her spine. She pressed against me harder, her need growing more urgent.

"By the gods, Aurora." My voice came out strangled.

She pulled back, eyes wild, a drop of blood glistening on her mouth. "I can make you forget them," she whispered. "The Voices. Make them disappear for a little while."

"How?"

"By giving you something else to focus on."

She grabbed the hem of my shirt and yanked it up. Locked her hands around my neck. Then her mouth was on mine again, demanding, needy. She nipped my tongue, and I groaned. And when she sucked on it, pulling my blood into her mouth, fire shot straight to my groin.

My control snapped. I fisted her hair, dragged her closer. Then I fell into her kiss. Wholeheartedly. Drunk on her.

Her hands moved between us, worked my pants open. I should stop this. Should be the better man.

But fuck it.

I let her push the leather down while I slipped my hands under her shirt, filled my palms with her breasts. My cock sprang free, hard and eager.

When she raked her nails over my length, a groan slipped through my clenched teeth. I twisted her nipple with my thumb. Felt the rush of heat to her core, ecstasy spreading through her body. She began stroking me more urgently, her scarlet eyes absorbing my every reaction.

"Aurora," I hissed in warning. If she didn't slow down, this would end sooner than either of us wanted.

She ignored me, shifted backward, and sank to her knees. She took my cock by the base and circled the head with her tongue.

Fuck. I saw stars.

A moan tore from my chest. All reason fled as I gathered her hair, twisted the thick rope around my wrist, and pushed deeper into the heat of her mouth. She looked straight into my eyes as she took all of me in, and I watched with rapture how her cheeks hollowed when her lips rose slowly over the tip and back down again.

"You feel so good," I said, and when she moaned for me, something warm unfurled in my middle.

She took me deeper, her eyes watering. I gave her hair a gentle tug, adding just enough aggression to match my need.

Her response was a heady groan that told me she enjoyed it as much as I did.

I increased my pace, thrusting into her mouth, chasing the crest of building pleasure. I needed to come more than I needed breath.

Aurora pulled away with a loud pop. "I want you inside me," she said, breathless. "Now."

I stood in a rush, pulled her up with me, and pressed her against the wall. I caught the hem of her top and tugged it over her head. The sight of her took my breath away—narrow waist, milky-white skin, and the most exquisite breasts that would haunt my dreams for the rest of my life. I dipped my head to taste her tight nipple, and she arched into my touch, her hands tangling in my hair.

If I didn't have her now, I'd lose my mind.

I pulled my hips away just enough to reach for the fastening of her pants. The fabric slipped down her legs, taking her panties with it, and I skimmed my fingers along the curve of her thigh. Her skin pebbled under my touch, and the anticipation building between us was stifling.

When I kissed her again, it was fierce and claiming. Nothing compared to my finger tracing up her center in a feather-soft touch.

Then, I gave her bud a gentle flick.

She cried out. With my chest, I pushed her harder into the wall, cupped the back of her neck and circled her sensitive spot, lightly, denying her release.

"Radu," she groaned against my mouth. "Stop teasing."

Her desperation drew a dark chuckle from me.

"As you wish, princess."

I lifted her legs around my waist, rubbing my length up her wet core, then retreated. Delicious shivers raked through her body, and I chuckled again. My tip barely nudged her opening, and halted... only then did I thrust.

Hard.

Fireworks exploded behind my eyes. Pleasure coursed through me so intensely I nearly tipped over the edge myself.

"Oh, God," she gasped, her head falling back against the wall.

The world vanished. She took me so well, every sensation so intense it bordered on addictive. Nothing existed beyond the two of us, beyond this moment that felt like coming home and losing myself all at once.

I pulled back before thrusting again. And again. Without mercy. Setting a rhythm that had us both clinging to each other. She met my movements, gyrating her hips and heightening the sensations.

"Fuck," I breathed, my accent thickening with need. "Just like that."

The soft tendrils of her magic reached toward my wolf. He stirred, acknowledged her with something like approval, then settled back, as if he'd recognized her as ours long before I'd made up my mind.

Our magic mingled, darkness and crimson dancing as one. As power surged, so did the pressure building with each hard thrust. I felt my control slipping through my fingers like sand.

My body wound tighter. Muscles tensed.

I could barely breathe through the intensity. I needed release, while also wanting this to last forever.

My movements grew more focused, more intense. The tide of pleasure rose as I pounded into her.

The climax hit me like a freight train. I groaned against her ear, lost in the overwhelming rush. She shook in my arms as we reached that peak together, her soft cries mixing with mine.

When I came back to myself, I slid us down to the floor, my back against the wall. She settled on top of me, straddling my hips, and I locked my arms around her and refused to let go.

It took me a long moment to notice the silence in my head.

The Voices had stopped. For the first time in decades, my skull wasn't splitting apart. And it was because of her. She was my salvation, my reprieve, and I could no longer see myself resisting the pull that had taken me into her orbit.

I buried my face in the curve of her neck, breathing in her scent. "You sealed your fate, princess. You can't get rid of me now."

She laughed and pressed a soft kiss beneath my jaw. "Who said I wanted to?"

"Good." I rolled us over, pinning her beneath me with a wicked grin. "Then we should probably do this again—and again."

She made a half-hearted protest when I started kissing my way down her throat.

Not that either of us believed it for a second.

AURORA

WE WERE MIDWAY UP the trail from Solomon's Rocks to Postavarul Massif when Quakelord's voice echoed through the forest. "Last one up does laundry for a week!" He leaped over a fallen tree, twisted in the air to cross his forearms above his head, and unleashed his magic. "Yee-haw! Eat dirt, losers!"

The ground rumbled like a waking beast. Dozens of earth pillars erupted from the forest floor with violent force, soil and stone geysering upward in jagged spears. Each column twisted as it rose, their pointed tips gleaming with moisture and moss. We were moving at no less than sixty miles per hour. A direct hit would punch through our bones like a spear through parchment.

"You better hide your cheatin' ass, 'cause when I get my hands on you——" Terraknight's threat died in a snarl. He planted his feet and swept his massive arm in a wide arc.

The earth responded as if part of his body. Every pillar Quakelord had summoned cracked, then exploded outward in a shower of dirt and rock fragments.

Pebbles pelted our faces as we ducked and weaved through the debris field. Clumps of mossy soil splattered against tree trunks, releasing the rich stench of damp earth.

Selena caught my eye and shot me a conceited smirk that said 'no one messes with my blood source.'

Then the ground bucked, and we lost our footing.

Terraknight's magic rippled outward in a seismic wave that sent us all tumbling down the mountainside in a chaotic avalanche of limbs and curses. Tree branches whipped our faces and caught in our hair as we crashed through undergrowth.

"Sorry, ladies!" Terraknight's gravelly voice shook with mirth.

"Sorry my ass!" Selena spat as she rolled to her feet. Dirt streaked her pale cheek like war paint. "When I catch you, Sabin, you'll be picking rocks out of your teeth for a week!"

"I'll hold him down for you, Lieutenant!" Gale's voice carried from further down where she swooped between the trees.

I laughed, a deep belly laugh, as I pulled twigs out of my hair. A beetle the size of my thumb had lodged in the collar of my suit—one of those things that fed on rotting wood——and I flicked it away with a grimace.

Quakelord's careful topknot had come undone, wild black strands flying in every direction. He cursed loudly enough to wake zmei, which were known for sleeping in the deepest caves, as he realized his cheating had backfired spectacularly.

"Betrayed by my own people," he groaned, then spat out a mouthful of leaves. "No one has any loyalty anymore!"

Quakelord was a lot like blood on white pants. He could be either grating or hilarious, depending on who had to deal with the mess.

Hummingbird circled overhead like a hunting hawk, then tucked his dove-white wings and plunged toward Terraknight's retreating figure.

"I'll make him pay for that, Projector," he promised with a wicked grin.

There was barely enough space for him to maneuver between the twisted branches, let alone line up a proper strike. But that didn't stop him...

Wood cracked in the aftermath of his air lance. A flock of birds exploded from their roosts in a panic of wings and shrieks just as a ninety-foot-tall Scots pine groaned, tilted, and crashed to the ground. The impact sent tremors throughout the entire mountain, and I palmed the nearest tree to find stability.

Terraknight's deep laughter boomed from ahead. "Hummingbird, you suck!"

"Eat me!" Hummingbird shouted back, his wings beating furiously as he banked between the trees. He tucked into a dive and slammed into Terraknight's broad back with enough force to send them both careening into a massive sycamore trunk.

They tumbled to the base in a tangle of limbs and feathers, loose bark raining down on their heads.

Small woodland creatures bolted from their burrows and scattered into the underbrush.

"You moron," Terraknight groaned. "That hurt!"

Quakelord rolled to his feet with cat-like grace and dug his fingers into the damp earth. The rich scent of moss and petrichor spiked around him as his magic stirred to life. Thick roots burst from the soil, followed by creeping vines that moved like living serpents. They coiled around Terraknight and Hummingbird's ankles, then climbed higher—calves, thighs—binding them tight against the very tree trunk they'd just crashed into.

Hummingbird tried to twist free, wings beating uselessly against the bark. "Oh, come on! This is just—" A root wrapped around his jaw and muffled the rest of the protest.

"What the—" Terraknight's cursed, but a thick vine snaked around his head and clamped over his mouth like a gag. Every time he flexed his earth magic to shatter Quakelord's bindings, fresh growth sprouted to replace what he'd destroyed.

"In love and war, everything is fair, ladies," Quakelord said with a wink. "Every man for himself!" He threw back his head and howled like a wolf before sprinting uphill with dizzying speed.

Every man for himself, indeed. Time to even the odds.

I reached out with my Blood Manipulation and seized control of his racing pulse. Not enough to hurt him, just enough to make his legs wobble. He stumbled, caught himself, then stumbled again as I played with his circulation.

"What—Projector!" he whined over his shoulder.

But Selena and I were already on the move, the trees blurring past us as we left Quakelord behind.

Three weeks and a day had passed since they'd told us the truth about the Tenth Ward. We were on a mission tonight, but my thoughts kept drifting to what came after. I'd corner Radu the moment we returned and make him understand that staying here while waiting for the inevitable death of his friends was no longer an option. I needed him to portal me back to the Republic.

I'd given my plan a lot of thought over these past weeks. The old smuggler's tunnel would get me inside. The same passage Lev, Katerina, and I had crawled through as children, shrieking with laughter as we hunted for pirate gold and hidden chambers. Back then, our greatest fear had been staining our silk dresses or missing afternoon blood service in the palace gardens.

Now I planned to use it for something far more dangerous than treasure hunting.

I was going to disturb a Creator in his Deep Sleep.

Not just enter Dracula's Sleeping Chamber. That alone would earn me a death sentence. No, I intended to do something infinitely worse. I'd feed him my blood, grant him access to my memories, and potentially trigger his awakening decades before the ordained time.

Pray his sense of justice would compel him to act.

The Blood Communion was strictly forbidden to anyone below the Council of Elders. Not impossible, any pureblood possessed the basic ability, but so heretical that even contemplating it was considered a sin. The ritual was sacred, reserved for moments of absolute crisis when the First Originals' intervention was the only salvation.

I'd say saving our race and the mixed-breeds qualified.

My Transmitter buzzed against the bone behind my ear, and I pressed a finger to accept the call. The Voices leaked through the connection with Harbinger, but since I wasn't Harmonized with him, they sounded muffled.

"Harbinger to Black Guild," Radu's voice came through the static, sharp with urgency. *"Confirm. Standard intercept formation. Wait for my signal."*

"Copy that, Harbinger," I replied. "We're in position."

He, Pearl, and Ember had split from our group at the base of the mountain to scout the rocky pass where Souleaters were spotted moving in a slow procession. Their numbers posed little threat to our combined strength, but Radu never left anything to chance.

The others continued their race, unbound now, but still shoving and trash-talking despite Harbinger's orders. Another aggressive tackle between Terraknight and Hummingbird toppled a tree, sending it crashing to the ground in an explosion of splintered wood and startled wildlife.

So much for stealth.

Could I blame them? They lived each day expecting it to be their last. If racing up a mountain and acting like fools brought them joy, who was I to judge?

Selena had a different opinion.

She pulled up beside me, muttered, "Damn boys," under her breath, and darted ahead. A trail of jasmine perfumed the air in her wake, mingling with the earthy scents of moss and pine.

"After your first decade, you learn to ignore them," Gale said, nudging me with her elbow. Her smile held a mix of humor and challenge that seemed to say, 'You'll see for yourself if you stick around long enough.' Then she spread her velvety wings and launched herself into the darkness above.

I watched the silhouettes ahead—Terraknight and Hummingbird still wrestling their way up to the top, Quakelord darting between trees on silent footfalls. For a moment, I wondered what it would feel like to join them. To forget duty and death and just exist in the simple joy of an innocent competition.

But the tension of pre-battle crept up my spine, chasing away any thoughts of play.

We reached the craggy peak and spread out along the ridge. Six sets of eyes focused on the monsters moving through the pass below. My Blood Manipulation swept outward, cataloguing the advancing horde. The count came back balanced. Equal numbers of each Souleater type, but not enough to warrant a full-scale attack.

I could see them clearly in my mind. Their auras pulsed with oily darkness, but I was getting better at telling them apart. Nebulas shambled in the rear. Ignises hid in the front and the center. Limuses prowled the flanks. And above, the Glacies hovered on massive black wings, the flapping sound covering the scraping of claws on stone.

"Where's the Gloom?" Quakelord whispered, leaning over the edge for a better view.

None of us had an answer, and the murky silence made my stomach clench. The Limuses always deployed the sand barriers during attacks.

Their absence felt... wrong.

In the shadows the Glacies cast on the ground, the Ignises' horns blazed like torches. When moonlight hit those outside the darkness, metallic hides gleamed with a sheen like beetle shells.

Wind carried the stench of rot and sulfur up from the valley, and my hands shook as I gripped the rocky ledge and tried not to breathe it in.

I pushed my blood magic further, sweeping every corner of the pass. "I don't understand," I said, frowning. "I don't sense any other Souleaters. There should be more—backup, reserves, *something.*"

Terraknight's voice came from my side. "Something's off. Could be a trap." His eyes swept the formation below. "Cap, what do you want us to do?"

"I don't hear any more of them," Harbinger's response crackled in my ear.

Air sizzled behind us. We turned as Radu stepped through his portal, Pearl and Ember behind him. Frost covered their hair, and Pearl rubbed her arms for warmth. Only Ember looked unaffected—her fire magic protecting her from the bitter cold.

Radu moved to the edge and studied the Souleater formation below. I found myself watching the way moonlight caught in his platinum hair as a gentle breeze whipped it around his face. His shirt pulled tight across his chest and shoulders, outlining every carved muscle beneath the fabric.

The man was a contradiction. Always silent, locked in his head, like the rest of us didn't exist. Now I understood why. The Voices gave him no peace, a constant chorus of the dead demanding his attention.

Knowing the reason didn't make him any less maddening to deal with. Still, I couldn't deny the effect he had on me. Those strange golden-scarlet eyes could leave me breathless with just a glance. It was foolish, really. Here I was in the middle of a potential battle, distracted by temptation.

Then again, meaningful relationships had never been my strength. Between Selena and the occasional Blood Pact—where conversation was hardly the point—I kept to myself. Hard to form connections when half the Republic saw you as the 'halfblood-loving princess' and the other half thought you were too far above their station.

"Too many Ignises in the front," Harbinger said, his deep, masculine voice disturbing my wandering thoughts. *"We'll strike from the rear, take our chances with the Nebulas. The Limuses are guarding the flanks, but they're too close to the canyon walls. No room for a side attack."*

I followed his gaze to the four-armed creatures lumbering at the convoy's rear. Their hunched backs and skeletal frames looked almost pitiful from this height. But I remembered when one of them crushed me to its chest. How massive they'd seemed when towering over me. How their rotting breath had made my eyes water.

Gale crouched at my side, wings spread in a scarlet blanket behind her. She shot me an infectious grin, and her whole face lit up. It was impossible not to return the smile despite the churning in my gut.

Another battle, another chance to save the people I vowed to protect—or fail spectacularly. The fear never got easier. Not only for my life, but for what my mistakes might cost others. Phoenix's face flashed through my mind; the moment my control slipped and those Ignises broke free.

I couldn't let that happen again. I wouldn't.

"On three."

Radu stepped forward, shoulders squared, jaw set, and scanned each of us with calculating amber eyes. When his gaze locked with mine, the world narrowed to just us. Battle-hunger flickered in his dilated pupils; the same predatory gleam I'd seen countless times before steel and portal magic met rotting flesh. His mouth quirked up at one corner, and I caught the silent message: *Trust yourself. Try to enjoy the slaughter.*

I'll try, I sent back with a nod. For Father, for Conin and Phoenix, for everyone we'd already lost to these monsters.

"One," he began, never breaking eye contact.

My pulse hammered against my ribs. The Souleaters' guttural snarls carried up from below.

"Two."

He stepped backward off the ledge, body twisting in freefall as his lips shaped a soundless, "Three."

I looked over the edge just as the portal swallowed him, then spat him out sixty feet below in a burst shadow. The blood-red gem at the pommel of his sunsteel blade glinted as he slid it free from its sheath. Then another portal claimed him.

Boots scraped stone. Gale and Hummingbird launched themselves over the cliff, wings pressed tight to their backs. They plummeted toward the horde of Souleaters, then snapped their wings open mid-fall. Copper and dove-white feathers caught the wind as they banked hard, diving straight into the circling Glacies.

Air lances sliced through the night and clashed with bursts of ice shards, followed by the wet splatter of severed limbs hitting the ground.

"Eat my dust, Terra!" Quakelord called out, spinning to face us with his back to the ravine. "Ladies." He tipped an imaginary hat and spread his arms wide, letting gravity take him.

For all his quick temper, Quakelord knew how to cut tension when he wanted to. A smile tugged at my lips as I craned my neck to follow his descent. Narrow platforms jutted from the cliff's face, softening his landing as he bounced down like a grasshopper.

Rich, fruity magic saturated the air so thick I could taste it on my tongue. I glanced over to find Terraknight to my left, knees bent, arms spread at his sides.

The rock underneath him appeared to turn spongy.

I gawked and reached out to test it. Cool to the touch, but it felt like rubber instead of stone. He tested it with a few bounces, building momentum like a diver on a springboard. His grin flashed white as he caught Selena's dumbstruck stare.

"Show-off," she muttered, but her lips twitched.

Terraknight's laugh boomed across the pass before he dove head-first into the abyss. For someone built like a battering ram, he moved without sound. Not even a pebble scattered in his wake.

"Ready?" Pearl asked.

Her eyes blazed sapphire-bright. Pearlescent scales rippled across her hands and forearms, catching moonlight as she wove complex patterns through the air. Water droplets materialized from nothing, thousands of them spinning and merging until a massive sphere of liquid hovered five feet off the ground. The soft murmur of churning water almost drowned out the battle cries rising from below.

"I can't believe I'm doing this," Ember spat and stomped one yellow rubber boot against stone.

She had good reason to worry. Fire magic worked fine for rooftop-hopping across ruins scattered throughout the wards, but more than a hundred-foot drop was a different story.

So, we had come up with another idea during our strategy meeting——use me as a pack mule while Harbinger and the others kept the Souleaters distracted——which she agreed, albeit reluctantly.

"Hop on," I said, patting my thighs and bending my knees to match her height.

"You think having a few decades on me gives you the right to be condescending? Stop treating me like a child!" Ember seethed, but she still grabbed my shoulders and hoisted herself onto my back.

A killer smile lit across Selena's face as she snorted behind her fist. I bit my cheeks to stop the laughter threatening to escape. "No one thinks you're a child," I cooed. More like a sweet, innocent young woman who could melt steel with her bare hands.

Pearl waited at the edge, only her head visible above the giant water sphere that encased her body. Saltwater sloshed around her shoulders as she moved.

"See you down there," she called, then rolled forward and plummeted. The massive bubble carried her like a cannonball.

"Our turn," Selena said, peering over the cliff's edge. "Rappel down to that ledge. See it?" She pointed to a flat outcropping jutting from the rock face about seventy feet down.

I nodded.

"Should be safe to jump from there if she holds tight. If not... at least you tried." She shrugged with typical Selena warmth. "Break a leg."

"I'm right here, you assholes," Ember muttered, but Sel was already gone, a dark blur dropping into the canyon.

I adjusted my 'cargo,' making sure Ember's grip wouldn't snap my neck on landing, then dropped to my knees. My fingertips found the first handhold, rough granite biting into skin as I supported both our weights. This would destroy my nails, but it might earn me a few points with the balaur.

The ledge stretched almost four feet across, plenty of room to land safely. Battle sounds rose from below, deafening now as we grew closer to the slaughter. Wings beat too close for comfort as Glacies circled overhead, their ice magic crackling in the night air. The Black Guild kept them occupied, but it wouldn't last long.

I breathed in the thick stench of rot and took a running leap into empty air.

"Hold on," I whispered.

Gravity seized us like a giant's fist, but even with Ember's added weight, the fall felt routine. I'd been jumping a three-hundred-foot drop from my bedroom window since age five.

This was nothing.

The landing jarred us both. Momentum pitched Ember forward, and her forehead cracked against the back of my skull hard enough to make me see stars.

"This changes nothing," she said, sliding off my back and rubbing her nose. Her lovely brows slid together as she assessed the battle, but the smile she tried to hide behind her hand told me I was on the right path to win her heart.

I flashed her a grin, blinking rapidly as the dizziness subsided. "Let's go raise some hell."

Ahead of us, Black Guild was already carving through the Souleater vanguard.

Gale stood at the center of a howling vortex, mahogany hair ripping free from her braid and lashing her face. Pearl worked in perfect sync from the ground, sending thick ropes of water spiraling up from the base. The liquid tentacles climbed higher and higher and twisted around each other like a massive serpent made of brine.

Pearl clapped her hands, and the water ropes snapped forward. They wrapped around Souleater necks and torsos before dragging them screaming into Gale's spinning death trap.

Salt spray mixed with the sweet scent of citrus as Gale spread her wings wide. When she launched skyward, chunks of stone tore loose from the ground, caught in the updraft of her takeoff. The trapped Souleaters spun faster, their gurgles and shrieks bouncing off the gorge's sheer walls as she carried them higher.

She hurled them against the cliff face with bone-crushing force. Rock cracked and boulders tumbled down, flattening the Limuses too slow to dodge.

Ember's boots squeaked as she rushed toward the battle, but I couldn't look away from Terraknight. He stopped dead center in a pack of circling hellhounds, tapped his boot once, and dropped into a fighting stance.

Dozens of Limuses circled him, their crimson eyes blazing with hunger, and the damp, foamy saliva from their snapping jaws made even my skin crawl. Behind them, Glacies dug their talons deep into stone, ice creeping down their claws to form spears that scraped the ground.

A massive stone pillar erupted in front of Terraknight just as the hellhounds pounced. He drove his fist straight through it, shattered three feet of solid rock into thousands of razor-sharp fragments, and sent the explosion of stone shrapnel ripping through Limuses.

But the Glacies were already raising their arms, ice spears aimed at his exposed back.

Sabin, you fool.

I thrust my Blood Manipulation forward and slammed into their minds. Glass-thin barriers tried to keep me out, but I cracked through like breaking a mirror. I raised my palms and twisted their heads toward each other, then clenched my fist.

The ice spears launched straight into their own ranks. They punched through gray flesh, some lodging deep, others bursting out the other side in sprays of black ichor. Bodies dropped, adding to the growing pile of corpses.

Terraknight spun, eyes wide as he searched for whoever had saved his ass—Souleaters didn't just drop dead for no reason. When his gaze found mine, that confused frown melted into a brilliant grin.

"Thanks, Projector!" he called with a sharp nod before sprinting toward where Hummingbird and Quakelord were cutting through the remaining horde.

Black gore drenched their clothes and painted their faces, but it didn't stop them from shouting kill counts at each other. They moved with vicious efficiency, competing to see who could deliver the fastest death blow. Watching them laugh and joke while butchering monsters should have been reassuring.

Instead, dread pooled in my stomach.

This was too easy. Souleaters never went down this fast, never fell into such obvious tactical blunders. Something was wrong.

Radu materialized beside me as if summoned by my thoughts, and I noticed the Voices hissing through my Transmitter had grown louder. What used to be background static now buzzed like angry wasps, impossible to ignore.

"Hold!" he barked, raising a fist.

Every muscle in his body went rigid, veins standing out along his forearms as he listened to something the rest of us couldn't hear. His eyes twitched, pupils darted back and forth like he was reading invisible text. The Souleaters around us continued their march, flowing past as if we were nothing more than rocks in a stream.

They were ignoring us.

What in the Underworld—?

I held my breath and sent my Blood Manipulation sweeping toward the canyon's exit. Nothing. No ambush, no reinforcements lurking within my one-mile range.

Radu broke formation and scanned the canyon walls with keen eyes. His knuckles went white around his sword hilt.

"We fall back," he shouted, voice tight. "I don't like being trapped in here. We'll draw them into open ground where we can—"

A blinding lance of light tore across the sky, turning night into day in a heartbeat. The beam sliced through the heavens, then erupted in a thunderclap that shook the mountains themselves.

The sound hammered my bones and turned my blood to ice. Realization washed over me. A burning sensation akin to fire ants spread across my skin.

Trap.

"RUN!" Selena's scream broke my paralysis. She shoved hard against my chest, and my numb legs finally responded.

The sky was falling, and we were about to die.

AURORA

DOWN THE RAVINE SEEMED the only escape route my terror-addled brain could process. I sprinted through the canyon as if the Shepherd itself clawed at my heels. My pulse hammered so violently against my throat I could taste copper with each beat.

I vaulted over a jagged crevice and craned my neck to track the electric lance as it arced downward. Toward us; the realization robbed me of breath and sent me stumbling over fallen rock.

The bolt was following the gorge's path, cutting through darkness faster than sound itself.

We were running directly into its trajectory.

The narrow walls pressed in on both sides, offering no shelter. I watched the blazing spear grow larger, brighter, close enough now that I could see bright blue tendrils of energy writhing around its head. The bolt would hit the canyon floor ahead of us, but if we stopped, we'd be as good as dead.

Then thunder split the air and ruptured my eardrums.

A frightened scream tore from my lips as I ducked my head, but there was nowhere to go except forward. Blood trickled warm down my neck, the ringing drowning out everything.

Every hair on my body stood rigid from the electric charge building in the air. Some primal instinct screamed that even raising my arms would strip flesh from bone. I forced my legs to pump harder despite the loose shale threatening to send me tumbling, knowing it was useless, knowing we were about to die.

Selena was right on my heels, hands pressed over her bleeding ears. Raw terror carved lines across her face as she looked up. Terraknight and Ember flanked her, leaping over the uneven terrain while Gale's copper wings beat frantically three feet above the ground.

Terraknight suddenly wheeled around, his mouth working in desperate shouts I couldn't hear. His wild gesticulations sent ice through my veins—

Impact.

The bolt hit the earth just as Harbinger materialized from a portal with Pearl clutched in his arms. Both of them staggered as the shockwave slammed into them first, then hurled the rest of us through the air.

I slammed into an outcropping of stone, my ribs screaming against the collision. Pain exploded across my spine as I crumpled to the ground.

Gasping, for one, two, three seconds, and then I forced my eyes open. The stars rolled overhead through the settling dust. Urgent, desperate voices penetrated my stunned mind.

"Hummingbird!"

"Quakelord!"

I clawed my way to my hands and knees, fighting the skull-splitting headache, and staggered to my feet.

Smoke and pulverized stone choked the air, thick as winter fog. My blood magic swept outward through the murk, hunting for familiar auras. Most of the guild pulsed with battered but steady life—all except two.

My heart stuttered.

Hummingbird's pulse fluttered weak and thready. His consciousness felt fractured, like scattered glass. Unconscious. Just knocked out.

Quakelord had vanished completely.

I stretched my magic to its absolute limit, probing past the Souleater survivors. Nothing. Not even an echo of his presence.

"Quakelord!" I joined the frantic chorus. "Hummingbird!"

With each unanswered call, the hollow in my chest grew bigger. My subconscious already knew what my mind refused to acknowledge. No living mortal could hide from my Blood Manipulation. If I couldn't sense Quakelord…

Suddenly, wind gusted through the ravine. Gale's wings beat in powerful strokes, her magic clearing the choking smoke. The gray veil lifted, revealing the devastation.

Beyond the crater's rim, a dark shape lay crumpled.

A strangled noise left my throat.

Even through the haze I recognized the sprawled limbs, the wild black hair now matted with blood. Quakelord's body lay motionless in an expanding crimson pool, his sharp features slack in death.

The sight punched through me like a blade, and the chambers in my heart squeezed shut. My knees gave out, but this time no one caught me as I crashed to the hard ground.

We were too late.

"Over here!" Terraknight's voice sounded rougher from the smoke and dust he'd inhaled.

He kneeled beside Quakelord, his large frame hunched in defeat. I couldn't tear my focus from the copper tang mixed with moss and rain—Quakelord's magic signature still clung to him. For the first time in my life, the smell of blood didn't trigger my fangs. Acid burned up my throat instead.

Everyone rushed toward Terraknight's call, but shock had locked my vocal cords. I couldn't make them understand there was nothing we could do for Quakelord.

Hummingbird's fading thread lay hidden somewhere beyond the crater. The others couldn't feel what I felt. Couldn't know he was barely breathing.

All they could see was Quakelord's broken body.

My legs moved without conscious thought, but not toward the others. I followed the thin blue thread my magic showed me—the barely there pulse that led to where the blast had hurled Hummingbird against the far cliff face.

"Aurora!" Selena called. "Where are you going?"

I stumbled over loose rocks, ignoring her call. A sob tore from my throat despite my hand pressed tight over my mouth.

Just like with Phoenix, I'd been too slow when it mattered most.

But Hummingbird was still breathing. That thin thread of life pulsing through my magic meant I had a chance. One last chance to do something right. I'd tear open my own veins if that's what it took to keep him alive.

I wouldn't lose another one.

A streak of red painted the stone wall from ten feet up to where Hummingbird lay twisted at its base. His head tilted at an unnatural angle, brown curls plastered to his skull with blood and grime. One dove-white wing sprawled beneath him, bone fragments piercing through torn feathers. His leather vest hung in tatters, revealing deep lacerations that had shredded the white cotton shirt underneath.

But the massive wound splitting his abdomen open made my knees buckle all over again. Pale intestines spilled through the tear in his flesh, steam rising from the exposed organs in the cool mountain air.

Dark Father, help us.

Quakelord's lifeless form... the extent of Hummingbird's injuries... A searing bolt of grief pierced me as I dropped to my knees beside him.

No. No, no, no.

We were going to lose him too.

There was no way his body could heal that wound fast enough to save him. I lifted his head gently into my lap and brushed the matted curls from his forehead. His amber eyes fluttered open, unfocused but aware.

"P-Projector," he whispered, blood frothing at the corners of his mouth. "Sorry I... I've been such an ass to you. Always was... shit... with outsiders. Especially purebloods."

"Hummingbird, don't talk. Save your strength."

"Too late," he breathed. "Can't... can't fly anymore." A weak smile ghosted his pale lips. "Tell the others... tell them I went down swinging."

"Don't you dare give up on me!"

He just looked at me with a crooked grin. Something sharp twisted in my chest; a thin line of pain stretched to the breaking point. It hurt so much I couldn't draw air into my lungs.

Hummingbird's body went rigid in my hands, and I felt the last flutter of his life slipping away.

No!

I seized that fragile thread of consciousness. With all my magic, with all the strength I possessed, with everything Derzelas gave me, I gripped that fading piece of Hummingbird and refused to let it go.

Vanilla and pennies saturated the air. Power vibrated in my very veins as I poured everything into his body, drove it deeper, forced his blood to multiply, to circulate, and his heart to beat.

I won't let him die. He will live. He must.

God, please don't let him die.

"Aurora, stop!" Selena's voice sounded from miles away. "You can't fight death like this!"

Try me. Hummingbird's life force sank further into the void. I poured more power into him. More... I needed more.

Copper coated my lips, and I tasted my own blood when I licked them. Pressure built in my head, my body's warning that I was running on empty.

"You're killing yourself!" she screamed, but I channeled more magic, pulled harder on the threads of his life.

His heart stuttered, then beat once. His eyelids twitched.

But something was wrong. His eyes, when they opened, held no warmth. No recognition. They stared through me like glass.

"Let me go," he whispered, but his voice sounded hollow, empty. "Please... let me go."

"This is how monsters are made," Selena said, closing a hand over my shoulder. "This isn't healing, A. You're binding his soul to a dying body."

The knowledge settled cold and certain in my bones. Selena was right. My chest tightened, and my stomach knotted, and I felt the blood I drank from Radu earlier edging back toward my mouth. I swallowed hard and took several deep breaths, disgusted with myself for even contemplating doing that to Hummingbird.

I wouldn't become the very thing I despised. Wouldn't create the abominations that haunted our darkest legends. Because what I was attempting had been tried before, centuries ago, by desperate purebloods who couldn't accept loss. The results were always the same.

Ghouls.

The word alone made my skin crawl. Creatures that existed in the space between life and death, their souls bound to decaying flesh by blood magic gone wrong. They weren't unlike Souleaters—pure hunger wrapped in rotting skin, driven only by an endless need to feed.

Ghouls lurked in the deepest tunnels beneath the Carpathians, as far from sunlight as they could burrow. The Council pretended they didn't exist, but every pureblood child learned the stories. Warnings about what happened when you tried to cheat death itself.

I wouldn't curse Hummingbird to that existence. Sweet Derzelas, I wouldn't wish that fate on Lev Wurdulak himself.

My shoulders sagged and rounded inward as I looked down at Hummingbird's pale face—so young, so fragile. "Let me go, Projector," he murmured again, weaker this time.

I severed the magic. The connection snapped like a broken cord and slammed back into me. In my arms, Hummingbird lay unconscious, his thread of life barely flickering. Blood leaked from my eyes and dripped down my face, mixing with the crimson pool spreading beneath his broken body.

Quakelord was gone.

Hummingbird didn't have much longer.

Standing felt like wading through molasses. Every muscle protesting as I forced myself upright. Even the ground seemed to resist my advance, as if it knew the weight of loss I carried.

This was my fault.

I should have seen the trap sooner. The ease with which those first Souleaters had fallen... it should have been a warning. They'd been sacrificial pawns. Passed through the canyon to draw us in where the energy blast could strike. The enemy had even predicted we'd attack from the rear.

A subtle, ruthless strategy unlike anything Souleaters had shown before.

My heart plummeted.

Sweet Derzelas, was this... was this an attack orchestrated by the Shepherd?

A Glacie dropped a dozen feet away, its hooved feet scraping against stone. Ice crystallized along its elongated arms as it flexed razor-sharp claws in our direction. Behind it, more shadows moved: Limuses prowling along the crater's rim, their barrel chests heaving as they scented fresh blood.

Fury blazed through my veins. "Sel, stay with him," I snarled, stepping between her and the advancing monsters.

My magic punched into the Glacie's mind. For a heartbeat, it resisted, then I crushed through its defenses with every ounce of power left in me. I seized control of its nervous system and made it drive its own claws through its skull.

The creature's beady eyes went wide before its head caved in, black ichor spraying across the mountain wall.

Behind me, jasmine and vetiver flooded the air as Selena's magic awakened. A faint crimson glow emanated from her palms as she pressed one hand against Hummingbird's gaping wound, the other over his forehead. The whites of her eyes turned completely black, fusing with her irises until they resembled pools of liquid obsidian.

"Make them suffer," she ordered, then bit into her wrist and positioned the dripping wound over his lips.

Three more Souleaters crept over the canyon's rim. Every movement was a beacon, an offering, to fulfill my rage and thirst for death.

My hand found the silver needle hidden in my hair. Rage narrowed my vision to a single point. The world went silent as my pulse slowed to that of a seasoned predator.

The first—a Limus—charged, snapping its jaws at the air. I sidestepped its clumsy lunge and drove the needle through its eye socket, twisting until brain matter gave way. It collapsed in violent spasms.

The Nebula came from the left, all four arms extended. Like smoke through flame, I caught two wrists and snapped the bones with my bare hands. Before it could react, I grabbed its throat and squeezed until cartilage popped beneath my fingers. Acidic saliva dripped onto my arm, burning through leather and skin. I barely felt the sting.

The third—another Glacie—hesitated, sensing the death of its packmates. Something almost like awareness flickered in its black eyes.

I grinned, cold and cruel, showing my fangs.

"Come on then," I snarled.

It lunged. I met it head-on, catching its claws against my forearms. The impact drove us both to the ground, but I rolled on top, pinning it beneath my weight. Leathery wings crumpled under my knees as I drove the needle into the soft spot beneath its jaw and severed the spinal cord with one clean thrust.

Chest heaving, I looked down at the corpse with satisfaction.

I would claim their feeding ground as my domain. Their growls would become whimpers under my carnage. Their claws would fall open, unable to claim another life. And I would end this. Even if I had to kill them one by one.

My hands balled into fists. Black ichor coated my palms and face and dripped down my neck beneath my collar. The remaining shapes near the crater's edge held back, watching with wary eyes. A few retreated into the hole.

Some primal part of me noted they should have attacked by now. But fury had burned away rational thought, left only the need to destroy something, anything, to make the pain stop. These weren't mindless White Sheep—they were Black Sheep with fragments of consciousness, smart enough to recognize a predator when they saw one.

Smart enough to retreat when the odds turned against them.

I stared at the bloodshed, a boulder in the pit of my stomach. The Academy had trained me to lead, to strategize, to protect. Yet here I stood, surrounded by rotten corpses, and still utterly powerless to save the people in my care.

No matter how many I killed, how much blood I spilled, none of it would bring Quakelord back.

Thunder split the night sky. I ducked on instinct as the heavens blazed white-hot again, turning darkness into blinding day. Familiar this time. Not a lesser threat, but at least I knew what to expect.

I shoved my grief into that locked chest in the back of my mind, along with every other pain I couldn't afford to feel right now. Spinning on my heels, I counted the globes of fire growing larger in the distance.

Five.

Five Magma Lances deployed from every direction, trapping us in. Too late to stop the launch, but I could still eliminate the source before they fired again.

My Blood Manipulation exploded outward so violently my body recoiled.

"Find shelter! Now!" someone roared—Harbinger or Terraknight, I couldn't tell through the ringing in my ears.

But there was no shelter.

Nowhere to hide in this narrow stone throat.

My magic penetrated the Ignises' empty minds. No resistance this time, as if whoever had controlled the previous Souleaters had vanished. Unlike in Brasov, I didn't waste precious seconds deciding methodology.

I wanted them gone.

Erased.

Extinguished to bits.

Their black, viscous lifeforce rushed to the surface of their armored hides as I commanded their vessels to empty. I couldn't see them—hidden beyond the towering canyon walls—but I sensed the ichor gushing through every pore, felt them drop like stones as our connection severed.

But this was no cause for celebration.

Whoever orchestrated this knew my limitations and positioned the Ignises exactly one foot inside my range. I couldn't sense what lay beyond that barrier. More Black Sheep? An entire army?

The odds looked grim either way.

"We need to run!" Selena's voice vibrated with hysteria.

Hummingbird's limp form lay over her shoulder, blood from her torn wrist smeared across his ashen face. His broken wing and boots dragged behind her as she rushed toward me.

Another thunderous explosion splintered the night. I jerked as Selena shoved my shoulder.

"Snap out of it! We have no time!" Her scent had soured with fear.

I stared up at the hundred-foot walls hemming us in. The gorge stretched barely forty feet wide in some areas, ancient limestone carved over millennia into a natural trap. Above us, jagged edges jutted out against the star-scattered sky, some as sharp as broken teeth.

Sweet Dark Father Almighty.

Time slowed to a crawl. Terror froze my blood as the true horror crashed over me. We were insects caught in a giant stone bottle, and someone was about to pour in liquid fire.

The Magma Lances struck through the limestone with earth-shaking force. Lava erupted through the fissures and poured down in glowing waterfalls. The narrow pass turned into a furnace. High above, centuries-old pines clinging to impossible ledges burst into torches before tumbling into the inferno below.

Two bulwarks of lava formed ahead and behind. Two from the sides. One slashing diagonally across our escape route.

The walls themselves had become weapons, caging us in a corridor of death.

Black spots crowded my vision. My body felt disconnected, floating, moving too slowly while reality shifted into fast forward. The approaching heat made the air shimmer like a mirage. I would die here without warning the Republic.

'You're going to lose this war, princess.' Radu's words echoed in my skull.

Nausea churned in my stomach, but I forced it down. One step at a time. *Get out alive first. Then find a solution to save a nation that didn't want saving.*

Selena's grip on my elbow was iron as she hauled me toward the cluster of bodies gathered on the other side of the crater. Through smoke and ash, I recognized Terraknight's grim features. Rich chocolate skin disappeared under layers of grime and blood, his hazel eyes stark in the hellish glow. He grasped my free arm and pulled me behind his massive frame just as Selena crouched to lay Hummingbird gently on the ground.

"How long do we have?" she asked, voice hard and focused.

I looked up at the converging walls of fire and felt my heart stop. "Not long enough."

At my feet, Gale kneeled with Hummingbird's head cradled in her lap. He was too pale, had lost too much blood. Being Changed could only do so much for a mixed-breed this badly injured. Their mortal blood hindered immortal healing, and if they lost all their reserves, they died. The gaping wound in his abdomen was too massive, the healing process too slow to suture itself together.

Selena's emergency work wasn't enough.

Blood coated Gale's arms to the elbows as she pressed down to slow the bleeding. Silent sobs shook her shoulders as her copper wings wrapped around them both, shielding him against our tightening circle.

Beside me, Ember gasped between cries.

I reached out to comfort her, but she pulled away, her gaze locked on Quakelord's motionless form. His black hair spread like spilled ink around his head, waxy skin stretched tight over angular bones. Selena had draped her leather coat over his torso, concealing the fatal wounds.

The stillness of his body was devastating—no heartbeat, no life left in those veins.

An invisible claw pierced my chest and twisted. Helplessness crashed over me as I fought back burning tears.

We'd never hear his voice again, cracking jokes or spewing hatred about the Republic. I'd rather be the target of his loathing than see him reduced to this empty shell.

Derzelas, hadn't there been enough death?

"Stay together. Don't leave the bubble," Pearl's firm voice brought me back from my spiral as cold saltwater foamed around our legs. Brine grew so strong it almost masked the spike in Harbinger's scent.

Ten yards away, darkness writhed and crackled, streaked with golden arcs flaring inside it. The air rippled with approaching hell.

In front of me, sweat beaded on Terraknight's nape, his dark skin gilded by the lava's glow. I focused on a droplet trailing from his hairline when something buzzed to our left, followed by another swish behind us.

Craning my neck, I spotted lightning bolts whizzing from four expanding portals. Pitch black surrounded us as golden strikes collided and retreated into the ever-growing gateways' depths.

Pearl's water bubble rose past my chest now, its pressure oddly comforting against the scorching air. I forced my breathing to steady, my heart to slow its gallop.

I understood their strategy now. Pearl had encircled us with her magic, just like in Sibiu. Plan B, in case Radu's portals failed to contain the Magma Lances.

All around us, the portals had fused into a single cylinder of stretching blackness. I tilted my head back to watch it soar toward the clouds, grasping Selena's hand and squeezing tight.

We'll make it. We'll survive this. We won't die.

The Magma Lances cleaved through the remaining forested mountainside.

As water covered my head, the last thing I saw clearly was the portal walls reaching past the lava tides—over a hundred feet high—blotting out the moon itself. Holding my breath, I waited for impact, for the sound that would announce our doom.

But nothing came.

The darkness felt crushing.

Terraknight jostled backward and stepped on my foot, so I pressed my hands against his broad back to steady him and realized he was bracing against someone else's weight. Reaching over his shoulders, I found Radu's soft hair and curled my fingers around his neck for support.

He was struggling to maintain the portals, shoulder muscles tensed like boulders. Underwater, his frantic heartbeat sounded like muffled drumbeats, reverberating through Terraknight's body and into mine.

Eyes squeezed shut, I sent my Blood Manipulation outward again, desperate to understand what was happening beyond the water shield and Radu's magic.

Silence. No more oily mental threads. I pushed further until my skull throbbed. No Souleaters moved within my one-mile range—as if they'd never existed, or the Shepherd had ordered a retreat.

This had been an ambush. A perfectly laid trap.

The Shepherd had cast its lure, and we'd taken the bait. Starved to cleanse the world of these monsters. A bitter sigh escaped me, the bubbles tickling my face.

Without Pearl and Harbinger's quick thinking, we'd already be ash. Even now, we weren't safe. Only Gale could have escaped on her wings, but knowing her loyalty, she'd never abandon the others.

The Black Guild's bond was stronger than forged steel.

The Shepherd had positioned those Ignises at perfect intervals—a five-pointed star with us at the center. When they launched their attacks, they'd left no escape route, no safe ground to reach.

The more I understood its strategy, the more my blood chilled. Terrifyingly intelligent. Utterly ruthless.

I kept my magic extended like a sensor, monitoring for any breach. Souleaters pressed differently against my consciousness than natural creatures; their corrupted essence always betrayed their presence. But there wasn't even a stir.

Inside Pearl's bubble, time moved slower than molasses. Death's proximity warped perception, made seconds feel like hours. When silver light began filtering through the murky water, relief flooded me. Silver meant moonlight. No lava walls.

Radu had done it.

He'd absorbed the Magma Lances and saved us all.

AURORA

PEARL'S WATER BUBBLE BURST with a wet gasp, and seawater rushed around our ankles before draining into the cracked earth. Steam rose from the scorched canyon floor, carrying the acrid stench of melted stone and charred pine.

Within moments, the thick and suffocating air, heavy with ash that left grit on my tongue, covered us entirely. I'd have killed for clean water. But I settled for wiping soot from my eyes and surveying the wreckage. Where Quakelord had fallen, only dark stains remained on the blackened rock. The water had carried away every trace of him—his blood, the copper tang of it, even the moss and petrichor scent of his earth magic. As if he'd never existed at all.

Black flakes drifted down and settled on our shoulders and in our hair. I touched my lips, my fingers coming away tarnished with ash.

Survival had never tasted this bitter.

"Give them space." Terraknight gripped both mine and Selena's shoulders and cleared his throat. "Let's step back."

He steered us away from where the other outliers gathered around their fallen guildmates. Family saying goodbye.

A broken whimper rose from Gale's throat. Radu kneeled beside Hummingbird's crumpled body, the iele's marigold eyes fluttering open—conscious again but fading fast. Blood frothed at the corners of his mouth with each shallow breath.

I couldn't make myself look anymore. The pain was suffocating, like someone had shoved cotton down my throat. Like a coward, I searched for Selena, hoping to draw strength from her.

She stood on Terraknight's other side, her face set hard despite the tears tracking through the soot on her cheeks.

Tears pooled in my eyes at the sight, and I looked away. She was supposed to be the tough one.

A little further ahead, Ember had collapsed against Pearl's shoulder, small fists twisted in the varva's woolen cardigan as she fought to muffle her sobs. Even though the Magma Lances had pierced through the canyon walls, they still amplified every sound. Each broken breath. Each stifled cry.

Pearl wiped at a tear and leveled a hapless gaze at me. But I didn't know how to make her feel better. Didn't have any answers to her pain. Before I could even attempt to offer comfort, another cry of anguish cut through the air.

Gale staggered forward, dragging her injured wing as she stumbled toward Hummingbird. Terraknight caught her around the waist and pulled her back. She fought his hold for a moment, then collapsed against his chest. Her anguish carried, and I couldn't hold back my tears anymore.

Hummingbird coughed again, a violent fit that shook his entire body. Fresh blood sprayed across his chest, adding to the crimson already soaking his tattered cotton shirt. His usual scent of clean ozone, as if he'd just emerged from a heavy storm, still clung to him, but underneath it, I caught the metallic sweetness of approaching death. His heart stuttered in an irregular rhythm that made my own ache.

"I know it's ha-hard," Hummingbird's voice came in fractured whispers between wet coughs, "but you have to do it." He tried to push himself up.

Radu's hand pressed gently against his shoulder, easing him back down. "Don't strain yourself. You'll only make it worse."

Hummingbird's eyes drifted closed, but a blood-stained smile ghosted across his pale lips. "Just... try to remember something good about me, yeah?" His breath hitched as he looked up at his captain. "And promise me—you'll take me with you?"

"I will."

Radu caressed Hummingbird's face with a hand slick with blood and dirt. A single tear traced down his cheek as he shifted to unsheathe the pistol strapped to his thigh.

They all carried guns. I'd learned why months ago when I'd asked if they used them to slow the Souleaters. They'd been evasive at first, uncomfortable. Then came the truth about Black Sheep and how they fed, and the real purpose of those weapons became clear.

They didn't want their souls trapped inside monsters. If it came down to it, if death was inevitable, a bullet to the head was the cleanest exit. Even if it wouldn't kill them outright, at least it would ensure the Black Sheep couldn't use their brains.

My stomach had sunk when they'd explained it, but I understood.

Now, watching Radu pull out his weapon with that shuttered expression, I learned there was another reason.

Another burden he carried.

It finally clicked why Terraknight and the others sometimes called him 'our Harbinger.' It wasn't just about foreseeing the Souleaters' approach or honoring their names. It meant something so much deeper. Sacred.

He would shelter their souls.

My heart broke for him. He would carry them—their names, their memories, their essence—until his own life ended. It was the most noble salvation these outliers could hope for. These people who lived knowing tomorrow wasn't guaranteed and that fates worse than death existed.

I felt his pain lodge in my throat, choking me. I wished I could ease his suffering, take some of that weight from his shoulders.

Radu raised the pistol to Hummingbird's forehead.

"Farewell, my friend." His voice cracked despite his efforts to steady it.

Silence fell. Thick. Oppressive. The hairs on my neck rose.

"STOP!" Selena's shout shattered the stillness.

We all whipped around to stare at her.

She stood rigid, jaw clamped so hard I could have honed a blade on the sharp line of it. Her obsidian eyes were wide with shock, as if she couldn't believe she'd just interrupted Harbinger from his dreadful task.

I couldn't believe she'd done it.

Astonishment sucked the air out of my lungs, and I stared at her, speechless.

Her fists trembled at her sides, the wet fabric of her top clinging to tensed muscles.

I expected the gunshot. When I turned back to Radu, he hadn't moved. His finger remained steady on the trigger, but he waited.

"I can save him," Selena whispered.

"Sel, he's not a pureblood," I replied, keeping my voice low. I was terrified of Radu's reaction, afraid I'd make things worse and rob Hummingbird of a quick, painless death.

When she spoke again, all uncertainty had vanished.

"Derzelas, don't I know that." She glanced at Hummingbird with uncharacteristic warmth before her clinical mask slipped into place, erasing any trace of emotion. Selena had entered work mode.

Then her cold, calculating eyes locked with Terraknight's. "I'm not a healer for nothing. It will work, but I'll need a lot of blood at the end."

He nodded without hesitation. "Whatever you need."

"I need to stabilize him for transport." She strode toward Radu, who still hadn't moved a muscle.

Crouching beside him, she raised a steady hand and gripped the gun barrel. Her heartbeat remained calm as she pushed it down and away from Hummingbird's head.

Radu's pulse exploded into a gallop, his body jerking as if she'd shocked him from a trance. The glare he shot her could have frozen oceans, but whatever he read in her eyes made his shoulders relax. Hope flickered across his harsh features, softening the hard lines around his mouth and eyes.

"I want you to trust me," she breathed. "Give me room to work." Her voice might've seemed harsh to others, but to me was everything. This was Selena's version of compassion: few words, decisive action.

Radu gave her a quick nod and rose to his feet. Metal clicked as he holstered the weapon. "You save his life, Lieutenant," he said, bending to lift Quakelord's lifeless body, "and I'll be forever indebted to you."

A portal opened ten feet away. Wind whipped our hair from the force of the darkness writhing within it. He paused, met her eyes once more, then stepped through with Quakelord and vanished.

Selena stared at the void, lost in thought. She bit the inside of her cheek and rolled up her sleeves. Then looked back at Hummingbird, who had passed out again.

"Everyone, listen carefully. We need to move fast." She swung a leg over the iele to straddle his thighs. "Gale, I need controlled air pressure on his wounds. Stop the bleeding, but don't compress too hard."

Gale nodded, tears still wet on her cheeks, and kneeled at Hummingbird's head, rolling her wrists. She lifted his head onto her knees as her dark eyes began to glow silver-blue. Orange and honey washed away the stench of death.

Blood slowed to a trickle from Hummingbird's wounds.

"Perfect. Hold that pressure steady—don't vary it, or you could rupture his veins."

The bleeding stopped completely.

Pearl dropped to Hummingbird's side, her muscles rigid. "What can I do?"

"Clean the wounds. Gentle streams. We can't risk more tissue damage."

Pearl nodded in quick, jerky movements, the multicolored strands that had escaped her braid framing her face. I realized then that she, Gale, and Ember were the only ones completely dry among us. The perks of elemental magic.

"Just tell me where," she said.

"Sel," I murmured. "What if you can't—what if he's too far gone?"

She looked up at me, and for a moment her mask slipped. "Then at least we tried."

Then she leaned forward and used her sharp nail to cut away what remained of Hummingbird's shirt. They worked together, gently tearing the fabric from his bloodied skin to reveal the true damage.

"Start with the smaller cuts," Selena instructed, brushing a curly lock from his forehead. A deep gash glistened beneath, filled with debris and ash. "This one here. Rinse out the dirt before we cauterize. Work your way down. I need everything cleaned so I can focus on his abdomen. Ember?"

"Here." The balaur crouched on Pearl's other side.

Selena remained hunched over Hummingbird's torn abdomen, inspecting the wound with gentle prods of her fingers.

"Wait for Pearl to finish, then seal the cuts. The heat will kill any bacteria in the tissue. Can you keep your hand steady?"

Ember shifted into position, tucking her legs beneath her. "I can do it."

Flames burst from her palms, casting us in golden light. Her bottle-green eyes took on a metallic sheen I'd never noticed before—almost reptilian. She extinguished the flames but kept the magic burning beneath her skin, maintaining the precise temperature needed for cauterization.

Hands clasped in prayer, I watched them work.

Gale remained statue-still while Pearl and Ember followed Selena's instructions with laser-like concentration. Hummingbird's complexion hadn't improved—his skin stayed pale as parchment—but at least his heart maintained its slow, steady rhythm. Still pumping blood to his brain. Still keeping him alive.

"What about me?" I asked, moving closer to Selena. "How can I help?"

She stayed silent, eyes twitching as her mind raced. Pearl had moved to examine Hummingbird's broken wing, where bone had pierced skin.

"Remember what I told you about Blood Transcendence?" Selena asked, never taking her gaze from where Ember was sealing a cut on the iele's bicep with her glowing finger.

"I do." What I didn't say was that I remembered her admitting she'd never successfully performed Derzelas' most complex, arcane magic.

"Wasn't it supposed to be nearly impossible? Something about controlling immortal blood?"

"It is, when the subject *is* dead," she confirmed, finally meeting my eyes. The bitter twist of her lips told me she was disappointed I hadn't figured out her plan already. "But Hummingbird isn't dead yet. His immortal blood is still flowing. It's his mortal genes that have gone into survival mode due to his injuries—"

"They're shutting down to preserve what's left," I finished. Then the full horror hit me, and my legs nearly gave out. "Sel, you want to force his body into a pureblood state while he's still alive?"

That's *exactly* what I'd tried earlier.

What she'd stopped me from doing.

For good reason.

"You know what happens if this goes wrong," I hissed.

Her jaw clenched. "I won't let it go wrong."

"That's not how this works!" Fear hitched up my voice. "What I almost did to him before—"

I couldn't say the word. Not with Gale and the others listening. *Ghoul.* The abomination that waited when blood magic failed.

"There's a difference between what you tried and what I'm proposing." Her obsidian eyes bored into mine. "You were trying to trap his soul in dying flesh with brute force. I'm going to temporarily override his mortality so his immortal side can heal him properly."

She leaned closer, lowering her voice. "I wouldn't attempt this if I hadn't witnessed your blood control. What you did to Harbinger in the war room—I felt you weave his molecules into threads even with a blade at my throat."

My stomach dropped. How had she managed to monitor my magic while staring down that portal-born yatagan?

"You'll separate his mortal blood and extract it while I work," she continued as if the task wasn't impossible. "Temporarily. Just long enough for his pureblood physiology to heal the damage."

"You're insane." When her expression didn't change, panic flooded through me. "This isn't some research experiment, Sel—this is Hummingbird's life!"

"I could extract the blood myself, but the healing requires molecular control that takes decades to master." Her voice hardened. "You don't have decades, he doesn't have minutes. So what's it going to be—help me save him, or stand there wringing your hands while he dies?"

Pearl and Ember had both finished their tasks and were staring at me with wide, fearful eyes. But it was Terraknight's anxious pacing and muttered curses that made it difficult to swallow the tightness in my throat.

What Selena asked of me was like demanding a pureblood in bloodlust to show mercy, to step back before draining their prey dry. The only reason I'd survived my own bloodlust after Brasov was drinking Radu's original blood. It had been the single thread that pulled me back from the edge. Without it, I would have kept hunting until there was nothing left to kill.

"Let me get this straight," Terraknight stopped mid-stride and dragged both hands over his short-cropped hair, "you want to drain Hummingbird's mortal blood, possibly killing him or turning him into some abomination, so you can make him immortal?"

"Only temporarily," Selena corrected, but didn't deny the other possibility.

Anguish carved deep lines across the vice-captain's face.

"Even if we avoid creating a monster, his body could still reject forced immortality," I said. "Sabazios' blood runs strong—it might fight back."

"Then we move fast." Her sigh carried defeat and determination in equal measure. "Look, I don't have any other ideas, he's running out of time. I can't promise this will work, but I'm confident I can heal him once every trace of mortality is removed. That much, I guarantee."

"Do it," Gale said, never breaking concentration. The silver-blue glow in her eyes remained steady as she applied pressure to his wounds. "I've known Hummingbird the longest. He'd want this chance. For all his jokes about death... he doesn't want to die."

"Agreed," Pearl said, shooting a pointed look at Ember when silence stretched between us.

The balaur stared at Hummingbird's blanched face, her throat working. When she finally spoke, her voice carried surprising strength. "Bring him back to us."

All eyes turned to Terraknight. He stood frozen, head tilted toward the star-strewn sky, the pulse in his neck throbbing visibly. The weight of deciding a friend's fate pressed down on those broad shoulders. He rocked on the balls of his feet, hands buried in his pockets, then dropped his gaze to Hummingbird. Color drained from his dark skin.

A sharp crack split the night.

We all flinched. No one spoke, but we knew.

Radu had given Quakelord peace.

The finality hit like an arrow to the heart. Until that moment, some desperate part of me had clung to hope. Maybe Selena could have saved them both. Maybe Quakelord was just unconscious. Maybe we'd misread his injuries. That single gunshot severed every thread of denial.

Quakelord was gone.

Ember's shoulders shook as she pressed glowing hands against a cut on Hummingbird's cheek. Tears hissed against her heated touch. "He was supposed to outlive us all. Always said he was too stubborn to die."

Pearl leaned back on her heels, her eyes the startling shade of robin's eggs, glistening. "He promised to teach me his favorite card trick. The one where he always cheated." Her voice broke, but she smiled at what was clearly a fond memory.

"He made me laugh during my worst battles," Gale said between sobs. "Said fear couldn't kill you unless you let it move in and pay rent." She whimpered. "I never got to thank him for that."

Terraknight's shoulders sagged as if the sound had stolen his strength. He stared at his hands—the same hands that had clasped Quakelord's nape in friendship just hours ago during their race.

"Fifty-nine years old," he said, voice hollow. "We never even celebrated his last birthday. Too busy fighting to live long enough for the next one."

The silence felt heavier than the ash still falling around us. We all understood what that gunshot meant beyond Quakelord's death. Some battles couldn't be won, some friends couldn't be saved, and some losses would hollow you from the inside.

We were running out of time to save the ones still breathing.

"Do it," Terraknight spoke again. "Save him."

My hand trembled as I pressed it to my mouth, worrying my lower lip. Could I really separate every molecule that made Hummingbird a son of Sabazios? And if I managed it, how would I contain it?

"Aurora?" Selena's sharp voice pulled me back to her. The deep frown lines between her eyes told me this wasn't the first time she'd called my name. "Terraknight said yes. What about you?"

Five sets of eyes focused on me. My heart thumped against my ribs, an unbearable weight crushing my lungs. *What if I make a mistake and kill him before Selena gets her chance? Should I extract his blood in stages or all at once?* I wanted to curl up in a ball and cry.

"We can't do this without you," she said impatiently.

I forced myself to nod despite my shaking hands. I'd controlled Radu's blood molecules before. I could do this. "Give me ten minutes."

"You have five. He won't last longer."

I took one last look at Hummingbird's sleeping face and closed my eyes. The world fell away as I slipped past his non-existent mental barriers.

His blood felt different from Radu's, though both carried dual essences, Hummingbird's were fundamentally at odds. Where Radu's pureblood and varcolac natures had found balance through true immortality, Hummingbird's immortal heritage clashed with his mortality. The immortal blood flowed thick through major arteries, while his mortal essence ran thinner, faster, through smaller vessels. Like oil and water forced together but never truly mixing.

I began the delicate work of separation, but this was far more complex than what I'd done to Radu in the war room. Then, I'd simply woven his blood molecules into microscopic threads—a blood mesh to control his motor functions.

Separation required something entirely different. Something new.

Instead of threading, I had to stack the mortal molecules carefully, forming dense knots that wouldn't rupture under pressure. Each cluster required precise control—too loose and they'd dissolve back into his system, too tight and they'd crystallize and tear through his veins like razorblades.

One hundred knots formed along his circulatory pathways. Nowhere near enough for a healthy person, but all his weakened system had left after the massive blood loss. I guided them through the maze of his body toward the open wound in his abdomen, where extraction would be safest. The mortal blood resisted, clinging to vessel walls as if sensing its impending exile.

My temples throbbed with the effort. But eventually, every droplet of blood yielded to me and flowed as I commanded it.

"Gale, I need you to create an air chamber for his blood. We'll contain it together until Selena finishes."

Her breathing quickened, but her reply was swift. "Ready. I've secured the space."

"Release the pressure. I'm bringing it out."

The invisible barrier Gale held over the wound relented, and I opened my eyes to witness the extraction. The knots I'd formed throughout his circulatory system had merged during transport, creating one dense crimson mass. It lifted at my order, encased in Gale's shimmering air bubble, and floated away from Hummingbird's body like a dark jellyfish suspended in glass.

Selena was already positioned over his abdomen, fresh cuts bleeding down her wrists while her hands worked above the gaping wound. Deep red light emanated from her palms as her eyes became totally black.

I'd never witnessed her healing powers before. Check-ups, yes. Nexus repairs, certainly. But never this—never watching her drag someone back from death's threshold.

Terraknight flicked his fingers and sliced razor-thin shards from the rocks on the ground. The fragments he'd created levitated toward Selena, seven inches long and sharp enough to split hairs.

"Keep them coming," she murmured. "I need consistent flow."

The shards kissed her forearms, opening precise wounds that immediately began sealing. Blood streamed from her into Hummingbird's torn belly, but her immortal healing fought against the process. The cuts closed within heartbeats, forcing Terraknight to slash fresh ones in an endless cycle.

I must have missed when she'd given him instructions, lost as I was in the delicate work of blood separation.

With a constant crimson supply flowing, Hummingbird's intestines began repositioning themselves. Gray-pink coils slithered back into place as if guided by invisible hands. New muscle fibers sprouted and wove between damaged tissue while blood vessels branched out, connecting in intricate networks that pulsed with fresh circulation.

"Holy Sea Goddess," Pearl breathed. "Is that normal?"

"Nothing about this is normal," I replied, gaping at Selena's regenerative powers.

Wound edges crept toward each other in waves of pale pink tissue. What should have taken days happened in seconds. No scarring, no misaligned flesh, as if the injury had never existed.

My jaw went slack. Pearl rose to her knees and slammed a hand over her lips. Ember's mouth moved around soundless words.

Selena's heartbeat began slowing.

I focused on her pulse, steady but weakening as she hemorrhaged. Crimson hadn't yet invaded her irises, but the black veins creeping along her hairline warned of our lack of time. Selena in bloodlust would be catastrophic after tonight's losses.

Four inches remained until the wound would close completely.

Terraknight had positioned himself behind her, knees bracketing her small frame. Each slash of his stone blades made him wince, but he never hesitated. His entire focus had shifted to tracking every tremor, every hitched breath, every pained hiss that escaped her lips.

I'd seen that protective intensity once before, in a mother bear defending her cubs. Ready to die for what was hers.

Selena's shoulders drooped, tipping her over Hummingbird's body. I reached out, but Terraknight was faster.

"I've got you," he murmured against her ear.

Her rigid posture melted at the sound of his voice.

Crouching behind her, he wrapped an arm around her waist and pulled her against his chest. The black veins in her hairline had darkened, her skin losing its luminous quality.

She'd lost too much blood.

"What's wrong with her?" Ember's voice hitched despite her attempt to whisper.

"Sel?" I called out.

Her irises remained their normal obsidian, but the hollows beneath her cheekbones had deepened.

"You can put the blood back now," she said, her words slurring slightly.

Gale's glowing eyes met mine. Together, we guided Hummingbird's extracted blood toward the narrow gap remaining in his skin. It slipped inside as if drawn by suction, helped by the vacuum Gale maintained to keep the area sterile. While I worked to de-stack the clot and distribute it through his veins, Selena sealed the final inches of skin, and the crimson glow faded from her hands.

Darkness settled over us again.

"He should be fine," she announced with a weary sigh, slumping back against Terraknight. "Rest, fluids, and food. That's all he needs now."

Color was already returning to Hummingbird's face. His heart rate strengthened, pumping renewed life through his system. The collective exhale that escaped us carried relief so profound my eyes burned with tears. Looking at him now—peaceful, whole—no one would believe he'd been dying moments ago.

"Time to keep your promise," Selena murmured, tilting her head back to meet Terraknight's gaze. The hunger in her eyes matched his own.

His smile held enough sin to damn a saint. "Take whatever you need, hellcat. You've earned it." He pulled her in his arms, and she wrapped her legs around his waist as he carried her into the darkness.

We watched them disappear in silence.

Gale was first to speak. "Guess we're carrying Hummingbird home ourselves."

"Guess so," Pearl replied with a shrug.

I kneeled beside Hummingbird and watched his chest rise and fall. Victory never came without cost. We'd saved one life tonight, but Quakelord was gone. A man whose journey had been carved by war and persecution; his life cut short when the world needed more people like him. No pretense, no games. What you saw was what you got.

His sacrifice couldn't be meaningless.

I wouldn't let it be.

May you rest in peace, friend.

Harbinger

Silver light hit the house's busted façade, throwing shadows across the peeling latticework. Years of weather had stripped the green paint down to rust, and that ugly shower curtain Rosebud had hung still flapped.

'TWENTY DOWN, TEN MORE TO GO. GLORY TO THE FUCKIN' REPUBLIC!'

Sabin——Terraknight——kneeled on one knee atop a compact platform of earth that he'd raised to reach the first floor. His broad shoulders blocked part of the moonlight as he worked, paintbrush in hand.

Ten had become nine after Rosebud. Nine became eight when Mandrake didn't come home. Seven after Phoenix. Now he was crossing out the seven.

Making it six.

He dragged the brush across the plastic. It scraped more than painted, as the paint on the bristles had long dried up.

I laughed, but it came out hollow. The baby zmeu in my lap whined and pressed his cold beak against my neck.

"Yeah, Boy. I know," I whispered. "I miss him too."

That tally had started as a joke. Our way of counting down while giving the Republic the finger. Ten stubborn bastards too dumb to die.

Who were we kidding?

It was a fucking cry for help.

The brush paused. Even from down here, I could see Sabin's shoulders shake. The earth platform quivered slightly under his weight as pebbles tumbled from the structure, responding to his emotions. He was taking this harder than the rest of us. Quakelord had been like a younger brother to him, his drinking buddy. His pupil.

With a long, taxed exhalation, Sabin lowered the brush and stared at his handiwork.

I should call up to him. Tell him to come down. But we all had our ways of saying goodbye.

The Voices clawed at my skull like trapped rats. I shoved them into background noise and focused on Boy's heartbeat against my ribs instead. Fast. Steady. Real.

Six left. The way we kept dropping, Terra would be up there again before the week ended.

Add another line. Cross out another number.

Another friend I couldn't save.

Sabin finished and leaned back on his haunches. The six looked crooked, rushed. He inhaled a long breath and exhaled slowly. Then he wiped his cheeks and rose. The platform crumbled as he jumped down, pelting dirt onto the overgrown grass.

I tilted my head back and stared at the sky. Moonlight shifted behind the clouds, racing shadows across the yard toward the cottonwoods.

Almost peaceful. If you ignored the bloodstains on the steps and bullet holes in the shutters.

If you pretended we weren't already dead, just waiting for the Republic to make it official and ship in the next batch of expendables to fill our spots.

The shower curtain snapped in the wind. Rosebud's message taunted us like a middle finger. *Glory to the fucking Republic.*

Even the stars seemed to mock us tonight. All that cold light, still shining while another of us was gone too soon. The world kept spinning like nothing had changed, like Quakelord's death meant nothing at all.

That's what pissed me off most. How beautiful everything looked when my heart was torn to pieces.

"Say what you want and stop hovering," I muttered, not bothering to look over my shoulder.

Sabin had been standing in the shadows since he'd jumped down, probably waiting for me to acknowledge him. Or lose my shit. Wouldn't be the first time. I was terrible company, but I didn't want to be alone either. Not that I'd ever admit it to him.

His boots crunched on scattered dirt as he moved closer. The scent of jasmine clung to him, thick, with the lieutenant's blood still on his skin. Part of me wanted to needle him about the target it would paint on his back if the Souleaters attacked us tonight. But I couldn't talk shit about her.

Not after she'd saved Hummingbird.

After dealing with Quakelord, I'd portaled back to the pass and saw Gale and Pearl shouldering a battered but healed Hummingbird between them. Then I came here and planted myself by this fountain. Couldn't face going inside yet. Couldn't face the empty spaces where Quakelord's voice used to be the loudest.

Sabin's heavy footsteps halted beside me, and I finally met his eyes.

The bastard had an inch on my six-three and never let me forget it. Built like a bear, muscles straining against his dark shirt. Dried blood marked his left cheek, flaking in his five o'clock shadow. His chin bobbed in acknowledgment, but those hazel eyes flickered with something that might have been worry.

"Did you find it?" he asked, voice careful.

Boy hurled himself from my lap, hit the ground in a tumble of wings and claws, and scrambled toward Sabin with excited chirps. The little sounds cut through some of the rage building in my chest.

Sabin dropped to one knee in the damp grass. "Come here, Sugar!" He spread his arms wide as the zmeu launched at his chest. The reunion lasted all of two seconds before Boy started squirming for freedom.

"Ungrateful little shit," he muttered, releasing him. Then his eyes found mine again. "Well?"

"Nothing left to take." I swallowed, and it felt like crushed glass going down. Thinking about the Shepherd, about what its power had done to Quakelord... My fingers drummed against my thigh, each tap sharper than the last, and I admitted, "There wasn't... much of anything left of him."

Sabin's face went blank. We'd all seen what that energy bolt could do to flesh and bone.

"Just grab something from his room then," he said, tucking his hands in his pockets. "Maybe pull the queen from his chess set. Bastard loved protecting her more than winning." His voice trailed off. We both knew Quakelord's favorite excuse every time he was about to lose a match. Something we'd all heard nightly for years.

"'What gentleman sacrifices a woman to win?'" we said in unison.

My vision blurred. Eyebrows trembled with the effort of holding it together. Not that Sabin hadn't seen me break before, or me him, but we both preferred avoiding each other's emotional wreckage when possible.

Real fucking warriors, the both of us.

He slumped down beside me with a long sigh. "He'd be cursing us both for sitting here moping."

The smirk tugging at his mouth pulled a snort from my throat.

"Remember when he flipped the board that night the girls got drunk? Said Phoenix was distracting him on purpose." I scrubbed at my face with dirty hands. "She wasn't even in the room."

"Course she was distracting him, he had the hots for her." Sabin's grin faded. "Twenty-eight years, and he never beat me. Not once."

"Maybe you should've let him win. Just once."

"Tried. He called me out every time." Sabin shook his head. "Said pity victories weren't victories at all."

The silence stretched between us, filled only by the rustle of wind through the cottonwoods and Boy's soft snuffling as he hunted for beetles in the grass. Somewhere in the distance, a night bird called—lonely, mournful.

Just like the rest of this godforsaken place.

Leaning forward, he rested his elbows on his knees and stared off toward the trees. "Damn. Not even a piece, huh?" His voice went flat, detached, as he pulled us back to his original question. The way it did when reality cut too deep to feel. "Figures, since he took that blast head-on." Sabin turned to face me, jaw muscles tensed. "I know you don't want to hear this, but I'll say it anyway—it wasn't your fault."

Then whose was it?

I gave him a fleeting glance and shrugged. He didn't need to know how deep this guilt went. How it dug its claws into me, eating me from the inside out. How desperate it made me to find the monster who'd taken my brother. To end this before I lost anyone else.

Conin's necklace burned against my chest. The black opal pendant had been my burden since I'd found his frozen body. A cruel reminder that his soul was still out there, trapped.

Because of him, I could hear the Souleaters.

But I'd almost been too late sensing those Ignises today. Too focused on what the Shepherd planned next instead of the immediate threat.

Could have lost everyone because I wasn't paying attention.

Turning toward the northwest, where Solomon's Rocks lay buried somewhere in the Curvature Carpathians—a hundred and fifty miles of jagged peaks and hidden valleys—I forced the words out.

"I heard him, you know." The admission tasted like curdled milk. "But I figured he'd hold the attack until he got closer, like he usually does. He was still too far out to matter, so I didn't..." I dragged my fingers through my hair. "Fuck!"

Restless energy shot through my veins, priming me for a battle I couldn't have. My knees bounced with the need to run after the bastard and face him once and for all. After today? I wasn't sure I could end him before he killed me. And if I died, I'd leave my guild defenseless. Conin's soul trapped forever.

"An attack like that could level entire cities," I continued, shooting to my feet. The words stoked white-hot flames in my chest. "Pointless against moving targets, a waste of energy on a single guild." I started pacing. "Had to be a test firing. Show me what he can do."

"While picking off two of ours in the process," Sabin said grimly. "We'd have been ash if he hadn't withdrawn."

"If this becomes his standard play, it'll be more than two next time." I stopped pacing, muscles loosening as the energy bled out of me. "The Republic won't stand against that kind of firepower. Millions of pure-bloods turned into feeding stock. Think about how many Black Sheep would evolve into Shepherds overnight."

Sabin stayed quiet, letting me work through it.

"Not that it'd matter to us—we'd be dead." I slumped back down beside him. "But the projector needs to survive. She's the only one positioned to stop them from reaching those walls—maybe even end this for good." My voice dropped as I added the last part.

"Think her plan will work?"

I thought about Aurora's face when I'd told her the truth about the war. That mix of horror and determination, the way she'd absorbed each terrible revelation and kept standing. The stubborn set of her jaw when she'd declared she wouldn't let any of us die.

"She's got the spine for it," I said. "But she's walking into a viper's nest. Even if Dracula grants her his power, the Republic might just put a blade in her back anyway. Or worse—use her as a scapegoat when this all goes to hell."

When Sabin's silence stretched too long, I turned and found him watching me with a bemused smile. Dark brows arched high, like he'd just figured out the punchline to a joke I didn't know I'd told.

"What?"

"Nothing." His lips twitched, fighting back laughter. "Just never seen you this worked up over a projector before."

Heat crept up my neck. "Maybe I don't want her to die with the rest of the fucking continent," I snapped. "Can we focus? We've got bigger problems than—"

"Easy there, Cap." He raised both hands, grinning wider now. "I know how fucked our situation is. But maybe I want to hear you admit what's really eating at you before you shatter my dreams of living past this century."

I glanced around, listening for footsteps or voices. The woods stayed silent except for Boy's soft snuffling in the grass. My gut told me Sabin wanted to dig into something that had nothing to do with the Shepherd's firepower and everything to do with Aurora.

Since we were alone, I decided to let him try. "Admit what?" I asked.

His eyes widened—probably expected me to shut him down—but he recovered fast. "What's going on between you and the princess?"

Straight for the throat. "Same thing that's between you and the lieutenant. I'm her blood source."

"Uh-huh." His gaze dropped to the ground, head bobbing slowly. Then he slapped his thigh and leaned forward. "Come on, man. We've known each other what, almost eight decades? Besides wiping our asses, we've done everything together." He shot me a sideways look that cut straight through my bullshit. "Since when do you give a damn if an original starves?"

"You've seen her in bloodlust. I'm doing all of you a favor keeping her fed, you should be thanking me."

He laughed outright. "And how deep are you in her when that happens?"

"Fuck you."

That only spurred him on. "Just admit you like her. Won't melt the skin off your bones."

"You first," I tossed it back. "I've seen you two together. There's more than blood sharing between you and Selena."

"By the Gods." He puffed up, mock-indignant. "You'd think at your age you're past acting like a brat with his first crush. Alright, if you want to hear a real man admit his feelings—" He flashed a nuclear grin and cupped his hands around his mouth to howl into the night, "I LIKE SELENA!"

And I'm the child.

I rolled my eyes, but he wasn't done.

"See? Wasn't that hard. She's the most beautiful woman I've ever had, and that filthy mouth of hers is both a curse and a blessing——if you catch my drift." He wiggled his eyebrows.

Despite everything—Quakelord's death, the Shepherd's power, saving Conin—I couldn't hold back a chuckle. It felt wrong to laugh when I should've been grieving, but it eased some of the weight crushing my shoulders.

"Alright, maybe I don't hate her like the rest of her kind." Boy looked up from his beetle hunt, ears pricked like he sensed the shift in mood. "I wish I could, but her compassion, that stubborn streak…" I scrubbed my face with both hands. "Makes me want to lock her away somewhere safe. I don't want her hurt, and my wolf's going insane trying to protect her every damn second. Unless…" I trailed off, not sure how to finish that thought without sounding like a complete bastard.

Sabin leaned forward, barely perched on the fountain's edge. "Unless?" he pressed, pushing me to say things I hadn't accepted myself yet.

"Unless she drives me so crazy, all I want is to punish her," I growled.

His mouth went slack. We just stared at each other in the sudden silence.

I can't believe I said that out loud.

"Go on. Please don't stop now," he mocked, which earned him a punch that he dodged without effort.

"I don't know what she's doing to me, man." I ran my fingers through my hair, pulling at the strands. "Every moment with her, I wish it never ends. When she's not around, I can't breathe." I tapped the soft spot below my sternum. "Like there's something expanding in here, pressing against my ribs. An ache that only stops when she's in my sight, or I catch her scent."

I kept my voice low, afraid the silent night would carry my words too far.

Sabin—my brother, my best friend—released a sharp breath and chuckled behind his hands. He stared at me with wide, glittering eyes, like a varcolac father watching his cub turn for the first time.

I itched to punch the smug expression off his face.

His chest expanded as if he wanted to speak, so I narrowed my eyes and shook my head in warning. "Don't you say it."

His grin stretched to his ears.

"Don't you fucking say it!"

He said it anyway. Worse hearing it from someone else than from the nagging voice in my head. "You're falling for her."

I was. Hard. After a lifetime of traveling and fooling around, I had to come to this battlefield to find the only woman who captured not just my interest, but my wolf's as well.

Just thinking about her—the way she moved, that stubborn tilt of her chin when she was about to do something reckless—made me drown in a tide of lust and need. I wanted her with an intensity that made no sense, wanted to crack open that careful control of hers and see what lay underneath.

Why was she affecting me like this?

Her blood was addictive, yes, and her ability to soothe the noises was everything I fought for, but this went deeper than feeding or relief. Deeper than losing myself in a warm body.

Six months ago, someone could've told me Aurora was walking straight into that snake pit alone, and I'd have shrugged. Good. Let the original do what she was bred for. If Lev got his claws into her afterward? Not my fucking problem. But that was before. Before I knew what she tasted like. Before she belonged to me.

And now I had no choice but to follow her into that cesspit so she could get Dracula's power. To make sure she gets back safely. To free my brother and save my guildmates.

Sabin saw my expression, and the humor drained from his face. "You know she's going to be Queen of the Republic someday, right?"

"I'm well aware."

"And that you're *the* enemy." Same grave tone.

I nodded. "That, too."

He sucked air between his teeth, curiosity cinching his brows together. "So, what's the plan, Cap?"

"Nothing to plan." I leaned back on my hands, stared into the distance. "Same as always—kill the Shepherd before he gets too strong. With or without Dracula's power, he needs to die. There's too much at stake."

"That's not what I—"

"I know what you meant. But right now, that's all that matters."

"Wait a fucking minute. You're okay with her going back?" Sabin's eyes went wide when I didn't answer. He let out a low whistle as he put two and two together. "You're going with her? That's suicide, man. What if you get caught? What if that bastard prince gets his hands on her again?"

"No one's going to hurt her," I snarled. My wolf clawed at its cage, demanding blood. Let the bastard cross my path. I'd relish killing him slowly, methodically, with my bare hands. "I'll be with her every second. Cover our tracks." My hands curled into fists. "Besides, I doubt they could keep up with my Chronoportal even with their best trackers."

"You've thought of everything, huh?" Sabin gripped my shoulder and offered me a toothy grin. "Never thought I'd see the Great Harbinger falling head over heels."

"Whatever," I muttered, shrugging him off.

"Alright, alright." He raised his hands in surrender. "But speaking of bastards we need to kill—what's your take on this long-distance power the Shepherd just showed off?"

I closed my eyes and focused on the constant buzzing in my head. Thousands of Black Sheep whispered their final moments, but I filtered through them, searching for one voice among the chorus.

Conin's voice.

Nothing came through. Just the endless murmur of the dead.

I opened my eyes.

"A strike of that magnitude has to drain him," I said. "He'll need time to recharge before another attack of that scale. That's why he used those Ignises at the end."

Sabin nodded. "Makes sense. That kind of power doesn't come free."

I scanned the horizon, toward where I could hear the last of it. Somewhere out there, my brother's consciousness was trapped inside a monster, planning world destruction with the tactical brilliance that had once made him Russkaya's youngest strategist.

"He's gone quiet now," I said. "Like he's pulled back to lick his wounds. Or plan his next move."

"You can tell?"

"From his voice, yeah. But mainly because he's not broadcasting anymore. I'll keep my focus on it, and make sure we aren't caught us off guard again." I scrubbed my jaw. "Though he probably won't try the same trick twice."

We hadn't met this Shepherd face to face yet, but we'd tangled with Souleaters under his command several times. Two of those encounters had cost me friends.

Sabin went quiet. I glanced over to find a thick vein pulsing at his temple, his lips pressed into a hard line.

"He found you," he said.

"Must have recognized me through that Nebula in Brasov. The one carrying Phoenix's soul." I turned my gaze back toward that distant mountain pass again. "Think he's known where I was ever since."

Sabin's lips clamped shut as he bit back a curse. "We need to move. Get out of his range before he decides to end us."

"Nah." A sardonic smile tugged at my lips as a memory surfaced. Conin and I hunched over his strategy board, him planning each move while I relied on instinct and luck. "He's playing games. Testing his pieces before the real match starts." A sharp stab pierced my skull, and I pinched the bridge of my nose. "He'll come for me next time," I continued. "Won't just blast me from a distance. That's cheating in his book."

I turned toward Sabin, and my vision blurred. The world went askew.

His hazel eyes bled into molten amber. Features I knew as well as my own reflection superimposed themselves over his face like a double exposure.

My pulse hammered against my ribs. No, not now.

I recognized the signs but couldn't stop the slide. The present dissolved like smoke.

My brother materialized across from me, hunched over the maple Go board we'd set up on the stone steps outside Dad's study. Moonlight carved shadows across his face—the same angular features as mine but softer, not yet hardened by decades of war. His jaw hadn't filled out completely, still carried that youthful sharpness that made the ladies whisper behind their open fans.

Silver-white hair cascaded over his forehead as he studied the board, identical to mine but longer, the way he'd worn it before his wolf awakened. When he looked up, crimson rimmed his citron irises. They flared bright before his fangs flashed with his smile—his tell when he was about to crush me at our game.

"Your move, brother." His voice carried the confidence of someone who'd never tasted defeat. "Though we both know how this ends."

Pine and snow drifted around us, mixed with the familiar musk of our home. I could feel the weight of the gold torque against my throat, warm from my skin, its intricate knotwork pressing into my pulse. The carved wolf heads at each end rested heavily on my clavicles.

"Do we?" My stone piece slid forward with a soft click, claiming territory he'd left undefended. "You always were too confident for your own good."

Conin laughed, a bright sound I'd thought lost forever. "Says the brother who taught me everything I know." He countered my move with effortless skill. "Tell me, Radolf—when you portal into battle, do you still hear Dad's voice? 'Strategy without honor is mere butchery?'"

Dad's favorite lesson, drilled into us during countless evenings just like this one. Back when the worst threat we faced was losing a challenge of dominance.

"Every time," I admitted, reaching for my next piece.

"Good." A predatory gleam flickered behind Conin's eyes. His familiar features wavered, replaced by something darker, more monstrous. A shadow with too many teeth that I couldn't quite focus on. Then his face returned, but wrong somehow. Alien. "Because what I'm planning for you and your guild—it's going to be beautiful in its precision. You'll appreciate the artistry, even as it kills you."

"Cap!" Sabin's voice pulled me from the vision with cold hands. "Snap out of it!"

The board vanished. Pine scent evaporated. My hand flew to my throat. No torque, just bare skin and the silver chain where Conin's opal pendant hung from.

The world snapped back into painful focus with Sabin gripping my shoulders, his face creased with worry.

"You back?" he asked, voice tight, before releasing me.

"Yeah." I scrubbed my face with hands that wouldn't stop shaking. "How long?"

"Few minutes. Your marks were showing, man." Sabin's jaw worked as if he were chewing gravel. "You never let it get that far. This is happening more often?"

More than I wanted to admit. The episodes had started in childhood, brief flashes where I'd see people I'd never met, places that didn't exist on any map. Strange landscapes populated by even stranger creatures, conversations in languages I didn't speak but somehow understood.

My parents dismissed it as an overactive imagination. Said they'd fade as I grew older. They did. Most of the time.

Then the war started, and they came roaring back. Worse after finding Conin's frozen corpse. What used to last a heartbeat now stole whole seconds, sometimes minutes. Pearl thought the childhood episodes were signs of latent magical sensitivity. Cracks in my mind that made me susceptible to inheriting my clan's powerful magic. That using Chronoportal, opening doorways between worlds, had widened those old fractures.

Made sense, and I never corrected her.

Because the truth had nothing to do with my clan's magic. In the space between sleeping and waking, I experienced lives I'd never lived, caught memories that weren't mine. But that was my burden to carry. Had been since the beginning of time.

"I'm fine," I said when Sabin's scowl deepened.

"Bullshit." He leaned closer, studying my face. "You were smiling while you talked to him. It's the first time I've seen you look at peace since we found his body."

My gut twisted. Even knowing what Conin had become, part of me still missed my little brother. Still wanted to believe I could save what was left of him.

"Don't lose your head when we're this close," Sabin warned. "I need you sharp for when the time comes. Don't let emotions get in your way. Not if you're really going along with Aurora's plan and risking yourself."

"I know." I straightened, voice firm. "Won't happen again."

His expression said he didn't believe me, but he nodded anyway. "Better not. Because if you crack up on me now, I'll drag you back to reality myself." He popped his knuckles for emphasis. "Even if I have to beat some sense into your thick head."

Despite everything, I almost smiled. Leave it to Sabin to threaten violence as a form of care.

"Sabin?" I cleared my throat, then forced the words out. "You know what you mean to me, right?"

"Woah." He pulled back, eyeing me with suspicion. "I love you too, man, but that sounds ominous as hell."

"The Shepherd won't stop coming after you to get to me." I broke eye contact, staring at the candlelight flickering through the wooden boards nailed over the window frames. "Every time he attacks, more of you die. And for what? Because I can't let go of my dead brother?"

"Stop right there." Sabin grabbed my shoulder, forcing me to face him. "You think we're here out of pity? Think we don't know what we signed up for?"

"You signed up to fight Souleaters, not to be bait for—"

"We signed up to follow you. Our Harbinger." His grip tightened. "Through whatever hell you drag us into. That includes your psychotic family reunions."

I stared at him, throat tight. "Even knowing how this ends?"

"Especially knowing how this ends." He released my shoulder, and for a moment I thought I saw tears in his eyes. When he spoke again, his voice sounded deeper than usual. ""What kind of fool throws in the towel just because the end's coming?'"

Quakelord's words. My throat constricted.

"We made our choice long ago," he continued, looking me dead in the eyes. "All that's left is following it."

I turned away, blinking hard against the sting behind my eyes. A laugh escaped me, raw, grateful. "I don't deserve you bastards."

"No, you don't." His expression softened, as did his voice. "Lucky for you, we're too stubborn to find better company."

I patted his shoulder and rose to my feet. "I need to go. The commandant is waiting for me," I said and walked toward the portal crackling in the middle of the shooting range. The cold darkness called to me, promising escape from the fire blazing in my chest.

"Better get up there and finish changing those numbers." I nodded toward the house where our shrinking count waited. "I'll see you in a few hours."

"Good luck," Sabin called after me. "And come back in one piece."

The darkness swallowed me before I could promise something I might not be able to keep.

AURORA

THE WATER SCALDED MY shoulders, but I cranked the handle hotter anyway. Each droplet dampened my growing concern. Pain demanded less effort than trying to figure out Harbinger's latest vanishing act.

Eighteen hours.

Eighteen damned hours since he'd stepped through that portal with Quakelord's body, and I hadn't seen hide nor hair of him since. When I'd cornered Terraknight this morning, asking where his captain was, he'd given me some nonsense about "patrol duty" while avoiding eye contact. Though he'd done his best to hide it, worry creased the corners of his eyes. The same look he'd worn when Hummingbird was dying. He'd fussed around me afterward, asking if I was hungry, needed anything, offering his wrist with that gentle protectiveness that reminded me why Selena had fallen for him—not that she would admit it if asked.

I'd declined as kindly as I could manage, even though my fangs ached with need. The man had already given enough blood to keep Sel from slipping into bloodlust after her healing marathon. And if I was being honest, after tasting Harbinger's blood, everyone else seemed watered down by comparison.

I shouldn't even be in here, anyway. My room didn't have a bathroom, so I'd been rotating between Selena and Radu's for the past weeks. But Sel was still recovering from saving Hummingbird, and I'd figured Harbinger's shower was free since he'd vanished to parts unknown.

Again.

I scrubbed at my arms until the skin turned raw. Gale's homemade soap, with its rough bits of oatmeal and dried herbs, stung my flesh, but not as much as the burning ache spreading through my chest.

This was bottling his blood all over again.

I'd been stupid enough to think things had changed between us after that night on his balcony. But nothing *had* changed. Sure, he let me feed from him—clinical, efficient transactions that kept me functional. A wrist offered without ceremony, withdrawn the moment I'd taken enough to survive. No lingering touches. Oh, there were heated glances—moments when his eyes would burn into mine with pure hunger—but hadn't acted on them. Not recently. And he sure as hell hadn't tasted my blood again, hadn't sought the connection that had shattered us both in the privacy of his quarters.

The signs had been there for days. I'd caught him staring into the fire three nights ago after the guild's outdoor dinner, chin plopped into a cupped hand, eyes distant. Whatever thoughts consumed him weren't of this world—or this century. The others had noticed too but said nothing. Terraknight shot him worried glances. Gale kept refilling his untouched coffee. Even Ember had held back her usual flirt.

But none of them had asked what was wrong. And I'd sat there like a coward, studying the hard lines of his profile in the firelight, wanting to reach across that invisible barrier he'd erected but too proud to make the first move. Too terrified of being dismissed—again.

The soap slipped from my wet fingers and slid along the tiles. I didn't bother picking it up.

I ran a hand down my face. My head hurt from the mixed emotions waging a war inside me. I thought I had him figured out. That's what I got for thinking.

Idiot. That's what I was. Checking shadows for glimpses of platinum hair, breathing in his scent when I entered his room to shower, listening for his footsteps in the hallway, hoping that he'd engage in conversation. I'd trained myself to read strategy and tactics, to analyze enemy movements and predict their next strike. But when it came to Radu? I was blind as a bat.

Aggravation coursed through me, ruffled my feathers, got my hackles up. More than anything else at that moment, I wanted to know why he'd pulled away—why he'd left me. Why he'd held me against him like I was the only thing keeping him anchored to this world, then retreated so far into his head I couldn't reach him even when he was sitting three feet away.

The water pressure dropped to a trickle as someone else in the house turned on a faucet. I pressed my forehead against the cool tile and tried to convince myself I didn't care where he'd gone.

"Keep telling yourself that, Aurora. Maybe eventually you'll believe it."

The truth was, I'd started looking forward to seeing him. To those stolen moments when his guard dropped and I glimpsed the man beneath the captain's mask. The way his eyes softened when he looked at me sometimes. How his voice roughened when he said my name.

I'd gotten used to being the focus of these small attentions. To mattering to someone who wasn't obligated to care about me.

And now I couldn't patch the cracks in my defenses fast enough to hide what his withdrawal had done to my heart. I hated feeling expendable.

I forced myself to shut off the water and stepped into the cold air. Cracked subway tiles bit at my bare feet as I reached for a towel. A lone half-burnt candle flickered on the plaster-barred windowsill, casting shadows that danced across the spotty mirror above the vanity. Steam clouded the glass, so I wiped it away with my palm and met my hollow stare.

Hell. That's what I looked like. Pale and drawn, with dark circles shadowing my eyes from too many sleepless days. Between learning the truth about the Black Sheep, experiencing the Shepherd's terrifying power firsthand, Quakelord's death, and Selena still unconscious since Terraknight had brought her back, my mind refused to quiet.

And now Harbinger's absence.

I needed to get dressed and find something to occupy my thoughts before I did something stupid like march downstairs and demand answers from Terraknight. Embarrass myself once again for being too naïve and falling for Radu's evasions.

My inner dialogue was not very kind when faced with stupid ideas.

The navy-blue top with delicate lace detailing slipped on easily enough. My leather pants were another matter. A war waged against stubborn material that clung to my still-damp skin. When I finally won that battle and pulled on my knee-high boots, my simmering frustration redirected from him.

At least he hadn't insulted me with his bottled blood this time.

But how long would he be gone? My fangs already ached with need. I would have to accept Terraknight's offer if my hunger became dangerous.

The hallway stretched before me, with flickering candles that danced in gilt-framed mirrors. Oil paintings lined the walls, portraits of the house's original owners. In the months of being here, I hadn't stopped to consider the people they once were. What had happened to them when war struck? Relocation, or had they fallen victim to the attacks that decimated the Tenth Ward's defenses?

Moving past their watchful eyes, I carefully stepped around the antique side table where I'd shattered the priceless Stefan Luchian vase weeks ago. The shards had been swept up, but the empty space remained like an accusation. Frayed carpet edges caught at my boots as I passed Phoenix and Quakelord's doors.

Too many empty rooms now. Too much silence.

With a heavy heart, I pushed open the door to my suffocating Victorian chamber. The familiar mustiness of old wood and dust greeted me, along with something that made my pulse spike.

Coffee and roses.

Powerful magic crackled like electricity before a storm.

My breath hitched as the portal tore open with a groan that split the air like bone snapping. Lightning bled from the edges, tendrils of white fire writhing. Sparks rained down, and I forced myself to take a step back from where they met the ground.

The wind rose in savage howls, almost tortured, and whipped my hair across my eyes, dragging the scent of frozen ozone through the room.

From the center of the portal's storm, a figure surged forward, crashing to the floor with a sound that made my stomach turn. Then, as suddenly as it had appeared, the gateway let out a violent hiss and collapsed in on itself, as if someone had severed the connection with an axe.

Harbinger.

One knee hit the floor hard as he tried to right himself, the sunsteel blade clutched in his bloodied fist. His head hung low, platinum hair seemingly longer than before, wilder, matted with something dark and foul. The stench slammed into me. Souleater ichor mixed with copper. My heart leaped into my throat. Instinct screamed to step back from the overwhelming reek, but my body moved forward.

"Radu?"

Silence. My racing heart was the only sound.

He didn't look up, giving me a chance to study him more closely. Heat poured off him in waves I could feel from six feet away. It took me too long to realize he wasn't wearing a shirt—and longer still to process that his bronze skin had turned obsidian black.

What in Derzelas' name—

He took a long breath, tilting his head enough to reveal bone structure more dramatic, more severe. Yet he remained devastatingly beautiful in that dangerous way that made smart women do incredibly stupid things. Golden glyphs traced up his neck in delicate spirals, pulsing like a second heartbeat as they curved along his jawline.

Ancient runes crawled across every inch of exposed flesh, spiraled down his arms, across his chest in intricate patterns that throbbed with each pulse. The markings seemed burned into his skin, speaking to some primal part of me that recognized ultimate danger at a cellular level.

My fangs snapped out in an involuntary snarl.

Was this his varcolac form?

Harbinger raised his head. Eyes that blazed like twin flames pinned me in place. His mouth was fuller, lips pulled back just enough to reveal razor-sharp fangs.

Of all the times to be terrified, this should have been one, but I felt nothing. No spike of adrenaline. No fear flooding my system. No panic attacks or nausea.

Beautiful.

His presence acted as a magnet. Every cell urged me forward.

I raised a tentative hand to his shoulder, expecting to be burned by the radiating heat. But as my fingers made contact with the golden markings, they flickered like dying embers and faded back into his skin. The obsidian coloring followed, leaving him looking like himself again—devastatingly handsome despite being covered in gore.

"Harbinger?" I dropped to my knees. "Are you alright?"

"I'm fine." Strained words. "Give me a minute."

Blood seeped between his fingers where he pressed his hand against his side. Each exhale was a grunt of pain. When he tried to rise, his massive frame tilted forward.

I caught his shoulders, taking his weight. His skin had returned to normal temperature. Still running hot, but not burning like a dying star anymore.

"You need Selena. Wait here. I'm going to—"

"No." His bloodied hand grasped my wrist. The blade clattered to the floor.

His face had gone white as bone. Bright red flared around his citron irises before spreading inward, battling the gold for dominance. Dark veins threaded down from his hairline, stark against his pallor.

Bloodlust. He was slipping.

"I need you." His voice rasped with strain.

I understood exactly what he needed. Pulling my hair over my shoulder, I bared my throat. "Take as much as you need."

His mouth moved along my neck with maddening slowness.

The scrape of teeth made me shiver. Fangs grazed my throat, their sharp edges creating friction that was both threatening and utterly erotic. The pressure increased, his tongue and lips finding every sensitive spot until my heart hammered and I pressed against him with matching need. A low rumble escaped him, so primal it made my nipples tighten against his hard chest.

"Aurora." His arms locked around me, and his voice turned darker.

Then his fangs angled, their tips teasing me in the most delicious way. My skin gave way under those needle points, and a sharp gasp tore from me as they sank deep.

The gasp became a moan as sensation flooded me. Heat poured from where we connected, racing within my veins to consume my entire body. Fever swept over me, making me dizzy, while unexpected waves of pleasure made my head fall back and my legs tremble.

My pulse beat frantically under his mouth, and when Radu took that first deep pull, ecstasy shot straight to my core with enough force to nearly break me apart.

His growl vibrated against my throat. His fingers tangled in my hair, keeping my head back as he drew again, sending fresh cascades of bliss through me. The world shrunk to this single point of contact, to the incredible sensation of my blood flowing into him.

Another pull dragged a cry from my lips, and I raked my nails down his back, clawing at him as need consumed me. I wanted all of him, and I rolled my hips against his thigh in silent invitation.

Radu's mouth was suddenly gone, and we moved in a different time, through different worlds. Before I could process what was happening, my back hit the wall, his body pressed against mine. Hard, unforgiving muscle and burning skin. This wasn't the composed captain I knew. He was a beast unleashed, driven by whatever haunted those golden-crimson eyes.

"I need more than blood." His voice was rough gravel against my ear, stripped of every pretense. "I need *you*."

His mouth claimed mine before I could respond. Coffee and copper flooded my senses as his tongue swept against mine with wild longing. His hands found the delicate lace at my neckline. Tore at the fabric with a sharp rip.

Heat exploded between us. His knee pushed between my thighs as calloused palms cupped my breasts. Thumbs circled the sensitive peaks until I arched into his touch with a broken moan. One hand twisted in my hair while the other roamed with possessive urgency. As if he needed to claim every inch of me. As if he needed to chase away whatever darkness clung to him.

My leather pants and boots joined the scraps of my top on the floor. His blistering fingers found me already slick with want, and I gasped, taking hold of his wrist as that familiar spark ignited in my core.

Molten lava spread through me, burning from the inside out. I guided his touch deeper, and a microsecond later, I found myself on the thread-bare rug.

This wasn't about gentle seduction.

This was possession. Dominance. Unadulterated need. Yet even in his frenzy, even with the way he pinned me beneath him like prey, he didn't hurt me. Just the opposite. Stinging tendrils of ecstasy spread throughout my body as he positioned himself above me, his breathing labored. One hand curled around my throat as he unfastened his pants.

"Tell me to stop." His hand braced against the wall above my head, our bodies poised on the edge of joining. "Before I can't."

Instead of answering, I pulled him down to me, plunging both hands into his hair and twisting my fingers in a firm grip. "Don't you dare."

He entered me with one powerful thrust.

Air rushed from my lungs. A jolt of pleasure bucked inside me, sharp and consuming. I breathed in the air he breathed out, tasted the essence of him—dark coffee and something uniquely male. My nails bit into his shoulders when he pushed too hard, too fast.

But he didn't stop.

This wasn't just about pleasure. This was about seizing control when everything else had spiraled beyond his grasp. His kiss grew as demanding as his thrusts. I could feel his restraint fraying with each movement as he clamped me to him, held me captive beneath his weight while he drove into me with increasing force.

"Is this what you need?" I whispered against his ear.

He hesitated. Faltered. My body cried out, wanting the peak it sought. Yet my heart wanted Radu—with me, not fighting through me.

"You should stay away from me." He nipped at my earlobe, the minor pain causing a sharp spike of arousal. "I am not who you think I am. Not what you think I am." His voice thickened with something deeper than desire—shame, maybe, or fear. "I'm so much worse than a monster."

I kept my arms wrapped around his head, refusing to let him retreat into whatever hell lived inside his head. "We're all monsters," I breathed and placed one hand on his steel-hard buttock, urging him deeper. He hissed. Pressed harder. "But if your beast needs to unleash whatever brought you here—then do your worst."

His eyes changed then. The fight left them, replaced by acceptance, maybe, or surrender. He kissed me with renewed intensity, raw and unguarded, as if I were his lifeline in a drowning world.

Pressure built as he buried himself over and over, each thrust more possessive than the last, as if he could chase away his demons by owning me completely.

The air vanished from the room. His movements became more desperate, the hand around my throat tightening just enough to remind me who was in control. The tide swelling inside me rose higher with each powerful stroke until it finally burst through, crashing against my bones like a boiling sea.

He groaned—part agony, part ecstasy—as he followed me over the edge, spilling into me with a shudder that shook his entire frame.

For a moment he lay breathless and spent. When he moved to pull away, I wrapped every available limb around him.

"Not yet," I whispered, directing his mouth back to my neck.

His fangs found a different spot, breaking the skin with a tender care that almost brought me to tears. The dual sensation of his bite and the aftershocks still rippling through me made me gasp. I lost track of time—him feeding while I listened to his heartbeat slowing, felt some of the tension drain from his muscular shoulders.

Then he pulled back, bit down on his tongue with a sharp fang until blood welled, and kissed me so fervently my eyes rolled back. His blood mixed with mine on our tongues. Our minds collided like old friends finding each other after a long separation.

His emotions poured through the Blood Pact like a shot of adrenaline.

Rage. Pure and consuming, directed at himself as much as whatever had driven him to my room. Hopelessness so deep it felt like drowning. Sorrow that made my chest cave in. Grief for losses I couldn't name but felt in every cell of my body. All of it tangled together, feeding the beast that had demanded dominance, control, something to anchor him when everything else had crumbled.

Then the visions hit.

A mountain village carved into steep hillsides, stone houses with wooden shutters now hanging askew. Smoke billowed from thatched roofs as orange flames devoured everything in their path. Bodies littered the narrow cobblestone streets. Civilians dressed in flowing robes and headwraps unlike anything worn in the Republic, some whole, others torn apart so violently I could barely make sense of the scattered limbs. Rivers of blood flowed between the corpses, pooling in the spaces where families had tried to hide.

The screams were the worst part. High-pitched wails split the night sky and mixed with the guttural roars I recognized in a heartbeat.

Souleaters.

Hundreds—no, thousands—of them swarming through the village like a plague of locusts.

A woman's voice rose above the chaos, shouting commands in what sounded painfully similar to Russkayan. I felt Radu's anguish as he answered her call, his magic exploding outward with such violence it nearly drained him completely. A portal tore open before him—not the sleek doorways I'd seen before, but a gaping maw that swallowed the horizon. His entire field of vision disappeared behind the massive gateway, infinite darkness streaked with lightning bolts, all converging on the same point.

But there were too many.

Even with his power, even with the fire arcs and earth spikes, water cannons and air strikes erupting from other elementals in the distance, the horde kept coming. I felt his muscles burning as he fought, portals opening and closing in rapid succession, sunsteel blade singing through rotten flesh. The exhaustion that came from hours of battle, from watching people die despite everything he did to save them.

Then the image shifted to aftermath. Houses reduced to blackened skeletons, smoke rising in dark tendrils toward the stars. More bodies caught in their homes, in their beds. Children who'd never had a chance to run.

His mental barriers slammed shut, and I gasped against his mouth as the waves of his anguish crashed against me. No wonder his beast had taken control. No wonder he'd needed to possess, to claim, to prove he still had power over something in this world.

Derzelas Almighty, he'd been fighting all this time. But the clothes, the architecture—none of it was familiar. Had he portalled beyond the Gloom? Were the Souleaters waging war on other nations as well?

So many questions crowded my mind I could barely breathe.

"Now you know," he whispered against my lips, and I flinched as his thumb brushed away tears I didn't realize I'd shed.

"Radu…" I traced the sharp line of his jaw, wanting to take away his pain.

"Don't." His voice was rough, pleading. "Please, don't ask. I don't want to lie to you."

I kissed him again. Poured everything I couldn't say into that desperate contact. Radu was weaving himself into my heart thread by thread, and I already dreaded the day he tore it apart. Because that day was inevitable, as certain as dawn following darkness. Whatever truths he kept locked away would eventually destroy what we were building.

Unable to piece together the whys and wherefores of his secrets, I decided not to think about it and embrace this sweet self-deception.

He relaxed, the last of his defenses crumbling as I felt everything negative drain from him. Every doubt, every fragment of anxiety from the hell he'd just escaped.

The four-poster bed protested as we moved to the mattress, rusted coils poking through worn fabric. But wrapped in his arms, surrounded by his warmth and the steady rhythm of his breathing, it felt like the finest silk. His presence was a salve that soothed my frenzied thoughts, calmed the roiling seas within me.

I'd never felt so at peace. So completely at home.

For now, questions about where he'd been, what he'd faced, could wait. Dusk was still hours away, and I intended to savor every moment of this rare calm before the storm inevitably returned.

Aurora

THREE HOURS LATER, WE'D made it back to his bedroom, both of
us scrubbed clean and thoroughly exhausted. Well, I was exhausted.
Harbinger looked like he was simply granting me a brief intermission. I'd
left him sprawled across his mattress wearing nothing but a damp towel
slung low at his hips, one corded arm folded beneath his silver head, while
I escaped to wash away the evidence of our marathon session.

Not that I was complaining.

Now, I stood before his cracked vanity mirror, studying my reflection
with fascination and disbelief. My lips were swollen from his devastating
kisses, wine-dark and tender to the touch. The woman staring back at me
looked thoroughly debauched. My hair was mussed, skin flushed, dried
blood from healed bite marks decorating my throat. I traced one with my
fingertip, shuddering at the sensitive skin.

Several revelations had emerged from our extended encounter. Who
knew the shower fixture could serve such inventive purposes beyond
basic hygiene? Radu's stamina bordered on the supernatural—even for
someone with immortal blood. But most startling was the growing

awareness of our deepening connection. Whether born from his lowered mental barriers or the cumulative effect of our blood exchanges, I'd begun sensing the subtle rhythms of his body. Every shiver of pleasure that danced across his skin, every tremor that built within him, every explosive release—all of it echoed through me with devastating clarity.

The sensation was completely foreign. Utterly intoxicating.

Molten warmth pressed against my back. I stilled, savoring the familiar burn of his proximity.

Radu's palms braced on the vanity counter, caging me within his muscled forearms. I melted into his solid chest and indulged in the luxury of simply admiring him through the looking glass. That mouth, full and wicked and designed for sin. Those liquid amber eyes, with their thick fringe of lashes, made the crimson flecks in his irises gleam like scattered rubies.

Pure fantasy made flesh.

His stare trapped mine in the mirror's surface while his fingers found the drawstring of my borrowed sweats and tugged. Slowly. Deliberately. His attention shifted to my mouth with the hunger of a child eyeing blood-candy, as he traced a finger along the waistband. His touch scorched everywhere it landed, and I couldn't help wondering if the heat came from his wolf or served as protection against the bitter cold of traveling between realms.

"Don't go back," he murmured, then caught my earlobe between his teeth. Just enough pressure to send electricity racing down my spine.

"Where? The Republic?"

"Mm."

His voice rumbled through my ribcage, and I struggled to process his words when every syllable, every caress, threatened to short-circuit my brain. He was pure temptation, and I was thoroughly addicted. I'd felt him move inside me, experienced paradise in his arms, and the memory was so vivid, so catastrophic, that I knew no other man would ever compare.

Underworld's balls.

I had to regain control before we lost ourselves again. Selena was probably wondering where I was. I'd heard her voice echoing from somewhere in the house around our fifth round, then promptly forgot everything else existed.

"Wait," I said, catching his wandering hand before it could wreak more havoc. He twisted his wrist and entwined our fingers, the simple gesture sending fresh heat spiraling through me.

"Planning to leave me hanging, princess?"

A breathless laugh escaped my lips. "Exactly."

"And what happens if I refuse to cooperate?"

"Radu." My protest sounded pathetic even to my ears. "We really should talk."

"So talk," he said, guiding our joined hands lower. "I'm listening."

His hooded gaze, my flushed skin, our joined hands disappearing beneath fabric, ignited a wildfire so vicious within me, I almost combusted. I writhed against his touch as he traced small circles on my sensitized flesh using both our fingers. Tangled my free hand in his hair and gasped his name.

He pushed my legs further apart, then bit into the soft curve where shoulder and neck met.

Fire consumed me from the inside out.

I waited for him to enter me and claim his own pleasure, but he held back. Drove me toward the precipice instead.

Our mental connection blazed to life again, weakened from earlier blood exchanges but still there. Two minds collapsed into one, and I felt the exact moment his pleasure merged with mine.

A sharp intake of breath. Cool air whispered against my nape as he shuddered.

His fingers filled my center while allowing me to continue the torture above. We were locked together now, sharing every sensation, every spike of heat. The connection built and built until release hit me hard. I bit down, muscles seizing as waves crashed over me and left me shaking.

Radu's guttural moan vibrated against my throat as our connection pushed him over the edge. I spun in his arms, fisted his hair, and dragged his mouth to mine. He wrapped around me, holding tight as his body found its own completion. For a moment he went rigid as stone, trembling with the force of it, before slowly melting against me.

"You were saying?" he murmured into my shoulder.

Breathless laughter bubbled up my throat. I grabbed a towel from the hook and cleaned off the traces of our joining while silently cursing my complete lack of self-control around him. But I couldn't deny the truth. He awakened things in me I'd never known existed. Made me crave him like blood itself.

Sweet Derzelas, what future could we possibly have?

The question drained the warmth from my veins. A knot of dread expanded in my stomach. I was still floating on bliss, still connected to him through blood and breath, yet my pragmatic mind was already spinning toward the inevitable.

Everything crashed over me then. How we'd begun. What he'd become to me. Why this could never work.

The first time I 'met' Harbinger, I was watching the Sparrows die through my Astral Visor, hundreds of miles away. What should have been a routine patrol had turned into a slaughter. Limuses ripped through my guild while I sat helpless in my command center, watching through Stoneheart's eyes as, one by one, my outliers fell.

Then the tide had turned. Crimson dots vanished from my scanner as Souleaters retreated en masse. Captain Harbinger had materialized like vengeance itself, cutting down enough enemies to save what remained of my guild.

The next time I saw him in action was in Sibiu. He carved through hundreds of Souleaters like death given form. Beautiful. Terrifying. I should have questioned his knowledge of enemy positions then, but the incredible power he wielded had mesmerized me.

Then Brasov happened. The moment that changed everything.

A Nebula had approached him on that blood-soaked square, raised its four arms, and said, *'Brother.'*

The word had thundered through the Harmonization, nearly splitting my skull. Everything clicked. His uncanny predictions, his secretive nature, the way Souleaters moved purposefully around him. He could communicate with them. With the monsters that had devoured our people for a century.

I'd searched his mind afterward, probed for deception, for betrayal. Found nothing but grief and determination. That's what made this so impossibly cruel. I trusted him, trusted his heart, his intentions, his love for his guildmates.

And that's exactly why I could never bring him home.

The Republic had murdered his mother for sympathizing with mixed-breeds. Condemned his brother to the camps. If they discovered what Radu was—what he could do—they wouldn't just execute him. They'd turn his death into spectacle. A public holiday celebrating their power to destroy even legends.

And me? I'd be executed right beside him for bringing a monster home. Treason. Consorting with the enemy. Endangering the state. Lev Wurdulak would use it as justification to tear down everything I'd tried to build, to cement his family's hold on power forever. My death would be slow, public, and serve as a warning to anyone else who dared question their authority.

But watching Radu die would destroy me long before they opened the hatch in the Oculus.

The weight of my feelings for him—most of which I was still not fully on terms with—led to only one conclusion.

I'd protect him the only way I could. By keeping him as far from my people as possible. Let him fight his war here, surrounded by those who valued honor over politics. Where his strength was celebrated, not feared.

Maybe someday the Republic would change. Maybe they'd prove worthy of someone like him.

But I wouldn't hold my breath.

"I have to go back," I said, determination hardening my voice. "Dracula needs to know what's happening in his territory. Without his Blood Aura, we don't stand a chance."

Radu had been trailing lazy kisses along my collarbone, his lips sending tremors through my already sensitized skin. I hated interrupting when he was being so thorough, but this couldn't wait.

"Radu." I caught his chin, forcing him to meet my eyes. "Are you listening to me?"

His mouth curved in a smug grin. "Every word, princess."

He reached for a towel, draped it over my damp hair, and started to rub. The massage made my eyes flutter closed, and I found my hands gripping his firm backside—purely for balance, of course.

"I've been thinking about the Shepherds," I said, trying to ignore the magical press of his thumbs against my skull.

"Have you now?" His tone was indulgent, distracted.

"The Souleaters were created with immortal blood—we know that much." I forced myself to focus, even as his ministrations threatened to turn my brain to mush. "The Black Sheep evolved by consuming more immortal essence. Which would make the Shepherds closer to a pureblood composition than the basic White Sheep. Still, everything you've told me about them seems too complex for Russkaya's resources. I feel like I'm missing something."

That got his attention. He paused in his massage, amber eyes sharpening.

"Regardless," I continued, "Blood Aura could seize control of a Shepherd's mind before it launches another energy strike. It doesn't have range limitations like my Blood Manipulation, and like any living being, the creature wouldn't be able to resist Dracula's power."

I'd spent hours analyzing this after witnessing the Shepherd's devastating capabilities. The Black Sheep had fought my mental intrusions, their consciousness slippery but not impenetrable. A Shepherd, though? I wouldn't dare attempt direct contact after seeing what it could do.

He let out a slow breath and fixed his citron eyes on mine. "That last attack was Conin announcing he'd found me. My brother was a great strategist. And now that thing is using his tactical genius to hunt me down." He tossed the towel aside, banded his arms around me, and crushed me to his body. "I've accepted that I might die. Made arrangements for it. But I won't watch my friends fall, and who knows what monstrosity he'll become once he absorbs my Chronoportal."

"Exactly why I need to reach Dracula." I let my hands roam up his spine, feeling the hard cords of muscle contracting under my touch. "Whether he grants me his power or wakes himself, Blood Aura is our only weapon against that thing. We could cripple the Souleater advance, save millions."

He studied my face for a long moment. Through our weakening bond, I felt his hope, his guilt, his desperate need to protect everyone he cared about.

"Use me," I said softly, making the choice for him. "Portal me outside the Seventh Ward. I'll find my way to the Sleeping Chamber and be back before—"

"Like hell you're going alone." His voice turned granite-hard. "I'm coming with you."

"What?" I jerked back. "Absolutely not."

He stared at me as if I'd suggested he sprout wings and fly. "If you think I'm letting you walk into that snake pit alone, you clearly don't know me at all."

"I can handle myself perfectly fine."

The instant those words left my mouth, I realized the irony. Wasn't my complete helplessness against Lev the whole reason I'd fled the Republic?

"Sure about that?" Radu's tone suggested he was thinking the exact same thing.

"Absolutely." I straightened, trying to project confidence I didn't entirely feel.

A low growl rumbled from his chest, raising goosebumps along my arms.

"You are the most infuriatingly stubborn—"

"Me?" My voice pitched higher. "I'm the stubborn one?"

He leaned down until we were nose to nose. "As a damn mule."

"Because I don't want to watch you die? That makes me stubborn?"

"Absolutely." He threw my word back at me.

My teeth ground together as his silver hair caught the candlelight, suddenly impossible to ignore.

"We'll be fortunate if the Nightwatch doesn't spot us the second you portal near the walls," I snapped, jabbing my finger into his solid chest. "You drop me off and leave. End of discussion."

"Can't do that, princess."

The urge to smack sense into him was overwhelming.

"Radu, please." I flattened my palm against his chest, feeling his heart thunder beneath my touch. "The Nightwatch are elite originals with shadow magic at their command. You can't hide from their Darklings, and speed means nothing when they can track your very essence. These aren't ordinary guards. They've devoted their entire existence to eliminating threats like you." My voice cracked despite my efforts. "They will kill you."

"Then we don't get caught."

I threw my hands up, staring at the ceiling. "They'll execute me right alongside you, you stubborn ass! Treason, consorting with enemies—they'll kill me just like they did your mother, only this time they won't bother hiding it. Is that what you want? How does that help anyone defeat the Shepherd?"

The change in his expression was catastrophic. I'd seen earthquakes level cities with less devastation. His eyes blazed crimson before settling into molten amber, the wolf rising so close to the surface the golden patterns flickered beneath his skin.

Fear clawed up my throat as every instinct urged me to run before the predator decided I was prey. I tried to step back, but his arms locked around me like iron.

"No one," he snarled, voice dropping to something animalistic, "touches you and lives. I'll burn the entire Republic to ash first."

His breath scorched my face, the heat radiating from him like a forge. I opened my mouth, but no sound emerged.

"This isn't a negotiation," he said, his words final. "You take me with you, or you don't go at all. Your choice."

I met his stare despite the warring emotions in my chest. Pondered whether punching him would knock any sense loose. "You have serious control issues." I pressed my nail into his chest hard enough to dimple skin.

His jaw ticked, but he remained silent.

Smart man. Or maybe he'd already decided this conversation was over.

"I need to check on Selena," I said, stepping out of his reach. "And you need a shower." I turned and left him standing in the bathroom, dread settling like lead in my stomach.

The shower roared to life before I'd even cleared the doorway.

AURORA

I MADE IT HALFWAY to Selena's room before her door swung open. She appeared in the doorway, one dark brow arched high, and the golden ear cuffs I'd gifted her for her hundredth birthday gleamed against her obsidian hair.

I swept my gaze from her booted feet, up her black leggings and oversized tee, to the crown of her head, making sure she was alright. Her creamy skin had regained its healthy glow, no longer bearing the black veins that had terrified me after she'd drained herself saving Hummingbird.

"Well, well, well. The prodigal daughter returns," she mocked, but opened her arms in invitation.

I chuckled and rushed to wrap her in my arms. Radu and I hadn't exactly been quiet during our extended... reunion.

Bending slightly, I pulled her tight. "You look good," I said, exhaling a loud breath as relief flooded through me. Though I'd known her condition wasn't critical after the healing, that she needed only rest to replenish her reserves, seeing her upright and sarcastic meant everything was back to normal.

"Sabin made sure to keep my veins happy every time I so much as twitched in bed." Sel delivered it in a humorous tone, but the underlying affection was unmistakable.

I glanced past her at the rumpled sheets twisted across her mattress. The mingled scents of jasmine and ripe berries lingered in the air. Proof of how *thoroughly* the vice-captain had been tending to her needs.

"He's good for you."

She let go, a strand of hair falling free from behind her ear as she nodded. "He is." Her eyes went dreamy for a second. I could only imagine what debauched thing she was remembering. Or maybe she was simply in love.

But it didn't last long. She took a sniff and fixed me with a shrewd stare I knew meant trouble. "You seem quite satisfied yourself," she drawled. "How's that whole 'I'll-only-use-Harbinger-as-a-blood-source-and-nothing-more' philosophy working out for you?"

"Oh, shut up. It's not like I planned any of it."

"What, to fuck him like there's no tomorrow?"

"Sel!"

She shrugged, reached over to the dresser mounted on the wall beside the door, and grabbed her medical kit. It was a small silver case with a fingerprint lock similar to the one that held my Nexus and Astral Visor.

Music drifted through the thin walls, a soft and melancholy song that made my chest tighten. It came from somewhere above us.

Selena looked at the ceiling and shook her head. "Come on," she said on an exhale, stepping into the hallway. "You can tell me all about your unplanned sex marathon on our way to check on Hummingbird. That stubborn fool completely disregarded my orders to stay in bed."

"Again?" I slapped a hand over my mouth at the same time she halted.

The stare she leveled at me was nothing short of murderous. "What do you mean, *again*?" Her voice rose an octave in three words flat. "This isn't the first time he's wandered off?"

Underworld's tits. I didn't mean to get Hummingbird into trouble. He'd barely stayed put since he'd come to, but I wasn't about to dig his grave deeper.

"I'm not snitching," I said, miming a zipper closing over my lips.

"You don't need to. Your guilty face says everything." She huffed and strode across the hallway to the console table that had housed the priceless vase I'd shattered. With the press of her finger on what seemed like a random spot on the faded wallpaper, a hidden door popped open.

My jaw hit the floor. "How did you know about this when I didn't?"

"Maybe because I pay attention to my surroundings?" she said, with all the sass she could muster, and disappeared into the dark stairwell.

I rolled my eyes and followed her up. What could I say? She had a point. The secret passage had been *right* in front of my room and I'd never noticed it.

A musty scent of old wood and decades of dust greeted us, stinging my nostrils. The sneeze that followed echoed in the corridor, and I half-expected a colony of bats to descend upon us. They didn't, but that didn't stop me from raising my hands protectively over my head just in case they changed their minds and decided to snag their little claws in my hair.

"So?" Selena asked without looking back. She had chin-length hair—she didn't care if she lost it to those flying rats. "Spill it. Giving in once I can understand. Blood Pacts can be intense. But an entire night?" Her voice dropped to a hush, as if that would help in a house full of mixed-breeds. "I thought you didn't want to 'cater to his every whim'?"

I let out a frustrated breath and tried to sort through the hurricane of thoughts revolving around Radu and me. "It's not like that. I don't know how to explain it. Things get... complicated around him."

She paused on the squeaky step above me and turned. We were nearly the same height now, her obsidian eyes glittering with curiosity in the candlelight filtering up from the hallway.

"Explain."

"Well, you probably don't know since you were unconscious, but he disappeared again. Eighteen hours without a word."

She nodded, but her brows furrowed. "Where did he go?"

I shrugged, but couldn't hide the irritation in my voice. "No idea. But it wasn't anywhere on our side of the Gloom." Which raised even more questions about him. If he could leave this battlefield, why choose to stay? The only explanation that made sense was his determination to free his brother from the Shepherd's control. Otherwise, why endure so much grief?

I swore to Derzelas, the man had secrets by the dozen.

"Beyond?" she shrieked.

"I think so. The glimpse I had of his memory was murky."

She paused, deep in thought. Then she tsked, shaking her head. "And after vanishing without explanation, you took him straight to bed? A, I thought you were smarter than this."

"What was I supposed to do when he portaled into my bedroom half-lost to bloodlust?" I whisper-yelled.

"What?"

"He was hurt, bleeding, barely coherent. He asked me to let him feed, and I—"

"Oh."

"Yes, oh."

Her stare could have reached into my soul; it was so laser-focused. "So, you satisfied his hunger and then happily let him into your pants?"

"Not happily," I lied through my teeth. "I wanted to demand answers, but then I felt his overwhelming grief and sorrow while he was feeding. Sel, they're battling the same war we are."

She startled. "Who's 'they'?"

It was almost comical—if the subject wasn't so serious—how her chastising expression changed into absolute confusion.

"I'm not entirely sure," I said. "I heard a woman speaking Russkayan, saw other elementals in the distance."

"Uh-huh. And you didn't think to ask for details?"

"He told me not to before I had the chance." I clamped my lips shut as soon as the words left them. It sounded as bad as it had in my head. Aurora zero, Radu one. I always forgot my brain when I was around him.

"Uh-huh." I could tell by her tone she knew exactly what had happened. "And you listened because...?"

I welded my teeth together. "And then I had sex with him. Happy now? I chose to postpone the interrogation and live in the moment."

"Well, you certainly seized that moment." She raised her hand and grabbed something invisible. "Hooonk. Hooonk."

"What are you doing?"

"All aboard the express zeppelin to Bad Decision Territory." She tugged the imaginary cord again. "Hooonk. Hooonk." Her voice dropped to mimic the deep, resonant sound of an airship horn.

"It won't happen again," I said half-heartedly. Maybe if I repeated it enough, it would become true.

"Like it didn't happen after Brasov? Or that time in his room? Face it, A—you're developing a pattern."

Elena's voice found that exact moment to echo in my mind. *Impulsive decisions lead to permanent consequences, Aurora.'*

I sighed. I hated when my mother's sayings randomly crowded into my head to sour my already bad mood.

"Men like him only enjoy the chase," I said. "And now that he's gotten what he wanted—"

"Multiple times."

"—he'll lose interest." I glared at her. "He'll finish his task and leave. It's over." My lips moved, but I wasn't entirely sure of the words that left my mouth.

"Men expecting to get bored don't seek out a woman's help when they have perfectly capable friends to turn to." She paused as if pondering whether she should say what was on her tongue next. "And they certainly wouldn't spend all night sampling the goods if they were already over it."

"It's the blood exchange. It complicates everything."

"So you keep saying." She waved dismissively. "It's obvious you're falling for him, I think you should tell him how you feel."

I couldn't deny it, so I didn't try. But... "I'm not telling him anything."

Her eyes narrowed into a challenge if I'd ever seen one. "Coward."

"I'm not a coward." I smacked her backside.

She shook her head and resumed climbing. "Bawk, bawk."

"Selena—"

"Bk, bk, bk—"

"Selena, seriously—"

"Bawk-awk!"

"I'm not telling him because I'm afraid, I just don't want things to get awkward when we still need to focus on killing the Shepherd. Which, by the way—"

"Yeah, keep telling yourself that, sweetheart." We reached a nonde-script door at the top of the stairs. With a smile drenched in saccharine, she winked, said, "Hold that thought," and twisted the brass knob.

The door opened to reveal a massive attic filled with hardwood furniture and priceless belongings under dusty white sheets. But what caught my attention was a grand piano taking center stage. Dozens of candles crowded its ebony surface, spilling their wax in washed-white rivers down the sides.

And right there, sitting on a burgundy velvet bench, under waving shadows, was Hummingbird. Alive. Whole.

His wings folded away with a soft susurration, settling behind him on the wooden floor like the richest cape woven with silk. Not a single bruise marred his pretty face, and I knew that under his forest green sweater his abdomen bore a red scar that still needed healing but was otherwise closed and without any sign of infection. The chestnut ringlets of his hair bounced as he turned to wave at us, a boyish smile lighting his features.

I smiled at him, but Selena shattered the moment by stomping her way in and promising violence. "I thought I told you to stay in bed," she barked and propped her hands on her hips. "Your intestines literally grew back from nothing. They need time to settle."

"I'm fine," came his reply, though it sounded breathier than usual. "See? I can sit up without—" A sharp inhale cut him off.

"Fine my ass," Selena muttered and dashed to check on him. "Scoot over."

She straddled the bench, pressed one hand to his forehead, and the other over his heart. A soft red light radiated from her palms at the same time her floral scent spiked.

"Projector." Hummingbird's face turned pleading when his eyes landed on me again. "Can you please tell the lieutenant I'm fine? She's been hovering like a mother hen ever since she woke up."

Selena cast a razor-sharp scowl in his direction that would wither a stout winter rose. "You ingrate," she muttered as she retrieved a syringe from her kit, flicked it a few times, and squirted out some of the yellowish liquid. Then she rolled up his sleeve and administered the medicine with practiced care. "I annoy you because I want to make sure you're healing properly."

You could say whatever you wanted about Selena—that she was cold, uncaring, headstrong—but when she took you under her wing, you could always count on her to have your back. I'd never met anyone more loyal than she.

Well, Harbinger, but that was beside the point.

"Can you blame her?" I pulled a squeaky chair from the maple dining set hidden under the covers. "You were dying. We almost lost you."

Sorrow of the darkest kind seeped into his eyes. His easy smile faltered, replaced by a gravity that made him look older. The kind that said he'd seen too many atrocities. "I remember bits and pieces. The energy bolt, Quakelord..." His voice grew airy with grief. "He saved my life, didn't he?"

The silence that followed felt heavy enough to crush us all. I'd found out later, after we'd returned and licked our wounds, that Quakelord had used his earth magic to catapult Hummingbird from harm's way. But he'd been too slow to evade the attack and save himself. That's why Hummingbird had landed so hard against that rock face.

"Yes," Selena said in a murmur. "He did."

Hummingbird's face crumbled before he pressed the heels of his hands over his eyes. His shoulders shook with silent sobs.

Survivor's guilt.

That terrible weight of being alive when others weren't. Of wondering why you deserved to breathe when they didn't.

Tears burned the back of my eyes.

"Hey." I leaned forward, squeezing his knee. "He made that choice. We all did. That's what being in a guild means. We protect each other, no matter the cost."

"Aurora's right," Selena added, her clinical mask slipping to reveal the grief underneath. "Quakelord knew the risks, he died doing what he believed in—keeping his family safe."

Family. That's what they were, and what I'd also started to feel in the short months I'd spent with them. Not bound by blood but by choice, by shared battles and unbreakable loyalty.

"How much longer before he's fully healed?" I asked Selena.

"Physically? Another day or two of rest should do it." She traced her fingers over Hummingbird's ribs, checking for tenderness. "But what he went through—regenerating entire organs—it's not something you just bounce back from. His body needs time to remember how all the pieces fit together."

What she didn't say was that emotionally it would take longer. Years, decades maybe. We'd all lost people we cared about. Me, my father, whose absence I still felt in my heart even after almost a century. My Sparrows. Phoenix, Quakelord. Others who'd fallen along the way. The dead left scars that never fully healed, phantom limbs of grief that ached in quiet moments.

"Quakelord's gone," he whispered as though he'd finally come to terms with it. Lowered his hands, then met my gaze. "We'll remember him by living, by fighting. His sacrifice won't be meaningless."

I felt a tear slip down my cheek. The conviction in his voice reminded me why I'd grown to care so deeply for these people. Not just for their strength or their loyalty, but for their ability to find hope in the darkest places. To keep believing in something better even when the world tried to crush that belief.

A soft knock disconnected the moment. We all turned toward the door as it creaked open, revealing Harbinger's broad silhouette.

"Sorry to interrupt," he said, his golden eyes scanning Hummingbird for signs of improvement. "How are you feeling?"

"Like I got struck by lightning and had my guts rearranged," Hummingbird replied, a lopsided grin tilting his full mouth. "But alive. Thanks to you. All of you."

Harbinger stepped into the room, wearing a light brown shirt that made his bronze skin glow and black cargo pants tucked into combat boots. If he looked like a dark god in leather, he was impossible to resist now. A warrior ready for battle. A commander who would do anything to protect his people.

"Actually," he said, his gaze sliding to me, "I came to talk to Aurora. About our conversation earlier."

My pulse jumped. "I thought you'd changed your mind."

"Never."

The room went silent except for the distant ticking of a clock somewhere under the sheets. Selena's eyes widened as understanding dawned. She gathered her supplies, arranging them in their designated spots in the metal box.

"The Republic? When?" she asked, closing the lock with a loud click. Her stiff shoulders told me she wasn't eager to go back, and I bet Terraknight had everything to do with it—not the chauvinist dickheads she used to work under.

"As I told Harbinger earlier," I said. "It's enough if I go alone. No reason to put you at risk as well." Her body relaxed a little, but her jaw was still set. "Besides, I'd much rather you stay here in case someone needs you."

"Aurora made a compelling argument," Harbinger said, ignoring my pointed suggestion that he stay put and let me go alone. "If Dracula can grant her the Blood Aura, if we can convince him to help... it might be our only chance to level the playing field."

"Or it might be a death sentence," Selena muttered, "for both of you."

The fear in her voice made my heart clench. She was thinking exactly what had kept me awake for the past two nights—of Lev, of the Tribunal, of all the ways this could go catastrophically wrong. I didn't blame her.

"Which is why we need to be smart about it," I said, coming to terms with the fact that Harbinger was going to tag along. I needed him to teleport me close enough to the walls to avoid being seen by the guards. There was no way he was going to stay put. "Quick in and out. I present the threat to Dracula, get the Blood Aura or do the unthinkable—wake him up—and we're back here before anyone realizes what happened."

"And if the Wurdulak prince tries to stop you?" Hummingbird asked.

"He won't get the chance," Harbinger replied before me. "I'll make sure of that." His eyes flashed with an amber glow, and I might have imagined it, but I thought I saw the golden patterns pulsing beneath his skin too. More and more, his varcolac was making an appearance.

Regardless, the promise in his voice made my breathing quicken. Possessive. Protective. Utterly serious. This coming after he'd so eloquently said he'd burn the Republic down if something happened to me... The predator in me purred with satisfaction.

"Good." Selena nodded appreciatively, then leveled her stare at Harbinger. "How precise is your magic? Can you portal directly to the Temple, where our Creators rest?"

He shook his head, and candlelight reflected in the silver of his hair. "Chronoportal doesn't work that way. It's not enough to know about a place. I have to physically visit it before I can teleport there again."

She let out a dejected sigh and looked at me. "In and out, my left toe." She pointed her chin at Radu. "You need him to get inside."

After seeing my confused expression, she raised her hand and started ticking off items with her fingers. "Even if he portals you outside the seventh ward, you won't be able to get in undetected. They have guards posted at every entrance—gates, tunnels, you name it. But even if you somehow manage to slip past them, you won't trick the blood wards."

My entire body sagged, my arms hanging like overcooked noodles at my sides. I'd forgotten about those damn blood wards.

"I gather that's bad?" Harbinger's gaze bounced from me to Selena.

"Bad?" I scoffed. "The government put them up after the Total Rendition to detect any mixed-breed who might trespass over our borders. The problem is they don't just sense mortal blood. They flare up at any type of blood."

Selena picked up where I left off. "They have an entire department dedicated to overseeing and reinforcing them. That's how they track if everyone crossing the inner gates has approval from the Obayi-fo—the Master of Keys, the man in charge of that sector."

"They linked the wards to the National Gene Bank," I continued, the full scope of our problem hitting me. "The institution that safe-guards every citizen's blood sample."

No way I could pass through without Lev knowing of my return.

"Radu, you said you remember the fountain in front of the Corvin Palace. Could you teleport us there?" I asked.

He nodded, but Selena cut him off before he could say more. "It's too public there. Too many eyes." She tapped her chin, her dark eyes unseeing as she fell deep in thought. "You said your mother took you out on the balcony to show you the fireworks. Do you remember your childhood home?"

"I grew up in Russkaya," he corrected, "but, yeah, I remember Ma's house."

"Then that's how you get in. It must be somewhere close to the palace since you could see the festival's show from your window. Any chance your family took you to Derzelas' Temple?"

He shook his head. "Even if they did, I was too young for it to make an impression. I don't remember."

It dawned on me that I didn't know Radu's age. But seeing as in the vision of him, Conin and his mother he'd been past the maturing age, and adding the long decades fighting Souleaters, he couldn't be much older than me. Maybe ten to twenty years. Fifty tops.

Hard to tell when every child of Derzelas stopped aging in their twenties.

Seizing the opportunity, I took my chance.

"And how long exactly do you reckon that was?" I asked, schooling my face to seem indifferent.

He read right through me. The bastard. "Where would the fun be if I told you that?" His chuckle was deep, like the rumbling of distant thunder, and soft as silk.

"Fine," I scoffed, and got back to serious matters. "Let's say we portal to your mother's house. We'd still need to cross half of the First Ward on foot to get to the Temple. And even if we manage to hide your hair somehow, people *will* recognize me."

"Not if you're with him, they won't." Selena slumped into the plush emerald armchair she'd unearthed from a pile of forgotten furniture.

Her face took on that collected expression that usually meant she was about to recite a sequence of events that would lead to us arriving safely at the Temple, and would probably start her story right around the Arrival of the Dark Sons millennia ago.

I held my hand in the air, stopping her before she could start. "That's exactly what I want to prevent. They will know what he is straight away."

Derzelas, was it too hard to grasp that if word got out that a varcolac was walking freely on the streets, mayhem would ensue? And not only that, but the future queen was the one who'd smuggled him inside the walls?

"Aurora, darling," she said with a sly smile. "How often have you been seen in the company of a man?"

I winced.

Thanks for that, Sel.

"That rare, huh?" Radu snorted, but his smug grin said he didn't mind it.

My cheeks flamed like a sacrificial pyre. "Oh, hush," I said and rolled my eyes. "I didn't want to give them more material for the gossip columns, they had enough as it was. People live and breathe for any dirt they can dig up about life at court."

"But they're especially curious about their future queen," Selena added. "Fully cloaked, you'd be just another couple keeping their infidelities a secret. No one would even consider it's you, believe me."

"And where in Derzelas' name will we find cloaks to wear here?"

"I know a place. Leave them to me," Radu said, and gave me a sinful wink. The most wolfish grin I'd ever seen crept across his face. Damn his varcolac heritage. "Your virtue is safe with me, Your Majesty."

A scorching wave rolled through my body from my toes up to my scalp. It wasn't fair for my traitorous body to react to him like that when I was still miffed at him for hiding things from me. But when he sank his teeth into his lower lip, my lower belly clenched tight, and I couldn't hold back the groan that escaped my mouth.

"Okay, that's enough!" Selena growled, jumping to her feet and shoving us apart. Her head barely reached Radu's chest, but the threat in her glower said his towering height did not intimidate her. "Keep it in your pants. We still need to come up with contingency plans. I know it all depends on the location of your mother's house, but we need to talk about what routes are safer in case you can't take the less obvious ones. How are you going to get inside the Temple without getting caught?

There are at least two guards outside the Sleeping Chamber. If they see you and alert the Nightwatch—"

"Lieutenant," Radu interrupted, "in my experience, the more you plan for these things, the more likely you'll get fucked when they don't work in your favor. The mind adapts quicker to new situations when you have fewer expectations. We'll portal to Ma's house and wing it from there."

"We won't wing anything," I choked out. "If we're doing this, you'll do what I say."

He shrugged, and I shook my head at him.

Then I continued, "He's right, though, Sel. Too many things can go wrong and throw a wrench in our plans. We'll avoid the main roads and keep to the quieter areas. I've already thought about this. We could enter the Temple through the tunnel on Moonlight Terrace. Remember the fountain?"

Her eyes glittered in recognition, and she nodded enthusiastically.

"Ravenwood Heights is far enough from the boulevard, and Sable Street leads straight to the square," I further explained. "If that doesn't work, we'll detour through Shadowbrook. It's riskier since we'll have to cross the bridge over the Blackwater Channel, but the crowds will thin out."

"Alright, sounds good to me," she said, nodding in agreement. "When do you leave?"

"The sooner the better." Radu's voice was firm. "I assume the Transmitters won't reach the Republic?" he asked her.

"No, they are close-range devices."

"Tonight then. After sunset." He looked at Hummingbird, and his lips curved in what might have been a smile if it held any warmth. "I don't want to be away too long in case the Shepherd makes another move."

Selena's face blanched. I could only assume it was because she realized they wouldn't have Harbinger to warn them in advance about the Souleaters.

"Tonight," I repeated, my stomach fluttering with nerves. "You won't even know we left."

AURORA

THE BUZZING OF THE house woke me before sunset. I'd grown accustomed to waking in complete silence during our time in the Tenth Ward, so the scraping and murmur of voices filtering through the walls startled me awake.

For a heartbeat, I expected to see Mother rifling through my wardrobe again, or perhaps the world had finally ended. Not that they were mutually exclusive.

Then awareness crashed over me. I was in Radu's bed at the Black Guild's manor, with very warm arms wrapped around my waist and an even warmer zmeu curled against my chest.

It wouldn't have been so bad if Shadow weren't a smidgen colder than the flames of hell itself. The ash-colored zmeu was barely a few months old, with wings to match her dusky hide. Everyone in the guild called her different names, but I'd settled on Shadow because she had this habit of watching us from dark corners. If it weren't for those owlish yellow eyes glowing in the dark, you'd never know she was there.

Unfortunately, she also snored like a drunken sailor.

I nuzzled the rough skin between her tiny horns, then carefully wiggled free from under covers, arms, and paws.

I'd fallen asleep after Radu had insisted I replenish my blood reserves. And by insisted, I meant him parading around stark naked and wet from the shower, teasing me with superficial cuts until I gave in.

And I had.

Several times.

He lay sprawled among embroidered sheets and thick feather pillows, his face the picture of innocence. True, it was a devastatingly sexy kind of innocence, but it did magical things to my nether regions all the same. I wanted nothing more than to steal one last kiss before the night began, but I couldn't risk waking him. I needed him sharp and focused to portal us hundreds of miles through Souleater-infested territory.

My gaze drifted up the angles of his body. He had his arm thrown over his forehead, his right palm open and facing the ceiling. Coordinates and checkpoint markers scrolled in black ink across his skin. The route he'd memorized to avoid Republic scanners and stay invisible to projector surveillance.

Taking one last look at those strong features, I gathered my scattered clothes from the floor and slipped out into the hallway, then to my room.

After dressing quickly in fresh leathers and braiding my damp hair back, I slipped on my knee-high boots and made my way downstairs. Voices carried from the back patio. Gale rushed out of the war room with a map rolled in her hands. The same one that served as both tablecloth and reference for the outer wards during strategy meetings.

I wove between marble-topped tables and velvet settees lining the columns of the foyer and followed the earthy smell of freshly brewed kafea. Candlelight reflected in the countless faceted teardrops of the chandelier and scattered patterns across the papered walls.

Outside, the air smelled rich with damp earth and night-blooming flowers. The stream burbled gently beyond the fence, mixing with the chirp of nightjars. Paper lanterns hung from the gnarled branches of the old oak, swaying in the breeze and casting warm amber light over the guild members gathered around the dinner table.

Radu had arrived before me——via Chronoportal——and stood with one hand braced against the worn wood as he leaned forward. "—fallback position is the Sparrow's base in the ninth ward. If the Shepherd breaks through our perimeter, you run there immediately. No heroics."

When he saw me approaching, he fastened heated amber eyes on me until Terraknight's gruff voice pulled his attention.

"We can traverse the river here," the vice-captain said, pointing at the map spread between last night's abandoned dinner plates. "But if it predicts our escape plan and ambushes us... we're fucked."

"Split into two groups to diminish the chance of being caught together." Radu traced routes with his finger. "One takes the Ialomita River, the other the caves."

"So, it's a gamble who faces the Shepherd," Ember said.

I stepped closer, studying the tactical positions on the map. The caves weren't far from Sibiu. "What about a decoy route? Send a small group to the outskirts of the city to draw its attention while the others slip through the mountain."

Radu's eyes flicked to mine. "That puts whoever takes the decoy route in direct danger."

"Everything we do puts us in danger. At least this way we control the risk instead of leaving it to chance."

He considered this, then nodded slowly. "Hummingbird and Ember could handle the decoy. Their magic creates enough chaos to draw the

Shepherd's focus, and he can fly her to safety before the Souleaters close in."

I swept my gaze over Radu's trademark black leather pants that hugged his firm ass and powerful thighs. A loose black t-shirt stretched across his broad chest, the opal pendant resting between his pectorals and catching the soft glow from the paper lanterns. Scuffed combat boots—the kind that had seen real action—completed the look. But the sunsteel blade sheathed around his forearm made me pause.

A lump longed in my throat.

He never went anywhere without it, but bringing it to the Republic... The only weapon that could kill an immortal. I didn't know how to react to that. Then again, if the worst happened and the guards caught us, did I want him defenseless? I hadn't sugarcoated the truth about the Nightwatch; they would act first and ask questions later if they considered either of us a threat.

I swallowed the ball of dread and dropped onto the stone balustrade, leaning back against a pillar. Above, the night sky stretched endlessly, uncaring of my earthbound problems. I tried not to feel bitter. Not very hard, but I did give it an ounce of effort before I gave up and let myself resent the hell out of the entire pureblood establishment.

Stress and fear were eating me alive. Especially when our entire plan balanced on one single variable—Dracula. One ancient, unpredictable Creator who might decide we weren't worth his time. One being who could crush us all if the mood struck him.

Just perfect.

Despite being only half full, the moon blazed with unusual brightness through the gray clouds drifting overhead. Even the damn sky was conspiring against me.

Another reason for my spectacular mood.

The Red Moon crept closer each night, already making the moon appear nearly double its normal size. It would continue to swell as it drew nearer than it had in five hundred years. Closer meant wilder magic, purebloods losing their minds to bloodlust, and originals vulnerable to eternal bonds.

The bane of my existence.

At least one good thing had come from the chaos my life had become since my hundredth birthday. I wouldn't have to bind myself to that vicious bastard who had stolen my throne. Though at this rate, there might not be a throne left to fight over.

A boot scuffed the ground, and I startled. The familiar scent of jasmine reached my nostrils before Selena's voice came over my shoulder.

"You ready for this?" she asked, clamping her fingers around my forearm.

Her grip felt like a vice, knuckles white with tension.

"As ready as I'll ever be," I said, forcing what I hoped passed for a confident smile.

Her dark brows drew together as she pulled me down closer to her height. "Listen to me carefully," she demanded in a hushed tone. "No detours. No side trips. And whatever you do, don't even think about checking on Commander Enescu while you're there." Her eyes narrowed. "You have your whole immortal life ahead of you to confront him. It's too risky."

"I'm not stupid, Sel. I'll be careful—"

"Projector!" Gale called from the roof, drawing everyone's attention.

She launched herself into the air with a flourish of bronze wings and mahogany braids, landing in the ankle-high grass. Dressed in form-fitting black clothes, Gale looked ready to pull off the heist of the century rather than like someone who'd just woken up.

She climbed the three stairs to the patio and wrapped her arms around my shoulders. "Both Hummingbird and I wish you good luck tonight. He said he would have walked you to the portal if the lieutenant hadn't threatened to rip him a new one for leaving his bed."

"Damn right I would," Selena said with fierce pride, making us all laugh despite the tension.

"Projector, come see what Cap brought for your disguises," Pearl called from the doorway.

The varva wasn't heavily built—none of the guild women were—but her arm muscles strained under the weight of the garments. A longer black piece spilled from the crook of her elbow, nearly reaching her studded boots. She wore a simple white tank and midnight silk shorts, her turquoise hair cascading in loose waves around her shoulders.

I jumped down and walked over to her. "Let me see," I said, reaching for the bundle with violet silk lining.

I slipped on the velvet robe, expecting its weight to drag at my shoulders. Instead, the supposedly full-length cloak barely reached mid-thigh, leaving the bottom half of my projector uniform completely exposed.

"Ah, Harbinger?" I croaked, flapping the oversized sleeves. "What exactly is this supposed to be?"

He covered the ten feet between us. "It's not exactly a buyer's market out there, princess," he drawled. "But it serves its purpose." He reached over and pulled the large hood up over my head. "See? It's doing exactly what it's meant to do."

I batted his hands away, catching a hint of his addictive scent. "What about my legs?"

"Pearl?" he called without taking his eyes off me.

Both dimples made an appearance alongside his grin. I couldn't decide if that smug expression made me want to slap him or grab his face and kiss him senseless.

Probably both.

"Here." Pearl passed him the black garment, and he held it up for me to see.

A strong whiff of mothballs wafted from the fabric, making me wrinkle my nose. I examined the long skirt with a critical eye. Layer upon layer of black lace spiraled down from the waistband, with a dark slip underneath providing decent coverage that trailed almost to the ground.

I shrugged and snatched the garment from his hands. "I suppose it's not terrible."

"Not terrible?" he scoffed. "It's perfect! You have no idea how long it took me to find something in your size."

"It's not—" I started to protest, then choked on the words as I cinched the waistband and found it was indeed a perfect match. The bottom layer of lace pooled slightly around my feet.

"What were you saying?" Radu wasn't looking at me directly, too busy securing his own heavy cloak at the base of his neck, but sarcasm dripped from every word.

His cloak was made of thick wool, dyed deep brown, with a silver trim that caught the moonlight when he moved. The oversized hood fell in a stiff triangle to his shoulders, and it reeked of mothballs just as badly as mine.

"Well look at that..." Terraknight's deep chuckle carried over the murmurs around us. He circled us like a predator, rubbing the dark stubble on his chin. "Cap looks like he's snagged himself a wealthy—"

"Widow?" I said, kicking one leg forward and rustling the layers of fabric.

"More like a rich man's mistress," Gale corrected with a grin.

Selena nodded approvingly. "Perfect. No one will give you a second glance."

She was right. The longer I studied our disguises, the more confident I felt. What we looked like now—a well-dressed gentleman with his expensive companion—was common enough to be invisible.

"Time to go," Radu announced, clapping Terraknight on the shoulder. His other hand began rotating in slow circles at his side. "We'll see you before sunrise."

The air sizzled and thundered behind me. My hair whipped across my face as his cloak fluttered about him. I didn't need to turn around to recognize the signs of his portal opening—I'd felt his Chronoportal enough times to know it anywhere.

Terraknight stepped forward and crushed me in what might have been an embrace or a wrestling hold. "You watch yourself out there," he growled in my ear, and I nodded quickly, eager to escape with my ribs intact.

We all exchanged farewells like we'd never see each other again, and the hollow ache in my chest expanded until it felt like it might swallow me whole. Strange how much it hurt to leave them, even for just a few hours. The bonds I'd formed with them had become stronger than I'd realized.

How everything had changed since that first day at the Initiation ceremony.

Selena hugged me next, then Gale, and finally Pearl. A few tears were shed, though I wouldn't name names. I didn't expect any show of affection from Ember, and wasn't surprised when she simply nodded curtly.

Selena caught my hand one last time, her grip fierce. "In and out," she said, echoing my earlier words. She forced a smile that couldn't quite hide the worry in her dark eyes. "Just like you promised."

"In and out," I agreed.

"Come on, Projector," Radu called, his hand extended toward me in front of the swirling portal.

I bent forward, gathered the folds of my skirt around my knees, and hurried to join him. My heart hammered against my ribs.

He took my hand, stroking my knuckles. "Don't be afraid," he whispered, pulling me closer to him. "I won't let anything happen to you."

The portal writhed like a living being, ice-cold air bleeding from its edges. Static electricity raised the hair on my arms. The void beyond looked hungry, patient.

And despite everything—despite not knowing what we'd find in the Republic, despite the growing dread that this mission might be our last together—I believed him.

Together, we stepped into the swirling darkness.

AURORA

IF SOMEONE ASKED ME to describe how it felt to travel through Radu's portal back to the Republic, I'd choose two words: cold and wrong. It was nothing like the brief journeys we'd taken before, when he'd snap us across a battlefield in seconds.

Oh, no.

I found this out later, when solid ground materialized beneath our feet, but he'd used his magic to teleport us moments into the future. All the while, we'd trudged through thick darkness, elbowing our way between the thin walls of different worlds. Radu pit-stopped in remote locations across the outer wards to keep the chill from freezing me to the bone, except it hardly helped.

Time didn't feel linear anymore. We'd been trapped inside a dark tunnel where invisible forces pulled us apart from all sides. A startled shock of electricity dumped adrenaline down my spine every time we snapped back together, like someone had stretched us like elastic and then let go.

I didn't know what was worse—feeling sick and ready to puke all the time, or tingling everywhere from the harsh cold.

On the sixth stop, the portal spat us out behind a rocky outcrop somewhere east of the main gate to the Seventh Ward, though still too far away to see the walls.

My legs wobbled as I tried to find my balance, but Radu's grip shot out to steady me. His fingers remained wrapped around my wrist longer than necessary, warm thumb tracing over my icy pulse, before he remembered himself and dropped his hand.

A smile tugged at my lips, but it vanished the moment I caught the scent. The night air was humid here, carrying pine and something that shouldn't be. Something that made my blood freeze.

Charcoal and sage. The stench of Darklings.

"Nightwatch guards," I whispered, pressing against the rock and pulling Radu down beside me. "Trackers."

His palm found his blade. "Patrol?"

"No." Dread pooled in my stomach. "They almost never leave their posts."

A lanky man with a short mohawk, bushy eyebrows, and a frown that said people did what he commanded if they wanted to keep their appendages probed the soil. Probably the leader. His dark armor gleamed in the moonlight as he turned his head, scanning the terrain with laser-focused eyes. Blackened greaves protected his legs while his gauntlets gripped a retractable baton, its tip sparking with spiderweb patterns of blue energy. The red cape he wore billowed around him, and wisps of shadow curled upward from his boots where his Darklings tested the air.

"They're hunting," I whispered.

Every fine hair rose on my body. If they risked crossing into the outer wards—this far from their stations—they were searching for someone important enough to justify abandoning their posts.

My pulse hammered against my throat. So much for the Commander's story about my death. The question wasn't whether they'd come for me. It was who had sent them. Mother would have dispatched a discreet envoy, someone who could bring me home quietly without political fallout. These were hunters in full battle gear, their armor forged from Carpathian iron.

Lev.

The bastard wouldn't settle for discretion. He'd want a public spectacle to cement his claim as my protector, probably spinning some tale about me being kidnapped by Russkaya's spies. The perfect excuse to lock me away until our wedding.

"They're looking for me," I breathed.

Radu's entire body went rigid. I felt the tension roll off him, his shoulder pressed against mine turning to stone. "How do you know?"

"Nightwatch don't patrol beyond the walls. Ever. Someone sent them. Someone important."

They spread out in a classic search formation—one at point, two flanking wide to cut off escape routes. Dark smoke puffed behind them as they popped in and out of shadow, moving with lightning speed that left trails of Darkling mist. The leader raised his gauntleted fist, and the others materialized from wisps of darkness, freezing as they listened for disturbance.

"I'd bet my crown it's Lev. He's probably convinced the Council I'm being held against my will."

"Then we kill them. Now."

He started to rise, but I shot my arm out and grasped his elbow, my fingers digging into the corded muscle there. Heat drifted off him like sand off a dune, his varcolac emerging in response to the threat. Golden patterns pulsed beneath darkening skin like molten gold threading through marble.

It should have frightened me—him losing control like that—but it didn't. The rational part of my mind catalogued the danger: muscles coiled for violence, predatory stillness that promised swift death, amber irises that had shifted from liquid honey to glowing suns. Other than having a glimpse of his varcolac form in my room, I hadn't seen Radu's full transformation. But I'd sensed his wolf countless times. Watching me when he thought I wasn't looking. Assessing me with impenetrable focus during our arguments.

Predator recognizing predator.

He wasn't the boogeyman of my childhood stories. The monster mothers whispered about to keep their children in line. Maybe it was my own immortal nature recognizing a kindred darkness, or maybe it was something deeper, a pull that defied every lesson I'd been taught about his kind. But for reasons beyond my understanding, beyond nature itself, I trusted not only the man *but* his wolf as well. The beast that could tear me apart was the same one that had caught me when I stumbled, that had saved my life and faced my starved monster head-on.

"Wait," I hissed, tightening my grip on his arm. "You can't just kill them."

The contact seemed to ground him. I felt the moment his varcolac retreated. The glowing glyphs fading beneath his skin. His breathing slowed, shoulders dropping as he fought to rein himself in.

When he looked at me again, his eyes had returned to normal. "Why not? They wouldn't hesitate to turn you in."

"Yes, but..." I scrambled for a reason, trying to ignore how his protective instincts made my stomach flutter. "They're innocent."

He looked at me as if I'd grown three heads.

"If I could talk to them, tell them the truth—"

"Absolutely not. You're not going anywhere near them." His free hand moved to cover mine where it gripped his arm, his touch surprisingly gentle despite the steel in his tone.

"But they're trained to look after the Republic's best interests."

"You said it yourself—they're Lev's dogs now." His fingers swept across my hand in an absent gesture. "The moment you show yourself, they'll drag you back to him. I won't allow it."

"Since when do you get to decide where I can and can't go?" I challenged with more bite than I'd planned. Though whether from irritation at his presumption or frustration at how his touch made my pulse race, I couldn't say.

He caged me between his body and the rock, getting in my face while he enunciated each word. "Since the moment you became mine to protect." His jaw was granite. "I don't care if they're honorable or loyal or whatever noble bullshit you're telling yourself. You reveal yourself to them, and I'll kill every last one to keep them from reporting back."

The possessive conviction should have made me angrier, not sent heat spiraling through my veins. The way he said 'mine'—like it was an immutable fact, like the sun rising or the tide turning. I bit the inside of my cheek to keep from leaning into him as his scent spiked.

He pulled me toward the writhing portal, but I dug in my heels as another fear bloomed in my chest. My fingers tightened around his, and he immediately stilled.

"If they find our trail back—" I started, and he must have heard the tremor in my words because he halted at the portal's mouth and cupped my cheek.

"They won't," he said, and I caved and turned my face into the warmth of his palm. "The guild is safe. Trust me. I know what I'm doing."

The word 'please' hung unspoken between us, but I heard it anyway in the way his searching gaze held mine. I looked toward the Nightwatch getting farther away, their red capes snapping in the wind, then back to those mesmerizing eyes that stripped away every defense I had.

"Portal us out," I said.

Thunder cracked around us, and the world shifted again.

ONE MORE STOP AFTER that, and then auburn walls caged us inside a massive room. The momentum sent me stumbling forward, but Radu's grip was like a vice around my bicep. It saved me from face-planting on the expensive rug, but didn't stop the world from spinning. I closed my eyes, taking deep mouthfuls of patchouli and cigar-scented air to fight the nausea. Ice melted off my skin, dripping in rivulets beneath my dress collar, making me shiver.

Radu's hand moved to rub warmth back into my arms.

"Easy," he murmured, steadying me until the worst of the dizziness passed. A different kind of shiver flitted over my skin like a caress at the sound of his voice. "The cold's always worse on the last jump."

Moving my face muscles to test if my nose hadn't fallen off from frostbite, I almost missed the soft click that filled the silence.

The back of my lids turned bright red.

Snapping my eyes open, I zeroed in on two filament bulbs shaped like inverted teardrops, flickering in the lamps mounted on each side of the four-poster bed. My adrenaline was flowing with the excitement.

"Electricity," I whispered, spinning on my heels to take in the riches surrounding us. Relief almost collapsed my knees. "Radu, we made it! We're in the Republic."

I couldn't contain my smile as I turned to face him, but he'd already moved to the window and wasn't paying attention to me. I swallowed my disappointment and took in the room instead.

Despite the arched ceiling, the bedroom felt suffocating. Furniture made of massive dark wood, polished to almost mirror shine, crowded every spare space. A tall wardrobe ran along one wall, stopping an inch shy of the ornate door to the ensuite. Opposite stood a dresser and desk separated by a black marble mantel.

A small fire crackled inside the hearth beneath, spreading a pleasant fragrance. I crouched to smell the potpourri sachets hanging from the fire grate, my skin tight from the tension radiating from Radu's silent form. It dawned on me it wasn't patchouli I'd smelled before but a mixture of spices and herbs left to heat near the flames.

Standing up, I craned my head back and stared at the familiar portrait nailed on the wall. Cold washed through my middle. Fear crawled up my spine and sent tingles of apprehension racing down my legs.

"Radu, where did you bring us?" I choked out, shaking my head and denying what my mind had already accepted.

This got his attention.

His steps were silent as he returned by my side, close enough that I could feel the heat from his body. He studied the painting with cold, calculating eyes before turning to me. "Where I was supposed to. You know him?"

I gave him a stilted nod, my tongue suddenly thick in my mouth.

The man in the oil painting was probably close to four hundred at the time of commission, but it was hard to tell. His hair, jet-black with a faint green undertone, was cut just long enough to style, although he hadn't bothered. No gray yet. His face was clean-shaven, not a hint of shadow to darken his angular jaw. A tall forehead, big nose, thin mouth, and scarlet eyes under thick, bushy eyebrows. Not conventionally handsome, but powerful. The first face you see when the Master of Keys grants you free passage into the First Administrative Ward.

"Marcel Hansen, my cousin Victoria's betrothed," I hissed and turned to clutch his arm, giving it a little shake. "Damn it, Radu! You brought us to the Obayifo's house!"

Fire kindled in his stare at the panic in my words. "I've no idea who that is, princess. But this," he twirled his finger in the air, and I caught his other hand clench into a fist before he hid it behind his back, "used to be Ma's house—see that?"

Grabbing my hand, he pulled me to the double glass doors by the bed, pointing from the large balcony stretching outside to the colossal building perched on the hill.

"Corvin Palace," I gasped. "This is where you watched the fireworks from?" My palms pressed against the cool glass, my eyes glued on my childhood home.

Floodlights placed at strategic points on the ground bathed the building in warm light, making it look even more imposing. A sense of longing thickened my throat.

Radu's voice went quiet in that way that promised blood. "Yeah. Me and Conin, Ma and Dad. The whole family celebrated along with their killers."

I stared at his hard profile in silence, watching the muscle in his jaw feather with tension. The pain radiating from him was almost tangible, and without thinking, I reached out and touched his arm. He startled at the contact but didn't pull away.

The massive expanse of the mansion was a testament to two things: the owners were rich, and they liked people to know it. But from my knowledge, it had always been the Obayifo's, first cousin to Anastasia Hansen, and second in line to inherit the throne when Dracula's rule ended.

"You're a Hansen," I whispered, and the shock sent my heart racing. I searched his face for the truth I should have seen before. "Radu, you're royal! Your mother was either a sibling or a first cousin. Sweet Derzelas!" I covered my mouth, gaping at him with wide eyes. "Anastasia's grandparents are on the Council... They sentenced their own blood to death—"

That realization ripped right through me. I felt like parchment that someone had split down the middle, folded the two halves together, and torn apart again. They'd failed her. Dear God, they had failed as the heads of their coven. Sacrificed a daughter, and for what? For trying to right their mistakes? For making the world a better place?

The balcony door rattled as Radu flattened me against the glass, his hand covering mine where it still rested against my mouth. His body was a wall of heat and tension against me, but his touch remained careful.

"Shh, princess. None of that matters now." His breath was warm against my ear, and I suppressed a shiver. "I'm a Lowe, I'll die a Lowe. All I've got from them is a pair of fangs and red annoying eyes."

"And immortality," I mumbled behind our joined hands.

He pulled away with a grunt, but his gaze lingered on my face as if he were memorizing it. "That's debatable. But we don't have time for that." Raising his palm between us, he wiggled his fingers. "Your hand. I don't want you getting even an inch away from me."

My heart did a somersault at the casual possessiveness, and I had to bite my tongue to not let it show. The way he said it—not demanding, just stating a fact—made my pulse skip. I complied and rested my palm flat in his, trying to ignore the flutter in my chest at how perfectly our fingers fit together.

Just then, loud, merry chatter echoed somewhere in the house, and my poor heart, which barely had time to slow down, jumpstarted again.

Radu's grip on my hand tightened. The mansion had four floors in total, three above ground and one buried six feet below, presumably for the cellar—or at least that was what the official papers said.

According to gossip?

It was a place of debauchery, intended for orgies, mass feedings, drugs, and various indulgences. While not illegal, if the rumors proved true, it would mean social suicide for the Master of Keys. Hence the secrecy.

But to each their own.

The commotion grew closer. Someone tripped, the sound of rushed heavy footsteps thudding down the hallway. More than one woman chuckled, but only one cooed between bouts of laughter, "Marcel, dear, I told you not to mix the wine with the stardust. Let's put you to bed."

He growled, snapped his teeth, and gave chase. The ladies squeaked in fright, faking like the talented actresses they were, and tapped high heels across the floorboards. Shadows flickered in the light flooding beneath the doors.

Something glinted in my periphery, and I snapped my head back to Radu. Clutched firmly in his other hand was the sunsteel blade, his expression purely murderous. I fought the urge to roll my eyes even as a deep-seated fear—not for my life, but for Marcel's—pooled in my stomach. I couldn't care less what happened to him. He was a despicable man who took advantage of young, defenseless women. But his murder would be a complication we couldn't afford.

"If I asked, real nice with a cherry on top, would you please not kill them?" I said, gently lowering his arm. The muscles beneath my palm coiled like springs, ready to strike.

His gaze dropped to my mouth, and the hunger there made it difficult to breathe, to concentrate, to resist him.

Then footsteps approached the door.

I had to get my head straight. The door handle jiggled, followed by the thud of someone colliding with the wood.

"Blink once for yes," I mouthed.

Another crash against the door. Radu didn't hesitate, slid the blade into its sheath and yanked the balcony doors open.

Before I knew it, my cape billowed in the wind as we perched on the stone railing. His arm wrapped around my waist, steadying me as the voices grew louder.

"Don't let go," he mouthed, his grip on my hand growing firm and reassuring.

The bedroom lock clicked open.

We jumped.

Two acres of perfectly manicured garden rushed up to meet us, crisscrossed by immaculate pathways and trimmed evergreen bushes. Adrenaline flooded my veins as I heard the giggles not far behind us, and we landed near a granite statue of a robust woman playing a harp. Radu was already moving, pulling me after him through shadows cast by jasmine-heavy trellises. Purple clusters of wisteria hung above our heads like festival decorations, their sweet fragrance following us to the line of cedars bordering the property.

We vaulted over the stone fence into the narrow alleyway beyond.

"That was close." I laughed, breathless from the rush.

Radu's gruff chuckle stunned me into silence, and I felt the stroke of his laughter deep inside where no one should have been able to reach. The shadows were thick around us, hiding his face beneath the hood. But hearing that sound from him was as rare as finding a natural pearl. It reached a space I'd kept locked away, the part of me that remembered what it felt like to feel safe, to feel joy without the fear of sudden loss.

"Let's not do that again," he said, studying the cobbled path that led down to the street below. The iron-cast lamp at the corner flickered and hummed. "Down?"

"Down."

Radu went first—the three-foot passage couldn't fit us both. Tall sandstone walls loomed over us, covered in blankets of five-leafed ivy.

Nostalgia mellowed my euphoria. I'd walked these passages as a child, searching for every hidden route in the Republic. In autumn all that green would turn blood-red.

"I'd pay good money to hear your thoughts right now," Radu said, halting at the junction.

"Take a left, then a first right." I was relieved to see that we were alone. "We're in the district next to Ravenwood Heights. The lane we just came from—I used to call them secret passages."

"Secret passages?" Amusement colored his tone.

"When I was five, I'd sneak out my window to explore without anyone knowing." We cornered onto the next street, where a few people walked on the far side, faces turned away from us. "It was all in my head, of course. Father ordered the royal guards to trail me, but they kept their distance."

"And you were looking for?"

"Every hidden route to the palace. To protect my kingdom." I raised my chin proudly. "No one entered my realm without me knowing."

"Stubborn brat." His laugh was low, warm. "Nothing's changed."

Before I could retort, hurried footsteps echoed from Nightshade Crescent. Radu tensed, pulling me closer to the wall.

"Eyes forward. Keep moving," I whispered.

The stranger turned right at Midnight Mist, disappearing from view. We climbed steep stairs, passing a group of cloaked purebloods who threw curious glances our way before dismissing us.

Three blocks later, Radu's mood darkened.

"Such comfortable lives," he muttered, surveying the polished facades around us, "built on halfblood blood."

Guilt flooded my body. It hit me like a winter fog, thick and murky. What must he think, returning to this wealth after decades of war? I glanced around, hyperaware of our privileges—the trimmed gardens, the pristine streets, the safety we took for granted.

"These families work for the government," I said quietly. "Army officers, administrators. Selena's parents live on the street over."

He didn't respond.

We walked in silence, fingers still linked, crossing streets when crowds grew thick. Ancient sycamores obscured the moon, their mottled trunks so wide that three purebloods holding palms couldn't span them.

"These trees are four centuries old," I babbled, nerves making my mouth run. "In another century, they'll cut them down and replant. Urban forestry management cycles every—"

The sigh of annoyance he released was long and meaningful.

"Am I talking too much?" I felt the night air grow colder. A storm was moving in, and I stifled the shiver that threatened to roll through me.

"Just a bit."

Heat flooded my cheeks. "Sorry. Adrenaline makes me chatty."

"I noticed." Despite his dry delivery, his thumb kept tracing reassuring circles on the back of my hand.

The gesture was becoming comforting.

Finally, the street sign I'd been waiting for appeared. Sable Street cut left—a one-way alley, wide enough for a motorized vehicle, though few bothered with wheeled transport when Darklings could travel faster.

"We're here!" I squeezed his fingers too tight, and he hissed through his teeth. "Sorry! I didn't mean to—Moonlight Terrace is right at the end. We should see the fountain in—"

Something rustled behind us. Charcoal and sage filled the night air, and my insides clenched like a fist.

"Stop right there!"

AURORA

Radu's grip jerked me to a halt.

"That's far enough." The voice drove the breath from my lungs. A pause, boots scraping cobblestone as they spread out. "Turn around. Face us." The flat authority of Nightwatch officers.

Lead poured through my veins, locking my joints. Behind us, five hearts drummed in unison. Slow. Controlled. Deadly. Once every three seconds. My pulse hammered triple-time against my throat.

The Nightwatch never moved in fives.

Panic clawed upward from my chest. They'd hear my racing heart, track the spike in my scent, follow the terror bleeding from my pores like hounds chasing wounded prey. In Lev's Republic, my royal blood made me simultaneously valuable and expendable.

Either way, we were fucked.

I turned toward Radu, meeting golden eyes that held the dull glow of a still wolf sizing its prey. His jaw set as if he were planning a siege.

That meant someone was about to die badly.

My stomach dropped. If he started cutting, we'd never leave this alley breathing. Five against two weren't fighting odds. They were execution odds. And I'd seen enough of Radu's diplomacy to know it involved creative applications of his sunsteel blade.

People feared the Nightwatch for good reason. Century-long training stripped every trace of compassion from them and left behind killers in pureblood shells. They saw through shadows, heard lies in heartbeats, eliminated without hesitation or remorse.

I caught Radu's wrist before his hand could find his blade. "There's a gap between the buildings thirty yards back," I mouthed. "If we can reach it—"

"Not with their Darklings." His lips moved, but no sound came out.

"Then we talk our way out," I whispered, but he didn't look convinced.

I shook my head under the hood, eyes wide with warning. *Don't you dare.* But his jaw stayed locked, stubborn as granite. Still, he angled his stance between me and the threat, shoulder blade pressing my collarbone. Always shielding me, even when logic screamed we were outnumbered.

That protective instinct would get us both killed.

"Officer." I stepped aside, keeping my voice conversational despite the deep-seated fear chilling my bones. Thunder rumbled overhead, storm clouds gathering thick and ominous. "Terrible night to be caught outside. Is there something we can help you with?"

The lead guard ignored my attempt at civility. "Identification. Both of you. Step into the light."

His tone held the kind of polite steel that brooked no argument. Metal clinked as he moved closer.

I dipped my head further, letting the hood's shadow deepen across my face. Through downcast eyes, I caught glimpses of his approach.

Wisps of shadow curling from thick-soled boots where his Darklings writhed in dark puddles. Red cape billowing around blackened greaves. The distinctive bulk of Carpathian dark iron armor.

Even from my limited view, the armor's generous proportions suggested serious bulk beneath—six-two of solid muscle moving with predatory confidence. The way he carried himself spoke of casual violence, the kind of man who enjoyed his work too much. The sort you'd cross streets to avoid if you were smart.

Radu's scent spiked, betraying the tension coiling in his massive frame. I felt his muscles bunch under my grip, ready to spring into violence the second I let go.

"By whose authority do you detain law-abiding citizens?" I released Radu's wrist and stepped forward, letting righteous indignation seep into my voice while keeping my face hidden. "We've committed no offense and were simply returning home before the storm breaks."

Steel clicked against steel as he drew his weapon. The baton extended with a sharp metallic crack. Blue energy danced along its surface, throwing jagged shadows across brick and mortar.

The guard's power lashed out, and I sensed the invasive tendrils of his blood magic probing for entry into Radu's mind.

The psychic attack felt like ice against my own consciousness. A ruthless search for weakness, for trauma to weaponize. But whatever fortress Radu had built around his thoughts remained unbreached, his mental walls harder than the dark iron encasing his attacker.

"Drop the disguise." His words sharpened to a blade's edge. "Final warning."

Four more batons snapped around us, harsh blue light strobing across the ground. I glanced back toward the gap between buildings—our only escape route now blocked by two guards who'd circled behind.

The alley walls trapped us completely.

"Get behind me," Radu said, and though his voice was soft, his tone was a whip-crack of command.

His hand found my arm, started drawing me backward with gentle pressure. When I resisted, raw strength settled the argument.

"You'll only provoke them," I hissed, but even as the words left my mouth, I knew it was too late.

"Remove the hoods. Now." The leader snapped his baton again.

I stepped back and squinted into the stark whiteness. That's when an armored arm came into view with a raised baton.

It rocketed toward me so fast that my one thought consisted of one scenario. If my math was correct, accounting for the weight behind the swing, and the length and crackling energy of the weapon thrusting toward me, this was going to hurt.

But the blow never landed.

Radu let out a slow breath—half sigh, half growl of a man pushed past his patience. "Princess, promise not to yell at me for what I'm about to do."

Terror seized my throat. I squeezed my eyes shut, waiting for the inevitable bloodbath.

But I'd seen him fight. Seen him drop Souleaters without breaking stride. When Radu promised violence, bodies hit the ground. The only question was how messy he'd make it.

The wet crunch of pierced flesh snapped my eyes open.

Crimson spurted around the lead guard's gorget, painting his stunned face. Radu's sunsteel blade jutted from the gap between armor and jaw, driven so deep only the bone handle remained visible. In the blue light of the batons, the pommel stone gleamed almost black—matching the shock dilating his pupils.

Sweet Derzelas.

Radu moved faster than my eyes could track, struck exactly at the one vulnerable spot in Nightwatch armor. The guard staggered, choking on blood, gauntleted hands clawing at the embedded steel. Black veins spread from the wound, crawling across his pale skin like spider webs as the sunsteel worked through his system.

Steel-shod boots scraped cobblestone. The other four charged, weapons raised, faces twisted in feral snarls. All matched their leader's intimidating height, but where he'd been built for speed and versatility, these were pure muscle, thick-necked brutes with arms like tree trunks.

The first one reached Radu and swung his baton in a vicious arc. Radu twisted away, the weapon's blue energy crackling past his ear, and drove his elbow into the guard's temple. Armor rang like a bell, but the man barely staggered.

"Stubborn bastard," Radu muttered, ducking a second swing.

He grabbed the guard's wrist, used his momentum to spin him around, then kicked him hard between the shoulder blades. The Nightwatch officer stumbled forward, straight into the path of his comrade's baton. Blue energy erupted across his chest plate, and he dropped like a stone.

Two more guards flanked wide. Dark smoke puffed from their boots as they vanished mid-stride and materialized ten feet closer. Their batons hummed with destructive power, casting writhing shadows across Radu's harsh features.

One feinted left. Before Radu could track the movement, the guard dissolved into wisps of darkness and reappeared at his right, baton already swinging. Radu caught the weapon's shaft bare-handed, his skin smoking where the energy affected him, and yanked the guard off balance.

The smell of burned flesh filled the air, but Radu's face showed nothing. He drove his knee up into the man's armored stomach, doubling him over, then brought both fists down on the back of his neck. The guard crumpled.

The remaining officer blinked out of existence. I tracked his Darklings as they streaked around Radu in a tight circle, ready to strike.

"Behind you!" I shouted.

Radu spun. His hand shot out, seized the guard's cape, and yanked him forward. The man's boots slipped on wet stone as he crashed into the side building hard enough to crack mortar.

But he wasn't done. Thick vines of shadows crawled up his limbs and torso as he pushed himself upright. He raised his weapon again, and I saw him blurring at the edges as his Darklings prepared to carry him through space.

Time seemed to slow as I forgot about my disguise and tilted my head up to look at him. Only to find his eyes on *me*.

His pupils dilated with recognition. Even through the blood streaming from his split scalp, understanding dawned across his features as he took in my exposed profile.

"Princess, get away from him!" he shouted. Shadows burst from him in a surge of charcoal-scented smoke, launching him toward me. "We'll protect—"

Radu's portal erupted from the ground, ten feet of hungry darkness, and swallowed the guard whole. Armor and weapons and half-formed curses disappeared into the churning void.

The other three guards scrambled to their feet. Dark wisps gathered at their boots, preparing to carry them away. But Radu was already weaving his fingers through the air. Three more gateways tore open and engulfed them in their depths.

One guard managed to grab a jutting ornament in the wall, his gauntleted fingers scraping against brick as the portal's pull dragged at him. Darklings hissed against the frigid cold and died out, needing solid ground that he no longer had beneath him. His eyes met mine for one desperate second before the abyss claimed him.

Radu fisted his hands, snapping all the gateways shut with a crash of thunder. Silence fell like a curtain.

The lead guard dropped to his knees with a loud clink of his armor. Blood frothed at his lips, smelling oddly close to my favorite synthetic blood blend—Hematech-9. Even dying, his heart stayed steady, disciplined to the end, trained never to show weakness even as his body betrayed him. Cold settled deep in my bones as shock began its slow ebb and the full ramifications of this nightmare sank in.

"The blade," I whispered, staring at how the black veins spread into his tight-braided hair. "It's killing him."

"Sunsteel doesn't just cut," Radu said, moving to stand over the dying guard. "It burns through immortal blood. Turns it toxic."

The guard's eyes found mine, wide with pain but filled with vitriol. *Traitor*, they seemed to say. I gulped, and it went down like a sack of rocks.

Radu pulled his blade free with a wet sound.

The guard convulsed once, then went still. But instead of settling into death, his body began to smoke. The black veins turned to cracks, like earth after a dry spell. Then he crumbled—armor, flesh, bone—his body reduced to ash and char.

I clamped both hands over my mouth, staring at the scorched remains scattered across the ground. It looked exactly like what sunlight did to our kind. But the sky above us was still dark, storm clouds blocking even the moon.

"You killed him," I gasped in disbelief. "He's actually dead."

"Deep wounds do that," he said before retrieving the weapon. "A cut bleeds you dry. A killing blow burns you out of existence." He cleaned the blade on his thigh, then sheathed it in the strap on his forearm.

His warning slammed back into my mind—what he'd said when I'd foolishly picked up the blade in his room. *'You've just held the only object known to kill an immortal.'*

I sat in stunned silence for a full minute and absorbed the meaning of what he said. An iron fist clenched my heart and was crushing tighter by the second. The walls pressed in around me. I could barely breathe, and I needed out of there.

"You let me touch it!" I dashed to him and struck his chest with everything I had. "You stood there and watched me pick up a weapon that could have killed me!"

The almighty Harbinger staggered, almost falling on his ass. Pride surged through me even as fear chased close behind.

"I thought I told you not to yell." He caught his footing, rubbed his chest. "And I didn't let you do anything. Your stubborn curiosity got seduced by a shiny ruby."

"I was not seduced by—"

I clamped my mouth shut, hoping he wouldn't see the flush creeping up my neck. He was right, damn him. Curiosity had driven me. I'd wanted to examine the weapon that could carve through monster hordes so effortlessly.

"This how it's gonna be?" He sighed like I was an unreasonable child. "You freaking out every time I save your life?"

"Excuse me?" I took a step back.

Blood rushed to my head, setting my cheeks on fire. I looked around for something to throw at him when Radu wrapped his arms around my elbows and crushed me to his chest.

"No, you don't." His breath was warm against my neck. "You won't get away until you admit I'm right."

Despite my fury, my traitorous body responded to his proximity. The scent of him made my head spin. His heat seeped through my clothes, reminding me of other times he'd held me this close.

"Let me go!" I writhed against steel-band arms.

"Say it first." He tightened his hold. "Without me acting on instinct, you'd be chained in some dungeon right now. And I'd be bleeding out on these stones. Don't feel guilty for their deaths, princess. They would've done worse once they found out who I was."

The concern threading his voice took the fight out of me. Beneath the gruff exterior, I heard genuine fear—not for himself, but for what might have happened to me.

"I'm not angry about the killing," I whispered against his chest.

"Then what?" He groaned in frustration. "Why are you so mad at me, woman?"

I bit back a smile despite the churning dread in my stomach.

"Answer me," he demanded when the silence grew.

"I got scared," I admitted, pulling back to meet his eyes. "Scared of what this means. Five missing officers will bring investigations, manhunts. Lev will spin this as an attack on the crown, use their disappearance to justify anything he wants. How many innocents will suffer because we couldn't find another way?"

He released my arms to cup my face. "Look at me, Aurora." His voice was gentle but firm. "More would have suffered once they dragged you back to the Council. They've killed for less."

He didn't need to elaborate. I'd seen the Elders pronounce his parents' execution in his memories during the Blood Pact. Unlike them, there would be no quiet death for me. I'd face a public trial, a grand spectacle where Lev could spin whatever story served his purposes best.

"If they'd taken me to them, the political fallout would have been huge. Martial law, mass arrests, every Tepes supporter brought in for questioning."

He gave a grim nod. "Either way, there would have been political consequences. At least this way, you're alive to fight back."

Five officers versus thousands of my supporters' lives. The math was brutal, but Radu was right. The worst Lev could do was blame faceless enemies for the missing guards. And if we could reach Dracula, get his power, none of this political maneuvering would matter. The real war was against the Shepherd.

"It's not only about politics." The admission slipped out before I could stop it. But now that it was out in the open, I didn't want to hold back. "It's about watching you throw yourself into danger for me. About not knowing if you're going to make it out alive."

He blinked. Then his jaw unclenched and his shoulders dropped. When he glanced at me again, his eyes had gone warm.

"Princess," he drawled. "Are you worried about me?"

I wanted to deny it, but after saving our lives, I couldn't manage the lie.

"Always," I whispered.

His gaze held mine for a long moment, intense and searching. Then he traced his fingers along my jaw, brushed his thumb over my lips. I saw myself reflected in those shifting amber depths.

Not a princess, not a projector, but something precious worth protecting.

The kiss was fierce and hungry as his tongue parted my lips and slipped inside. He tasted dark and dangerous, like coffee and smoke. When he pulled back, we were both breathing hard.

"Then we understand each other," he murmured. "Because there's nothing I wouldn't destroy to keep you safe."

My feet glued to the floor. My stomach somersaulted.

I believed him. The conviction in his voice—and his action—left no room for doubt, and somehow that didn't scare me anymore. I realized I wanted that protection as much as he wanted to give it.

Thunder rolled across the sky, closer now. The storm was almost upon us.

"We should deal with the evidence," I said, though neither of us moved to step away.

"What evidence?" Radu's hand rolled behind my back.

Magic hummed behind me, raising the fine hairs on my neck. I turned just in time to watch the remains of the guard swirl into the portal. Lightning split the gateway's edges as it snapped shut, leaving only clean stone and the sharp bite of ozone.

"Where did you send the other four?" I glanced over at him as a rumble shook his chest. He was laughing, his eyes gleaming with mirth.

"Somewhere they'll have plenty of time to reconsider their career choices." The grin Radu flashed me was amused and a touch feral. "Assuming they survive the landing in the Gobi Desert."

My eyes widened. "Solanthia?"

He shrugged.

I should have been appalled. Should have lectured him about the sanctity of life or the unnecessary violence. Instead, I found myself almost smiling back. Those men had been following orders to drag me back to Lev, but their good intentions would have gotten me killed just the same. Whatever mercy they received in the desert was more than the Council would have shown me.

"Derzelas, your ruthlessness is becoming attractive," I muttered.

His laugh was rough and warm. "Careful, princess. Keep talking like that, and I might get ideas."

His hands slipped out through the front panels of his cloak, fingers wiggling like he'd done in the Obayifo's bedroom. "Where's my hand?"

I rolled my eyes as though his request couldn't be more bothersome, when it really made my stomach flutter. Taking his hand meant accepting what was growing between us, impending heartbreak or not.

But I'd made my choice. Had probably made it that night in my bedroom when he'd asked me to let him feed.

I laced my fingers through his, felt his grip tighten with satisfaction.

"Time to pay a visit to your Creator," he said, leading me toward the soft glow of Moonlight Terrace at the end of the street.

"Let's do this."

AURORA

Moonlight Terrace embraced us through its stone archway. Water bubbled from the fountain, jasmine strangling the air from the blooming vines creeping up the buildings. A mesh of fairy light twisted overhead, throwing fractured shadows across cracked cobblestones.

"Is this the way in?" Radu jabbed his finger at the overflowing basin.

His whisper ricocheted off the walls. Wings beat somewhere in the darkness above us. My gaze snapped to the windows overlooking the terrace, zeroing in on the amber light leaking from one frame.

I held my breath. Counted heartbeats. But the drapes didn't twitch.

Relief hissed between my teeth.

I pressed a finger to my lips and nodded, then circled the fountain's base. Father had mentioned hundreds of secret passages honeycombing the Republic—great-grandfather Traian's paranoid genius designed for sieges that never came. I'd cracked this one through sheer stubborn persistence, Lev clearing spiderwebs while I fought with the mechanism. We'd used this entrance for our treasure hunts into the catacombs, slipping past guards who never thought to watch a fountain.

Octavian Hansen's masterpiece rose from the basin—Marcus' Arrival on Earth carved in marble that gleamed like fresh bone. The Creator commanded a hull-shaped chariot, arms flung wide as he drank from a *plosca*. Water burst from his mouth in an endless jet, the eternal power of blood made manifest.

Hansen had carved every ridge of muscle with obsessive detail, down to the locks that flowed like frozen rapids. But Marcus' perfect torso wasn't what I needed.

Below his vessel, dozens of figures captured in worship supported his divine weight. The mortals he'd reanimated during his time on earth. And one carried the switch that would crack the passage open.

"There."

I hiked my skirt above my knees and swung a leg into the fountain. Water lapped against my calves, tugging at the hem despite my grip. Radu followed without sparing his cloak, jumped straight in and sent water cascading over the rim.

I shot him a glare for the noise and waded closer to the base, trailing my fingers along carved marble until they found the chain.

"That's it?" he whispered, crouching beside me.

I traced the links of the diamond medallion circling the supplicant's throat. Found the clasp. Pressed.

Stone rumbled beneath us with a grinding sound that crawled up through my bones. The water level dropped with a mechanical hum. I grabbed Radu's shoulder as the basin floor trembled, then split apart like flower petals. Hidden stairs descended into perfect darkness, carved smooth by centuries of use and running water.

"After you, princess," he murmured against my ear.

I shot another glance at the windows—still no movement—then descended. Purebloods lived to report suspicious activity to the Nightwatch, but even if someone spotted us, the officers would need hours to comb the tunnel network. We'd vanish long before then.

I jumped from the last step as mechanical parts ground through the walls. Radu landed beside me, his boots splashing in the shallow puddle at the base. My pulse steadied as the ceiling sealed above us with a final click.

"What now?" Radu scanned the corridor, stretching in both directions.

Besides water dripping from his cloak, silence pressed against us. The tunnel reeked of stale air and decades of abandonment. That earthy cave scent that clung to forgotten places. Humidity thickened the smell as our boots stirred centuries of dust.

"Now we follow the tunnel eastward." I reached for his hand without thinking. His fingers locked around mine before my mind caught up with what I'd done. The satisfied rumble from his chest tugged a smile across my lips. "Every laneway leads to the palace. In the catacombs, every corridor leads to Derzelas' Temple."

"Clever." He sounded genuinely impressed.

"Great-grandfather's paranoia. Father said he spent his final years convinced we'd face conquest or cosmic annihilation."

We passed the first junction and climbed the gentle incline toward the Temple's foundation. Every few steps we stopped, listening. Nothing but our own breathing echoed back.

"Wouldn't be the first ruler to crack under power," Radu said.

"Or ennui claimed him. Immortals fear boredom as much as sunlight."

We were close. The last mile curved upward toward our Dark Father's place of worship, but each step brought new tunnels crossing our path.

"Think you'll go mad from immortality too?" he asked.

"I might not live long enough to find out." The prospect hollowed my stomach.

He stopped so abruptly I nearly collided with his back. In the cramped space, he had to duck slightly to turn and face me, his shoulders filling the width of the passage. "Isn't that why we're here? To claim your power so nothing can touch you?"

I kept my gaze fixed on the darkness ahead, where the tunnel split in three directions.

"Very soon, I'll face an opponent just as cunning and powerful as the Shepherd," I said, choosing the center passage. "That battle, I take alone."

He tightened his grip on my hand. Midnight roses and dark roasted beans filled the air. "Lev."

I nodded and forced myself to meet his stare. What I found was the lethal focus of a predator that had chosen its prey. The same look he'd worn in Brasov when he'd carved that crimson line across his chest to bait me.

"The Wurdulaks didn't just steal my throne," I confessed, and my voice echoed off the stone walls. "They destroyed my coven's reputation. Trampled Father's legacy into dust. Madness runs in my bloodline, but cowardice doesn't. I'd rather die fighting to restore our honor than let that bastard win."

"You won't fight alone," he growled. "That's not how this works."

"How what works?" I asked, confused.

"Us." He raised my chin with a knuckle. "Thought we'd established you're mine to protect."

"Arrogant ass," I said even as butterflies swarmed inside me.

He gave my hand a gentle squeeze. "Your arrogant ass."

His smile was warm fire after bitter cold. Those damned dimples scattered every rational thought I had.

Which explained why I nearly missed the blue electric lights flickering in the distance.

The last junction lay a hundred yards ahead. A crossroads where four tunnels met in a curved X formation. Blue lights pulsed along the uneven stone walls of the eastern passage, seeming to race toward us.

No footsteps. No voices. Just that eerie blue glow cutting through the darkness.

A knot of fear climbed my throat, and I swallowed hard to think clearly. Even if the government had wired the catacombs since my last visit, why install sensors in this forgotten side passage? It wasn't even a major route.

The realization hit like ice water.

Those weren't electric lights.

I grabbed Radu's arm, fingernails digging into his sleeve.

"We need to move. Now—"

A large, calloused hand clamped over my mouth, dragging me backward.

My heart nearly exploded in my chest. I recognized Radu's addictive scent, the heat radiating from his body, but instinct still screamed at me to fight. Every fiber demanded I break free and run before the Nightwatch patrol spotted us trapped in the open intersection.

Then a man's voice echoed from around the bend.

Radu's arm locked around my waist and lifted me clean off my feet. He moved with dizzying speed, my hair whipping forward as he rushed us back down the tunnel. He pressed me against the wall of a shallow alcove we'd passed moments before, his body covering mine.

His scent turned sharp and bitter—the telltale sign of magic use—as he threw up a portal to shield us from view. If the Nightwatch decided to explore our passage, they'd find nothing but empty stone.

I forced my breathing to slow, every muscle coiled tight as voices grew closer.

"Do you think she's really dead?" the voice asked, and it wasn't hard to figure who this 'she' was. The Commander's narrative to avoid Mother's inevitable search parties. How perfectly that had worked in our favor.

Armor clinked and echoed in the silence. I stopped breathing altogether.

The guard's voice carried a high, slightly pitched timber that young men possessed before transitioning to deeper, more authoritative tones. Though if he hadn't managed it by now, he never would. Every Nightwatch officer had at least half a century on me.

I twisted my head until Radu freed my mouth, but didn't dare draw breath for fear of discovery. Nervous anticipation made me nauseous. I would make a terrible spy.

I knew they couldn't reach us without teleporting through Radu's portal, but if they raised an alarm, my plan to petition Dracula for the Blood Aura would crumble to ash.

Every beat of Radu's heart hammered against my ribcage. He pressed his furnace of a body against me so tightly our bodies molded together. The scent of him wrapped around me, making my head spin despite the danger lurking mere yards away. Less than an inch separated me from darting my tongue out to taste that delicious golden column of his throat.

The voices grew louder, boots scraping against stone as the patrol moved closer to our junction. Radu's grip tightened impossibly, and I felt rather than heard the low growl building in his chest.

His hand moved from my mouth to cradle the back of my neck, fingers threading through my hair. He pulled me closer to his chest still and rested his chin on top of my head.

My heart melted, body sagging against him. Even in hiding, even with enemies prowling nearby, he surrounded me like a shield.

The Nightwatch guard came to a halt not far from where we'd stood seconds ago, his armor clinking as he fumbled with the buckles. Metal clanged as pieces hit the ground, followed by the unmistakable sound of him relieving himself against the tunnel wall. I rolled my eyes and grimaced in disgust at every trickle and splash.

Two more officers approached the junction, their footsteps barely audible against the dirt-covered floor.

"We wouldn't be here if the higher-ups thought she was dead, would we?" another man answered. From his no-nonsense tone, he was clearly the leader. "It's not our job to have opinions, officer. We follow orders. The prince put considerable resources into hunting her. Even Governor Tepes has his own dogs following her trail. It's just a matter of time before someone finds and drags her back where she belongs. Now finish your business and shut up."

A droplet of water from Radu's drenched cloak hit the dirt at our feet with a wet clink. Then another. And another.

We both stilled. And I hoped his portal would dampen the sound.

The third guard paced around, her footfalls lighter than her companions'. She took a loud sniff, bristling the fine hairs on my nape. Each deep inhalation felt like drawing back the string of an imaginary bow, taking careful aim. Fear slammed into me, locking every muscle.

"Do you smell that?" she said, stepping into our tunnel and pausing just inside the entrance.

The first guard snorted. "Yeah, I'm taking a piss."

"Not that, you idiot!" she snapped. "Someone's been here recently. It's faint, but there's something bitter, acidic. Burnt chocolate, maybe?" Her voice carried a note of uncertainty. "It's... off somehow. Not quite mortal, not quite immortal." She inhaled again, deeper this time. "And underneath that... sweetness. Like those peach pastries from the bakery on Dawn Avenue."

My blood turned to ice. If she could detect Radu's dual nature, then every pureblood with a functioning nose would recognize the anomaly the moment they caught his scent. I'd grown so accustomed to his uniqueness that I'd never considered the implications. How foolish I'd been to think he could walk among my people undetected.

Yet here we stood, barely a dozen steps away, and she couldn't pinpoint our location. She should have traced the scent straight to us by now.

Then, understanding hit me.

The portal.

A heavier set of boots stopped beside her. He inhaled deeply, held his breath for several seconds, then exhaled slowly through his mouth. "Their trail passes through here." The leader.

I fisted my hands in Radu's shirt and pressed my face against his chest, trying to make myself smaller.

Steel rattled again, and the first guard rejoined his team. "Do you think it's her, sir?"

"Intel says she's traveling with a female companion. The dominant scent here is clearly masculine." Their leader stepped back, the others falling in behind him. "Let Joseph handle whoever's down here—this is his territory. Let's move. The faster we clear this quadrant, the sooner we're back on the surface."

Their footsteps faded to whispers until the female guard spoke again.

"You think she's running or being held? She's been in the outer wards for months."

"Doesn't matter," the leader spat. "Prince's orders are clear—question every outlier about the princess, then execute them. Someone will break eventually."

"Good." Her voice held satisfaction. "Those half-breed scum deserve—"

The voices grew distant as they moved away from our tunnel, but their words thundered in my skull like hammer blows.

'Question every outlier about the princess, then execute them.'

The thought cinched my ribs around my lungs. Bile burned my throat. Outliers were dying because of me. Mixed-breeds who'd already sacrificed everything for the Republic were being slaughtered to satisfy Lev's twisted need for control. Because I'd been weak. Because I'd chosen to run instead of staying to face him.

I pressed my fist to my mouth, biting my knuckles to distract myself from the fierce burning behind my eyes. How many had already died? How many more would follow while I hid in shadows? Their blood tainted my hands as surely as if I'd wielded the blade myself.

Then ice shot through my veins. How long until they reached the Tenth Ward? What if they'd already threatened the Black Guild?

"You alright?" Radu asked, tightening his arms around me.

But I couldn't find comfort in his warmth. Not when innocent people were paying the price for my freedom.

I nodded stiffly and shoved my emotions back into that steel box I kept for moments like these. When I couldn't afford to break down.

I had a plan to focus on.

"We need to keep moving." I pulled away, not meeting his eyes.

Inside the alcove, I couldn't smell the guards at all. Out here, without the portal's buffer, I nearly staggered from the assault on my senses—pine, bergamot, lavender, and underneath it all, the acrid stench of urine. The foul smell snaked around me like poisonous gas, and I couldn't decide which would be worse: breathing through my mouth or nose.

I wrinkled my nose in disgust and gestured toward the junction. We returned to the crossroads and took the right passage. The spiral staircase at the end led us to a hidden door set deep in the fortified perimeter surrounding the Temple.

Balmy tropical air hit us as Radu forced the rusted lock with his shoulder, and we stepped into the inner courtyard.

The sacred ground pulled at something deep in my chest. Every time I set foot on this hallowed earth, I felt Derzelas' presence, as if all my burdens lifted, leaving only the essential core of who I was. His Sons had first touched earth on this hill. Here, too, He would rise when His time came.

"Fucking hell, princess," Radu muttered, stopping beside me. His gaze swept the massive stone walls bristling with defensive towers. "Thought we were entering a holy place, not storming a fortress."

Despite everything weighing on my mind, I couldn't suppress a chuckle. "Another gift from great-grandfather Traian's paranoia. He fortified Derzelas' sacred temple like a military stronghold." I gestured at the imposing battlements. "Wait until you see the moat he dug around the outer walls."

The Temple stood out like a peacock among pigeons. Twenty stories of red tuff and sandstone stretched skyward, pointed turrets crowning its bulk like spears thrust at the heavens. It resembled the fortified churches of old Solanthia, except great-grandfather had abandoned the traditional cross-shaped floor for open rectangular space. Dense strands of ivy and honeysuckle climbed the walls, their leaves gleaming under the bright moon.

"I'll give you credit," Radu said, inclining his hooded head. "You people know how to build shit to last." He pointed at the arched windows, where warm light filtered through stained glass. "Looks like someone's home."

"There's always someone inside," I said, reaching up to smack his chest as if this should be obvious. "The High Priestess and her acolytes live here."

Radu gave me a pointed look, his irises flickering from glowing yellow to brilliant red like they couldn't decide on a color. "Then how do you plan to do this without getting caught, smart ass?" He caught my wrist and linked his fingers with mine.

My heart did a flip, and I swallowed. The way he stroked my skin with deliberate, silky touches soothed the bleeding wound left by the guards' words. More and more, I found myself drawing strength from his presence exactly when I needed it most.

Without him, I wasn't sure I could face Dracula.

I squeezed his hand and started toward the temple entrance.

"This is a place of worship," I reminded him. "It's always open to any-one wanting to pay respects to our Father. There's no judgment inside. Covered or bare, Derzelas doesn't care. We're all his children regardless of how we present ourselves."

He grunted, "Fair enough," as we approached the grand archway.

An intricate carving of our Dark Lord dominated the pediment. Derzelas seated on his massive throne, draped in elaborate cloth, arms outstretched in welcome. Gilded words gleamed above the entrance: *'Devote yourselves to me, my beloved children, and the gates to my kingdom shall forever remain open for you.'*

"We'll walk straight through the front door and blend in. Are you spiritual?" I asked.

"To your God?" He scoffed. "Hard pass."

"Figured as much," I muttered. He might not have grown up with our customs, but he didn't need to be such an ass about it. "Then you handle unlocking the crypt door while I pray. It's behind His statue. You can't miss it."

We passed through the porch, where sturdy wooden doors stood open. Sinuous carvings depicting the underworld and the three Creators decorated its surface, embellished with golden hardware that gleamed from centuries of devotional touch.

"Fine. I'll do all the work while you slack off," he teased, but his words died as we stepped into the atrium.

And with good reason.

Warm sand-colored tiles stretched beneath our feet. Soaring ceilings reached toward the heavens, supported by slender gray columns that rose like towering trees. Our finest sculptors had carved them to branch into a canopy of stone, transforming the massive space into a mesmerizing forest that stole your breath.

I pressed the back of my free hand against my mouth, stifling laughter. "Not quite what you expected?"

He didn't answer. I doubted he could. Even after all this time, the sight still left me speechless.

Flowing water whispered around us. Dappled light filtered from above as we moved deeper into the temple. An indoor garden stretched on either side, with lush grasses and night-blooming plants spilling from curved raised beds surrounded by a gently winding pond.

Radu stopped dead, jerking me to a halt beside him. He pointed at a lily pad. "Is that—"

"A koi fish? Oh, yes," I said. "There should be goldfish and frogs as well. Also, a turtle, if it survived. It's been decades since I bothered checking on the aquatic residents."

The air carried lavender and lotus. Dragonflies and tiny insects darted between flowers like scattered jewels.

He leaned close, his whisper meant only for me. "Do people know there's a legion of bloodthirsty creatures waging war outside their borders? Who the hell has time to maintain all this?"

His tone lacked that visceral hatred I'd grown accustomed to, but I knew him well enough to catch his disapproval. Irritation sparked inside me, but his grip tightened on my hand, sensing I wanted to pull away.

"The priestesses maintain the Temple. They created a space for peace, tranquility, and reflection. Stop being such a condescending ass."

As if summoned, a woman appeared from a side door. Tall, thin, ramrod straight. She wore a blood-red gown, the splits down the sides revealing white flowing pants and silken flats. Her onyx hair fell in complex braids to her mid-thighs, swaying with her purposeful strides.

She carried that weight purebloods gained after several centuries. But her eyes betrayed her true age. Sharp. Merciless. Like Elena's.

Those eyes locked onto us with unwavering focus, raising the hair on my nape.

"Welcome to the sanctuary of our Dark Father," the High Priestess said and paused to tend wilted flowers at Derzelas' statue. "Please, let me know how I may assist you."

I dropped into a curtsy, my hood shifting forward as I pulled Radu down beside me in a respectful bow. "We humbly thank you, High Priestess. We've come to offer our respects."

Her head dipped in acknowledgment. "Your presence honors Him. Please, let me know if you require guidance with your offerings and prayers."

I nodded, not trusting my voice to betray us. My pulse hammered with fear that Derzelas would strike us down for lying in his sanctuary. Or worse—she'd sense something amiss and summon the guards. She seemed satisfied with my silence, though, moving on with her work while humming.

I nudged Radu forward. We headed straight for the knee-high podium at the nave's rear, my breath coming in shallow bursts while he brooded beside me.

Derzelas' statue towered above us, fifty feet of ivory marble reaching toward the ceiling, hands open at his sides as if drawing us closer. Moonlight streamed through the high stained glass, painting the polished stone in shifting patterns of color and shadow.

Radu stopped five feet away and planted his feet. Other purebloods began their prayers from the middle aisle, and I let him stay put.

Approaching Derzelas' gigantic feet, I grabbed the ceremonial blade from the pedestal among the flower arrangements and incense.

Please, Father, accept my offering as an apology for what I'm about to do.

I slashed my palm. The wound sealed almost instantly.

It took several more cuts to keep blood flowing long enough to anoint His feet. The blood trailed down the statue's slight incline, gathered in the narrow groove and dripped into the silver bowl below.

Dracula will know I wouldn't disturb his Sleep unless the danger was imminent and our people faced extinction.

My blood wasn't powerful enough to wake him—I hoped—but it would let him share my memories. He'd see what had happened since the war began. The injustices we'd committed, the lies we'd believed. Most importantly, how close we were to another attack.

He was the most merciful of the Sons. He'd forgive my transgression. He—

"High Priestess!" a high-pitched voice gasped from the atrium. "You're needed outside. Please, come quickly!"

Something clattered to the floor. My heart slammed against my ribs. This was it—our window. The humming cut off, replaced by the sharp tap of hurried footsteps on stone.

Adrenaline flooded my system.

"Time to go, princess," Radu whispered against my ear. His fingers pried the blade from my death grip and returned it to the pedestal.

AURORA

THE HEAVY GILDED DOOR behind Derzelas' statue hung marginally open, held by Radu's black opal pendant. The hinges stayed silent as he widened the gap for me to slip through.

My heart pounded against my throat as I stepped into the dimly lit corridor. Golden light from wall sconces softened the rough sandstone jutting from both sides.

I strained to hear any approaching footsteps. None came.

Radu scooped up his necklace and followed.

"It was supposed to be locked," I muttered as the door hissed shut behind him.

He pulled back his hood and fixed me with piercing eyes. "What do you think I've been doing all this time?" The corner of his mouth quirked up, showing a maddening dimple. "I'll admit I hadn't pegged you for being this pious."

"Oh, hush." I waved a dismissive hand. "Someone needed to play the part since you avoided the shrine like it carried the plague. Besides, there's nothing wrong with honoring the God who gave us life. Yours included."

"No further comment," he said, reaching for my hand as he passed. His silvery hair fell across his forehead, and my palm itched to run my fingers through it. Until he opened his mouth again. "Now let's move before that woman comes looking for us."

I smacked his shoulder. The sound echoed. "She's one of the most revered women in the Republic," I hissed. "And cover your head before the guards spot you."

He caught my wrist before I could pull his hood up.

"There's no one down here, princess."

I skidded to a halt and stared at him. "What do you mean?" I whispered, then resumed walking. "There should be two Nightwatch officers guarding the Sleeping Chamber."

He shrugged, falling into step beside me. "Maybe they got called away with the others, that bastard's keeping the entire force busy hunting for you."

"Something doesn't feel right," I said. "We barely saw anyone crossing the ward to Moonlight Terrace. If we hadn't encountered the Nightwatch—"

"Twice," he cut in, holding up two fingers.

"Right. I would've said this was almost too easy. I don't remember the Temple ever being this deserted."

We rounded a sharp bend and faced a long staircase. A ceramic bowl of warm lavender oil sat on an ornate pillar. I breathed in the sweet scent before voicing what had nagged at me since we'd surfaced from the catacombs.

"Radu, what if they already know we're here?"

"More reason to move fast." Before I could blink, he swept me into his arms and launched himself down the entire flight. A portal flickered mid-leap, cushioning our landing at the bottom. He set me down and kept walking like nothing had happened. "We go in, you claim your power, we portal out. We're too close to quit now."

My knees turned liquid, but that had nothing to do with needing assistance and everything to do with the way he'd manhandled me. Which was outrageous, and I'd analyze it later once we were safe.

Seriously?

I'd survived a century on my own. I could handle a steep staircase.

"You're right," I forced out, rubbing my arm in comfort, and crossed the empty vestibule to the archway where golden words gleamed, *'Herein lie the Great Sons in eternal dream.'*

My heart stopped, then galloped at full speed. I drew a sharp breath, read the inscription once more, and stepped through.

The Sleeping Chamber swallowed us whole. Our footsteps thundered against barren walls, and a gasp escaped my lips.

The sheer scale... cream walls stretching endlessly upward, space yawning in all directions, crushed me down to nothing. My chest hollowed. Invisible hands wrapped around my throat and squeezed.

"Fuck me," Radu breathed behind me. "How big is this place?"

I couldn't answer. This was what an ant must feel like facing a giant's doorway, watching titans pace beyond the threshold.

Because it wasn't just the room's vastness that locked my knees and stole my breath. Power surged from the center, hitting us like a blast furnace. Even Radu grunted, but whatever he said was lost to me.

I could barely stand.

Drawing another breath, I forced my legs forward.

Thirty feet ahead, the stone gave way to three vast sanctuaries carved into the earth—the resting thrones of the most powerful purebloods who'd ever walked the earth. Their sarcophagi gleamed with consecrated gold, each lid etched with sigils that pulsed faintly with power, as though they still breathed the names of their makers. The air trembled with quiet divinity.

Between the tombs, a colossal amphora of burnished silver blazed with undying, living fire. Its flames moved, not with the wind, but with a will of their own—spiraling in reverent, hypnotic rhythms, shaping halos of light that reached out and reflected on the ceiling and walls like prayers given form.

Time slipped away.

I blinked and found myself at the triangle's center, where the Creators' magic hit me full force.

Underworld's tits and balls, what a rush.

My hair stood on end, scalp tingling with electricity. Goosebumps exploded across my skin. The crushing magnetism yanked me downward.

My legs gave out. White-hot agony tore through my thighs and hips as my kneecaps cracked against the hard floor.

"Aurora!" Radu's voice sounded underwater, muffled by waves of power crashing between us.

I still had enough mind-clarity to know that if I couldn't resist their combined force, his varcolac blood wouldn't stand a chance. Worse, they might sense him as a threat and obliterate him.

"Stay back!" I screamed, wrestling my trembling hands upward against the crushing force.

He froze a foot from Dracula's chamber, his cloak whipping around him. The stubborn bastard had watched me collapse and still reached out, testing the charged air with his palms. He jerked his hands back as if he'd grabbed molten steel.

A string of curses erupted from him—those I heard crystal clear. "Fuck! You okay, princess?"

I started to nod when the magic surged, a familiar current that my body recognized down to the marrow.

Dracula was testing me. His power spiked.

My head whipped back, mouth opening in a soundless scream as every bone in my body turned to grinding glass. Agony with a capital A bleached my vision. Muscles and tendons stretched to their snapping point as violent spasms tore through me.

Despite the fire consuming me from the inside, I heard Radu's roar. The air splintered as he slammed against the magical wall erected to keep him from reaching me. Blood streamed from his burned knuckles.

"Let me through!" he shouted. "Aurora!"

I couldn't take much more. With shaking hands, I yanked the sharp needle from my sleeve and jabbed my fingertip. A fat droplet of crimson welled up.

I squeezed, dragging my arm forward, forcing more blood out before the wound could seal. A fifty-fifty chance to get out of this alive was fifty percent better than certain death in the Tenth Ward.

The blood hit Dracula's golden lid and sizzled into nothing.

Everything happened at once. The agony crested, threatening to tear me apart. My vision went black. This was it—death on my knees before I could save anyone.

Then silence.

His magic drained away like water through sand, flowing back into the floor. The flames froze in their vessel. Radu's struggle stopped. Ominous quiet settled over the chamber.

A circle formed around the golden lid, and Dracula's chamber erupted in blinding light.

I fell through collapsing dimensions, my body dissolving and reforming. I screamed, but no sound emerged.

Darkness devoured me, then spat me onto endless cold marble.

The throne room made the Sleeping Chamber look like a closet. Black columns stretched into shadow, carved with figures, sentries, that writhed when I wasn't looking directly at them. Crimson torches burned without warmth, making the obsidian walls pulse.

An invisible force slammed into my back, and through my lashes, I glimpsed him.

Dracula sat atop a throne carved from a single ruby, nine feet of lethal power wrapped in midnight robes. Dark hair fell past broad shoulders. Razor cheekbones, diamond-sharp jaw, straight nose, and skin white as fresh snow. No beard softened his features, only the cruel perfection of a god who had never known weakness. His crimson eyes burned ancient and merciless, holding power that could unmake worlds.

He was the first vampire, the original pureblood, the template from which we'd all been carved. He could silence a nation just with his name. This was what he chose to be—terrifying, magnificent, untouchable.

When mortals dreamed of dark gods, this was the face that haunted their nightmares. His presence radiated absolute authority, pitiless intelligence, and the calm certainty of someone who had never been challenged. He could have been death itself wearing flesh.

I owed him everything; he had made my people. Yet when he looked at me now, every instinct screamed to kneel. To prostrate myself in submission.

It was like standing before the birth of darkness itself. When the power of those eyes had touched my ancestors, they had no choice but to worship. Now those eyes fastened on me, stripping me bare, peeling away flesh to examine my soul.

"You dare wake me from sacred rest?" His powerful voice shook the walls.

My arms trembled, supporting my weight against the crushing force pinning me down.

"You've been gone too long, my lord," I gasped each word. "You need to see what's happening."

"Your petty concerns are beneath me." He leaned forward. The air turned arctic. "Why shouldn't I erase you for this transgression?"

Ice coated my lungs, crystal shards blooming up my throat and coating my tongue. My heart pounded against my ribs as the full weight of my stupidity struck me. I'd woken a god, an ancient, indifferent god who could unmake me with a thought. What had I been thinking?

Terror locked my throat. When I finally managed to speak, it came out as a harsh whisper.

"Because we're fighting our own dead now. Every time one of ours falls, they join their ranks. Because we're losing the war, through lies and betrayal, while the real enemy grows stronger." My voice strengthened the more I talked. "If you don't act, there won't be a Republic left when you wake."

His eyes narrowed. The pressure lifted slightly, enough to let me rise on my heels.

"You speak of defeat. Have my children grown so pathetic?"

"Our defenses are non-existent. Our leaders are corrupt. We're losing because we don't understand what we face." I fought the pain and struggled to my feet. "You made us from your blood. Help us finish this."

Black seeped into the white of his eyes. I stepped back, expecting him to annihilate me.

"Approach."

Blood Aura crashed into me with that one powerful word. Every muscle seized, then moved at his command as his power carried me up the steps.

My thoughts scattered. I was clay in his hands.

I stopped at the base of his throne, gasping as he released his hold. He towered above me even seated, but when he rose to his full height, I had to crane my neck just to see his face.

He struck without warning. Iron fingers clamped around my throat, hauling me off my feet. A debilitating fear paralyzed my body.

My hands clawed at his wrist, but his skin was harder than stone, and my nails splintered against him.

"Your blood will show me truth or lies." He tilted my head, baring the vein pulsing beneath my skin. "Pray you speak honestly."

His fangs drove through my throat in one clean bite.

I expected my blood to burn, to feel the same searing agony as when Lev tore into me.

But this felt nothing like Lev's violation. Dracula's grip remained clinical, purposeful. No grinding hips, no groaned threats, no savage thrusts that ripped flesh. No bloodlust-crazed eyes demanding I 'bite back.' He held me like a specimen under examination, not prey to be devoured and defiled.

I stopped fighting and surrendered. The pain evaporated as his all-powerful consciousness invaded mine. Every secret, every fear, every moment of war flashed behind my eyes. He sifted through decades in heartbeats, discarding worthless moments, cataloguing what mattered.

My vision dimmed as he drank deep. Then his fangs withdrew with a wet sound, and color returned to my world.

"You speak truth," he said, releasing me so I slumped to my unsteady feet. Crimson stained his lips as ancient eyes blazed with stolen knowledge. "This enemy has grown bolder. Wields power that shouldn't be available to him." Shadows pulled around him, melding with his robe. "I will give you what you need, even as your blood has already been touched."

I stumbled backward, hand flying to my throat. "Touched?"

A chill ran down my spine. Someone had tampered with my blood? When? Who? What does that even mean? Dread filled my stomach, but his dismissive wave silenced my spiraling thoughts before I could voice them.

"Power demands sacrifice. Swear to me you will devote yourself to the Republic until this threat ends."

The air itself seemed to hold its breath. "I swear it."

"Swear you will be my instrument of war. My will made flesh, my heir in all but name."

His offer siphoned the breath from me. Power to save them all. Power to end the lies, the corruption, the meaningless deaths.

"I swear."

"So be it." He sliced his wrist with one claw. "Come, my child." Brimstone and copper filled the air as dark blood welled up, so rich it looked black. "Drink. Let my blood bind you to your oath. Forsake it, and you'll never see another dawn."

I didn't hesitate.

I pressed my mouth to the cut. His blood hit my tongue, and my body became an inferno. It burned down my throat, flooded my system.

Power erupted beneath my skin. His Blood Aura punched through my bones and ripped through my body. Every cell tore apart and reconstructed. The magic swelled until I'd split open. It ripped a scream from my throat, but only blinding light poured out.

My vision went white.

Shaking, I clutched at my chest. *Focus. In, out. Count the breaths.*

One, two, three.

The marble split beneath me. Silver light bled through the cracks. Something was awakening inside me. Something I could never walk away from.

My sight cleared slowly.

I stared at my hands and gasped.

Red lines bled under my skin. A faint glow traced their jagged edges across my palms and fingers. I felt them burning beneath my sleeves. They raced up my arms, seared across my chest, and spread down my back, thrumming with his divine power. His mark.

When they melted into my bones, I felt empty and overflowing. His terrible power was now part of me.

The throne room dissolved, and I fell back into my body.

My head sagged as I slumped back on my heels. I would have killed for a moment to breathe, but the fates weren't listening. Strong hands grabbed my shoulders and dragged me back to a hard chest.

"Come back to me." Radu's voice cut through the fog. I blinked, trying to clear my vision. He exhaled hard. "You're okay, thank the gods."

I could sense the worry gnawing at him. Tilting my head back, I met his gaze. Storm clouds had gathered in his eyes, dulling their brightness. His wolf stared back at me, the golden feathers spinning around blown pupils.

Radu tightened his arms and pressed his lips to my forehead. "Goddammit, don't scare me like that again," he said. "Did it work?"

I let out a shaky breath. "It worked."

He kneeled in front of me, and despite our height difference, I spotted the smoky threads of Darklings gathering over his shoulder.

Instinct kicked in. I yanked Radu's hood over his head.

"Aurora," he started to protest, then caught the scent.

Geranium and mint.

He went rigid.

I saw her first. The High Priestess emerged from the darkness, crimson robes bleeding from shadow. Her floral perfume couldn't mask what I smelled beneath it—fear. Sharp, metallic fear.

Her eyes swept the crypt. When they locked onto mine, something cold slithered down my spine.

Radu exploded upward, dragging me with him. His sword sang from its sheath, the blade pointed in her direction. He growled, a low rumble that came from his throat but sounded completely feral.

"One word and you're dead," he snarled.

She didn't flinch. Didn't even breathe hard. But she sank into a curtsy so deep it looked like worship.

My heart stopped.

She knew.

"Princess, you must leave now," she whispered. "The Nightwatch have surrounded the temple. My sisters can't delay them much longer. Hurry."

Heavy footsteps thundered above us, muffled by stone but growing closer. We had seconds—maybe less.

"Go," I told her. "If they catch you here, they'll know you helped me."

She didn't argue. Shadows swirled around her, and then she vanished.

I turned to face the man by my side, trying not to read too much from the way his arm had fastened like a steel band around me. Like he was afraid I was going to disappear if he let go even for a second.

"Radu," I called.

"No."

"Portal out."

"No," he repeated, his mouth set in a grim line. "We leave together."

I pulled away from his touch, my heart racing in my throat. The loss of his warmth knotted my stomach.

Confusion sparked in his eyes. I watched him fight the urge to follow, to close the distance I'd created. His hands twitched at his sides, but he held himself back.

"What are you doing, Aurora?" he whispered.

Shouted orders accompanied the clank of armor. A spike of adrenaline made me nauseous. If I fled now, it would make me look guiltier. Too many people had seen me at the Temple. And even though they didn't know my identity, it wouldn't take long for the Elders to figure it out. I was the only woman of rank with the power to release the officers stationed to guard the Creators. The Council wouldn't know the chamber had been left unguarded.

I couldn't defend myself if I ran away. Lev could spin whatever story he wanted about what happened here. Besides, no one would listen to warnings about the Shepherd from a fugitive princess hiding in the outer wards. The Council needed to hear the truth, needed to face the real threat. And they'd only listen if I confronted them with the dignity my title demanded.

I'd stand and fight.

The guilt was already eating me alive for the lives lost because of my cowardice. More outliers would die if I continued to hide.

I had information the Republic needed and authority they'd respect. My name would protect me from immediate execution.

And most importantly, I had Dracula's power to prove my innocence. If I learned how to summon it in time.

I'd always known capture was a possibility. Better to face them alone than drag Radu down with me and get us both killed.

"I'm staying," I said with all the conviction I could muster.

"Like hell you are." He moved toward me.

But I stepped back. Out of his range.

His eyes almost appeared pleading. "I'm not leaving you here."

The pain in my chest turned to acid. It seeped into tiny cracks and poisoned my blood. I swallowed, not an easy task given that all the spit had dried up in my mouth. I felt like puking. I had to make him go. Had to save him. They would kill him without hesitation, tear him apart while they'd make me watch. And there was only one way to make Radu leave willingly.

I had to shatter his trust.

"This was always temporary." I forced glacial ice into my voice. "Did you think it was real?" I lifted my chin, making myself meet his eyes even as mine burned with unshed tears. "That I could actually care for someone like you?"

He clenched his teeth, the confusion marring his features turning to pain. "Aurora..."

"You're a varcolac." I spat like it was toxic. My hands trembled, so I fisted them at my sides. "Your kind murdered my father. Killed thousands of innocents. Did you really think I could forget that? Forgive it?"

He went utterly still. The kind of stillness that came before violence. "You don't mean that."

"I don't?" A cruel laugh scraped from my throat. "I used you. Your guild, your protection, your blood. It was all just... convenient. You were convenient."

His mouth opened, closed, opened again. I watched the devastation bloom in his eyes.

But I knew this wouldn't be enough to make him leave. So, I twisted the knife deeper.

"The only reason I let you touch me," I retorted, letting the hatred I felt for myself seep into my voice, "was because I needed your portal magic." I gestured toward Dracula's chamber with a dismissive wave. "But now I have what I came for. I don't need you anymore. I can finally reclaim my throne."

He shook his head. His hands curled into fists at his sides. "You're not like them, I *know* you."

The pleading in his voice nearly broke me. I wanted nothing more than to throw myself into his arms and beg forgiveness. My whole body ached as if rejecting me and the poison in my words.

Yet even after everything I said to him, a stubborn flicker of doubt burned in his gaze. The guards were nearly here. *Leave, damn you.* I had to cut deeper, reach where it would hurt him the most. Destroy any chance of reconciliation.

"You hear their voices!" I shouted, uncaring the Nightwatch could hear us. "You belong with them just like Conin does now. Maybe that's where you should be too. Listening to your brother beg for death in that thing's voice every night. At least then you'd be useful for something."

He took a step back; his breath turned ragged. The silence that followed was excruciating. Even the door exploding above us seemed muted, distant against the roaring in my ears. Radu stared at me with winter in his eyes, icy enough to flay off my skin. His chest rose, his jaw working soundlessly. I could almost hear the walls he'd always kept erected around me slamming up. Locking me out.

"I see." His voice turned hollow, stripped of everything that had made it his. He straightened to his full height, rolling his shoulders back. "Should have known better than to trust a pureblood."

A portal cracked open behind him. Jagged. Violent.

His beautiful golden eyes met mine one last time, and I saw nothing there. No warmth, no recognition. Just emptiness. "Goodbye, Your Highness. Hope your throne keeps you warm at night."

He stepped toward the portal, then paused without turning back. His shoulders sagged for just an instant—so brief I almost missed it.

"For what it's worth," he said quietly, "I would have died for you anyway. Didn't need to lie about it."

Then he crossed. His form dissolved into thick darkness, and the portal snapped shut, leaving only the acrid smell of burned coffee and the shards splintering my chest.

I stared at the spot he'd vanished, my heart a bleeding ruin, as the Nightwatch poured into the chamber. Guards surrounded me, electric batons drawn, but I barely saw them through the tears blurring my vision.

I did the right thing. I'd saved him. Whatever Lev did to me, whatever the Council decided, I'd saved him.

Even if I'd just murdered the only good thing in my life.

More guards wearing the silver armor of the royal knights rushed in, filling the spaces between the pillars. The force Lev had spared would've flattered me if their menacing glares didn't remind me how much trouble I was in.

Behind me, the air fizzled with Darklings, vomiting four more originals into the chamber. I recognized their scents instantly. Lev, and his loyal dogs: Alexandru, his right hand in political matters; Tristan, head of the royal guard; and Sevastyan, the eternal sycophant.

I turned to face them, barely containing my disgust.

Dressed in black silk that made him look like spilled ink against marble, the most hated man in my universe fixed me with the focus of a predator who'd finally cornered his prey. Death seemed to waft off Lev like smoke off dry ice. His straight hair fell past his shoulders, hiding the shaved side underneath, and the dark-purple shine of it matched the silk on his lapels.

Silver rings, one on each finger, caught the torchlight as he dragged his thumb along his lower lip. Triumph flickered across his face, and my stomach clenched.

Then he went still. Nostrils flared as he scented the air. His scarlet eyes turned polar, moving from Dracula's chamber to me. The scowl he hit me with could have convinced a seasoned Nightwatch guard to empty his bladder.

"Aurora, what the fuck have you done?"

TO BE CONTINUED...

Acknowledgements

WRITING A MANUSCRIPT IS a solitary endeavor, but creating a book is a collaborative journey. Bringing you deeper into the world of the Crowned Republic of Transylvania has been an incredible ride, and I'm indebted to many who made this possible.

To my beta readers—Jenny, Magnolia, Nermeen, Mona, and Nat—thank you for your sharp eyes, brutal honesty, and unwavering enthusiasm.

To Alexandra, who read every version and never let me take the easy route. Your challenges made me a better writer.

To my editors, Lauren and Ellie: Working with you has been transformative. Your expertise sharpened every line, your encouragement lifted me when I doubted, your professionalism elevated this manuscript into something I'm proud of. Aurora and Radu are stronger because you refused to let me settle.

To my street team and early readers—your excitement fuels the entire *Beyond the Gloom* series. You make the hard days worthwhile.

To my husband, for believing in this story from day one and giving me the space to see it through.

Finally, to my readers: Thank you for returning. Thank you for trusting me with your time, for embracing these flawed, fierce characters, for following Aurora, Radu, and the outliers deeper into the Gloom.

This is just the beginning. Stay with me.

About the author

Denisa Mih always knew creative arts were her calling, but becoming an author was an unexpected turn. With a background in Landscape Architecture, she stumbled into writing when an idea refused to let go. One page turned into ten pages, ten pages turned into chapters, and before she knew it, her first novel, *Blood Sings*, drew breath and came to life.

Born and raised in post-Communist Transylvania, Denisa grew up surrounded by stories of resistance and change. These experiences, along with Romanian folklore and Dacian mythology, heavily influence her writing. With inspiration from her time in Australia, she blends these elements and creates unique, paranormal tales.

Denisa currently lives in Transylvania with her husband, eagerly awaiting the arrival of their twins. When she's not writing or preparing for parenthood, she can be found exploring the mystical landscapes that fuel her imagination.

www.ingramcontent.com/pod-product-compliance
Lightning Source LLC
Chambersburg PA
CBHW031318210726
48287CB00005B/1597